4/19/24

Kathy, enjoy
the read — it's
Montana at its best.
Semper Fi,
Bob

SPRINGER'S HEART

SPRINGER'S HEART

BOB MANION

The Write Place
Spokane, Washington

Published by
The Write Place
Spokane, Washington

ISBN: 978-0-9788507-4-6

Printed in the United States of America

Ed. Rev. 122220

DEDICATION

This book is dedicated to those who signed the blank check to their country and walked in the service of the United States of America whether they be Marine, Soldier, Airman, Sailor or Coast Guardsman. They are my brothers and sisters; Semper Fi!

ACKNOWLEDGMENTS

There are many who have helped me in this endeavor. I must always recognize my children: Bob Jr. (Colonel, USMC), Randy (bicyclist), Samantha,a special thank you to Wendy my life partner, friend, and poet. Those of my writer's group: Marion, Betty, Richard, and Gail, who read, commented, and edited for me. Gail, I couldn't have done it without your wise assistance. And, of course, those men and women who wear Marine Green, savor your time with the Corps; it ends so quickly. Ooo-Rah! Devildogs!

To the cowboys and cowgirls with whom I have had the privilege of sharing a trail or chasing a few steers together. The ground does not get any softer as we get older. Stay in your saddle, share your stories and a bit of time, you won't regret it. Be kind to your horse; it may be the only way to get home.

CHAPTER 1

The eighteen wheel semi-truck strained its way up to the mountain pass. The glare of rain water on the dark highway reflected the trailer's tailgate and the flashing warning lights. The driver of the light blue SUV squinted to protect his night vision from the reflected brightness of approaching headlights. Piles of dirty snow lined both sides of the two-lane highway.

John Anderson could feel the SUV's tires hydroplane as they crossed wide streams of water from rain and melting snow. Anderson maintained a safe distance from the semi-truck's trailer. Water thrown up by large tires created a dirty mist he couldn't avoid on the SUV's windshield. John used the window washer fluid sparingly, afraid it would run out before reaching a service station where he could replenish it.

Joan Anderson reclined in the passenger seat and dozed beneath a plaid car blanket. The trip had been long and tedious through nasty driving weather of mixed snow and rain. Since leaving San Francisco, this was the third and last mountain pass on their way home to Dutton. A line of trucks labored their way up the long twisting highway to the pass summit.

John looked forward to getting home after six days away at the four-day conference with a hard day of driving on each end. Joan rarely accompanied him on a business trip. This was a vacation for her from her hum-drum life in Dutton. He glanced at his wife when she coughed in her sleep and snuggled deeper into the seat pulling the blanket closer about her. He couldn't help smiling; Joan was still beautiful and shapely after giving birth to three children. When the twins were born the doctors told Joan she couldn't conceive again; yet ten years later Mary Ann arrived, a precious gift to the family.

Thoughts of their children brought a smile to the man's face. Michael and Margie, their fifteen year old twins, and five year old Mary Ann. Mary Ann was the family's sunshine, always smiling, laughing and asking questions.

John spotted a sign for a passing lane two miles ahead. He noticed Joan was awake and commented, "If we can get ahead of these trucks, it should be clear sailing down the other side of the pass and clear highway all the way to Dutton."

Joan leaned toward her husband and reached out her hand to touch the back of his neck. A lock of his dark hair had slipped out of place curling against his forehead; it gave him a youthful look. A boyish smile belied his nearly forty years.

As before John saw the passing lane sign, the trucks ahead of him moved as far right as they could. John drove closer to the truck and prepared to pass. He pulled out into the passing lane and increased his speed. The SUV accelerated and began passing the slow-moving trucks. He was passing the fourth of five semis when he saw an out of control semi-truck appear from around a curve ahead headed downhill. The truck's trailer was sliding, the driver losing control.

The driver of the truck John was passing saw the oncoming truck barreling down at them; he stomped on his brakes to give John room to slip in between his truck and the truck in front. John slipped into the pocket to the right between the braking truck and the truck ahead. He slipped as far into the opening space as possible. The out of control downhill truck and trailer were upon them. It struck the lead truck in front of John knocking it off the road to the right. The truck's trailer whipped to the left striking the Anderson SUV and knocked it out into the path of the oncoming semi-tractor.

John heard Joan's scream as the front bumper of the semi-tractor smashed into the SUV. The heavier truck bounced up, rode over the smaller SUV, collapsing the passenger vehicle like a cardboard box. Joan died instantly. John Anderson died a second later as the SUV roof smashed down upon him. The semi-tractor with the SUV under the engine continued down the highway for a quarter mile before coming to a stop. The SUV was ground into a wet steaming mess in the center of the downhill lane.

* * *

Officer Duane Garvin knocked on the door. A middle-aged woman answered his knock. She identified herself to the officer as Mrs. Wilkins who was watching the Anderson children while their parents were attending a convention in San Francisco. She explained they were due to return that very evening. Officer Garvin asked Mrs. Wilkins to step outside. He told her of the fatal accident on the mountain pass a hundred and fifty miles from Dutton. According to the officers at the scene, the accident victims were John and Joan Anderson of Dutton.

Garvin asked if Mrs. Wilkins knew of any relatives of the Andersons. She didn't know whether the Andersons had any living relatives to be notified. She did know both of the Andersons were raised in an orphanage and it was doubtful if any relatives existed. They were interrupted by Garvin's radio when he was informed by dispatch that the State Orphanage facility in Dutton would be notified to insure the children were protected and cared for. It was left to him to make arrangements with Mrs. Clemons, the Children's Home Director, to meet with the children. He was to remain at the Anderson home until Mrs. Clemons relieved him of responsibility.

Mrs. Wilkins gave the officer her cell phone number and said she would not tell the Anderson children until after talking to the Home Director, Bess Clemons. Officer Garvin returned to his police cruiser, where he retrieved Mrs. Clemons's telephone number from his computer.

"Ma'am, this is Officer Garvin of the Dutton Police. We have a situation involving three children; it appears their parents have been killed in a vehicle accident. We are waiting for confirmation of the identities of the deceased, but it's 90 percent positive they are John and Joan Anderson of Dutton. The bodies will be fingerprinted at the scene and the prints forwarded to NCIC." He was interrupted by the dispatcher informing him there was a fingerprint match for a John Anderson. Garvin passed the information to Clemons along with the names of dependent children and the address. She said she'd meet him at the Anderson home.

Thirty minutes later Bess Clemons joined Officer Garvin on the sidewalk in front of the Anderson home. Mrs. Wilkins had been watching through the curtains. Her heart sank when she saw Bess Clemons park behind the police car. The attractive blond woman and the older police officer slowly climbed the steps to the broad porch of the neat, well maintained Cape Cod house. They reluctantly rang the doorbell.

Bess met the three children accompanied by Mrs. Wilkins. Bess told the children about the accident and inquired about any relatives. The children had never met or heard of any relatives of their parents. Bess elected to leave the children at home and return the next day to discuss options with them. She relieved Officer Garvin of responsibility and he returned to his patrol. As she climbed into her car, the tears came. This was the hardest part of her job. She hated each time she informed a child about the death of a parent. She drove to the Children's Home to begin the paperwork for the state to assume responsibility for the children.

CHAPTER 2

Twenty-three years earlier, when John Anderson was celebrating his seventeenth birthday, Sergeant Hank Springer, Marine Security Guard, stood next to the reception desk in the American Embassy lobby. The telephone in the guard office rang. Hank excused himself from the two tourists he was talking to and entered the office to answer the incoming call.

"Marine Guard, Sergeant Springer speaking, how may I help you?"

"This is Lori O'Donnell in 345; would you tell Ernie Holder I'm sorry I won't be able to meet him for lunch. Something has come up and I'm going to be busy."

Hank immediately understood the message and answered, "I'm sorry too Lori. Is this something I can help you with?"

"Yes, I'm sure you can."

"Okay Lori, I'll pass the word on to Ernie, thanks for calling." Hank gently put the handset down on the telephone. There was no Ernie Holder with the Marine Embassy Guards. Ernie Holder was the emergency help code for embassy employees. Hank glanced out the window and was glad to see Corporal Ken McCarthy coming up the steps and about to enter the embassy lobby. Hank reached into the safe, pulled a spare pistol from the rack and a loaded 9mm magazine for the Beretta M9 pistol. He closed and locked the safe. When Ken came through the door five seconds later Hank handed the pistol and magazine to the Marine in civilian clothes. "We've got an Ernie Holder problem on the third floor, P Section."

Ken immediately took the pistol, slapped the loaded magazine into the grip and jacked a round into the chamber. He lowered the pistol's hammer to prevent an accidental discharge. Ken followed Hank across the lobby, the pistol by his leg out of sight of the two tourists and receptionist. McCarthy followed two steps behind Hank around the main floor corridor to the stairs to the third floor.

The two Marines stopped on the second floor stair landing one floor below room 345. The next flight of steps would bring them to the stair exit across the hallway from Lori O'Donnell's office. The Marines made a quick plan; McCarthy, keeping the pistol hidden inside his windbreaker jacket, would go first to the office of the Chief of Station and inform him of the situation in Miss O'Donnell's office. Using the connecting offices, McCarthy would pass through the Assistant COS office and into O'Donnell's office.

Corporal McCarthy hastened up the flight of stairs and acted unhurried, leisurely walking toward the corner office.

Hank waited, allowing McCarthy time to get into position; then Hank went up the stairs, crossed the hall to stand in the doorway to O'Donnell's office. "Hey Lori, what's up. We missed you at dinner last night." Behind Lori was a short sloppily dressed man with dirty brown hair attempting to look at papers on O'Donnell's desk. The intruder was wearing a tan sport coat and his body odor struck Hank from seven feet away. The man stood behind O'Donnell holding something in his hand. When he saw the six foot one inch 190 pound Marine with the heavy pistol on his hip, he hesitated then started to raise his hand as Corporal McCarthy came through the inner door with his pistol pointed at the man's head.

Hank came around the desk and grabbed the man by his wrist and the back of his neck in a take-down. Hank slammed the man onto the floor while McCarthy pulled Lori out of her chair and pushed her out of the office into the hallway. McCarthy then turned his attention to help Hank with the intruder.

"Okay Mister Smelly, let's see what you've got." Hank pulled the man's coat down, trapping his arms in the sleeves. The Marines found a small automatic pistol and switchblade knife in the sport coat.

The two Marines dragged the man out into the hallway, took him to the floor and searched him more thoroughly. Besides the small pistol and the switchblade knife, they found the man's Iranian passport in the inside pocket of his jacket.

Hank addressed Lori, "Call the security office. Get the Gunny up here and tell him to bring restraints."

A crowd began to gather and Hank ordered them to clear the hallway. Three minutes later Gunnery Sergeant Manly in civilian clothes came out of the stairwell from his office in the security section on the second floor. McCarthy held a weapon pointed at the man. Hank proceeded with an abbreviated strip search to find any additional weapons or other threat the man might have on his person. Hank tossed the man's coat to the Gunny to make sure nothing was missed.

Hank removed the prisoner's belt, pulled his trousers down to the ankles and opened the shirt checking for any hidden items. The Marine turned the pants pockets inside out. The pockets contained a few coins and a hotel receipt from one of the shabby hotels near the city's train station. Hank pulled the man's arms behind him, used the flexible plastic ties instead of handcuffs Manly brought with him. To add security, Hank cuffed the intruder before he pulled him to his feet. Hank pulled the dirty brown pants up so the man could hold them in place with his secured hands. The three Marines frog-marched the intruder around the building to the elevator. They tried not to breathe the foul odor from the man's unwashed body. Hank noted the intruder's hands and face were clean where the rest of the man was unwashed, not a good sign. When the elevator doors opened into the lobby, the Gunny went ahead to open the locked Marine Security Guard Office while Hank and McCarthy marched their prisoner across the lobby.

After the host country's police were notified, the Embassy security officer released the intruder to local custody. The three Marines conducted a quick security inspection of the embassy building. Ten minutes later, four off-duty Marines arrived from the Marine House, armed and wearing camouflaged utility uniforms. The Marines conducted a thorough security check of the building and Embassy grounds. An hour after the incident, the embassy offices had returned to normal business.

It was determined the man entered through the Consular section on the first floor eluding the local policeman posted there. Hank sat at the Marine Guard desk to complete the paperwork required when actions by Embassy Marines resulted in aggressive contact with American citizens, the local police or foreign nationals.

Finished with the reports, Hank went to Lori O'Donnell's office to see if she needed anything and recovered from her experience with the intruder. Her office was empty, all the file cabinets closed and locked. The Station Chief's secretary told him Miss O'Donnell had taken the rest of the day off. She added when Miss O'Donnell left she appeared fine, a little shaken up by the experience, but okay. After making her incident statement ,the security officer sent her home in an embassy staff vehicle.

* * *

On a Saturday morning, three weeks after the intruder incident, Hank was again on duty at the Embassy on the day watch when Miss O'Donnell entered the lobby. This was the first time he had seen her since the incident in her office. When she stepped through the embassy lobby doors he was stunned. She wasn't the most beautiful woman he had ever seen, but to him she was perfect.

He smiled and simply said, "Good morning Ma'am."

Lori looked at the tall Marine in the undress blue uniform: blue trousers with the red stripe, tan shirt and the white pistol belt and white holster cover. She noted the heavy automatic pistol with the scarlet and gold lanyard clipped to the pistol's grip. His brown eyes smiled at her from under the highly shined bill of the white hat with the gold Marine Corps emblem at the peak. Her smile broadened and blue eyes sparkled. Her blonde hair made her face look like it was surrounded by a golden aura. Hank didn't fail to notice the shape of her legs silhouetted in her light summer dress by the morning sunlight streaming through the lobby windows. The sun bathed her in a warm glow like an angel. It was magic. Hank instantly lost his heart.

Lori signed into the building, giving her office as her destination. When Hank looked at the sign-in log he noticed she had also added a smiley face by her extension number.

The Marine paced the lobby glancing at the clock behind the receptionist's desk. Finally enough time elapsed to justify another physical security check of the work spaces of the building. He locked the main door, told the receptionist he'd be on a security check. Hank checked all the offices on the second floor before he climbed the stairs to the third floor. He crossed the hallway to O'Donnell's office and stood in the doorway.

Miss O'Donnell stood beside her desk reading a document taken from an open safe. She turned her head in response to his soft knock. A bright smile illuminated her face at the sight of the Marine. She straightened to her full height of five feet six inches. Her expression radiant, tiny smile lines appeared at the corner of her eyes. A faint dusting of freckles decorated the bridge of her nose.

"Hello Miss O'Donnell." Hank made small talk he wouldn't remember two minutes later; taking his heart to task, he asked if she would like some coffee or a soft drink.

"A soft drink would be wonderful if it's not out of your way, Sergeant?" She waited for him to fill in the question with his name.

"Springer ma'am, Hank Springer," he said blushing. When he realized he was blushing, it only made it worse. His face turned red. "Be only a few minutes."

"Fine Sergeant Springer, please call me Lori." Hank nodded, afraid to open his mouth and embarrass himself further.

After the good-looking Marine left, Lori sat behind her desk and ignored her work, thinking about the Marine. He is so young; of course I'm only twenty-two she thought. Too much time around all the old fogies in the State Department is making me feel old. The State Department orientation she attended was more a lecture for senior citizens. Minutes later the sergeant was back with two large containers of soda.

"I didn't know what you like, so I brought light and dark. Coke or 7-Up?" He had literally run to the lobby, checked on the receptionist, went down the stairs to the cafeteria and back to Lori's office. On duty Marines did not use the elevator and he was a little out of breath, which embarrassed him further. After setting the drinks on her desk, he took off his hat and ran his hand over his dark brown buzz haircut.

Lori laughed, and pointed to the chair beside her desk inviting him to sit. Hank's face lit up but quickly the smile turned upside down. He explained, Marines weren't allowed to sit in any office but the Marine Guard office while on duty. "I'm sorry, but I have to get back to my post in the lobby." Taking a chance, Hank asked, "We are having a party for one of the Marines at the Marine House next Friday. Would you come?"

Lori rewarded him with her amazing smile. "I'd be delighted; does that mean you're my date?"

His face echoed her smile. "You bet!"

From that Saturday, Lori and Hank were together whenever duties permitted. Within the first month the entire embassy knew they were a couple. For Hank and Lori the two-year assignment flew by.

With their impending marriage, the couple were popular and in demand for many social events. On the day after Hank's official assignment as a Marine Security Guard was completed, they married. All the off-duty Marines and selected embassy officers and staff attended and congratulated the newly wedded couple with toasts and boasts.

Sergeant Henry (NMI-No Middle Initial) Springer received his permanent change of station orders assigning him to the 1st Marine Division, Fleet Marine Force, at Camp Pendleton, California.

The newly wedded Springers were a union made in Heaven. Both were orphaned, raised by foster parents. In Lori's case she was adopted by an elderly couple without children; Hank was fostered by close friends of his parents. Both of Lori's adoptive parents had passed away a few years earlier leaving her a sizeable inheritance. She invested the entire amount, living on her Foreign Service pay.

Hank's own parents died in a private airplane accident when their small plane encountered wind shear, flipping the plane upside down. The plane was too close to the ground for the pilot to recover. After his parents' deaths, it was Jim and Maya Sutterland who took the orphaned boy into their home and raised him as their own son. Hank learned the ranching business from Jim and became an accomplished cattleman, horseman and rodeo competitor.

When Hank received the insurance money from his parents', he put the entire amount in a managed investment account. So far he hadn't touched the money. He declined to attend college and joined the Marines; the Sutterlands supported his decision. The Marines provided for all his needs. At the beginning of his second enlistment he received orders for the U.S.

State Department Marine Security Guard School at Quantico, Virginia. After completing MSG school, Hank was assigned to an Eastern European embassy as a watch stander on a two-year assignment; where he met the light of his life Lori O'Donnell.

CHAPTER 3

Hank reported to the Brooklyn Navy Yard to terminate his U.S. State Department assignment and establish dates for travel and leave. Able to get his orders endorsed by the Duty Marine Liaison Officer, he requested and received thirty days leave plus eleven days travel time to the West Coast. Hank would accrue another thirty days leave before his leave days expired, leaving him a total of 60 days of leave due after his initial leave. He wanted to spend at least four weeks in Montana. He could request more time if he and Lori wanted to stay longer.

The Lazy B ranch lay a few leisurely hours by car northwest of Missoula, Montana. Jim and Maya Sutterland owned and operated the Lazy B cattle ranch since the late 1950s. The Lazy B was on the east slope of the Cabinet Mountains, part of the Rocky Mountain chain of the Continental Divide. The closest city of any consequence was Missoula, an easy three hour car ride east of Spokane, Washington.

Each year since he joined the Marines, when not deployed, Hank spent at least two weeks of his annual leave at the Lazy B; most years he spent all of his 30 days leave at the ranch. If he could arrange it, he arrived during the roundup and branding. Jim often said` Hank knew the cattle and horse business better than he did and the Lazy B would always be his home.

The road to the Lazy B ranch was as Hank remembered from his last visit three years ago. The bent and crooked pine tree hit by lightning exactly ten miles from the ranch gate was still there. The ranch was 60 miles from the town of Lone Horse, population 3,157. Lone Horse was a community of retired ranchers, retired cowboys and businesses that supported ranch and farm operations of the area. A small elementary school and an even smaller high school sat side by side near the center of town.

The day after graduation from Lone Horse High School, Hank and his friend Ralph Bentley were on their way to the Marine Corps Recruit Depot at San Diego, California. Now Hank drove the familiar road toward his boyhood home to introduce his bride to his parents. As he passed through the gate and up to the ranch house, he noticed a new single story house across the parking area and the main house's front lawn. His attention shifted to the front porch where Jim and Maya waited to welcome him home.

Jim was in his mid-sixties and a couple of inches under six feet with a slender waist and broad shoulders of a working cowboy and the energy of a man half his age. A smile was always ready to break out on his sun reddened face. The crimson accentuated his green eyes. Hank teased him about his face; he said Jim's eyes looked like green olives in a bowl of tomato soup. His once-dark brown hair was now salt and pepper on its way to silvery white. Jim wore it a little long, like many of the cowboys who worked for him.

Maya—slender like Jim and nearly as tall—wore her white hair short and brushed back. She always said long hair was a nuisance on a ranch. Maya's gray-blue eyes were lively and danced with mirth. She wasn't above a practical joke when she thought it appropriate and could get away with it. Maya wore faded blue Wranglers and a green and black plaid shirt with the sleeves pushed up to her elbows.

As soon as the SUV stopped, Hank was out the door, double timing around the car to open the door for Lori and help her from the SUV.

"Hey boy, what you got there?" Jim called and received a friendly slap on the arm from Maya for his lack of manners.

"Now you go welcome Hank home like you know how to do." Maya pushed Jim toward where Hank stood holding Lori's hand, a foolish smile on his tanned face. Lori wanted to wear a dress to meet Hank's parents, but he insisted she wear her comfortable jeans and one of his sweatshirts she appropriated.

"Mom, Dad, I would like to introduce you to my wife, Lori Springer. That's Mrs. Henry (NMI) Springer," Hank said proudly. "Lori, these are my folks, Maya and Jim."

Maya pushed Jim out of the way, gave Hank a quick peck on the cheek then took Lori by the arm and led her into the house leaving the two men alone gawking at each other.

"I suppose you noticed the new house over there," Jim said and pointed unnecessarily toward the house across the yard. "You two will be staying there while you're here. I built the house as a guest house and I guess you're a guest, or at least Lori is. Better start unloading the car before Maya starts issuing orders." Jim laughed. "Besides, if you want to run around naked in the house, you can. Nobody to bother you."

Hank laughed at his foster father's choice of words and the image they brought to his mind. "You sure it's okay to use the guest house and maybe run around naked?"

"Damn straight." Jim laughed and slapped Hank on the back. "Maya had me build it for you so you'd have a place of your own when you came home." Jim reached into the back of the SUV and removed two of the suitcases and started toward the front door of the new house. Jim called over his shoulder, "You sure brought a looker home with you."

* * *

Jim and Hank did some team roping together in their spare time. Hank worked with one of the new bunch of young horses to break them to the saddle. He was gentle with the horses and they looked for him whenever the door to the guest house opened. In the morning they'd be lined up along the paddock fence waiting for Hank. By the second day, Lori accompanied him always with a treat for the horses. On the fourth day the horses were waiting for Lori along the fence.

Jim wanted to bring down a herd of cattle to the ranch and cull out the steers ready for market. The Lazy B crew of four cowboys worked full time plus Jim hired a few part time hands. The second week, all the men left the ranch house area and rode to the high grazing ranges. They spent the next four days gathering and bringing the herd down from the high country. Checking brands, they sorted out the neighbor's cattle and spent most of the day getting them back onto their own range. Hank earned his usual $100 a day for work as a ranch cowboy. He promptly endorsed the check and handed it back to Maya who put it in Hank's account which continued to grow from when he first came to the Lazy B.

The cattle not being shipped to market were returned to the high pastures after getting medication and new ear tags. Hank volunteered to ride fence with one of the hired hands, but Jim insisted he take Lori on a tour of the ranch's land. Lori had done recreational riding while in college, so they decided to go on horseback. Hank took one of the pack horses and the two saddle horses recommended by Jim. Hank escorted Lori on a three-day trail ride. As they rode around the edge of the ranch, Hank occasionally repaired a section of fence. By the second day Lori could mend fence as well as some of the cowboys working for the Lazy B.

Hank took her to some of the more remote places. The waterfalls and pool near the farthest point away from the ranch house offered secluded swimming and a good campground.

Hank was mildly surprised when Lori chucked her clothes, threw them in a shallow pool to soak and jumped into the clear, cool water. A minute later, Hank, minus his own sweat and saddle-stained clothes followed her into the pool. They spent the afternoon making love in a mossy glen next to the pool. For dinner, Hank fixed steaks and baked potatoes cooked in a rock oven beneath the fire. He put up the tent, but Lori dragged their sleeping bags out of the tent and under the star-filled sky. They talked together as a full moon rose over the land. Under the white light of the moon they made love.

"I don't ever want to leave this place," Lori whispered to her new husband. "I feel so close to nature and God here. And of course you." She giggled and tickled him, which resulted in a gentle wrestling match and after the moon set they held each other under the bright stars of the Milky Way.

* * *

Three weeks later, the day before Hank and Lori planned to depart for Camp Pendleton, California, Lori jumped up from the breakfast table and ran to the bathroom. Maya followed her and found Lori with a death grip on the toilet bowl. "How long has this been going on?" Maya sat on the edge of the bathtub.

Lori looked up: dark rings under her eyes stood out against her pale face. "For the last four days. I thought it was a touch of the flu, but now I don't know."

Maya stood up abruptly, a look of surprise and enjoyment spread over her face. "Lori, I think you're pregnant."

"No, no I can't be. We planned to have children after two years, not now." Lori stared up at the older woman. "What will Hank say, we had all these plans."

Maya got down on the floor with Lori and put her arms around her. "Hank will be overjoyed. I know him; you are the sparkle in his eyes. Hank's just like Jim. My only failure was being unable to give Jim the children he wanted. Hank came along and filled that void in Jim. I thank God everyday for bringing Hank to us. Thank you for making my son happy."

Together, the two women leaned back against the bathtub until Jim knocked on the door demanding an explanation from the woman folk. They could hear Hank mumbling in the background. The worry sounded in his voice and his pacing could be heard through the closed door.

"We'll be along shortly; you two go back and finish your breakfast. We are having some girl talk and we don't need you two snorting and pacing around." Maya turned her attention to Lori then back to addressing the door. "Jim, you and Hank clear and wash the dishes if you must be in the house." Quietly she said to Lori, "That should get them out of the house—neither one of them likes to do dishes."

At the evening dinner, Jim cracked a bottle of red wine to go with the rare meat. Lori refused to have a glass. Hank knew Lori liked to have wine with dinner as they so often had in Europe. He looked confused, and then a light went off in his face. "My God, you're pregnant!"

The two women looked at each other; each wore a non-committal smirk. Lori couldn't stand the suspense any longer and nodded her head to confirm Hank's outburst. Jim jumped to his feet, grabbed Lori's glass and turned it upside down on the table. Then he started pounding Hank on the back until the younger man began coughing.

"Baby, when, how?" Hank blurted between the coughs.

"Quite recent I would guess and you know very well how!"

Jim looked from one woman to the other. "Oh crap, it's the mother thing and there's two of them. Lord save us!"

Hank knelt down by Lori's chair. "Honey, is everything okay, do you need anything? I don't think you should go riding anymore."

Maya shook her head. "Oh for Heaven's sake Hank, leave the poor girl alone. If she wants to ride, she can ride. She's not going to give birth tonight or tomorrow. I do think you should stay here for another couple of weeks. If I know Hank, he wants to get where he's going sooner than later. I bet he has at least a month leave still coming to him after this one." She scowled at Hank. "So, Mr. Smarty, you call the Marines and tell them you want another two weeks leave. No make it three weeks." When Maya wanted to make her point, she made it.

"Okay, I'll call and request an additional two weeks."

"Good. Lori and I are going into Missoula shopping tomorrow, sans you two. I did say three weeks, didn't I?" Maya scowled at the two men.

Jim rolled his eyes, included Hank in the gesture. "Yes ma'am." He grabbed Maya by the arm and dragged her along with the wine bottle and glasses out of the room onto the porch.

Hank remained beside his wife's chair. He looked up into her blue eyes to see tears brim ready to spill out. Lori's lower lip quivered. "You're not mad—all our plans?"

"No I'm not mad, I'm elated, happy, ecstatic and all the other words to show you. I love you and this baby too."

Lori stood up and put her arms around Hank's neck. He hugged her close; then he released her. "I didn't mean to squeeze you so tight, is it all right?"

"Hank, you're not going to break me. Besides your hugs are wanted, now and always." She put his arms around him and pulled him closer. "Now, that's better, tell me you love me."

"I love you with my whole heart, there will only be you forever." Hank looked deep into his wife's eyes. "I promise: forever."

CHAPTER 4

Sabrina Michelle Springer was born at 1414 hours on Saturday the tenth of May. She weighed six pounds seven ounces and was twenty-one inches long. The Naval Hospital Maternity Ward at Camp Pendleton had a shortage of babies; Sabrina Springer was the only baby in the ward. Staff Sergeant Springer, dressed in dark blue scrubs and hospital slippers, had been holding his wife's hand since 0130 never leaving her side unless ordered by the doctor or nurse on duty: Hank always ready with a damp face cloth or ice chips to wet her lips. He told her stories of some of the funny things his Marines had done. Lori knew every one of Hank's Marines and invited them and their wives and girlfriends to the Springers' home for old fashioned barbeques.

In the months since Hank had joined the Headquarters and Service Company of the 5th Marines, Lori had become as much a part of the platoon as anyone other than the Marines themselves, always there with a shoulder to weep on for a wife who was becoming disenchanted with the Marine Corps or with family troubles.

Hank finished telling a funny story about his lieutenant when the nurse and doctor came into the room. "We are having a bit of a problem Staff Sergeant Springer. It seems there is a platoon of Marines in the lobby with wives and girlfriends all wanting to see Mrs. Springer. They all claim they are relatives, mostly cousins or brothers and sisters. You don't really have forty brothers and twelve sisters?" The doctor grinned at the new mother and father. "Listen, if you're not too tired I could let them come up three or four at a time."

"I think that's wonderful, please and thank you doctor. They are my family." Lori gave the doctor and nurse one of her beaming smiles, her eyes like rays of sunshine. The doctor left shaking his head while the nurse prepared for an intrusion into the maternity ward.

Every man, wife and girlfriend in Hank's platoon came with a small gift, some for Lori and some for Baby Sabrina. Marines from the rest of the company dropped by too. Hank thanked each person with a handshake and Lori by a hand squeeze and addressed each by name. The nurse stood against the wall next to the door and made sure no one overstayed. When all the Marines and women had visited, she arranged all the gifts and flowers around the room so Lori could see.

"I want a writing table and five boxes of note cards. Hank, please go to the gift shop for me." When Hank was gone, Lori broke into tears. The nurse watched, knowing how Lori felt about the love and thoughtfulness of Hank's Marine's and their families; their devotion touched her heart.

* * *

Sabrina learned to crawl on schedule followed shortly by running; she skipped the walking all together. Sabrina didn't walk, she ran everywhere. Words began to flow from her mouth non-stop.

Lori discovered she was pregnant with her second child as Hank completed his assignment with the 5th Marines. He received orders to the 1st Marine Division Intelligence Group. With the assignment orders came a Warrant Officer's Commission and temporary duty orders to the Warrant Officer Basic School at Quantico, Virginia. Lori and Sabrina went to the Lazy B while Hank was at Quantico.

Whenever possible, the Springer family toured the Southwest visiting lesser known but interesting historic places. Hank taught Sabrina to swim in a small pool on a tour of the Grand Canyon while camping at an isolated campground on the Colorado River. Hank held Sabrina by the hands and swished her through the pool. He never tired of hearing her squeals and giggles. He'd sat on the sandy beach and watched Sabrina play in the water doing the mud crawl and swimming under water.

Sabrina was an adventure, keeping Hank and Lori on their toes; one of them had to be with her at all times; she knew no fear. She was definitely Daddy's girl and Hank loved it. Lori enjoyed watching father and daughter walking together hand in hand.

Brent James Springer, named after Hank's father and Jim, was born on August 10 two years after Sabrina. Hank took a week leave and spent almost all of it with Lori at the hospital for the two days she was there and around the house while she recuperated at home. Sabrina stayed with neighbors in base housing until Hank missed her so much he brought her home. He taught the spunky two year old to fold baby clothes and to get her own breakfast of Cheerios or corn flakes and milk.

During Lori's second time in the hospital, the same doctor and nurse were on duty, but this time the maternity ward was full to overflowing. Brent had to share the nurse's time with two dozen other babies. Lori could tell Brent was still the favorite by the way Nurse Lieutenant Janice Lawson U.S. Navy (Medical Corps) always seemed to have him in her arms.

When Hank drove into the driveway of their quarters in base housing with Lori and Brent James Springer, men from the 5th Marines and Marines from the Intelligence Group were there to welcome Brent into the Culture of the Marine Corps, the Booty Platoon. Nurse Lawson showed up to join the party. Lori sat in a comfortable chair holding Brent; Sabrina, next to her, held her mother's arm, occasionally peeking into the blanket to make sure Brent was still there.

Randy Henry Springer was born to CWO2 and Mrs. Springer on the last day of July two years after Brent's arrival. Both Nurse Lawson and Doctor Waitman, the doctor who had delivered Sabrina and Brent, had been transferred to the Naval Hospital at Balboa in San Diego. Nurse Lieutenant Janice Lawson, now Nurse Lieutenant Commander Waitman, arrived before Lori left the hospital to congratulate the Springers. Sadly, Hank was on deployment as an infantry battalion Assistant Intelligence Officer.

When the Marine Expeditionary Unit returned to Camp Pendleton, Hank received orders for an overseas assignment to Okinawa, Japan for thirteen months, an unaccompanied tour with the 3rd MEF (Marine Expeditionary Force). One afternoon, when Lori returned to their quarters there was a message from Hank with a dozen roses. He planned to be home within the next 90 days and would take 30 days leave and visit Montana and introduce Randy to the Lazy B. Jim and Maya had come to California for the children's births. Maya stayed to help Lori with the children.

*　*　*

It was time Brent learned to swim and Sabrina pestered Lori to get her formal swimming lessons at the base pool. On Tuesday, Thursday and Saturday mornings, Lori packed up the kids and took them to the pool. Sabrina was the youngest in the class but one of the strongest swimmers. Hank had seen all his children drown-proofed while still on the short side of one year. Lori approved Hank's approach to child rearing and supported his plans even though they seemed a bit much for young children. Sabrina led the way with the Age Group Swimming Team. Hank never missed a swim meet unless required to be somewhere else.

Family vacations in Montana were some of Hank's happiest memories. Lori spent time with Maya and listened to the stories about Hank's teen life. The two women sipped tea and talked while the children napped or played on the front lawn. The driveway was crowded by several toys: a red wagon, small bicycle and tricycle and a small red pedal fire engine were neatly parked on the edge of the grass.

Hank worked with Jim gathering cattle from the high range. The older man watched the younger with a father's pride. From a shy newly orphaned boy to a man, Hank had grown into a wonderful husband, father and respected leader of Marines.

"What do you have planned for tonight?" Jim asked Hank and Lori while sipping coffee.

"Not much, just watching the moon pass over the mountains." Hank smiled down at Lori. The kids were in bed, tired after playing in the hay barn. Maya napped on the day bed, exhausted from playing with her grandchildren.

Today Lori, for the first time, spent the day with Hank and Jim gathering cattle. She lay on the couch with her feet in Hank's lap while he massaged her feet and toes and rubbed the ache from tired, sore muscles. Lori dozed. When Jim asked what they planned for tonight, she sat up. Jim very seldom inserted himself into their evening plans.

"I've got George Honey to babysit and we're going to Lone Horse for a night out. We haven't done much of that since you came to us Lori, and it's about time we did." Jim looked at her expectantly. "You up for a little dancing? I love to watch your husband glare at all the cowboys drooling over you."

"Since you put it that way, yes. Get this old cowboy to let go of my feet so I can take a shower and get all prettied up for my date with my two favorite gentlemen." Lori stuck her big toe onto Hank's nose then jumped to her feet before he could grab her for a little retaliation. "Ugh, you need a shower too there cowboy, you coming?"

Hank never refused an invitation and followed her with a smirk on his face. He wiggled his eyebrows at Jim. Maya, who woke during the conversation, punched Jim on the shoulder. "You ready to wash my back Old Man?"

CHAPTER 5

Hank's tour with the 3rd MEF on Okinawa, Japan was filled with training evolutions in Korea, Thailand, the Japanese Home Islands and exercises with other Southeast Asia armed forces. The thirteen months passed quickly and Hank was on a Marine Corps C130 transport on final approach to the Miramar Marine Corps Air Station north of San Diego. He wondered if Randy would even remember him. Sabrina was eight years old and a third grader. Brent, two years younger, was in the first grade and Randy, four, was ready for his own trip to preschool. Hank thought Lori wanted to keep Randy home for another year before he began kindergarten. Randy was still learning to talk and putting long sentences together. Lori's letters said she couldn't shut him up. He was constantly interrupting his brother and sister insisting they play and talk to him.

Lori waited at the gate when the pilot shut down the engines of the large blue/gray transport plane. When Hank stepped down from the plane's ramp, Lori was in his arms almost before he dropped his Valpak. They kissed and held each other, warmth and love flowed between them.

The customs officer from the San Diego office, a Marine Corps Reserve officer, cleared Hank and welcomed him home with a handshake. Lori noticed Hank wore the silver and red bar of a Chief Warrant Officer 3. "Wow, you really made it from gold to silver." She kissed him again.

"Yep, silver looks a lot better don't you think. Where're the kids?"

"I left them with Sue. I know how horny you lipstick lieutenants are so I thought I'd be prepared this time." She laughed.

Hank lifted Lori, holding her to his hip, carrying his Valpak in his left hand. "Where's the car?"

Lori pointed toward the second row of cars in the large parking lot. "Are you sure you don't want to stop for a beer at the club before you come home?"

They were still laughing when an enlisted Marine saluted Hank. "Good morning Gunner."

Hank answered with his usual smile and, "Good morning Devildog."

Hank set Lori on her feet and patted her bottom. "You run ahead and get the motor started. Both the car's and yours." Hank watched her walk quickly to the car, open the door, start the motor and release the trunk lock before he caught up.

"What's holding you up, cowboy? You're burning daylight." Lori laughed.

It seemed to take forever to get to his quarters at Camp Pendleton. Opening the door to the kitchen, he grabbed Lori, kissing her and holding her against him.

Lori pointed to the bathroom, "Get your butt into that shower before you come near me. You are stinky, you smell like oil and Av gas."

Hank, disappointed, did as instructed. He was soaping himself when the sliding door opened and Lori slipped into the shower. "Got enough room? There's a water shortage on base and we've been requested to conserve water so I thought we'd better shower together." She looked down. "You get that thing away from me." Lori pushed down on him then sank down on her knees. Minutes later, Lori slid up his water—slick body. "Now that you're clean and you look considerably more at ease, you can wash my back." She turned her back to him. "Now keep your hands doing what they are supposed to be doing, washing me."

Hank's hands, as if with a mind of their own, moved to more private places. Lori turned to face him and kissed him lightly on the lips. They dried each other and moved toward the king-size bed with the covers already turned down. They made love with tenderness, whispering all the love their hearts stored up for the long thirteen months.

The sun slipped toward the ocean's horizon when Hank pulled Lori closer and whispered, "As much as I love being here like this, can we please go get the kids?"

"Of course Lover, I'm surprised it took you this long to bring it up."

"It didn't take long to get it up; it was getting it down that took so long. Now, let's get the kids. I've been away too long."

"Okay, but we need another shower. You go first; I've got a couple of things in the dryer. There are steaks from the freezer thawing for dinner. The kids want a barbeque to welcome you home. Hamburgers for them and blood red steaks for us. You'll need your strength for later." Lori slapped him on the butt as she left the bedroom and slipped into her robe. She talked to Hank as he shaved. "Brent has learned to swim better and wants to show you, we can do that tomorrow at the pool. Sabrina is on the swimming team and has a youth swim meet Saturday. That's the day after tomorrow; I know how you get messed up with the International Dateline crossing."

"How about Randy, what's he got to show me?"

"He rides his three wheeler all over the place and he'll want to race you around the block. Oh yeah, he wants a battery operated jeep for Christmas. Brent wants a horse and Sabrina just wants her daddy home. Me, I just want to get laid. Think you can handle all those orders there Mr. Chief Warrant Officer of the Third Power?"

"I know I can handle the last one—the rest I'll have to work on."

An hour later, Hank walked up the sidewalk to the Bennett house; the children poured out of the house, swarming over him, knocking him to the ground where they wrestled until the kids tired. Joan had their clothing and toy bags in the hallway. After welcoming Hank, she shooed them home saying they needed family time.

Sunday, the day following Sabrina's swim meet, where she won three ribbons in her age group, the family left for the Montana ranch. Jim told Hank on the phone he had horses for both Sabrina and Brent. The horses were what Jim called, bomb proof. Hank and Lori were keeping the news from the children to let Jim and Maya have the joy of giving the horses to their grandchildren.

Brent frowned when Hank only loaded Randy's three wheeler in the back of the Ford F250SD on Monday morning. While Lori napped with Randy, Hank with Sabrina and Brent for company took the truck to the Ford dealer and had a DVD player installed so the kids could watch movies on the long trip.

Hank wanted to scream after the third time hearing the Baby Einstein disk. He thought it was the most irritating thing he had heard until Randy elected to watch Strawberry Shortcake.

"When did he start watching Strawberry Shortcake?"

"When he was learning to talk, I thought it was cute listening to him sing along with the DVD. After hearing it for the thousandth time, I was ready to throw out the DVD, the player and Randy too."

"You should have thrown the disk away."

"I tried, but he found it. I put it on the top shelf of the closet but he convinced Sabrina to get it down for him." Both parents groaned as the opening of Strawberry Shortcake and Blueberry Muffin started, again.

* * *

The second day at the ranch, Jim gave Sabrina and Brent their new horses. Jim took Brent to the round pen to teach him how to sit on the horse while Hank took Sabrina to the large arena. Hank rode one of the ranch horses while Sabrina was alone on her new horse, Jeff. Jeff was fifteen and wasn't as fast as his former owner thought he should be. Sabrina fell in love with the sorrel.

After a two hour lesson, Sabrina was still fresh and Hank was tired: the tension of watching Sabrina alone on the horse. Hank was proud of his daughter but he couldn't relax, as he watched Sabrina. He called it a day and helped Sabrina wash, groom and care for her horse. He noticed Jim had done much the same with Brent when the boy had enough riding for one day.

"Look how Jeff shines Daddy, isn't he beautiful? He's the same color as a bright new penny."

"I think you should thank Grandpa Jim and Grandma Maya. They found Jeff for you."

Time at the ranch passed quickly. Jim, Maya, Lori and Hank were able to get away for a few days' ride up into the mountains surrounding the Lazy B. Old faithful baby sitter George Honey was more than delighted to watch over the children. George was a great cook and full of stories to keep the children busy and contented.

*   *   *

The Springer family, like many Marine families, experienced weeks and months with the father away on deployments and training exercises. Hank was assigned to the Navy Marine Corps Intelligence Training Center at Dam Neck, Virginia, for four months. Lori joined him for a week over the Fourth of July holiday. The children were sent to the ranch for safe keeping. On the long holiday weekend, they toured the coast visiting historical sites and old friends at Quantico. Lori returned to Camp Pendleton after picking up the children while Hank finished his class. He was sent from Dam Neck to Fort Bragg and then home. Orders were waiting assigning him to Marine Corps Base Twenty-nine Palms, California, for duty with the 7th Marine Regiment of the 1st Marine Division. The Regimental Commander wanted Hank on site immediately and he left for the high desert base the morning after returning from Fort Bragg.

Lori became expert at packing alone and directing the movers: putting the things they needed as soon as they were in their new house on the truck last so those things were first off. With the moving company's help, Lori packed up the household effects and the family moved to the desert base. Much of the training at the giant base was live fire exercises and desert environmental survival training. Hank was able to spend almost every night at home. He expected the next set of orders would assign him to an East Coast Marine Corps unit. He was not surprised when he received orders to Iraq. He had missed Operations Desert Shield and Desert Storm but was assigned to a follow-on mission on a one year assignment with the Marine Headquarters of Central Command in Iraq.

Lori and the children stayed at Twenty-nine Palms in base housing while Hank was deployed. He missed Sabrina and Brent's birthdays but hoped to be home for Lori's. Because his overseas control date was affected by the Iraq tour, Hank didn't expect another Fleet Marine Force tour but a base or station assignment. He received orders to Marine Corps Recruit Depot, at San Diego as a series officer in charge of three recruit platoons and the drill instructors assigned to each platoon. It was a rare assignment for a Marine Warrant Officer and he was deep selected for promotion to CWO4.

The family moved from the desert to San Diego, bought a house in Mission Valley and settled in for Hank's two year tour at the Depot.

That summer, Lori took the children and went to Montana for the children's summer vacation. Hank caught a couple of flights to Fairchild Air Force Base outside of Spokane WA and drove to Montana for long weekend visits between recruit platoon training.

Sabrina was in her first year of high school, Brent two years behind her and Randy three years behind Brent. Sabrina started doing age group competition in barrel racing while Brent was forever playing with a rope. When he broke one of Maya's vases, the rope was banned from the house to the tack room.

Nearing the end of Hank's MCRD assignment, he received orders as the Intelligence Officer for the 22nd MEU. The work-up would last three months, and then Hank would embark aboard ship for duty in the Indian Ocean and Persian Gulf. The good part: Hank would only be gone six months and then return to Camp Pendleton. Lori and children stayed in San Diego but would move to a house they purchased in San Clemente while stationed with the 5th Marines. Hank was sure he would be stationed at Camp Pendleton when the MEU returned. Hank passed his twenty years in the Marines and decided he would continue to thirty years.

Lori and the children were at the dock in San Diego when Hank boarded the helicopter carrier USS Peleliu LHA 5. The staff officers were the first to board along with the command element enlisted staff. The infantry battalion would fly out to the carrier on a helicopter lift off the beach at Camp Pendleton. Lori as usual put on a happy face for Hank and the kids.

"Tell me this is the last deployment, please Hank. I feel like life is passing us by. I want to move to Montana and the children do to. You've got plenty of years to retire and we don't need the money." She put her arms around his neck and held him. "I'm scared Hank, I want you to think about it. You know I'll go along with whatever you decide, but please think about it."

"Okay honey, I'll do that. Maybe it is time I retired and became a cowboy full time." He looked into her eyes. "God, I love you Lori. You'll own my heart and my soul, forever." With that said, he kissed her and walked up the steep gangplank, saluted the Ensign and the Officer of the Deck, then disappeared into the cavern-like hanger deck of the ship.

Lori sighed. "Daddy will be home in a few months." She held Brent and Randy's hands; Sabrina cried silently, already missing her father. Lori led them to the car and drove home to begin the long wait for Hank's return.

CHAPTER 6

The call came over the ship's address system: "Chief Warrant Officer Springer report to the MEU Commander's quarters." CWO4 Springer was in the Communications Center reading the daily administrative radio traffic. Springer addressed the Master Sergeant in Charge of the Comm. Section, "Top, would you call the SCIF and let them know I'll be there as soon as I see what the Boss wants." Springer handed the message board to the Communications Chief and left to report to his Commanding Officer on board the *USS Peleliu* northwest of Diego Garcia in the Indian Ocean.

It was common for the CO to send for him. Intelligence reports and summaries from higher commands were a way of life for the MEU and the Intelligence Section. CWO4 Henry (NMI) Springer hurried anyway. When the Colonel wanted him it was for a reason and it was never a good idea to keep the boss waiting.

Hank Springer crossed the line into officer's country where the deck tile went from green to blue and passed the stateroom he shared with another Chief Warrant Officer. He ducked and passed through the watertight hatch. Hank was always cautious stepping through the hatches, known as knee knockers. He walked to the Colonel's stateroom and mentally ran through the items on the Daily Intelligence Summary.

Hank rubbed his hand over his short cropped dark brown hair and checked his uniform before he knocked on the CO's door. He waited the required fifteen seconds and entered. Sitting behind his desk, Colonel Syler looked up and then rose when the Chief Warrant Officer stepped into the tidy office. Hank noticed the Chaplain who sat on the side chair rose too. The Chaplain being there indicated bad news for one of his Marines, a death in the family or other emergency.

"Chief Warrant Officer Springer reporting sir," Hank said formally as he always did when there was another in the office with the Colonel.

"Hank, take a seat." The Colonel nodded at the Chaplain who moved a step away from the side chair. "Hank, I don't know how to say this, so I'm just going to say it. I received notification from the MEF G1 (Personnel), there's been an accident and Lori was involved. She's in critical condition at the Camp Pendleton hospital and the doctors don't think she's going to make it. Sergeant Major Griffith at MEF jumped channels to get this message out before the official notification. I called the Admin Officer and you have emergency permissive orders for transportation to Diego Garcia and for transport to Marine Corps Air Station, Miramar. A Marine C130 preparing to return to Japan has been rerouted to Kaneohe Bay Marine Corps Air Station and on to Miramar."

The Colonel walked around his desk and put his hand on his friend's shoulder. "Your orders were cut to North Island Naval Air Station in case you missed the Marine C130. The ship's captain has a CH53Echo Super Stallion helicopter ready to fly you to Garcia. The Admiral signed your priority orders." Hank could see giving him this news was almost as hard on the Colonel has it was on him. After taking a few calming breaths, the Colonel finished. "The Admin Chief has your leave papers and is waiting in your quarters. The plane will refuel in Hawaii and if you desire, you can go commercial. I think the C130 will take less time even though it's a hundred miles per hour slower, your decision."

The Chaplain put his hand on Hank's other shoulder. "Hank, our prayers for Lori go with you. If there is anything I can do, you have only to ask."

Springer dropped onto the side chair in shock. He stared at the two men.

"God Hank, you know I think the world of Lori. Sandy will be there for you and the kids if you need anything. The Gunny checked and you have twenty-five days of leave due plus another thirty at the end of this deployment. Take all the time you need."

Stunned by the news, Hank stood up slowly, shook the offered hands and quietly left the Colonel's quarters. Gunnery Sergeant Scholoski waited with his signed orders. "Gunner, we can send your personal effects later if you desire. I don't think the Colonel wants to assign another Intel Officer so your Intel Chief can handle the office with your concurrence. All you have to do is say the word."

"After I see my wife." Hank was still confused with shock. "I think I'll be coming back and rejoining the MEU in the Gulf. Oh Hell Gunny, I don't know, I'll have to get back to you. Would you pass the word to the chopper pilots, I'll be ready in fifteen minutes."

After Gunny Scholoski left, Hank sank into a chair and held his head in his hands. After a minute, he got up and packed his Val-pack with personal items. While walking across the flight deck to the helicopter, the impact of losing Lori struck him and he almost dropped his bag. Hank managed to get aboard the helicopter and strapped-in. The pilot engaged the overhead blades and thirty seconds later the helicopter lifted from the deck, pointed the nose southeast toward Diego Garcia, pushing the helicopter to maximum speed.

* * *

Hank Springer, still wearing his utility uniform and smelling of Av gas, strode down the hallway of the hospital toward the critical care ward. A nurse stopped him, read the name tag on his uniform and got out of his way, pointing to a doorway twenty feet away.

Lori lay on the bed with tubes running into both arms and a breathing tube down her throat. Her eyes were closed; at least the one eye he could see was closed. He dropped to his knees beside the bed. "God Lori, don't leave me," Hank whispered, tears streaming down his unshaved cheeks to drip unnoticed onto the floor beside the bed. He sensed movement and saw Lori's eye open, a tear pooled there. Hank watched the tear slip over and run down her cheek to disappear into a bandage. Lori's doctor placed a gentle hand on his shoulder. Hank had met him a number of times officially when members of his unit at Camp Pendleton were injured.

"Gunner, can I talk to you in the passageway, please."

"Yes sir." Hank reluctantly let go of Lori's hand and followed the doctor out into the hall.

"Gunner, can I call you Hank?"

"Yes sir, of course."

"Hank, Lori has a lacerated liver, we had to remove her spleen and her lungs are damaged in addition to the broken bones. But what is killing her is a rib pierced her heart—if we remove it she will bleed to death. We have no way of fixing her; it's only a matter of time."

"How soon Doc?"

"Today, no later than tomorrow. She should have died by now with her injuries, but she waited for you. She wouldn't leave without seeing you."

"Can she speak?"

"If I take the breathing tube out, yes. It's her decision, and yours. My suggestion is get your family together and spend the time she has left with her. If she wishes, I'll remove the breathing tube. After that it will be fast, less than an hour at best." The doctor laid his hand on Hank's arm. "I am so sorry Hank, we've done all we can. I wish we could do more. Do you want me to get the Chaplain?"

"No, Lori isn't very religious and I'm sure she'd want to spend time with the children. Is there a problem getting them in here?"

"No, not a problem. If you need to make some calls, use my phone." The doctor handed Hank a cell phone. "I'll be here when you need me."

An hour later, Hank heard Sabrina telling Randy to be a little quieter. Hank stepped into the passageway and was met by three pale and confused children: Sabrina, Brent and Randy holding Sabrina's hand. Jim and Maya Sutterland followed the children, their faces and eyes red.

When they'd crowded into the room, the doctor entered and stepped to Lori's bedside. "Lori, I'm going to ask you some questions. Blink once for yes and twice for no, do you understand?" Lori blinked once. "Okay I need to ask a control question, are you a horse?" Lori blinked no and a smile radiated from her eye. "Do you know what's happening to you?" Again one blink. "Do you want me to remove the breathing tube so you can speak?" One blink. "You realize that removing the tube will shorten your remaining time to probably less than an hour?" One blink. The doctor gently removed the breathing tube from Lori's throat. She gasped, and then her breathing, still labored, evened.

Lori strained to speak, her voice rough and weak but easily understood. "Hank, I love you. Sabrina, you are going to have to take care of Brent and Randy." She looked at Maya. "Please help Hank, thank you, you've been wonderful. Hank, watch over our children. When I can I'll watch too. Hank, I don't want you to grieve too long, I know you will. Get on with your life and love our children."

Maya broke down and started sobbing and was comforted by Jim. Sabrina had tears running down her cheeks. "Mom, don't die, please we need you, and Daddy needs you." Sabrina held Randy close so Lori could touch him with the tip of her fingers.

She reached for Brent and then Sabrina, who were both crying. "I need to be alone with your father—there's some things I need to tell him. I love you." Lori saw her children for the last time.

Jim and Maya gathered the children and took them to the waiting room next to the nurse's station. Hank watched them go then turned his full attention to his wife. "You tricked me; I always thought I'd be the first. God Lori, I love you more than life. If I could trade places I would in a heartbeat."

"No!" Lori whispered. "You are a good father. Take care of them, Brent is just like you and so is Sabrina. They will get through this; Randy will need a little bit more time. Maya and I talked after her brother Ben was killed, she'll help take care of the children." Lori's breathing had become labored; Hank rang the bell for the doctor. Twenty seconds later he came in. When Hank looked back, Lori's eye was fixed; he watched the pupil dilate and the blue iris of her eye almost disappeared. The doctor checked for life signs, found none and slowly shook his head. The doctor closed Lori's eye and left Hank alone with his wife, a crushed man crying unashamed holding her cooling hand.

* * *

Lori's funeral was held at the Camp Pendleton Base Chapel. Many of Lori's and Hank's Marine family filled the small chapel. Hank sat surrounded by his and Lori's children. Jim and Maya sat behind Hank, Jim's hand steady on his shoulder. Randy crawled onto Hank's lap, and a moment later Brent and Sabrina were crowded together with Hank holding them to him. The Navy Chaplin conducted the brief ceremony and Hank sat unaware when the man finished. Jim squeezed his shoulder. Hank sat with Randy in his lap, Sabrina had her arms around Hank's neck while Brent held onto to his free arm. As the family said goodbye to wife and mother, Hank rose with the children; each laid a red rose on the small cherrywood table held Lori's urn. After Hank put a rose on the table he stepped back, sat down on the bench and held his children close while friends filed silently past leaving a small token of a rose on the table. Hank's Intelligence Marines brought a live rose plant the family could plant wherever they called home. As they passed, they touched Hank on the shoulder or mumbled a heartfelt word of condolence.

Jim and Maya stayed with Hank and the children after all the others left, then took the children out to wait by the cars. When the chaplain placed the urn into a cherrywood box, Hank broke down and sat with his head lowered; tears came and he sat still until he remembered the children. He rose carefully like an old man and left the chapel. The chaplain would bring the box packaged and the rose plant for Jim, Maya and the children to take to Montana. Lori loved the ranch and Hank thought she would be happiest there.

Hank picked up Randy and hugged him until Maya gently took him from Hank's arms. Jim took Brent's hand and they began the lonely walk to the cars. Sabrina stayed with her father clinging to his arm. She dried her tears and led him to the car to follow the rest of the family home.

Hank elected not to have a reception at the house after the chapel service. The children's things were packed and ready for the trip to Montana. Jim would drive a rental truck with some of the household items Hank wanted to keep. The children would fly to Missoula with Maya where Jim had left the ranch truck he used to drive from the ranch to the airport for the trip to California. The children would stay at the ranch until Hank finished with the Marines and came home to the Lazy B.

Two weeks after Lori's funeral, Hank returned to the *USS Peleliu* in the Persian Gulf. He resumed his duties as the MEU Intelligence Officer.

Hank didn't want to retire from the Marines yet; but the children needed him. He knew the children were used to the culture of the Corps and their school and friends were part of the Marine Corps family. But it was time to start a new life without Lori and for him to devote time to his family. CWO4 Henry (NMI) Springer put in his papers to retire at the convenience of the Marine Corps or in six months. Three weeks later, his request for retirement was approved and he left Camp Pendleton for the Lazy B and Montana.

CHAPTER 7

The years without Lori were hard and lonely years for Hank. He buried Lori's ashes near the mountain pool where they spent many happy hours together. He devoted his life to his children. Jim built an indoor heated swimming pool for year around swimming. Sabrina continued with her swimming when she didn't have her nose in a book. She excelled in her studies especially the sciences. Sabrina wanted to attend medical school and become a thoracic surgeon. At sixteen Sabrina began competing in barrel racing on the Northwest circuit.

Brent, a so-so student in his first high school year, excelled during his last three years with exceptional grades. He worked as a cowboy on the Lazy B and competed in calf roping and as one half of a team roping pair usually with his father.

Randy learned the ranch business and was an excellent high number team roper, but enjoyed roping only as an outlet for excess energy. He didn't take roping as seriously as Brent. When Randy entered college, he stopping roping competitively to concentrate on his studies.

Hank's hair was still thick and liberally frosted with gray. His once 195 pounds of muscle was now 175 pounds, lean and hard from countless hours in the saddle. He no longer wore the camouflage uniform or Marine Green, but his heart was still that of the young sergeant who had held the love of the most beautiful girl in the world. Lori's rose plant reproduced to more than a dozen bushes. Maya planted them around the main house, and the roses added vibrant color to the ranch.

Sabrina finished with medical school and did one year of her internship at a Missoula hospital. She applied for and was commissioned a lieutenant in the U.S. Navy Medical Corps as an internist and surgeon. She requested and was assigned to the Marines. After her Navy orientation course at the Great Lakes Naval Training Center, she received her orders to report to the Naval Hospital Balboa in San Diego, California, and await further assignment to the Naval Hospital at Camp Pendleton.

Hank moved into the bunkhouse when Randy started college. He liked sharing space with the cowboys working on the Lazy B. As the foreman, he was entitled to his own room and used it as home and office. Hank's room's walls held pictures of the Springer family surrounding a picture of a smiling Lori. But Hank's favorite was of five year old Sabrina walking hand in hand with him down a forest trail. The two were perfectly framed by the loving mother and wife who had taken the picture. That picture showed the tone and strength of his relationship with his wife and family.

After Brent graduated college and received a reserve commission from the Marines as a Second Lieutenant, he completed his three years of active duty requirement and elected to remain a Reserve Marine Intelligence Officer working for the Joint Intelligence Center at Fort Lewis, Washington. Brent planned on working for the Lazy B as a cowhand until he decided what he wanted to do with the rest of his life.

Like Brent, Randy graduated in three years from the university in Missoula. He worked for the U.S. Forest Service assigned to the Kaniksu area of the Colville National Forest in northeast Washington State, the panhandle of Idaho and the northwest corner of Montana. He continued his education with graduate classes in fish and game conservation and law enforcement. He planned to transfer to the Federal Bureau for Fish and Game Enforcement after gaining valuable experience in the forest.

*   *   *

With Brent's return to the Lazy B, life took on more meaning for Hank. Jim and Maya worried about him after Randy left and the vacations stopped. Hank missed his family and Lori. He thought of her every day. When the roses bloomed, Hank kept a rose on his desk in Lori's favorite bud vase.

When Brent returned home, the team-roping team picked up again. Hank and Brent had team-roped together all through Brent's high school and college years. Sabrina did barrel racing and some team roping with Hank through high school, but concentrated on studies during college in Missoula and medical school at the University of Washington in Seattle.

Randy liked to pack trip alone with his horse and a mule. Occasionally Hank tagged along and listened as his son as he pointed to the different flora and fauna of the forest.

Except for missing his wife and children, Hank's life was good. He took on family responsibilities. It was Hank, who Maya relied on when Jim had a heart attack and during his convalescence. Hank kept things running while Jim recuperated in Hawaii. Maya was born in the islands and wanted Jim to retire there and let Hank run the Lazy B.

*   *   *

Ralph Bentley, longtime friend and retired Marine, was the foreman at a neighboring ranch. Ralph planned to pick up Hank at the Lazy B bunkhouse and they would ride together on the sixty mile trip to the town of Lone Horse. Brent would pick Hank up at Millie's, Monday morning on his way back to the Lazy B. Hank kept some of his good clothes, hat and boots at Millie's for his rare night out with friends.

Sharply at 0600 on a crisp April morning Ralph pulled his old green Ford pickup next to the hitching rail in front of the Lazy B bunkhouse. Hank waited on the porch in his favorite straight-back chair leaned against the bunkhouse wall. Hank wore a Ford Motor Company give-me hat pulled down to shade his eyes from the morning sun. The early spring sun warmed him as the fiery orange globe broke over the eastern skyline. Dressed in faded Wranglers, a worn and pressed denim work shirt and his well worn sheepskin denim jacket, Hank was ready for town. He still wore his graying hair a bit shorter than the rest of the men on the ranch. Hank shaved every day, even when he was riding fence or on a roundup. His eyesight had faded some, but he didn't require glasses, yet. Hank said he kept his weight down so his horse wouldn't have to carry the extra tonnage.

"Been sitting there long?" Ralph inquired as he pushed open the creaking, groaning driver's door and stepped down from the old Ford.

"Nope, been sitting here watching the sun come up; right pretty don't you think?" Hank's use of the language had regained much of its distinctive western flavor over the years since his retirement. "When you going to put some oil on that door. It sounds worse than a treed wildcat."

"Don't you worry about my truck's door." Ralph gazed over the hood of the pickup at the eastern horizon. "Yep, the sun and those clouds make for a pretty sunrise. Now are you about ready or are you going to keep us here jawing together all day?" Ralph looked around. "You got a bag or anything?"

"Just this." Hank picked up a small black gym bag from beside the chair. He stood up, twisted and stretched in place to ease some of the morning knots in his muscles and back. He stepped from the porch and walked with a noticeable limp. Hank went to the passenger door and pitched the bag into the back next to Ralph's old tan suitcase. The suitcase was tied shut with a piece of old yellowed clothesline. "You ever going to get another suitcase? That things older than I am." Hank joked as he climbed up onto the passenger seat. He nodded approval when the passenger door opened and closed without a whimper. "You should have kept your old sea bag; at least you knew how to pack one of those. And what's with the beard, you going to be a mountain man now?"

"Hey." Ralph grinned. "You don't fault my beard and suitcase and I won't fault that little sissy black thing you tote around. I am a mountain man or haven't you noticed being so busy and all." Ralph rubbed his gray and white beard, a match for his iron gray and white hair.

"We going to sit around here all day jawing at each other or are you going to drive this thing?" Hank pulled the new seat belt across his lap. "Put on your safety belt you old fool."

Ralph fastened the belt and stepped on the starter. Once the truck ran on all six cylinders, he put the truck in gear and drove around the yard past the corral and out the gate.

Ralph grinned. "I like the green color best you know." Ralph remained quiet for only a few heartbeats before he started to expound on the merits of his truck. "You know this here truck reminds me of the trucks we used to drive when we were in the Marines. Almost the same color don't you know?"

"My, you are getting darn right talkative in your old age. But yep, same color does bring back memories." Hank's face took on a faraway look. "Some good, some bad."

"Well, begging the Gunner's pardon—didn't mean to twist your tail and get you all melancholy," Master Gunnery Sergeant Ralph P. Bentley USMC (Retired) said, a boyish grin spread across his chiseled face.

"Shut up and drive Master Gunny." Hank stared out the split windshield as memories flooded his mind.

A companionable silence settled over the two men as the old Ford raced at a steady fifty miles per hour down the dirt road toward the town of Lone Horse. The trail of dust slowly floated back to the ground and marked the truck's passage.

Hank and Ralph served together off and on since they shared the experience of Marine recruit training. As old Marines have a saying for everything, the two men had shared the mud, the blood and the beer together. Each man enlisted at seventeen and served twenty plus years in the Marines, traveled many miles, saw a few battles, and lost a few friends.

When the two old friends retired, they each returned to their roots, cows and horses. The cattle country of Montana was the boyhood home of Bentley. Hank's early years were in the cattle country of Central Washington State. Hank and Ralph joined the Marines on the buddy program right after graduating from Lone Horse High School.

Upon retirement, Ralph returned to Montana and went to work at a neighboring ranch. Hank didn't know how much he was paid for his work at the Lazy B and didn't care. Hank took $200 a month from his wages and didn't spend half of that. The rest was held by the Lazy B in his name, along with his Marine Corps retirement and his investments in a different investment account. The sizeable investment account included his wife's invested portfolio, the heritance from her own adoptive parents. He also invested the insurance policy money from when Lori died and the money from the sale of their houses in California. His ranch wages, except for the $200, were invested with the Lazy B or in a managed investment account; he really didn't know what was in it. The children all obtained scholarships to college and worked at student jobs for spending money. Neither man paid much attention to monetary investments. Hank shoved his monthly statements into a dresser drawer and hadn't looked at a single one in some years. Maya filled out Hank's income tax forms and he signed where indicated.

* * *

Sabrina Springer: a newly minted Lieutenant (MC); a Navy doctor assigned to the Naval Hospital at Camp Pendleton, working temporarily at the Balboa Fleet Hospital in San Diego. Sabrina had honey blonde hair and clear brilliant blue eyes like her mother. She was intelligent, shy at times and outspoken like her father when challenged. She cut a broad path through boyfriends in high school and suitors during college and left broken hearts in her wake. At times, Hank thought Sabrina may have set her sights too high, but he was confident she would find someone and happiness. For the present, medicine was her calling and her passion.

Each year, Brent and Hank roped for a month on the Northwest Pro West Rodeo and some Professional Rodeo Cowboy Association (PRCA) circuits and participated in jackpot ropings together. The Marines and hard ranch work kept Brent's six foot two inch frame to a respectable 195 pounds. He liked to wear his dirty blonde hair short. He said it was easy to dry after a morning shower. His eyes were the same shade of blue as his mother's. With Sabrina and Randy working away from Montana, it was Brent who spent time with their father to ease the sorrow of Hank's separation from this eldest and youngest.

Proud of his children—a medical doctor, a cowboy and Marine, and the youngest a caretaker of the nation's forests and wildlife, Hank worked at a job he loved. He couldn't ask for a better life; if only Lori were there to share it with him. Memories of his life with Lori occupied Hank's mind much of the time when he rode fence alone with only his horses for company.

Randy's six foot one inch height made him a physical match and copy of his father, as did his attitude toward things. With brown eyes and light brown hair, as he aged, he looked more and more like his father.

Ralph breaking for a red light snapped Hank back to the present. Hank brushed the cobwebs from his mind.

"What time is Brent picking you up?" Ralph asked.

"Five o'clock in the morning day after tomorrow. We'll go back to the ranch and pick up the horses then head for Sioux City and on to Oklahoma City and some jackpots in between. We'll finish off with some Pro West roping and maybe a couple of the local PRCA rodeos going on in the area and then back here. Brent planned it all out." Hank paused. "You know you're welcome to come with us."

"Yeah, I know but this is your time with Brent." Ralph clapped his friend on the shoulder.

Ralph dropped Hank off at Millie's, wished him luck and a howdy for Brent. Hank watched as Ralph drove the old green Ford away and disappeared around the corner, leaving a blue cloud in his wake. Hank picked up his gym bag and strode up the walk and steps to the heavy dark wood door. He pulled the small rope ringing the bell in the hall and entered. He found a note addressed to him posted on the house bulletin board. Millie wanted him to know his room was ready, food was in the icebox and she would be back tomorrow afternoon.

Hank trudged upstairs to his room and found Millie had washed and ironed his clothes. His clothing bag sat on the room's lone chair. Hank's dress boots and a new white straw hat were on the shelf in the closet. He dropped his bag on the double bed and went down to the kitchen. He poured himself a glass of milk and ate a dinner of potato salad and cold fried chicken. A strawberry-rhubarb pie with his name on a card stuck in the pie called to him. Hank was going to watch his diet and calorie intake, but the sweet tartness of one of Millie's special strawberry-rhubarb pies was too much of a temptation. He cut a large piece and sat at the kitchen table to enjoy the treat.

The next day passed quickly. Ralph came by to visit. Hank, Ralph and Millie decided to go out for a steak dinner and a little honky-tonk'n. Hank returned to his room early leaving Ralph and Millie to make a night of it. He expected Brent to arrive on time and wanted to be bright and ready. Hank wasn't surprised about how much he looked forward to spending time with Brent. He hoped Sabrina and Randy would be able to get time to visit before the summer was over.

CHAPTER 8

Bess Clemons sat at her desk in the Dutton Children's Home office and stared at the list of children and dates when the State Social Services Department would take control for placement of the children. The names of three children stood out: Michael Anderson, sixteen; Marjorie Anderson, sixteen; Mary Ann Anderson, five. The three children were orphaned by a horrific automobile accident almost five months earlier. Bess had just one more month to find a suitable foster home for adoption of the Anderson children.

Mary Ann was a beautiful blonde haired, blue eyed girl, curious, and outgoing. A number of families expressed interest in adopting her. Marjorie was sixteen, a twin with brilliant brown eyes, soft light brown hair, on the verge of womanhood. Three couples expressed the desire to adopt Marjorie immediately, but Bess didn't trust their intentions or the altruism they expressed. One of the men had the appearance of a pedophile the way he looked at Marjorie when they were introduced. The others appeared to be only gold-diggers.

Michael, Marjorie's twin, was almost a carbon copy of her except he was nearly six feet tall to her five feet six inches. He was beginning to fill out through the chest and shoulders, his light brown hair cut shorter than the style of the day. There was directness to Michael as if he had to challenge everything; he had a sizable chip on his shoulder. Michael kept the two girls close to him whenever possible. He made sure they wore clean pressed clothes every day. Michael took the iron and ironing board from his former home with his personal items to the Dutton Children's Home. Bess was able to get him a semi-private room and he shared the room and bath with another boy who arrived the week before the Andersons.

Bess knew almost 75 percent of the people willing to adopt or foster the Andersons were interested in the girls alone, not Michael. Michael's goal was to keep the family together. Bess's biggest problem was the nearly one million dollars each child would inherit from the insurance company and the liquidation of the family assets.

Bess received a letter that afternoon relating to the Anderson children. The state set the date when the children would no longer be the Dutton Children's Home's responsibility. It was the state's intention to divide the children between three interested couples. At that time the fostering couple or adoptive parent would gain access to the children's inheritance. The overworked state agency would release all authority over the children to the adoptive and fostering couples. The couples would have the authority to use the money any way they saw fit in the care of the child. Bess telephoned the State Child Services Administrator and was informed the decisions were already made and if Bess hadn't fostered or found a family to adopt the children, the State would release the children in thirty-three days.

Bess could not see a solution to the children's problem. Michael would probably remain at the Home until he was eighteen, the girls fostered or adopted away. She needed to find that unknown family who was willing to take all three children. The district court judge who oversaw the Dutton Children's Home, Judge Hoskin, was sympatric with Bess' situation, but his hands were tied unless Bess could find a suitable family who would take all three children.

Sometimes I hate this job, Bess groaned. She looked at the clock above her office door, sighed and picked up her cell phone. She tapped speed dial for her daughter Bev. Bev would be leaving work as an elementary school teacher in the next few minutes to help at the Benefit Roping Jackpot for the Dutton Children's Home starting the next day.

"Hi Mom, no I didn't forget. I volunteered to watch the competitor's gate this afternoon after school. You still going to be the cashier for the barbeque tonight?" Bev asked.

"Yes, of course. I know I've been a bit distracted these past few weeks, but the Anderson children are nearing the end where I can keep them together. Four more weeks, I've only got four more weeks to find them a family." Bess paused, took a deep breath. "I'm sorry to dump on you, it's just so frustrating. I know there is someone out there for these kids, I can feel it."

"I know, Mom. It'll work out, you'll see. Maybe you can find a man for me too. It wouldn't hurt to find one for you either. I'll meet you at the fair grounds at 5:30. I've got to be on the gate to relieve Norman by 3:30. It's 2:45 now and I have to change. So, love you, bye."

Bess smiled for the first time since receiving the letter from the State Child Service Agency. Bev had an effect on everyone she came in contact with. Bess was glad Bev had ended the brief romance with one of the Dutton Dam's construction workers; Craig Baston wasn't for Bev. He was crass, profane and a braggart, but he was Robert Redford handsome and had the Redford charm and personality. He made up for his lack of brains by using his looks and boyish charm. Bess saw through him immediately but it took Bev a couple of months to see Craig's phony ways.

When Craig's job ended at the dam he left and cleaned out Bev's savings using one of her blank checks and a credit card to transfer her money to an account in Boise, Idaho. By the time Bev found out it was too late to recover the money. It was gone and so was Craig Baston.

CHAPTER 9

Hank stepped out onto the boarding house's large front porch. He looked at Brent's forty-five-foot gooseneck trailer hooked to the diesel F350 dually. Hank wore his freshly pressed Wranglers, newly oiled boots, pressed, and starched blue denim shirt and his new straw hat. His travel bag was on the porch beside him ready to be stored in the trailer's living space.

"Now, this is a horse rig!" Hank laughed and indicated Brent's truck and the new trailer, both bearing American flag and Marine Corps decals.

"Every cowboy or lieutenant is supposed to have a new ride." Brent teased his father. "The mileage may suck but neither rain, sleet nor snow shall keep this cowboy from his rodeo."

"Yeah, like the Marines gave you plenty of time off for the rounds. How did you like those big gray boats on your last tour?" Hank laughed at Brent's disgusted expression.

"They sucked. Let's get this show on the road, Pop."

"That is Chief Warrant Officer to the Fourth Power Pop to you sonny." Hank slapped his son on the shoulder.

Hank's rope horse and tack and Brent's horses were already loaded in the back after being stabled in Lone Horse overnight. Jim had one of the hands trailer Brent's horses and Hank's tack and horse to Lone Horse early the day before. Brent wanted a professional farrier he knew to put shoes on Jackson and Beany and included Jake.

"I need to stop and buy some ropes," Hank said when he saw the hardware and tack store appear on the right.

"Not a problem Pop. I got you six heel ropes, four strand, 3/8 scant, medium soft, right?"

"Yep, you got it, thanks. We need any more we can pick them up on the road."

* * *

Over the next four weeks, Hank and Brent competed in team roping events. Brent also competed in the tie-down or calf roping. Together the father-son team won enough to pay all their expenses and a bit more. More than enough to stop at Starbuck's for a cup of their best coffee.

On the home leg of their roping tour, Hank drove while Brent napped when they entered the town of Dutton. A large banner stretched across the main street announced a Jackpot Roping and Timed Events. It advertised, "$500 paid for first place, each event. Loads of fun. Benefit the Dutton Children's Home."

Hank glanced at his sleeping partner, reached over and shook his shoulder. "Hey Brent, wake up and look at this." Hank pulled the truck and trailer to the side of the street. Brent leaned forward and looked up so he could see the banner. "Well, what do you think?" Hank asked. "Could be fun and we've still got some time. You have anywhere you need to be in the next few days?"

"Nowhere important—sure Pop why not?" Brent leaned back in his seat. "We're way ahead on time and money so let's do it. Most of these small towns have stalls available at the local fairgrounds. The horses could use a breather and time away from the trailer for a couple of days." Brent rolled down his window and asked a passing couple where the rodeo grounds were located.

It was late-afternoon when Hank pulled the truck and trailer through the rodeo grounds gate. An attractive young woman at the entrance stepped up to the side of the truck. "What can I do for you gentlemen?"

"Howdy ma'am." Hank asked her if there were camper hookups for electricity and water available, and if there were any stalls for horses.

She pointed at one of the barns. "We have spaces and hookups for trailers available. There's a barbeque feed, all you can eat for ten bucks if you're interested. Stalls are ten bucks a day, all proceeds to the Children's Home. I'll have one of the men come by to help get your horses settled. We'll hay them and for a dollar more grain them too, your call. The stalls are covered with 24 by 24, cedar shavings, any other questions?" When Hank shook his head, she continued. "No? Okay, let me get on the horn to the stableman." She talked into the portable two-way radio, "Harold the stableman is near the camping area and will be there by the time you are. He'll help you get set up with water and electricity and show you the stable."

"Thanks, we might take you up on the barbeque. We'll definitely take advantage of the stalls for the horses." Hank smiled at the pretty young lady dressed in jeans, wearing a western shirt and a well-used straw hat. A blonde braid fell down the middle of her back. "My name's Hank Springer and this ugly sidekick is my son Brent." Hank and Brent both tipped their hats.

Brent was far from ugly and the young lady duly noted the smile, close cut hair and his clean hands. Brent tipped his hat again. Hank drove down the lane the girl pointed to. A man stood in the middle of the road waving; Hank figured it must be Harold.

An hour later, the truck and trailer were in place and the horses were bedded down after being fed and watered with Harold's help. Hank thought about the girl at the gate. "Hey Brent, would you go ask that young lady at the gate if there's a drugstore open this late." Hank didn't have to ask twice. Brent was out the trailer door and double-timed toward the gate before the last word left Hank's mouth.

Ten minutes later Brent returned followed by the gate girl, bringing a smile to the old cowboy's face. Brent introduced his father to the girl. "Pop, this is Beverly Clemons. Beverly, this old wreck is my father Hank Springer."

"It is a pleasure to meet you again, Mr. Springer," Beverly said in a clear strong voice. "I hope Harold got you settled properly. He's a good man, gets confused sometimes but he works hard and takes good care of the livestock. I'm sorry we only had the one stall open."

"That's okay miss, the horses are used to each other so it won't be a problem."

"Please call me Bev, Mr. Springer." She smiled. Her cheeks dimpled at Hank and blushed when she glanced at Brent.

"Okay, I'll call you Bev if you call me Hank, deal?"

"Yes sir, Hank."

"No sir stuff either." Hank put his hand out.

"No problem Hank." Bev took his hand in a firm handshake. So many of the women he met shook hands like they were extending an old wet washrag. Bev didn't leave right away, so Hank got personal. "What does a pretty young lady do for work in a town like Dutton?"

"Why I'm the local school marm." Bev laughed.

Hank decided to go along with her patter. "Well, I do declare, the school marm! Well Miss School Marm what do you think of that there young Springer standing there turning red?" Hank enjoyed teasing his son. "Now would you be the old maid school marm or is there a Mister School Marm?"

"I guess I'd be the old maid school marm pining away for an unnamed cowboy. Now that wouldn't be you, would it Hank?"

"I can tell you if I had a few years back it sure would." Hank laughed and glanced at a red-faced Brent. "If you would accompany my son to check on the horses, I'd like to go in and take a shower before going to that fine barbeque you were telling me about. Can you point me at an open drug store?" Bev answered him but her attention was on Brent.

Bev took Brent's hand and pulled him toward the stalls. The horses didn't need the attention, but it gave Brent an excuse to be with Beverly Clemons. The girl entered the stall and went directly to Jake who was eyeing her but not turning his head. Bev rubbed the horse on his neck and the spot between his ears and moved her hand down to rub his soft nose. When she turned to lavish attention on the other horses, Jake nickered at her as if to say, Hey, come back I need some more of that rubbing.

Brent introduced her to his horses after explaining that Jake was his dad's horse. She dutifully petted Jackson, his calf roping horse, and Beany, his head horse for team roping. Bev excused herself telling Brent she needed to clean up before the barbeque and she would see him there. Brent watched the sway of her hips as she walked away then he turned and ran back to the trailer to shower and change into clean clothes. Hank had finished showering and shaving. He sat on the couch, his feet on the coffee table wearing his new fancy boots. Hank didn't say a word, only smiled at the rushing young man. Ten minutes later Brent came out of the tiny bedroom still tucking in his shirt, his hair wet from the shower. With a smile and wave, Brent went out the door, leaving his father to fend for himself.

Hank walked the quarter mile to the drug store and bought a can of bag balm for the horses. He used the balm for his own sore muscles and scrapes when occasions warranted.

* * *

Hank entered the food barn and spotted Brent sitting with Bev at a table by themselves. Hank looked around and spotted a pretty woman alone at a table with a cash box in front of her. He approached the table. "This the place we pay for that great-smelling food?" He looked down at the attractive blonde middle aged woman who smiled up at him with startling blue eyes.

"Yes sir, you Mister Springer?" she asked.

"Yes ma'am, guilty." Hank couldn't help grinning, a sparkle in his own eyes.

"That good looking young man with Bev happen to belong to you?"

"Yes ma'am, guilty again." Hank handed her a ten dollar bill.

She smiled and pointed. "There's the start of the line, silverware and paper towels are at the end. Hope you enjoy. By the way, are you staying for the dance?"

"Dance? Sorry I'm afraid I'm not much of a dancer—been a lot of years since my last two-step."

"Don't let the word dance scare you, there aren't any experts here. We do boast a pretty good five piece western band, so stick around."

Hank filled his plate with barbeque beef and pork, corn on the cob and baked beans, then picked up a bunch of paper towels, a plastic knife and fork. He carried his haul to the table where Bev and Brent were whispering to each other, their heads close together. Hank pulled up a steel folding chair and sat down. "Hope you don't mind my joining you." He smiled.

"I guess you met my mother. Watch out Hank, she's the town's widow, while I'm the old maid school marm." Bev laughed and even Brent smiled as his father blushed.

Hank stayed for the dance. Bev's mom was even able to get him into a Texas Two Step a time or two. In spite of himself Hank enjoyed the evening and the company.

The next morning Brent disappeared, mumbling something about a breakfast date. Hank made his way to the pay window after checking on the horses. He put down the $100 per man per event entry fees for Brent in the calf roping, and him and Brent in the team roping. The team roping event was scheduled for the afternoon. The calf roping was scheduled as the last event, the fast time getting the only paycheck. The rest of the money went to the Children's Home. Team roping paid $500 for each the header and the heeler and the calf roping paid $500.

The team roping was a three-steer event, with the second round that afternoon. The short or final go for the top five teams was the last scheduled event prior to the calf roping. Hank looked over the entry list and saw he and Brent were the only ropers rated above three, so they would be favored.

The father and son sat on their horses and watched the other team ropers. Two teams other than Hank and Brent qualified for the final. With a combined time of 11.2 seconds the father and son team were firmly in the lead. Hank watched another father and son team catch their last steer. The man and boy were well mounted, but Hank could see the patches on the man's shirt and the boy's pants. He saw winning wasn't just for bragging rights but survival—they needed the prize money to live on. All Hank and Brent needed to win was to catch one leg with a reasonable time without breaking the barrier.

Hank looked over at Brent in the head box, and raised an eyebrow. Brent wore a puzzled expression, looked around, saw their competition and caught his father's meaning and smiled. The gate opened and Brent broke the barrier, but caught the horns and turned the steer perfectly. Hank rode the corner and Jake put him in the sweet spot. Hank threw and singled, losing first place by six seconds after the additional five second penalty for the single leg.

Grinning, Hank and Brent watched the father and son pick up the winner's checks at the pay booth. Hank was about to walk over and congratulate the winners when the man followed by his son approached Hank and Brent. He put out his hand. "You and your son are the best ropers I've seen. You should have won, Mr. Springer."

"Call me Hank and this is my son Brent. You won it fair and square. Your son has real talent and you're pretty well mounted. You should be winning again if I'm any judge of horse flesh and talent."

"Well sir, this here check will let us keep those two horses and then some. It's a pleasure to shake your hand Hank. My name's Ben Withrow and this is my son Robby. I hope we meet again. Robby shake Mister Springer's hand and meet a gentleman."

Robby and Brent listened while the two older men talked about other things, ranching and horses. Then Brent was called to the calf roping. Hank didn't fail to notice the blonde hair under a well used and sweat stained straw cowboy hat follow Brent. Bev caught up and took his hand as they walked to where Jackson waited. The horse was stamping his foot, impatient to get this fool human stuff over with and get back to the real important things in life, eating and hanging out with his buddies. Of course, chasing steers could be fun too.

Brent easily won the first place $500 check. With a nod to his father, Brent endorsed the check and gave it to Bev for the Children's Home.

* * *

"Hey Pop!" Brent shook his dad's shoulder. Hank groaned, sat up and put his feet on the rug below the pull-down bed. The sun was just breaking over the eastern hills and cast its bright light through the window. Hank squinted, reached over and pulled down the window shade. He rubbed the sleep from his eyes and ran fingers through his sleep mussed hair. The old man studied his number one son.

"Dad, you mind if we stay here in Dutton a few more days?"

Hank grinned at Brent as he shifted uneasily from foot to foot. "No, I suppose that will be fine." He decided not to tease Brent as he usually did when the opportunity presented itself. "Any particular reason other than the obvious?" Maybe a little tease.

"No sir. I would like to spend a bit more time with Bev." Brent sat down in the passenger chair.

"Maybe you should just spit out what you need to say. I think it's always easier that way," Hank prompted.

"Yes sir, gosh Dad I think she may be the one. I want to be with her all the time. I can't think, I can't eat." Brent looked miserable. Hank knew it was bad when Brent dropped his hat on the floor and left it there.

"What are we talking about here? Have you talked to Bess Clemons? She's Bev's mother and my dancing partner at the barbeque." Hank watched

Brent's eyes widen and then crinkle around the edges in smile lines. When the dance started Bev and Brent were checking on the horses and somehow never made it back to the barn for the dance.

"No, just Bev, not Bev's mother." Brent slowly moved his head from side to side. "You best be on your best behavior Pop." It was the son's turn to tease his father.

"Let me get this straight, you've talked to Bev about all this?"

"Yes sir, she feels the same way. I just don't know what to do—is it okay?"

"Why don't you sit down with your school teacher and the two of you decide what you want to do with your lives, especially for right now. One suggestion, she could come up to Montana. I can get the guest cabin at the ranch and she can stay there. You two can get to know each other and maybe a little less stress with nobody but the cows watching you two flirting." Hank watched emotions play across Brent's face. "Hey, it's just an idea. I don't want to be pushy." Brent always had his dad's support and Hank never failed to give good advice.

Hank's mind slipped back a bit into a memory of when he and Lori started their life's love story almost from the moment they met. Brent was quick with decisions just like his mother and father were. The brief time Hank had known Bev, he saw she was very much like Lori in temperament and personality. Bev seemed a good match for Brent and Hank liked the feisty school teacher too.

"I've invited Bev and Mrs. Clemons to join us for dinner tonight, okay Dad?"

"Sure son, you set it up and I'll be there."

Relief showed on the younger man's face. Brent left the trailer feeling it was a great day. He whistled a tune as he walked toward the stables to check on the horses.

Hank spent the day at the Dutton Sweet Air Laundromat after meeting Bess for an early lunch. She and Hank talked about their children and their jobs. Bess told Hank she was the Dutton Adoption Director for the State Social Services Department. Her office was at the Children's Home and she invited him to visit the Home.

After lunch, Bess needed to return to work and Hank needed to finish his laundry. Later at the trailer, Hank was folding his clothes and the iron was cooling when a knock on the door interrupted him. Hank in his stocking feet, faded Wrangler jeans and sleeveless sweatshirt answered the door.

"Well damn my sore eyes, Colonel Wheatly. What are you doing here in Dutton?" The Springer and Wheatly connection went back to the time when Hank was a staff sergeant and the colonel a butterbar second lieutenant.

The sergeant took the young LT under his wing and taught him what it meant to be an officer and leader of Marines. The two men served together often in subsequent years and when Gunner Springer retired, Wheatly was a lieutenant colonel and commanding officer of the infantry battalion of a Marine Expeditionary Unit aboard ships in the South China Sea.

"Yep, it's me. Are you going to invite me in or leave me out here with the critters and things that go bump in the night? Better call me Calvin, or Cal."

"Oh yeah, sure come on in." Hank stepped out of the way so Wheatly could enter the trailer. The last time he saw his guest was more than a dozen years before at a Marine Corps Ball. Hank showed his guest to the swivel chair. He unplugged the iron and plugged in the coffee maker after putting the ironing board in the narrow broom closet.

"Damn Cal, it's been years. Tell me what you've been up to. I know it's something, you always were one to get mixed up in the more interesting things."

The former Colonel took the offered chair. Hank looked at his friend: pressed Wranglers, plaid Pendleton shirt, shiny dark roper cowboy boots polished to a deep rich brown.

"I heard you were in town and I've been looking for you since the team roping event. I was afraid I'd missed you. I asked the man on the gate if you were still here, he pointed this way and so here I am."

A knock on the door interrupted them. Hank opened the door; Harold, the maintenance man stood back from the open door. "Mr. Springer, there was a man looking for you."

"Thanks Harold, he found me. He's an old Marine buddy."

"Okay then." Harold left, none of his business. Harold liked to keep his own company, but he liked being watchful and helpful even more.

"Sorry about that, where were we?" Hank prompted. "Wait a minute, do you live in Dutton and to what do I owe the pleasure of this visit?"

"Sit down Hank, I've got a story to tell and it concerns you, Brent, Bess Clemons and the rest of your family."

"What about Brent and Mrs. Clemons?"

"Hank, when I retired from the Corps I got a job as an investigator for an insurance company, and the company has been very interested where money goes after it is awarded in accidents. I sort of represent the children left behind and make recommendations in some difficult or unclear cases. Follow me so far?"

"Yeah, I think so. Go on. Wait, where do I fit in this?"

Cal shifted to a more comfortable position. "If what I have in mind happens I think it will be a win-win for everyone." Wheatly gathered his thoughts. "I saw you dancing with Mrs. Clemons; you know she is the State Social Services Representative and the director for the Dutton Children's Home?"

Hank smiled. "Yeah, I know. What's your point?"

"I've got a story to tell if you're willing to listen."

"I'm always ready to listen to a good story, shoot!"

Wheatly took a deep breath and began. "Five months ago there was a horrendous accident on the highway a hundred and some miles from Dutton. A man and his wife died. They left three children: twins, a boy and girl now sixteen, and a younger girl, five. The children are here in Dutton at the Children's Home. Bess Clemons is their case officer and she is running out of options and time to find a foster family suitable for the children. She only has six months from the date the state assumed legal responsibility for the children to find a safe place for the kids."

Hank raised his hand. "That shouldn't be too hard to find a family to foster them. What's the problem?"

"The problem is in two parts. First, the children want to stay together and the girls are high risk. The younger girl could be placed today. There is no shortage of people who are volunteering to foster the girls. That brings us to the second problem. Each child has an insurance payout of $700,000. With the current state laws the foster family will have access to the money as there is no trust to prevent it."

"I see, lots of people are willing to take the money. What about the kids?" Hank asked.

"The kids are being obstinate and antisocial so only the gold-diggers are hanging in there. In little more than a month the state will select a foster family and dump the kids." Wheatly sat back and watched the expression change on Hank's face.

"I don't know what I can do. I'm not married and I live in a bunkhouse in the middle of nowhere. I chase cows for a living and my family is raised. I am definitely not the ideal foster parent if that's what you have on your mind."

"I think you underestimate yourself Hank, if it's a question of heart; that you have in spades. I've seen you with your own children and you are a great father and would be an ideal foster parent and I know you are more than just a cowboy at the Lazy B. Think about it and talk to Mrs. Clemons, but don't take too long. Time's running out for those kids. Once they leave the Children's Home it will be too late." Cal Wheatly rose to his feet. "I've got another place I need to be. Think it over Hank. Semper Fi Buddy." Wheatly let himself out and left Hank with his head full of thoughts of what ifs, how tos and why fors to contemplate.

Using his cell phone, Hank called Jim Sutterland and said he needed an extra week for personal reasons. Maya on the extension phone butted in before Jim could say yea or nay. "You take all the time you need Hank. I hope she's pretty too." She hung up without saying goodbye. Jim laughed so hard it took some time for him to get his breath.

"I guess Maya has already made my decision for me. I'll see you when I see you." Jim laughed. "I hope she's pretty too." He hung up. Is everyone concerned about my love life? Hank thought.

*   *   *

Hank and Brent sat quietly in the only upscale restaurant in town. Brent's eyes skipped to the entrance anxious as he watched for his guests to arrive. The men saw Bess and Beverly enter, two beautiful blonde women who attracted every male eye in the room. Hank and Brent rose to their feet. Mother and daughter saw the two men wearing identical smiles as they stood by their table and waited for them. The ladies' faces brightened, lighting up the room like Christmas lights, a good comparison in Hank's mind. Mother and daughter wore wide smiles when their eyes met the men's eyes. Hank was surprised, when without warning his heart skipped a beat as he watched the ladies kiss his son on the cheek. When Bess Clemons turned her attention to Hank, he knew he wore a crazy one-sided grin. He could feel the heat of a blush steal over his face. He waited a mite bit too long. Bess smiled and indicated her chair. Hank hopped to hold it for her. He caught the scent of her perfume. The delicate scent shocked him and brought another missed beat to his heart.

Dinner was wonderful, the conversation full of promise. Hank couldn't help it, his eyes were on Bess as he drank in her blue eyes, shoulder length golden hair and the faint scent of her perfume and he listened to the music of her voice. He asked about her work and her life in Dutton. Bess again offered Hank a tour of the children's facility. She told him about the three children she considered her top priority. When Brent asked, Bev agreed to visit Montana as soon as the school year ended. Hank surprised himself when without forethought he invited Bess along. She didn't accept but she didn't refuse either. Hank felt a tingle, the first time in years, of hope for companionship for himself.

The men escorted the women to the house mother and daughter shared. After saying goodnight, the men returned to the rodeo grounds and their lonely trailer. The next morning Hank had telephone calls to make. Noon found Hank in the local telephone office using the public computer and telephone. He first called his investment advisor for an update and found out he was a millionaire many times over: three million dollars in liquid assets and another eleven million plus in long term investments in the original account from Lori's family, and a second account with another two million in liquid assets and seven million dollars of Microsoft and Starbucks stock. Thanks to his wise accounts manager, Hank was well heeled.

After the pleasant surprises of the weekend and the discovery of his wealth, Hank called Jim at the ranch and asked about the land Jim had mentioned he would be willing to sell to the right person. Jim had been talking about selling 10,000 acres for tax purposes. Hank also reserved the guest house for Bev.

Bev and Brent spent the day horseback riding in the hills surrounding Dutton; the two definitely bonded. Brent told his father over their morning's breakfast, he thought he wanted to spend his life with Bev.

In the afternoon after lunch, Hank met Bess at the Children's Home. During the tour Hank saw the twins watching a small girl play on the swings. The boy called the younger girl and they huddled together in a corner of the play yard. Hank watched them as Bess talked about the difficulties in placing older children.

Hank and Bess went to the movies after sharing dinner with Brent and Bev. The younger couple wanted to go dancing at a local nightspot. Hank asked Bess again to ride up to Montana with them. Bess surprised him when she agreed.

CHAPTER 10

Saturday morning found the foursome on the road to Western Montana. Next week Bev's class was on spring vacation and the following week she scheduled the class to be taught by the substitute teacher.

Bess would be on the first week-long vacation she had taken in seven years. Hank drove and talked with Bess. They stopped every two hours to check on the horses and water them. Brent took over the driving in Boise, Idaho. Hank and Bess moved to the back seat and both were asleep before Brent got the truck and trailer back on the highway; Bess's head leaned on Hank's shoulder. Hank fell asleep smelling the freshness of Bess's hair and her perfume.

The foursome arrived at the ranch in the early afternoon. Hank and Brent turned out the horses in the acre—sized paddock, throwing hay over the fence to augment the grass and filling the washtub with fresh water. Hank helped the ladies settle into the guest house; the men would sleep in the bunkhouse. With the ladies settled, Hank went to the main house and sat down with Jim.

The Lazy B Ranch was spread over 100,000 acres with shared borders with Federal Bureau of Land Management (BLM) open range and three bordering ranches. The open range gave the ranch an additional 250,000 acres of land for cattle grazing shared with the neighboring ranches.

"Hank, you've been working full time for over twelve years. I've been holding your wages except for a couple of hundred per month the whole time. I invested your wages along with mine and I think you'll be surprised. The total in your account is over $500,000. I've been planning to sell off 10,000 acres. I'll sell you those fenced acres and meadow in the northwest corner for $200,000. The Olson ranch bordering the east side of your land is willing to sell 500 acres. I talked to Arley Olson yesterday and he'll take your note." Jim thought a minute. "That will give you an initial 10,500 acres of your own plus the BLM land to use." Sutterland paused. "After paying me you'll still have $300,000 to get started with and buy those additional 500 acres."

Hank interrupted, putting his hand up. "Yes sir, don't short yourself. I'll pay what the land is worth and your offer is more than generous."

Jim grinned at his foster son and new neighbor. "No sir, having you close to home is worth a lot more than a few dollars. If you want to finalize we'll shake on it." Jim put out his hand and Hank took it. The deal was made.

Hank was now a land owner. "I want to throw in the 200 head of cattle you saved last year during the sleet storm as seed, so to speak. No arguments son, now go see to your guests." Jim smiled. It had been far too long since Hank brought anyone home to meet him and Maya.

Hank hurried to the guest house to tell his son and new friends, and then he remembered Bev and Brent had taken the truck to show his girl the moonlight over the valley. Maybe even watch the submarine races. Hank smiled at the thought. *Maybe Bess would like to see the submarine races?* Nah, but nice thought.

*   *   *

Brent stopped the truck at the edge of the mesa overlooking the valley and the small meandering river. The moonlight reflected on the ribbon of water. It shone like polished silver as it wound through the valley. Bev scooted across the seat, put her arms around his neck and pulled his face down to her lips.

The young man groaned. "God Bev, you drive me crazy."

She sat up so she faced him and looked into his eyes. Bev watched his face relax as he drank in her beauty. He was speechless when she reached forward, took his face in both her hands and gently kissed him. First on the lips, then his eyelids, chin and nose.

Brent gently put his hand on the back of her neck and held her to him. He kissed her and he felt her mouth open for his searching tongue. His tongue met hers and they held the kiss for a long moment. Bev put her hands on the back of Brent's neck, fell back on the seat and pulled him with her. They held each other and basked in love's embrace.

Bev gave a brief shiver and Brent sat up and took off his jacket and wrapped it around her. He held her until she quit shivering and snuggled deeper into the warmth of his arms. She felt this was where she belonged, here with him, like this forever.

Bev ran her hands under Brent's shirt and felt the fine hairs on his chest. His breath quickened as she slipped her arms around him and pulled him closer.

"God Brent, you drive me crazy too. You know, I had a boyfriend until a year ago. He was not what I thought he was so I sent him away. I knew in my heart the man for me was out there and now he has found me. Don't send me away Brent, I've never felt like this with anyone. I want you with me, I want you beside me."

"I'm not exactly pure either Bev. But from the first time I saw you standing at the gate to the rodeo grounds in Dutton I knew. You are the most beautiful woman I've ever seen. You take my breath away. I love you Bev. I never want to be away from you." He surprised himself at his own words, but Brent meant every one of them.

"Shut up, hold me and kiss me." Bev pulled his head down to kiss him. The two lovers sat close together in the truck, her head on his shoulder. His arm around her shoulders, he was content to watch the moon follow its track across the night sky. The howl of a wolf echoed off the mesa's stone walls and sent an involuntary shiver up Bev's spine. She snuggled closer and pulled his head down to kiss his lips again.

A watching coyote sniffed the air, turned and trotted away in the unique liquid movements of the wild. In the distance the wolf called to his mate, she answered; the echo of their call reached out across the valley.

* * *

The following morning over the breakfast table, Hank told them about buying the property from the Lazy B to start his own ranch. Bev and Bess wanted to see Hank's new purchase.

"I'd really like to show you but it is away from any improved road. The Forest Service maintains a fire access road through the area but use is restricted during fire season. There is a family living in a canyon but they are the only people within miles."

Hank stopped, a thoughtful expression on his face. The interplay between Brent and Bev caught his attention: something had changed. Every time he looked they were touching, not possessively but intimately as lovers do. With an effort, Hank got his mind back on the subject of his new ranch property. "I've been thinking," he began.

"Nobody would have ever guessed," Brent interrupted and laughed.

Hank ignored his son's remark. "Like I was saying, I've been thinking. We could take the horses and make a three—day camp trip. You can see the most beautiful part of Montana and the land I bought too, if you're up for a little trail riding. I want to check on those two college kids working up country anyway."

"I'm sure Jim isn't going to make you work now," Brent said as he shook his head.

"I'm still cattle boss of the Lazy B until Jim says I'm not. Somebody needs to check on those two boys. George Honey is riding the south and east fence and won't be finished for five or six days," Hank explained. "Yeah, I know they have cell phones with them and will call if they need anything. I'll talk to Jim this afternoon."

"Sounds good to me" Bess said. "I would like to do a camp trip for a few days. I haven't been on an overnight trail ride in years."

"Okay then it's set, if you children care to come along." Hank asked Brent and Bev to join them.

"Sure, I'd like that. I suppose there are extra horses around here." Bev looked at Brent and raised her eyebrows and waited for his answer.

Brent smiled and thought of his yet unscheduled weeks of annual active duty for training with the Marine Reserves. Brent should receive independent orders for the active duty at Quantico, Virginia. He grinned. "I'd like to do a good ride before my feet meet the mud and the critters of Quantico again. I must say the company here is better than Virginia." Brent laughed and grinned at his father. "I bet you'd like to come along to Quantico. I know you'd love a couple of weeks running around the woods in the mud sleeping with the snakes." He knew his dad would give an arm and leg to do a couple of weeks at Quantico and maybe Fort Bragg as dessert. You can take the man out of the Marines but you will never get the Marines out of the man.

"Okay then, if the ladies agree we'll leave the day after tomorrow early. Why don't you pick a couple of horses and tack for Bess and Bev. Jilly might be good for Bess. I've got a visit to make this afternoon, should be back for supper. Tomorrow we'll make a general store run to town." Hank was interrupted by a knock on the door.

Brent opened the door and found Jim. "Sorry to disturb you, but I thought you might like to show your guests your new land."

"Come in Jim, we were just discussing that," Hank replied. "Thought we'd ride out and camp a couple of days. Be back Saturday or Sunday."

"Maya and I would love to ride along if we wouldn't be intruding." Jim looked expectantly at Hank.

"Absolutely Jim, we would love to have you and your wife join us," Bess said and stood beside Hank. Jim met Bess and Bev earlier when Hank brought them to the main house to introduce his guests. Bess missed meeting Maya who hadn't returned from visiting an ill neighbor.

"Great, I'll leave you to your day. I'm sure Maya would want to get together with you to plan. Whenever the cowboy, there, will let you out of his sight, why don't you come to the house? Maya's been looking forward to meeting you and won't stop fussing at me. So for my sake, please come to the house, sooner is better." Everyone laughed along with Jim. With a wave he pulled the door closed behind him.

"Brent, why don't you and Bev see to the horses and tack," Bess said. "Maybe take a ride this afternoon. I think I'll just ride along with Hank after

Bev and I talk with Maya." Bess sent a beaming smile at the man. "That is if he'd like my company?"

"Darn toot'n Missy," Hank said grinning.

"Good, now just let me finish up these breakfast dishes." She turned to Hank. "You want to wash or dry?"

CHAPTER 11

The morning of the trail ride found Hank and Brent up before the sun. Brent brought two horses and tied them to the hitching rail in front of the house. The day before, he and Bev went on a day ride and Hank and Bess left before dawn to make a trip to Missoula, while it was still morning. Hank conducted his business and Bess did some shopping. On the way home they stopped in Lone Horse for grocery supplies and dry goods.

Bev came out of the house and stood on the porch to watch Brent. He checked all the horse legs. Running his hands up each horse's leg he felt for any swelling or heat, which indicated an injury or soreness. Brent lifted the horse's feet to inspect for loose or worn shoes as he cleaned each horse's feet. He felt Bev's eyes on him and turned. Bev's impish smile and the promise in her eyes quickened his heart. A blush rose from his collar to match the one that rose from her blue denim work shirt. Bev dropped her eyes only to immediately bring her eyes back to look at the man with whom she was falling in love.

Bev skipped down the porch steps, took the lead rope from Brent. Jilly was the ranch horse she'd ridden the day before. Bess would ride Jilly on the camp trip. Bev checked the tack seeing the headstall was adjusted properly. Next the saddle blanket: she looked for any folds or foreign objects beneath the blanket to irritate the horse. Bev patted Jilly on the neck and rubbed her hands over flanks and rump. She reintroduced herself to the sorrel gelding and left the cinch snug but not tight. Bev sidled up to Brent and gave him a quick kiss when he turned his head.

"Do you think your dad needs any help with the pack horses?"

"No, I think he's waiting for your mother to come out so he can help her. Don't take his pleasure away. I wouldn't like it if you were sent on some other errand just to get you out of the way." A mischievous gleam sparkled in Brent's eyes.

Hank left the pack animals tied to the hitching rail. He noted the gleam in his son's eyes. Well how about that? The kid's in love. Wonder if he knows it yet but he's a goner; aw, he knows it, he thought. The ladies in Missoula will have broken hearts, there will be weeping and gnashing of teeth. The thoughts had not faded from his mind when Bess came out onto the porch. She was dressed for the trail: Wranglers, and a pair of new roper boots on her feet, a worn blue plaid Pendleton shirt and the straw hat she and Hank bought at the general store in Lone Horse. She wore her blonde hair in a pony tail low on her neck and a smile on her face. Hank realized his own heart beat a bit faster when Bess appeared. *Damn, I'm too old for this. Besides we might be related soon judging from the way those two are looking at each other.*

Hank inspected his and Bess's horses and the pack animal for sore spots and lameness. After all the recent time spent traveling and the good food of the past few days, Hank felt like a stuffed turkey. He looked forward to the exercise of the ride and hated the heavy feeling from the lack of exercise. *I'm turning into a regular food blister,* he thought.

Brent moved Jackson and tied him next to Jilly on one side and Beany on the other. He helped load the last of the supplies on the pack mule. Each rider carried a bedroll and rain gear behind the saddle. The bedroll also contained a full set of spare clothes rolled up inside. Saddlebags contained more personal clothing and other items including three quarts of fresh water. The men tacked up their horses and put their personal rifles in the scabbards hanging from the saddle horns. Brent carried a vintage lever action 30-30 Winchester, Hank his favorite Winchester Model 94 .45 caliber rifle. Jim slipped his own 30.06 Winchester bolt action rifle in his scabbard. The rifles were protection in case an overly aggressive bear or mountain lion attacked them or the horses. The land was a primitive area complete with large predators who looked for easy pickings.

Bev walked up behind Brent and slapped him on the butt. "I hope you aren't going to make a habit of saddling my horse. I'm not a dude you know."

"Hey, want me to take the saddle off so you can saddle Beany yourself?" Brent said seriously, and then burst out laughing when Bev stuck her tongue out at him.

"Snot!" She playfully punched him on the shoulder.

Brent grabbed his arm and staggered back. "Easy there Supergirl. I'm only human you know."

"Smart alec. I don't know about that." Bev watched Brent blush. She took Beany's reins out of Brent's hand and retied him to the hitching rail using a halter and lead rope. Beany, a ten year old dun gelding, rolled an eye and nickered at the two immature humans.

Maya climbed onto the saddle and walked her horse around the parking area. She adjusted her tack as she rode. Bev put the headstall on Beany, tightened the cinch and tied the halter to the saddlebags. When Brent climbed into the saddle, she mounted Beany and moved out of the way.

Jim rode up. "Hank, you know the way better than anyone else, you're Trail Boss."

"Yes sir." Hank turned so he could speak to the gathered riders. "I'll lead followed by Bess on Jilly, then Maya, Jim, Bev with Brent riding drag. I'll lead the pack horse, Brent the mule, Jim you're backup. Don't let the horses bunch up; make them walk, space about a body length nose to tail. First leg is to Pony Meadow about three and a half hours out. We'll break there; anybody need to stop for cinch tightening or anything else sing out. We'll stop after about 20 minutes to check and tighten cinches. Brent you help the ladies, Jim and I will check the pack animals."

The trail to the high country crossed the meandering stream. At the crossing, the water reached the belly of the horses and resulted in some wet boots and socks. Hank called a break under some alder trees at an old campsite. He put up a quick picket line, and helped Brent remove the saddles and headstalls to be replaced with halters. They tied the horses to the picket line. The pack animals were hobbled and the panniers lifted off. They left the light pack frames on the pack horse and mule. Hank and Jim examined each horse's legs, hooves and shoes.

Maya, with Bess's help, took prepared lunches from the panniers. Hank checked the time and the distance covered and decided to extend the lunch break an extra hour.

Before eating, Hank told them to remove their boots, check their feet and let their socks dry. Hank noticed Bess was still wearing her boots. He walked barefoot to her and offered to help remove her boots and socks. Brent had already helped Bev and the two had their heads together in conversation.

"Now, isn't that sweet?" Hank mumbled as he watched his son and sat down next to Bess.

"You leave them alone you old cowboy or I'll tell them how much of a softy you really are." Bess leaned over and slow punched Hank on the shoulder.

The breeze would dry their boots and socks while they ate and rested. Lunch was cold fried chicken and cups of potato salad. A soft breeze washed through the trees and rattled the leaves and made a soothing sound. Hank noticed some of his charges had been lulled to sleep by the peaceful setting.

Time passed quickly. Hank woke Brent and Jim to help him bring in the pack animals. They put the panniers on the pack frames and rechecked the horses for sore spots: legs, backs and feet. Hank made it a habit to check the horses before and after each time they were ridden and at breaks during rides. He passed the habit on to each of his charges as Trail Boss. Bev's horse was a touch tender around his withers, nothing serious, and Hank would massage and work on the sore spot at that night's camp.

When the riders were once again in the saddle, Hank set off up the trail with Brent again riding drag, accompanied by Bev.

Sunset found them at the night camp on the step plateau up country from the ranch house, only six miles as the crow flies. They were on Hank's new ranch land which extended across the meadow from where they sat by the campfire. A fire ring of stones with a rock oven in the middle served as the center of the camp. Jim and Maya's tent faced the fire on the left, Bess and Bev's tent was in the middle with the tent Hank shared with Brent on the right.

Hank put all the saddles and tack together and covered them with a blue plastic tarp. The meat and other food tempting to bears and other critters he pulled up twelve feet off the ground suspended from a cottonwood tree limb.

Brent and Bev went for a walk around the meadow. At the edge of the plateau they found a large rock still warm from the afternoon sun. They were content, sitting together and talking about their lives before they met in Dutton.

Hank and Bess watched the young couple wander off fully absorbed with each other. The Sutterlands, Hank and Bess sat next to the campfire and talked. Finally, Bess got up and began to clean up, but Jim and Maya shooed her away. Bess and Hank were left to themselves. Hank thought it a good time to ask Bess her opinion about his plans for the ranch and the suggestion Cal Wheatly made.

They sat together against a log on their saddle blankets. "Bess, can I ask for your opinion and recommendation on a couple of things I need to take care of? If you don't want to it's okay, no hard feelings or anything."

"Sure Hank. You can ask anything. I think you know that," Bess replied and smiled.

"Okay, I bought the ranch for of a couple of reasons. First off, it's time I stopped riding fence for somebody else, even if it is for my folks and start building something I can leave my kids."

"I can understand that Hank, but why do I think there is more to this?" Bess looked up into Hank's eyes; she knew they were brown with light hazel flecks even though in the light of the campfire they looked gray with their touch of green.

"You're right, there is more. You know those kids whose parents were killed in that car wreck about six months ago?" He paused until Bess nodded. "Well, I want to foster them, here in Montana as soon as I have a place for them to sleep."

Bess stared at the man, taken completely by surprise. "Wow, now that is a big thing. You know the kids are technically wards of the state and you want to take them out of one state to another state. That my friend will be a major undertaking." Bess stared at the man who sat in front of her in the moonlight.

"Bess, I need your help to do this."

"Is that why you asked me here?" Bess asked, her mouth pressed into a firm line.

"No, yes, well sort of, not exactly." Hank stammered. "I wanted you to come with us for Bev and Brent and me, all of us."

The tension on Bess's face eased. "Maybe you'd better start over, from the beginning."

"Okay, but you may not believe some of it."

"Try me!" She wasn't letting up or making it any easier.

"When Brent and I were just getting to know you I got a visit from an old friend." Hank wasn't sure if he should identify his visitor. "Actually someone I have known for a long time, many years. Anyway, he came knocking on my door, while we were in Dutton."

"Is it important for me to know this person?" Bess interrupted.

"No, not really. He suggested I look into the welfare of three orphaned kids." Hank paused; he wondered how to explain all this to Bess. He decided to just tell her, and to explain his goals. "He told me there were three children recently orphaned by an auto-accident which killed both parents. They were at the Dutton Children's Home and you know them. The Anderson children, twins and a younger girl."

Bess interrupted again. "Those children are scheduled to be separated and adopted or fostered out." She looked directly into Hank's sad eyes. "There are two families who want to adopt the girls. I don't think we'll be able to get an adoption for the boy. Nobody wants a sixteen year old boy with a chip on his shoulder."

"Bess, will you help me foster those kids? I don't want to adopt them, just give them a home. It will keep the family together. I know there are two states to consider."

"Hank, you have no idea, but the states are not the only problem. You are an unmarried man and as of now without a job. You do have property but no place to live, that means a house." Bess stopped talking when she saw Hank's shoulders sag. "Hey, there may be ways around most of those things. A lot depends on recommendations of the courts, social workers, available financial resources, and access to schools, lots of things."

"Look, money isn't an issue; I'm a retired Marine Officer and have my retirement pay plus some investments I've made over the years. I'm pretty sure we could live for awhile on the investments." Hank watched Bess's mind process the information.

"So you have enough money to support the children?"

"Yes ma'am, not a problem." Hank smiled.

"Okay, I'll see what I can do. Get your bank statements together and a list of personal character recommendations to include your last three employers and any other testimonials you think will help."

"I've only worked for the Marines and Jim at the Lazy B, so two will have to do."

"That will be fine. Get your tax information for the past five years too." Bess hesitated. "It will help if you know a judge who will give you a good character recommendation." She was flattered that Hank relied on her help. Bess continued to be surprised by the man and every time she looked at him she felt a little flutter in her stomach. Not an unpleasant feeling, but a surprise just the same.

"I'll think on it. I really appreciate your help, Bess. I don't know if I can do this alone." Hank stood. "How about we take a stroll and use up some of this moonlight?"

"My pleasure, cowboy." Bess laughed, a pleasant sound on the high meadow.

* * *

After breakfast and the dishes were cleaned, Hank felt the ashes in the fire pit to make sure there were no hot coals to start a flame after they left. The trees, grass and bushes were dry from the below average rainfall after a harsh winter. The heat from the morning cook fire had dissipated, only a slight warmth remained. Hank poured the last of the coffee over the coals, rinsed the coffee pot with water from his water bag and poured the rinse water over the ashes before he put the coffee pot in a pannier. Hank mounted Jake and nudged the horse forward with his knees. Jake, accustomed to leading, set a leisurely pace leaving the other horses to follow and their riders to their thoughts.

Bess's mind was consumed with Hank's revelation from last night. The man was definitely a man of honor and surprises. He would make an exceptional foster parent. Now all Bess had to do was convince the powers in control to give Hank a chance. She firmly believed the children would have a second chance at a normal life. Actually, she thought it would be an exceptional life full of adventure and love.

As her horse followed the pack horse led by Hank, she realized she was personally interested in the cowboy. The flutter in the pit of her stomach might have been an omen. Bess knew Hank loved his late wife. Maya had told her when Lori died the man threw himself into his work and family.

Bess's thoughts brought a smile to her face. She knew from the way Bev had been talking and behaving, she and Brent were considering a life together. It shocked her to realize she and Hank would then be related by marriage. Wonder how that works? The thought surprised her.

Similar thoughts were wandering through Hank's brain as another part of his mind kept track of the hundred little things a Trail Boss was responsible for. Since crossing the meadow at last night's camp they rode on Hank's land. An hour later Hank led them through a stand of lodgepole pine trees and out onto a pristine meadow divided by a swift flowing stream. The meadow, almost twenty acres of flat grassland, was bordered by a forest of mixed cedar and fir trees with stands of aspen and alder along the banks of the stream. The land rose gradually into the foothills of the mountains.

Hank pointed to an old campsite not far from the stream. "We'll camp there tonight. We can put the horses in the old corral." He pointed at an old weathered corral nearly invisible against the darkness of the forest. "I repaired it last spring; with a few minutes work, we can use it for tonight." Jim and Brent dismounted and walked their horses to the corral. They tied the horses to the top rail and removed the saddles and other tack. There was plenty of room to put the saddles on the two hitching posts installed last year next to the corral gate. Hank got out the rope hobbles they used the night before and tossed them to Brent. "We'll hobble the animals and let them graze. The grass is rich and sweet and we shouldn't have to grain them. If anybody is up for a hike? A couple of miles up there," he pointed up stream, "is a really pretty waterfall and grotto. The trail up is rocky and steep in places so we'll have to leave the horses here."

"I forgot just how pretty this area is." Jim teased. "Maybe I should have kept it."

"Too late now Pop." Hank grinned.

"Hank, it's worth it to have you close to home," Jim replied seriously. "But the Lazy B gets free water."

"Water, water sure you can have all the water you need. Are you going to drink it or heaven forbid, bathe in it?" Hank laughed and held his nose.

"I know what you should do with it." Jim responded with a crude gesture. "Say, anybody up for a swim? There is a deep, wide place in the stream over by those aspen trees; ladies first."

Bess, Maya and Bev retrieved their saddlebags from where they'd put their tack. The women set out for the swimming hole. An hour later, they were back wearing clean clothes and smiles. "Your turn," Maya called. "Jim don't forget to wash behind your ears."

While the ladies bathed, the men had set up the camp, collected firewood for the evening and inspected the horses for soreness and any potential problems; Hank tended to the sore spots on a couple of the horses.

The men visited the swimming hole and were soon back. Bess organized a hike and Hank led them on the trail to the waterfall. Jim remained at the camp and fussed with the fire. He wanted the coals just right for the steaks and potatoes Maya brought for dinner. The steaks were wrapped and packed in ice accompanied by four bottles of wine, two for dinner and two for later.

The trail up to the waterfall passed through a field covered with large rocks. Hank led and they soon could hear the roar of a waterfall. Bev was the first to exit the trees and see the forty foot stream of water pounding down on the rocks in the pond at the bottom of the falls. From the water's edge they saw brook trout flash in the shallow pool. The mountain stream was full of the fish: no one came this high up to catch them. Some of the fish Hank saw from the bank were over a foot in length. "I should have brought a fishing pole; we could have fresh trout for breakfast."

Bess burst out laughing. "You don't need poles to catch fish. I'll see we have plenty for breakfast. I assume there are fish in the stream at the meadow?"

"Yeah, there are a lot of fish in that stream. I've got to see you catch them without a pole." Hank snorted before a smile spread over his face.

"Oh ye of little faith, we women have our ways." Bess poked him in the ribs.

Hank looked at Brent; the young man shook his head. "I'm not going to touch that."

"Smart man you raised there Mister Springer," Bev remarked.

The water was cold, but not cold enough to keep the ladies from wading as they scoured the bottom for agates and other small treasures. Hank interrupted their search. "If you're interested, gold has been panned out of this stream. Swish your feet around and you might just find a nugget or two."

"Yeah, sure," Bev said but she did swirl her feet around the bottom. She spotted a bit of yellow on the bottom and picked it up. "What's this?" She showed it to Hank.

"Well, I'll be. Bev found a nugget, small but a nugget just the same."

Bev, excited, rushed to show it to Maya and her mother. "This trip is full of surprises. I think I've found treasure." She took Brent's hand and gazed up into his eyes and she showed him her nugget.

The trip back to the meadow was much faster than the trip up the hill. Bev had the nugget wrapped in her handkerchief, excited to show Jim her find. Maya told Bev Jim was an authority on the lore of the east slope and she remembered something about a mine in the area. Jim would know.

When Jim saw the returning hikers appear from the trees, he stirred the fire making sure there would be hot coals over the stone oven in the center of the fire ring. Bev entered the camp and went directly to Jim to show him the small nugget of gold. Jim nodded. "After dinner, I'll tell you about the lost mine. There is a vein of gold up here and the stream gives up bits of gold occasionally. But first ladies, would you set the table?" While they were gone, Jim rigged a table out of some old boards he took from the partially collapsed line shack across the meadow.

Followed by Hank, Brent, Bev and Maya, Bess led them to the stream before the sun dropped below the tree line. The light was still good but the shadows were long. Bess rolled up her pants legs and her shirt sleeves, rubbing her hands together until she felt the heat. She stepped slowly into the water and bent over and held her hands close to the bottom. It was not five minutes and a ten inch brook trout came to investigate. The fish nosed around the palms of Bess's hands. A quick flick with spread fingers and the fish landed on the grassy bank. Bess put her hands back in the water. Soon there were enough fish for each of the campers. "Now ladies and gentlemen, that's the way a real fisherman does it."

"Mrs. Clemons I am truly impressed. I will never again underestimate the talents of a woman. May I assist you with the cleaning of your catch?" Hank offered.

"Nope, sorry Hank, but this is woman's work. But you can loan me the use of your knife." Bess dropped to her knees beside the stream. Bev borrowed Brent's knife and knelt beside Bess while Maya used her own knife and took her place beside them. "Haven't you someplace you need to be." Bess smiled up at Hank.

When they finished with the fish, Maya put them on the ice in the panniers to stay fresh for breakfast.

"Women!" Hank wandered away toward the corral where Jake had his head over the rail watching him approach. Hank opened the gate and let the horse out. Jake stayed next to Hank until he touched the horse on the flank. The horse slowly wandered toward the stream where the grass was sweet and green. Hank inspected Jilly and Beany and let them out to graze. The two trotted over to Jake and soon the three were munching grass together. Brent saw Hank release the horses and let Jackson out to graze with the rest of the horses.

Jake walked in a circle and found a good place and lay down and roll. The horse regained his feet, shook himself and took off at a dead run along the stream's bank and across the meadow. The other horses followed and tried to keep up. Reaching the far end of the meadow, Jake stopped and looked back toward Hank. Snorting and whinnying, he tore across the meadow and came to a sliding stop in front of Hank. Hank put his arms around the horse's neck and they stood together until Hank broke contact. Jake trotted across the meadow to the stream to rejoin the other horses. Jake was a stallion, all the other horses geldings. With new riders, Hank didn't allow mares in the mix. It was far too dangerous with a stallion and possessive geldings.

The meadow was close to the edge of Hank's land. In a box canyon three quarters of a mile away lived a family of five. The parents of a boy and two girls were Hank's closest neighbors. Access to the canyon was a fire service road, not much more than a Jeep trail. When the father could find work, he drove an old rusty Chevy truck to and from the canyon. He was a good cowhand, but had a lame leg after being thrown from a horse two years ago. With no insurance, and limited medical attention the leg healed badly. Hank seriously thought of hiring the man to run his cow operation. Hank would train horses unless he found a good horseman to run that part of the ranch's operation.

The men set up the tents while the women cooked. Maya set the grill over the red-hot coals. Bess placed a stew pot of water in the coals next to the grill and soaked ears of corn. Maya took the seasoned steaks, unwrapping them from the butcher paper and put them on the grill and seared the downside. Properly seared, she turned them over to cook. Bess put soaked corn around the edge of the grill to cook in their husks. Each part of the meal cooked together. Bess turned the corn every few minutes. She dunked the cobs into the water to keep the corn moist and the husk from burning.

Maya checked the steaks; when they were each cooked to her satisfaction, she removed them from the grill and put them on a hot metal tray where they sizzled. She placed the tray on the grill at the edge of the fire.

Bess used two sticks to lift the thin stone cover from the oven beneath the coals. Earlier she'd put six large foil wrapped baking potatoes in the oven after soaking them in a bucket of water. She wasn't surprised when each time Hank built a fire ring he dug a hole and lined it with rocks for an oven. Bess hadn't seen an oven like that since before her husband died twelve years before. Bess tested the potatoes with a fork—a few more minutes. She replaced the rock lid and scattered red hot coals over the oven. A few minutes later, Bess used her sticks to open the oven and remove the potatoes, putting them on the grill next to the steaks and replaced the cover stone of the oven.

The smell of the seasoned steaks drifted over the meadow. Bev put a large colander of greens on the makeshift table: dinner was ready. Bess looked up to see the three men standing watching the ladies' every move. She couldn't help laughing to herself, the image created a memory.

Bess felt someone behind her. "Ma'am, your table is ready, may I seat you?" Hank took her arm and escorted her to her place.

Jim stood at the head of the table, a bottle of wine in each hand. "Ladies, for your dining pleasure this evening, we have red wine." He lifted the bottle in his right hand. "Or we have red wine." He lifted the bottle in his left hand.

Bess laughed. "I think I'll try the red wine, thank you."

Maya took charge and motioned Jim to sit down. "Hank, since you are the Trail Boss you start. Brent, of course you are drag." The men laughed at Brent's hang-dog expression. The men looked at each other and ignored her instructions and each speared a steak, a potato and snagged an ear of corn. Within a minute each man was happily chewing on a piece of beef.

"Ladies, we had better get ours before these gluttons go for seconds." Bess laughed at the men's offended looks. But the women didn't waste any time getting their food. A minute later the only sounds in camp were the happy sound of chewing and contented grunts of appreciation. The large pot of coffee added its warm aroma.

After cleanup they spent the time in light conversation around the fire. The moonless sky was alight with billions of stars. The Milky Way illuminated the meadow in the clear mountain air. The stream reflected the starlight as it weaved a meandering silvery pathway through the meadow and disappeared into the forest. The quiet bubbling sound of the stream's current lulled the visitors to the meadow into moments of silence.

Bev asked Jim to tell the story of the lost mine and some of the history of this part of Montana. Jim began with the story of the Lost Mine and the mysterious hidden vein of ore, the probable source of the nugget now in Bev's shirt pocket wrapped in a tissue for safe keeping.

Maya retrieved the fourth bottle of wine from the pannier. "This is the last." She opened the bottle and poured a portion for each of Jim's listeners. She used the wine that remained from dinner to augment the last bottle. "Okay Jim, tell your story, I'm all ears." Maya smiled at her husband of fifty years.

Jim spun his story to an audience of rapt listeners. Even Hank was spellbound by Jim's talent for storytelling. After the Lost Mine story, Jim told tales of the badmen of Montana—outlaws, many of whom had become legend. Murderers, bank robbers and rustlers, each had their story and Jim seemed to know them all. With the last sip of wine gone, the campers were ready to call it a night.

* * *

Hank rose early and gathered the horses. He put them into the corral. Brent and Jim joined him and the men brushed the horses looking for any ticks or other critters the horses might have picked up overnight. Brent checked each horse's shoes. He found one of the pack horse's shoes loose. With Hank's farrier tools he reattached the shoe.

With a father's pride, Hank watched his son work. Jim stood beside him. "If you don't hire that kid, I'm going to."

"Not a chance. You think I spent all those hours training him to let you steal him away? You might borrow Brent on occasion though." Hank looked serious at his foster parent, and then burst out laughing at Jim's made up hangdog expression before he too laughed.

"What are you two so happy about? Why aren't you cooking breakfast?" Brent eyed his father and Jim.

"Never mind kid." Hank placed his arm around his son's shoulders and gave him a fatherly squeeze. He let Brent go and joined Jim at the fire. "Have I ever told you how much it means to me, you and Mom fostering and taking care of me all these years?" He put his arm around the older man. "I love you Pop."

"Hank, you are the son Maya and I never had. We couldn't love you more if you were our own blood. Watching you and your family grow up has been the brightest part of our lives. Don't forget the Lazy B is your home too."

"I don't think I could, Maya or you would be knocking down my door." Maya watched and tried to hide the tears that formed in her eyes.

Coffee done, Jim poured while Hank held the mugs. "You think Brent and the girl will tie the knot?"

"Don't know, won't be surprised though. Bev is quite a girl. She's a school teacher you know." Hank was impressed with Brent's choice. "That young man is smitten as any marginally intelligent person can tell at first glance. I wouldn't be surprised if they got married when he gets back from Quantico. I hope he comes back here to the ranch and raises enough kids to fill a school bus or school house with Bev."

"That's Bev, what about Bess?" Jim smiled at his son.

"What about Bess?" Hank eyed Jim and pushed his hat back.

"Hey, I can tell she likes you. She didn't take her eyes off you when we were on the trail."

"She was supposed to watch me, I'm the Trail Boss. Besides, Bess is helping me with a project in Dutton." But the seed was planted in Hank's mind, a fertile seed in a fertile mind.

* * *

Late in the afternoon, five saddle-weary riders passed through the ranch house gate. On the way back, Hank rode off to check on the ranch hands and set the schedule to bring the high country herd down for culling and branding. Hank decided to stay overnight at the line shack. His plan was to return to the ranch in the morning. He wanted to be back before Bess and Bev left to catch their flight to Spokane and home to Dutton.

The following morning, Bess stood by Brent's truck and watched the trail. She looked for the dust cloud that would signal Hank's return. Brent had the truck loaded with Bess and Bev's luggage. "What time does the plane leave?" Bess asked Bev for the tenth time.

"Pretty much the same as before Mom," Bev answered and rolled her eyes, so only Brent could see. "Hank will be here. Don't worry." She glanced worriedly at Brent and received a shoulder shrug to her nonverbal query.

Brent looked at his watch. "We need to be going or you're going to miss your flight to Spokane." Bev shushed him but climbed into the truck and sat in the middle of the bench seat. A disappointed Bess climbed into the truck and settled onto the passenger seat. She pulled the seatbelt across her lap to snap into the lock. Brent jumped down from the truck said he needed to make a pit stop before they left.

Minutes later, Bess watched Brent exit the bunkhouse and walk toward the truck. He stopped and pointed to the high meadow trail. A cloud of dust drifted up through the trees and shortly a rider appeared, the horse at a steady ground—eating lope. Hank was definitely in a hurry and Jake was intent on getting him where he wanted to be.

Bev and Bess were out of the truck much faster than they entered. Bess stood next to Bev and watched Hank draw closer. Hank pulled Jake to a sliding stop and dismounted next to the truck. He dropped the reins, grabbing Bess in a bear hug.

"Didn't think I'd make it. A little trouble pulling a cow out of a mud wallow on the way down."

"Dog-gone it cowboy, don't you ever cut it so close again!" Bess scolded and then threw her arms around Hank and planted a kiss on the surprised man.

Bev and Brent leaned toward each other and Brent whispered, "I think we'd better get married before those two decide to make you my sister." He laughed at Bev's stricken look.

"Don't you dare tease me like that!" Bev snorted and started to turn away before Brent caught her arm and turned her back around facing him.

"Who's teasing? We could skip over to Coeur d'Alene, Idaho, before I have to go to Quantico." Brent's smile made him look like he was still teasing.

Bev and Bess, who had climbed into the truck, climbed back out. "You fellows keep surprising a girl and you are going to have to install swinging doors on this truck," Bess said. Brent came to stand in front of them. Bess stared at Bev and then Brent, her eyes full of question.

"Are you asking me to marry you Brent Springer?" Bev asked, her blue eyes wide.

Brent looked Bev in the eyes and dropped to one knee. "Yes ma'am, I am."

Bev launched herself at Brent and knocked him backwards onto the driveway dirt. Bev fell on top of him as she kissed him repeatedly all over his face.

"I would suppose that's a yes don't you think?" Hank drawled. Bess punched him on the shoulder then grabbed his arm and leaned against him as they watched the two newly engaged hug and kiss in the dirt in front of the ranch's guesthouse.

"Wow, this could complicate things," Bess mumbled.

"Why? You're still going to help with the fostering thing?"

"Yes of course I'll still help," Bess said quietly.

Bev and Brent were on their feet and still clung to each other. Bev recovered first. "Mom, we need to go or we'll miss our flight. The sooner we leave the sooner I can get back here before he changes his mind. Besides, a little separation never hurts, except at first." Bev looked up adoringly at Brent as his arm encircled her waist.

"While you're in Dutton, I am going to see if I can start my annual Marine duty right away. So when you get back here, I'll be done for the year. Besides, I think I have some shopping to do." He helped Bev climb back up into the truck for the third time. His father shook Brent's hand and Bess kissed him on the cheek. Brent walked around the truck and climbed into the driver's seat, started the engine to let the truck warm up. With the engine warm and running smoothly, Brent drove the truck out through the ranch gate.

Hank stood next to Jake and watched the truck disappear. He watched until the dust settled back down onto the road. He picked up Jake's reins and led him to the water trough where the horse drank. Jake pulled his head back and dripped water onto Hank's boots leaving a coat of mud over the toe. When the horse was brushed and turned out to pasture, Hank went to the bunkhouse and packed his gym bag. Carrying the bag, he went to the ranch house and knocked on the door.

"Hank, come in." Maya answered the door. "I see Bev and Bess got away all right."

"Yes ma'am. Is Jim available?"

Maya nodded and left to fetch Jim from his office. She returned with Jim. "What can I do for you son, neighbor?" The man saw the bag. "Going someplace?"

"Yes sir. I need to go to town for a day or two and was wondering if I can use the old truck?"

"Heavens no, here take the new pick-up." Jim fished the keys out of his pocket. "I'm not planning on going anywhere in the foreseeable future so take your time." The two men shook hands. Hank found the truck parked next to the workshop with a full tank of fuel.

The next day Hank went shopping. He bought a fleet of seven trucks: new F150s, F250 diesels a F350 diesel to be picked up later and four F150 4X4 trucks for end of the month delivery. One of the F150s was a special order. He made arrangements for a local well digging company to drill a water well at the meadow site where he planned to build his house and submitted a request to the county for a building permit and to the U.S. Forest Service for permission to improve the road to the meadow.

Hank stopped at the hardware store and ordered a turbine generator to place in the stream to provide electric power. The turbine would have little or no effect on the wildlife or environment. He planned to bury all the power lines to a utility shed and on to the house and an outbuildings.

Hank used the next day to do all the legal work required in putting a ranch together, getting the correct permits from the state and the county. On Friday, Hank picked up his statements from the bank. His investment firm forwarded the information of his finances and liquid assets to the bank. He found his retirement pay on automatic deposit had accumulated to a half million dollars cash available.

Hank called friends from his past as character witnesses. All the statements were faxed to Millie's fax machine with copies to Jim's fax at the Lazy B. He spent Friday evening with Jim and Maya and stayed in the guest house. Maya insisted Hank as a fellow rancher consider the guest house his home until his own house was completed.

CHAPTER 12

Thursday morning before sunrise, Hank climbed into his brand new F250 diesel truck and set out for Dutton. He stopped only long enough to order two additional diesel pickup trucks to add to his truck fleet, a F250 and a F350 dually. He had plans and the trucks would help seal the deals, hopefully. All the trucks were fleet standard color except for the F150s, one ordered in black and tricked out with special wheels and tires. The other F150 trucks could be available colors. The last truck was ordered tricked out with a special paint job not yet specified; all the trucks Hank ordered were four wheel drives, a requirement for Montana ranch work.

Hank parked in front of his room at the Dutton Blue Bird Motel after he drove non-stop from Lone Horse. After a hot shower and eight hours of uninterrupted sleep he was ready to confront the day and make a positive change in his life. Last night he had debated with himself about calling Bess and decided to wait till morning.

Bess telephoned Thursday and caught Hank at Millie's. She contacted the district court judge and the judge agreed to meet with Hank and consider assigning temporary custody of the three children to Hank, dependant on the documentation of finances and character references.

Up and showered before the sun cracked the horizon, Hank sat in a booth in the Dutton Café with his third cup of strong coffee. Bess walked in and looked around. She spotted him at the same time Hank noticed her; he rose and watched Bess approach. He was awed by her beauty and self-confidence.

Bess tossed her heavy black handbag onto the booth's bench seat and threw her arms around his neck. She planted a kiss on him, leaned back and looked him directly in the eye, her own eyes misted.

"Doggone it; you sure know how to sweep a girl off her feet. Why didn't you call me last night?" Bess asked not taking her eyes from Hank's smiling face.

"Gosh Bess, I was really beat, it was late; I thought this morning would be okay."

"Well you were wrong, last night would have been better." Bess paused. "But now you're here, sit down." Hank sat back down and Bess pushed him over and sat on the seat beside to him.

"Excuse me Bess, you want breakfast or just coffee?" Jean, the waitress asked, hardly able to contain her enjoyment at Bess's smiles and excitement.

"I don't think I can eat right now. Just coffee Jean, thanks."

Hank was surprised at how much he looked forward to being with Bess and the tiny electric shock her kiss delivered.

"I hope that briefcase," Bess pointed to Hank's brown briefcase, "has all the documents we need."

"Yeah, I have all the documents not faxed to you already. All I have are five character statements and my financial statements. The investments are pretty diverse; you know some from here, some from there."

"Hank, why don't you let me look them over."

"Sure." He pushed the breakfast dishes aside to clear room, reached across and lifted his briefcase onto the table. Hank pulled out two folders and a tablet and put the briefcase back on the other seat. The folders were pretty thin and Bess looked a little disappointed. The folder labeled character statements contained only five typed faxed papers. The other folder wasn't much thicker.

Bess opened the statements folder and glanced at them. She looked at each statement and back at Hank, her eyes wide with surprise. "These will certainly do. Hand me the other folder." Bess opened the folder and her eyes grew even wider. "Damn Cowboy, you do know how to impress a girl. I made an appointment with the judge for nine o'clock this morning just in case."

Hank looked at his watch. "That gives us a couple of hours. I've got a couple of other things you can help me with."

"Sure, what do you need?"

"You remember the father-son team who won the team roping? Do you know where they live?"

"Sure, the Withrows. What about them?"

"I want to talk to Ben Withrow. If he is what I think he is, I want to offer him a job. The impression I got in the short time we talked, he could use a good job."

Bess hesitated before she answered. "I don't know if I should say this but." Bess sighed and looked Hank straight in the eye. "Ben Withrow was accused of taking money from where he worked a couple of years ago. In defending himself he lost nearly everything. The case has never been resolved legally. There was never any evidence to convict him but the damage was done. Ben lost his job and his home. He has been training horses, buying prospects at auction. He trains and sells them barely making enough to feed his family and keep enough horses to train and sell."

"Do you think he took the money?" Hank asked. A hardness passed over his face and was reflected in his voice.

"No sir, I don't think he did it. His boss was having an affair with the secretary who also had access to the money. She quit and left town shortly after Ben was accused."

"Would you recommend him for a responsible job?"

"Sure, I'd hire him if I had a job to offer him," Bess replied seriously.

Hank's face relaxed and the man Bess knew returned. She glanced at her watch. "We have enough time for another cup of coffee. I don't want to be late and I want to see the look on His Honor's face when he reads what you brought."

Bess led Hank into the suite of offices marked District Court. "Is he busy?" she asked the clerk sitting at the oak desk placed in front of a closed door.

"Good morning to you too Bess, he's expecting you." The clerk looked Hank over. "Aren't you that cowboy from Montana?"

"Yes ma'am, guilty." Hank smiled and shook the hand she offered.

"Say, you aren't busy this evening are you?"

"Easy Claudia, he's with me," Bess said.

"Oh yeah, well some people have all the luck." Claudia knocked on the inner door and opened it. She gestured for them to go inside.

Bess introduced Hank to Judge Hoskin. The judge motioned to the two brown leather chairs arranged in front of his desk. They sat and the judge took the file folders Bess offered.

The judge snorted. "This all there is?"

"Yes sir," Bess said. "I think you'll find everything you need."

"Humph!" Judge Hoskin opened the first file of character statements. As he read his eyes widened. "You actually know these people?"

"Yes sir." Hank kept his face calm.

"Humm, let's see. A United States Senator, the Commandant of the Marine Corps, the president of a Fortune 500 company, a Federal District Court Judge and who's this Jim Sutterland? He is in some pretty stiff company." Hoskin opened the financial folder and read the bottom lines. "According to these you are pretty well heeled too. Now tell me why you want to foster these children and your long-range plans."

For the next hour Hank explained his plans for the ranch and the opportunities he offered the children and answered the judge's questions.

"You have the papers with you Miss Clemons?"

"Yes sir, I brought them just in case." Bess handed the folder to the judge.

"I see you set up a monthly evaluation schedule for the first year and annually after that. That's good; I want those evaluations sent to me or the court by the tenth of each month and August first for the yearly report, any problem?"

"No sir." Hank and Bess watched Judge Hoskin sign the papers that gave Hank the custody of three children.

"It has been a pleasure meeting you Mister Springer, you take good care of those children."

When Bess and Hank left the courthouse, Hank was in a mild state of shock. He and Bess, against the odds, had done it. He was now legally responsible for three children. Half-formed plans for a ranch and the cattle and horse operations spun around in his head. A second family to raise. Children to educate, house and see to their safety; in his heart he knew he and Bess had done the right thing.

Hank followed Bess to the Children's Home and her office. They discussed the best way to break the news of the fostering to the children. One important benefit: the children would remain together.

Bess thought it best if she told the children that day and Hank meet them the next morning. Bess told Hank how to find the small ranch the Withrow family rented a few miles from town. She would join him later for dinner. Hank called Jim to inform him and Maya about the fostering of the children. Jim told him Brent was helping the survey crew establish the boundaries of Hank's new ranch and directing the drilling operation for the water well.

Hank left town and drove out the gravel road east of Dutton. He spotted the small two-story ranch house about a hundred yards from the main road. As he pulled the truck onto the driveway, he saw Ben Withrow working a young horse in a round pen. Hank watched the man work and noted the gentleness and the willingness to please of the horse. He saw new patched planks on the pen, the neatness of the yard and the serviceability of the equipment. Hank stepped down from the truck and leaned against the tail gate as he watched Ben work the colt. How the colt responded was the mark of a patient horseman. When Ben finished he opened the gate and walked out followed by the horse; the horse wore a halter but no lead rope.

Ben approached and stopped in front of Hank. Ben was about 6 feet tall. His brown hair was cut short, definitely a home barber cut. He had the typical slim build of a ranch hand used to spending long hours in the saddle. His sweat-stained brown Stetson spoke of hard work and better days. The horse stayed in his place, head at Ben's shoulder. "Hey Mr. Springer, what brings you out this way?" Ben and Hank shook hands.

"You do Mr. Withrow. There a place we can talk?"

"Yes sir, let me put Frisky away and we can use the kitchen. If I know Wilma she's put a pot of coffee on as soon as you pulled into the drive. Coffee okay with you sir?"

"Now I've said it before, name's Hank. Mind if I call you Ben?"

"I would be pleased if you would, thank you Hank."

Hank followed Ben into the barn. A barn cat lay on top of a stack of hay. Ben brushed the horse without having to tie him. Finished, Ben led the horse to a vacant stall, took the halter off and put it with a folded lead rope on a wooden peg beside the stall door. Hank noticed the two horses he'd seen Ben and his son ride at the jackpot. Only three horses: the man was living pretty close to the edge.

Ben led Hank into the warm, neat kitchen; the smell of freshly brewed coffee added to the hominess of the room. A tall woman with ash blonde hair and striking pale blue eyes, came into the kitchen. Ben introduced Hank to his wife, Wilma. The three sat at the kitchen table.

"What's on your mind, Hank?" Ben asked.

"I've got a proposition for you to consider." Wilma got up and started to leave the men alone. Hank stopped her. "This concerns you too Mrs. Withrow, Wilma. Please sit down while I explain." Wilma sat back down and gave Hank her attention.

"Okay, here's the deal." Hank began. "I just bought a ranch in Montana. I've got 200 head of cattle, some BLM land available and a bit over 10,500 acres of my own. My plan calls for a combination cattle and horse ranch. Right now it is only the land, no buildings, but I have picked the site for the ranch buildings. The survey crew is finishing up as we speak. Brent, my son, is with the drilling crew for the water well. Okay, my proposal; I'd like to hire you as my horse manager, to include breeding, buying and training. I'll furnish you a house, a truck and fifty thousand a year. I have three foster children so your children will have schoolmates. The downside is you might be in tents for a couple of months while your house is being built."

"How soon do you have to know?" Ben asked and glanced at his wife.

"I'll be leaving Dutton day after tomorrow. I'd like to know if you want the job tomorrow if possible, but before I leave at the latest."

"Other than the horse breeding and training, what would you expect from me?" Ben's voice betrayed his excitement.

"I'm not sure yet, but you might need to help push cattle once in a while. I'm going to hire a cattle boss too. I know you two will get along if you accept the job." Hank thought he'd said enough for the Withrows to make a decision.

Ben looked at Wilma raised his eyebrows. She smiled back and nodded. Ben turned back to Hank. "You just hired yourself a man."

"Great. I would like you to ride up to Montana with me. You can be back here by the end of next week or early the following week." Hank and Ben shook hands, closing the deal.

Ben looked at Wilma, an unasked question in his eyes. "Ben you go; Robby, Sue and I can run things till you get back," Wilma said. "I'll start packing, we don't have all that much."

Taking out his wallet, Hank counted out fifteen hundred dollars and handed the money to Ben. "Here's your first ten days salary. No, we'll call it travel money and moving expenses."

"You sure you can trust us like this?" Ben asked. "You know I was accused of stealing."

"Did you steal the money?"

"No sir."

"Okay, so what's the problem?" Hank grinned.

"Nothing I guess. You want me to meet you in town?"

"No, I'll pick you up here. Almost forgot, when you move bring your horses. If you want to sell them I'm buying, otherwise they're yours. Now folks, I've got a date so I'd better be getting or I'll have one upset lady on my hands."

"Then you aren't married, Hank?" Wilma asked.

"Nope, but I think I'm about to have a lady in my life so I'd better get to getting."

                                    *   *   *

Over dinner, Hank and Bess decided the best way to explain the fostering to the children was to just tell them. Hank could tell them about his plans, the ranch and answer their questions. Bess decided she would take four of the fourteen weeks of vacation due her and fly with the children to Missoula. Hank planned to ask Ben Withrow to take the children's belongings from storage and bring them when he moved his own household effects.

Bess reminded Hank the children each would inherit $700,000 on their eighteenth birthday, from their parents' estate and insurance money. Additional money from the sale of the house and other assets would be applied and added to what each child would receive. As their legal guardian, Hank would be overseeing the inheritance, submitting a yearly statement to the District Court in Dutton. Bess and the children would stay at the Lazy B until the new ranch house was completed. Brent hired a construction crew to build the houses and put the barn and stable together. Except for the houses, Hank bought them as modular buildings. He thought the buildings could be built and finished within a month, two at the most.

"You know Bess, I really appreciate what you've done for me and the kids. Volunteering to stay up in Montana for your vacation is great too." Hank, not usually at a loss for words, fumbled to get his feelings out.

"Hank, it really is my pleasure. Besides, Bev and Brent may decide to elope to Idaho and I want to be there of course." Bess hesitated to tell Hank that she and Bev had been talking about Bev's relationship with Brent and their plans for the future. She decided now was a better time than later. "Bev and Brent have decided they will live in Montana and not in Dutton. Bev has already given her notice to the school board, which accepted her resignation and hired her replacement. Bev is working with her replacement preparing the next year's class schedules. Her students think it's neat she's marrying a cowboy. The school board asked Bev to complete and submit the lesson plans for summer school before she leaves. Bev wants to leave Dutton as soon as possible." Bess paused to let it all sink in. She excused herself and went to the restroom. Bess returned and found Hank still thinking about Brent and Bev and their budding relationship.

"Brent called Bev this morning. He's not sure when he will go to Quantico and do whatever it is that Marines do when they go to camp. I have the feeling it's not the same as the Boy Scouts." Her comment brought a smile to Hank's face. "Bev has applied for a teacher's certification for Montana already."

Hank's mind was busy playing catch-up and new ideas were forming. "Wait a minute, you're saying Brent and Bev are getting married this summer and she's moving to Montana?" Hank's mind shifted into high gear. "Ben Withrow is going to work for me and he has two kids. I'm going to ask Josh Reynolds to work for me too and he has three children. The Finleys have five, the Johnsons four and I'm sure some of the other families on the east slope have kids too. Right now the bus drives sixty-five miles one way to Lone Horse for school. What do you think about building our own school? I'll donate an acre or two by the road and see to it the schoolhouse is built. I think there are already at least seventeen students and closer to thirty kids in grades one through eight." Hank was excited and as usual way ahead of himself. Excitement overtook him again. "I bet we can cut travel time on a bus to less than an hour a day as opposed to the three to four hours they travel everyday now."

Bess couldn't help it: she felt some of Hank's enthusiasm, but patience won. "Slow down cowboy. There is a lot more to a school than just a building. You need certified teachers and state approval, not to mention funding, besides the land and building. There are books and support materials, the list goes on and on."

Hank's excitement continued. "I'm going to offer Brent an opportunity to build up a dude business and teach rodeo roping. Team roping is one of the fastest growing sports in the world. The best thing is it dovetails in with the other projects at the ranch, like horse training, sales and boarding. City

Slickers on a real live working ranch. I heard there are several ranches making enough money from the dudes to pay wages, the upkeep on the horses and additional buildings." Hank winded himself in his excitement.

"Looks like you have another project to occupy your mind Mr. Springer," Bess said. She reached across the table and squeezed his workman's hand.

The food eaten, conversation unneeded, Bess and Hank strolled around town, stopped for an ice cream at a hamburger stand. The crescent moon helped set the mood as Hank walked Bess home.

The couple stood on the porch to Bess's rental house and looked into each other's eyes. Hank leaned forward and kissed Bess on the cheek, said goodnight and turned to leave.

Bess reached out and captured his arm. "Don't you want to come in for a cup of coffee and maybe watch a movie on the tube?" Bess asked. She felt uncomfortable, but didn't care. She wasn't going to let this opportunity with Hank pass untested.

"You sure about this Bess? I'm not much for movies and it's kind of late for coffee."

"Oh shut up Hank. Come in." Bess led him by the arm into the house. "Bev's asleep in the front bedroom; my room is in the back and opens onto a veranda." Hank followed her quietly through the house, down the hall past the bath and into a room decorated as Hank would have guessed. A queen-size bed, bedside table and lamps and a desk, with a new computer against the wall below a curtained window. Sliding glass doors opened onto a veranda that overlooked the backyard and flower beds.

Bess closed the door and turned to Hank. "I don't usually bring men home. Really you're the first." She stammered, embarrassed. "I don't know how to go about this."

"Shush." He quieted and reassured her. "I guess we'll both find out—it's been some time for me too." Hank dropped his cowboy hat on the desk, took Bess's hand and pulled her gently to him. He looked down into her eyes and she up into his. The two studied each other, questions sought answers until Bess reached up and put her hands on his cheeks, her finger tracing the small scar below his right eye. She moved her hands to the back of Hank's neck and pulled his face down to her.

They kissed softly at first, Bess pressing her body against his as their kisses became more urgent. She broke the kiss. "I really want this with you Hank." She pushed his coat off his shoulders and he let it drop to the floor. He stepped back, never breaking eye contact. He unbuttoned her blouse pulling it up out of her skirt.

Bess realized she was standing before a man wearing only skirt and bra while he studied her. The heat of a blush washed over her, she turned her head aside. Hank leaned forward kissing the space between her breasts. When she felt his breath on her flesh, a shiver covered her and raised goosebumps. She reached behind her and unhooked the bra, letting the straps slide down her arms. With a shrug she let it drop to the floor.

Hank's hands caressed her, fingers lingering on her nipples, erect, ready for his touch and kisses. Bess stood still while he took his time; he touched, kissed and licked her nipples gently and the flesh around them. Tiny currents of electricity swept up her spine. Bess unbuttoned his shirt so he could discard it onto the growing pile of clothes.

She grabbed his hand and held it when he reached for the button on the side of the skirt. When he stopped she held his hands and looked into his eyes. The moment passed, she released his hand and closed her eyes giving herself to him. The skirt joined the pile of clothes; Bess now wore only white panties. She unbuckled Hank's belt and unzipped his Wranglers. He stepped back and heeled off his boots, the denim jeans slipped down to gather at the ankle. He stepped out of the jeans and pulled her against him crushing her breasts against his chest. For a long moment they stood holding each other before Hank slipped her panties down so she could step out of them.

Bess looked down at Hank's boxer shorts and smiled. She dropped to her knees and pulled the boxers down. She was looking directly at Hank's erection. She looked up and smiled. "How old are you? Humm, liar!" Hank reached down and lifted Bess to her feet and gently pushed her back onto the bed. He found her blonde pubic hair short and trimmed; the faint smell of her perfume tickled his nose.

She surrendered herself to his ministrations until convulsions overtook her body. As he entered her she wrapped her arms and legs around him pulling him close as multiple orgasms took her.

It was some minutes before her mind cleared. They were still on the cover of the bed. Hank lay on his side, looked into her eyes: love shone in their depths as he pulled her tight against him again. This time the love making was slow and long-lasting, until each was sated. Bess pushed the cover onto the floor and moved up the bed onto the cool sheets.

They fell asleep in each other's arms, spooning until the rising sun woke Hank. He moved the hair from the back of Bess's neck and kissed her until she stirred against him, moving back into the curve of his body. Another session of love making occupied them until they heard Bev move around the house as she prepared for work.

When the front door closed, Hank rose and stumbled to the bathroom. Before he did, he kissed Bess, ran his hands over her breasts, leaned down and kissed each nipple. "Good morning ladies, I trust you are awake by your alert appearance." He laughed when Bess pulled his face down to her breasts, the nipples alert and ready for more attention.

"Sorry, I've got to go, I mean go." He got up and headed to the bathroom. Minutes later Bess heard the shower come on.

Hank was soaping himself when the shower curtain was pulled aside and a naked woman slipped into the shower with him. "My, is this a full service shower?" Hank teased.

"You bet, Lone Stranger." Minutes later, they soaped each other and learned the secret places that brought pleasure. Bess turned the cold water on full and got a quick reaction from Hank. He escaped the shower and grabbed a towel to dry himself. When Bess emerged, Hank dried her gently with an oversize bath towel. The towel smelled faintly of Bess.

Hank left Bess in the bathroom, dressed and made the bed, then went to the kitchen and waited for her. Twenty minutes later she came into the kitchen, and Hank handed her a cup of coffee brewed earlier by Bev. They sat at the kitchen table and nursed their coffee. Each wore a silly grin as they gazed at each other, words unnecessary. "I need to go to the motel and get fresh clothes. Do you want to come with me or meet me at the café?"

Bess considered. "I'll meet you at the café. I have a couple of things I want to go over before we go to the Childrens Home. I want the papers recorded at the courthouse separate from the judge's office. That way they are a part of the public record, above board and not subject to challenge by any of the other couples who have tried to get their hands on the children."

"Okay, it won't take but a few minutes at the motel and I want to get some more cash from the bank. I gave all my spending money to Ben yesterday. The kids are going to need some money for the trip too." He rose from the table and rinsed the cup at the sink. He stopped to kiss Bess and left the house to walk the few blocks to the motel.

On the way, Hank visited the Dutton Bank. He returned to the motel with $500 in cash and a credit card in Bess's name issued from a Missoula bank. The card was a no-limit purchase credit card with a $100,000 cash withdrawal limit. He checked to make sure the card and cash were there and then sealed the envelop, before he left the motel to meet Bess.

At breakfast, Hank gave Bess the envelop saying it was for emergency stuff and put it in her purse. After eating, they headed to the Children's Home in Hank's truck. He smiled as he admired her legs and the flash of the top of her stockings when she hiked up her skirt to climb into the truck's cab.

I like him looking at my legs, Bess thought and raised the skirt a bit higher than required to climb up to the truck's seat. She was wearing her blonde hair in a ponytail and it gave her a youthful look. Hank suddenly felt years younger.

While Bess talked to the children, Hank waited in the visitors' lounge. Bess entered followed by Michael; the boy walked with confidence, but Hank could see the anxious look in his eyes. Marjorie entered holding five year old Mary Ann's hand. Bess introduced the children and Michael shook Hank's hand, a firm man's handshake. The boy was tall, nearly six feet, dark brown hair, slim build and matching brown eyes. Hank could see Marjorie deferred to her brother as head of the family. She was a female copy of Michael, definitely his twin. She was tall; he guessed about five foot seven inches, brown hair with reddish highlights and brown eyes, a girl on the edge of womanhood.

Tightly clutching Marjorie's hand was Mary Ann. Definitely under five feet, dishwater blonde hair in pigtail braids. She looked up at Hank with clear blue eyes, no fear just curious. All the children's clothes had been freshly laundered and ironed. When Hank looked closely at the twin's body language, he read some anxiety and fear. He guessed it was the fear of being separated and possibly moving into the unknown. The twins sized him up as he did them.

"Bess says you're our foster parent." Michael opened the dialogue, surprising Hank with his directness.

"Yes sir, that's right. The judge signed the papers and you can come up to Montana and live with me on my ranch. I'm not forcing you but inviting you to come live with me. That way you can remain together. If you decline my offer, I'll have to go home alone. I don't want to but if it is your wishes and decision then that's the way it will be."

"Do you have horses?" Marjorie whispered.

"Yes ma'am, I do. You'll have to pick out your own if you want to ride. My ranch will have both cattle and horses. The two current horses I own are both ranch horses and one is my roping horse. I usually don't let others ride him but there are plenty of other ranch horses you can borrow until you get your own."

"Does that mean we will have a say in what we do and you don't have many horses, yet?" Michael picked up on the implied "yet."

"I am still putting the ranch together. I have two hundred head of cattle, ten thousand plus acres and right now only the two horses I mentioned. Oh yeah, there is a mule, a pack horse and my son Brent's two rope horses. They will be on the ranch too. But they are Brent's horses, not mine, so if you want to ride one of them you need to talk to Brent."

Hank paused, and then shifted the focus a bit. "Do you know the Withrow family?"

Marjorie sat up straighter. "I went to school with Susan Withrow. She's a little younger than me and Michael. I think the boy is still in high school and he will be a senior, or at least a junior. I think he's seventeen or really close to seventeen, because Susan and he aren't twins, well they might be twins." Marjorie paused thinking of what to say next. "I heard the father stole some money and he was fired from his job or something."

"Well yes he did lose his job, but he didn't steal any money." Hank glanced at Bess. "Mr. Withrow is going to work for me at my ranch. His wife, Wilma and his children Robby and Susan will be living on the ranch too."

"Where will I go to school? I want to go to school," Mary Ann said as tears began to roll down her baby cheeks.

Bess rushed over to pick up the five year old. Michael stared at Bess but didn't say anything.

Hank addressed Michael and Marjorie. "Okay, is it a deal or not? You coming with me or are you staying here?"

Michael and Marjorie looked at each other, shrugged and smiled. They stepped forward and each shook his hand. "Deal!"

"Okay, here's the plan. Mrs. Clemons, Bess, will travel with you. You'll take an airplane from here to Spokane and another flight from Spokane to Missoula. I will pick you up at the Missoula airport next Friday. Marjorie, if you want to, invite Susan Withrow to travel with you. Mr. Withrow will be driving to Montana with me; Susan can help her dad fix up a place for her family. That sound okay?" Marjorie and Mary Ann were obviously excited, Michael still reserved.

"I wish I could take you all with me right now, but there are a few things to be done in Montana before you get there. At some point in the future, you'll each have a truck of your own; or I should say a ranch truck of your own. Michael, I'm sorry buddy, but you get basic black. The trip to the high school in Lone Horse is more than a hundred miles round trip." Hank frowned. "Do you have a driver's license, Michael?"

"No sir. My dad was going to teach me and Marjorie to drive, then there was the accident." Michael sighed.

"Bess, do you think you can get a couple of the defensive driving manuals for Michael and Marjorie?"

"No problem. The laws are different between here and Montana, but similar enough, passing the driver's test shouldn't be a problem." Bess paused then asked, "Have either of you driven before at all?"

"Both Marjorie and I drove a little during driver's education at school. It was a required course before getting a driver's license. I have my driver's booklet in my stuff." He looked at Marjorie who nodded—she still had her booklet too.

"I'll make an appointment at the examiner's office in Lone Horse for both of you to take the written and driver's test. Insurance and a valid driver's license will be in effect before you put your butts in the driver's seat, understand?" Hank waited until both teenagers acknowledged his rule. "Okay, I won't be seeing you until you get to Missoula. Bess is in charge with Michael her assistant. Mary Ann, you watch over these two bigger kids, okay?"

The little girl swelled up, puffing out her chest. "You bet, I'll watch'm, won't we Bess."

"Yes dear, we will."

Hank put out his hand to each child individually, including Mary Ann. They shook hands again confirming the deals they'd made. Hank went to the office where there were some papers to sign while Bess returned the children to their rooms. She told them she'd pick them up in eight days for the flight to Montana and their new life there.

*   *   *

After he checked out of the motel Hank stayed with Bess that night. Bev was not surprised when she found Hank in the kitchen drinking coffee when she entered. "I suppose you know I spent the night with your mom? It's just something that happened and I hope you don't think less of her for it."

"No Hank, I think it's great. Mom really likes you and you are going to be my father-in-law soon."

"Yes—about that. I'm not sure your mother and I being together is such a good thing. I feel strongly for her and wouldn't hurt her for the world, but I have some demons to overcome." He set the coffee cup down on the table, sadness in his eyes. "I think you and Brent are meant to be together and have a whole passel of kids and for that I thank the powers that make it all possible. Your mother is a beautiful woman and she tears at my heart. I want to be good for her." Hank got to his feet, washed his cup at the sink. "So I'll see you in Missoula." He kissed Bev on the cheek and left the house.

Bev heard the diesel truck start as her mother entered the kitchen. "Did Hank leave already?"

"Yes mother, that's his truck warming up."

Bess was out the door before Bev finished talking. She ran to the truck, jumped up on the running board. Hank rolled the window down. "What, you're trying to leave without a kiss or a goodbye?"

"I didn't want to wake you. You need your sleep and I've deprived you of a lot of sleep lately." He smiled at her: hair messed from her pillow, no makeup, she was beautiful. "I'm going to miss you until next Friday. You've got the envelop if you need anything for you or the kids. The cash is for burgers at the airports. I think there is a layover in Spokane of a couple of hours. Damn Bess." He reached through the window and pulled her head against his forehead. He kissed her hard. "Better get in the house or the neighbors will talk." She stepped off the running board, backed away and watched as Hank put the truck in gear and drove down the street. She watched until he disappeared around the corner. She could hear his diesel engine until it too faded.

Chapter 13

Hank saw Ben Withrow in the stable grooming his horses when he turned into the driveway. Hank stood in the entrance to the breezeway of the stable and watched Ben brush his horse. He saw a bucket with a curry comb and brush beside a second stall. Hank picked up the bucket and entered the stall with the horse Ben's son used at the Dutton Jackpot Roping. Hank let the horse sniff him and waited until the horse let Hank rub his face. After the horse sniffed the curry comb and the brush, Hank started brushing the horse's flank. He brushed gently until the horse relaxed. Then he brushed the horse's face working carefully around the eyes and nostrils. He looked up to see Ben watch as he brushed. Ben nodded and went back to grooming his horse. The communication between horsemen, horses and each other was important especially around another man's horse.

Ben liked what he saw; his new boss was a horseman. Both men finished with their horse and worked together on the third horse. Ben put the brushes away in the small tack room.

"Morning Ben." The men shook hands. "Why don't you say goodbye to the family and we'll be on our way."

Ben nodded. "My gear is in the hall. I thought I'd bring along one of my saddles if you've got room?"

"Good idea, put the saddle in the back. There's a new saddle cover behind the front seat. I'll get it, where's the saddle?" Hank asked.

"The saddle is the older one on the top rack in the tack room. I'll go up and say goodbye to Wilma. If we have time, she has a cup of coffee ready for you and I'll get my things loaded."

Hank knocked on the door and Wilma answered. "Morning Mr. Springer."

"I thought we got this straight the other day Wilma. Name's Hank, not mister, just Hank or, 'Hey you!' when you want to get my attention."

The woman smiled at Hank, laughed and replied, "Yes sir Hank and I suppose the sir is out too?"

"Now you're thinking like my friend. Ben said there might be a cup of coffee lying around somewhere unclaimed."

Hank and Wilma were at the kitchen table making small talk when Ben came in. "Is Robby back from the Thompson's pasture yet?"

"He hasn't come in yet. It takes time for him to finish his job and get back here from the Thompson's ranch down the road," Wilma explained to Hank. "Robby spends a couple of hours each morning feeding the Thompson's animals before school. He's been doing that for the past two years. He earns enough to furnish his needs at school. It's a big help."

Robby Withrow came into the house through the back door. He removed his boots before he entered the kitchen in his stocking feet. Hank noticed the socks were just a little large and had been mended several times by the color of the yarn. The boy poured himself a cup of coffee and asked his dad if he could join them at the table. Ben looked to Hank who was busy looking at the wallpaper.

"Sit down Robby, Mr. Springer and I will be leaving in a few minutes. I'm taking the old saddle with me. I also have that repaired headstall and a set of roping reins." Ben looked inquiringly at Hank. "Do you think I should bring some saddle blankets?"

"No, I think we have plenty of blankets. The saddle idea was good though. We do have some spare saddles and I think we are going to need them."

Susan Withrow came into the kitchen. "Morning Mama, Daddy. Hello Mr. Springer." She greeted Hank. "Daddy, I put your denim coat in the hall, the tear on the sleeve is mended." Susan started to cry. She put her arms around her father.

"This is the first time we have ever been separated, except for a trip to town and to deliver a horse," Ben explained.

"Well, I have some news for you Susan. I'm pretty sure Marjorie Anderson will be calling to ask you to travel with her, Bess, Michael and Mary Ann next Friday. The airplane tickets are all taken care of, but you're going to need some spending money for the trip." Hank removed five twenty dollar bills from his wallet and handed them to Susan.

Susan looked at her mother then her father before timidly accepting the money. "I'll see you next Friday Daddy." On impulse she kissed Hank on the cheek and ran from the kitchen to disappear down the hall.

Hank was a bit embarrassed by Susan's kiss; he sure wasn't expecting it. But this attention from the women folk was pleasant. "Come on Ben before these women get me all melancholy." He drained his coffee, shook Wilma's hand and left the kitchen. Hank picked up Ben's bag on the way out of the house. He noticed the bagged saddle in the truck bed and tied it to one of the truck's tie downs with a piece of hemp rope.

Hank started the truck and waited for Ben. The family stood together on the porch, and Susan came through the door as Ben said goodbye to Wilma and Robby. Susan threw her arms around her dad and then retreated into the house. Ben carried his coat and another small bag. He climbed into the truck and put the bag and coat in the back seat. Tears were in his eyes too. The two men waved and Hank drove onto the gravel road and turned toward the main highway.

The men were quiet, each in his own thoughts, when Ben broke the silence. "I want to thank you for this opportunity and the money. Wilma slept all night last night. The first time she's done that since the trouble started a couple of years ago. If nothing else, thanks for that," Ben said sincerely. "Susan is so excited about traveling with Marjorie I don't think she'll sleep until they leave next Friday. You're sure it's all right for Susan to go with them?"

"Yeah, I'm sure. Marjorie needs the company too. It's a big change for the kids, all of them. I'm sorry I couldn't do more for Robby."

"Robby knows he's needed here to get things ready for the move. He needs to talk to the Thompsons about getting someone else to help with the feeding until Mr. Thompson is back on his feet. He's been ill with the cancer. The word is the chemo he's been taking has worked but he needs to regain his strength."

* * *

Hank and Ben were having dinner at a café outside Boise, Idaho, when Hank decided it was time to get the air cleared with Ben. The other man had been quiet except when he thanked Hank for hiring him. Ben answered questions when asked but did not volunteer much or open a conversation. "Listen Ben, I may be the boss but I'd also like to be your friend. I can't imagine you doing anything that might change that. I hired you because I think you can do the job. I think your family and mine can have a relationship that is more than employer, employee." Hank looked into the eyes of the man across the table. "Your job is to keep me from making mistakes with the horses and the management of the horse operation. But above that I want the Withrows to be part of our extended ranch family. You see something wrong, tell me. If I'm making a mistake when dealing with someone, give me a heads up. That's a heads up in private." Hank sat quiet for a couple of minutes. "Your kids, Robby and Sue will be like my own. I expect them to treat me like they would treat you. I know I'm not doing very well explaining this, but try to understand. I want your family to be like my own. I expect you to make decisions, which will be treated the same as if I made them."

Ben looked a little uncomfortable, and Hank could see the confusion in Ben's hesitation. Hank sighed: "Look Ben, your first job after bringing and settling your family is to go to the horse auction in Billings and find us some good breeding stock. You may have to make a few trips before you find stock of the quality we need to build with. Good stock you would be proud to sell with your guarantee. If you don't find any horses you like, then don't buy them. If and when school permits, I want you to take Robby and Michael with you and teach them what you know about horses. I also want each of them mounted with good strong ranch horses; the ranch horses I'll buy, others they want, they buy. There are other auctions besides Billings you might elect to attend, your call. Check the private sales too; there are a lot of horses being sold outside the auction circuit we might be interested in. See any problems there?" Hank could see the man relax; now he knew what Hank expected of him.

"Not a problem Hank. I think it will be good for the boys. How many horses you planning on having at the ranch? Working horses and horses you plan on selling?"

"I think horse numbers are something you and I can discuss later. I'm not actually sure what we'll have. The cattle operation will also have some impact on what we do as far as the horses. When we sell a Rolling H horse you trained you are entitled to twenty percent of the net profit. You and I will also guarantee each and every horse. Ones that don't work out go back to the auction. We'll work everything else out later as we go."

"You mentioned we might have to live in a tent for a bit—what's that about?"

"I haven't built the houses yet. You might have to help with that, but as soon as your house is built you move your family in. We'll probably be building all the houses pretty much at the same time. The outbuildings will be second except the hay and equipment barn. The summer months should be pleasant in the tents. I expect all of us will be using them for awhile." Hank grinned. "I hope Wilma won't be too mad at us: your decision to join me and mine for not having her house done."

"Not a problem. The way things were going in Dutton, we'd have been in tents pretty soon if you hadn't come along." Ben looked Hank straight in the eyes. "I owe you a lot Hank. I swear you will never have a reason to regret your trust and friendship."

"Ben, from now on you're my friend first, employee second. Your family is my family too. Do you understand my meaning?"

"Yes sir, I do." Ben went back to attacking his steak. The set of his shoulders told Hank all he needed to know about the man sitting across from him.

* * *

The trip from Dutton was uneventful. They stopped in Lone Horse long enough for Hank to take possession of the F350 he ordered before leaving for Dutton. Ben drove the new truck and followed Hank to the Lazy B. Two F150s including Michael's truck would be ready for pickup by the end of the week. The dealer promised if a surplus of trucks could be found, he would have all the vehicles Hank wanted by the end of next week. A green F250 diesel 4 by 4 was on the showroom floor and Hank decided to buy it. He told the dealer Josh Reynolds would be picking it up unless Hank sent a message saying otherwise.

At the Lazy B, Hank settled Ben in the bunkhouse. With Maya's help he got the guesthouse ready for Bess and the girls. Michael and Robby could stay in the bunkhouse. The next morning, Hank and Ben drove up to the new ranch site followed by Jim in his own truck.

While Hank was in Dutton, Jim used his bulldozer and improved the fire road to the ranch site. He took out most of the low spots and widened the road in the turns.

From Hank's description of the road access to the meadow, Ben thought it would take hours to reach the new ranch site. They drove out of the trees and spotted Brent's truck and tent near the stream. Brent's horses were pastured with Jake and Loco. The horses grazed along the stream where sweet grass grew knee high. Brent sat in a lawn chair beside his tent eating a sandwich and talking on his cell phone.

Hank reintroduced Ben to his son.

"Welcome to the ranch! No houses yet but we got land, and a well," Brent said. "Bev's not coming with Bess and the kids. She needs to stay for an extra couple of weeks to get the new teacher settled in. The school board is getting a little sticky about Bev resigning before the end of the school year and giving her a good recommendation for another job. Politics! Who needs it?"

"I thought you were on your way to Quantico." Hank frowned and raised his eyebrows and waited for an explanation.

"Nope, the unit got a message telling me not to report now. It seems there is a school at Fort Bragg that, Headquarters Marine Corps wants me to attend as part of my ATD at Quantico." Brent walked over to the F250. "Nice truck Dad, did you get me one too?" he teased his father.

Hank explained Ben's job at the ranch. "Ben is our new horse manager. You two will be working together a lot. About horses, Ben is the boss. About the money situation, Brent speaks with my complete confidence. I really don't see a problem with you two. If you do need a referee get Wilma if I'm not around."

"Who's Wilma?" Brent and Jim asked at the same time.

"Gee Brent, Wilma is Ben's wife and if Ben doesn't object, I'll hire her to be my ranch assistant." Ben and Brent looked at each other and shrugged.

"I'll be back in a while. Jim why don't you take Ben on a tour, point out where the horse corrals might go along with where you think the houses need to be. I'm sure you and Brent have discussed everything already. Brent, remember its Ben's decision for a final location on the stables, corrals and his house."

"Where're you going Dad?"

"I want to talk to Josh Reynolds—have you seen him around?"

"Yeah, Josh dropped by yesterday, wanted to know if he could hook onto the access road since it crosses your ranch. He looks a lot better than the last time I saw him. He rode in on that old paint horse of his."

"Jim, do you know if he took the job on the other side of Lone Horse?" Hank asked. "I know he considered it because he said he would."

"I don't think so. The work he was doing for Forsters finished up the other day. I wish there was something we could do. That family has had more than their share of hard luck," Jim said.

"Say Pop," Brent broke into the conversation, "this has got to be costing you a lot. You know I've got all that money just sitting there in the bank."

"Yeah, I know son, but you and Bev will need your nest egg." Hank sat still as he appraised his son. "Son, are you thinking of having Bev go back to Quantico and some of those other assignments that pop up on occasion?"

"No sir, if it's okay, I'd like her to stay here with you. She says she's done with Dutton and likes it up here, even if I'm not here." He grinned. "She even said she liked you, although I can't for the life of me figure out why. If I get an assignment to Dam Neck I might have her travel back there with me. The BOQ is right on the beach and it would be a nice vacation for her away from these pesky mountains."

Hank addressed all the men. "You did hear that I am fostering three children from Dutton whose parents were killed in a car accident. They'll be here Friday along with Bess and Ben's daughter Susan."

"Yeah, I heard from Bev. Wow Pop, a new family." Brent laughed and slapped his father on the back.

"You're not upset about it are you?" Hank's face showed concern.

"Absolutely not, I think it's great." Brent grinned. "What about Bess?"

"No, I'm not fostering her." Hank was barely able to keep a straight face. "But she's going to stay here for a few weeks and help get the kids settled. Ben, take that tour with Jim. Brent, I'm sure you've got plans. I'll be back in an hour or so."

Jim and Brent took Ben on a tour of the meadow. From what Hank told Ben, he expected to see the drilling rig still there, but it was noticeably absent. Brent explained they hit water with a supply rate of over two hundred gallons a minute; it was good clear water and at sixty feet. They drilled to eighty feet, but there was no reason to go deeper.

* * *

Hank drove up the double rutted trail as close to the canyon cabin as the trail allowed and parked next to Josh Reynolds's old red pickup. Hank looked at the thirty year old truck and wondered how Josh managed to keep it running. Hank stepped down from his truck and looked around the canyon; it was much as he remembered. He sighed, stepped onto the path and walked the quarter mile to the cabin.

Hank approached the cabin and could hear the sound of wood being split. He walked around the cabin and found Josh splitting wood for the winter. Josh's son Jesse was stacking the split wood in the racks close to the back porch entrance.

"Hello," Hank called. Josh stopped splitting and smiled when he recognized Hank. Jesse stood with his mouth open and stared at Hank. "Better stack that wood you're holding because it's going to get real heavy in a minute." Hank smiled at the boy.

"Howdy Hank, what brings you out this way?" Josh asked and sank the axe blade into the chopping block. Josh looked like a man used to hard work outdoors: narrow waist, broad shoulders and sandy colored hair. He wasn't a tall man, 5 feet 9 inches; his game leg made life hard.

"Wanted to stop by and tell you, you are welcome to use the road. I'll have Maya draw up an easement paper for you so there will never be a problem about access."

"Thanks Hank, that's right nice of you." Josh addressed Jesse. "Run and tell Mom we have a visitor and warm up some of that honey bread."

The boy jumped onto the porch and through the back door carefully shutting it.

"Let's go inside so we can talk." Josh led the way, his lame leg causing a pronounced limp.

"I don't want to interrupt Charlene's day now Josh. We can sit out here."

"No trouble, Charlene will want to see you. We don't get many visitors you know." Josh opened the cabin door and motioned Hank into the cool inside of the humble but immaculate cabin.

Charlene looked over her shoulder and smiled as she took a fresh loaf of honey bread out of the cast iron stove's oven. A pot of coffee was just beginning to perk over the fire box. Josh limped over and opened the cold box and removed a pint of home—churned butter and put it on the table. Charlene set the bread next to the butter along with a knife for each man and two cups. She sliced four thick pieces of the warm bread and put the knife on the side of the bread board. Hank noticed the first gray hairs in her brown hair. Her green eyes showed her grit, where humor was difficult in her hard life.

Josh and Charlene sat down at the table. "My goodness it is good to see you Hank. It has been much too long since you've visited."

"Thank you Charlene for those kind words. It has been awhile. I suppose you heard I bought about 10,000 acres. I'm going to do some cattle and some horses. That brings me to the reason for my visit; although it should be social." Hank apologized for not visiting before.

"What is so important you made a special visit?" Charlene asked, then added, "Josh said you are building on that meadow a mile over that way." She pointed by nodding her head in the proper direction.

Hank smiled. "Okay Charlene, Josh, here's the deal. I want to hire Josh to be my cattle manager. Of course Josh will have to help out my horse manager on occasion as he will have to help you." Hank paused and continued. "I'll pay you fifty-five thousand a year. My horse manager gets fifty thousand but I furnish a house for him to make up the difference. As the need arises, you can hire temporary wranglers or permanent if you think it's necessary. Oh yeah, the job comes with a new F250 pickup, you can drive to and from work. Hell, consider the truck yours and use it as if you owned it." Hank looked at the couple who sat quietly and stared at him, stunned by his offer. "Did I say something wrong?"

Charlene was the first to snap out of shock. "No sir, Hank." Charlene jumped up from the table and disappeared into the other room. When she returned her red eyes told all Hank needed to know. He waited for their answer. Josh and Charlene looked at each other and began nodding their heads up and down in answer. Hank took out his wallet. "I want you to get with Ben Withrow and find two or three good ranch horses. I think you're going to need them."

"When do I start Hank, or should I be calling you Mr. Springer?"

"Not if you want to keep your job. I'm Hank to my friends even if they work for me. You start right now."

Charlene couldn't hold back any longer: an emotional dam had been broken; Hank could see the stress evaporate from her face. She leaned over and threw her arms around him.

After a moment, Hank remembered the wallet in his hand. He pulled out some bills and counted ten one hundred dollar bills onto the table. "Tomorrow go into Lone Horse and get whatever you need to work. That money is not an advance. When you get back find Brent—no wait, there is a F250 truck that needs to be picked up at the dealer. Better yet, wait until noon and take your truck to town. Charlene, you go along too so you can bring your truck home. Buy the kids a pizza or something. Got any questions?"

"No sir. Hank you are a life saver," Josh said.

"Almost forgot, Charlene, I'd like to hire you for a month to help settle in the Withrow family. I'll pay you seven hundred dollars a week for four weeks. While you are in town Josh, go to the dealer and buy an SUV for the ranch. The dealer should be okay with that. That will be the school bus next year. Charlene, you'll need it to get around too. Consider it your rig, at least for now."

"But Hank, I don't have a driver's license," Charlene said meekly.

"You know how to drive?"

"Yes, but it's been years, but yes I can drive."

"Okay, as soon as you get to town go get a license or if you want to wait, Josh can take you to town sometime next week. Oh heck, you and Josh take care of it." Hank glanced longingly at the bread.

Charlene noticed Hank's look, took a piece, buttered it and handed it to him. She got up from the table and stepped into the kitchen, removed a loaf from the cupboard and wrapped it in waxed bread wrappers. She set the bread in front of Hank. He nodded; a verbal thank you wasn't necessary and the appreciation on Hank's face was enough.

"Josh, if you can get away, I would like you to follow me to the meadow and meet Ben. You two can figure out what to do about the horses." Hank stood up, Charlene handed him the bread, which he took smiling and carefully carried it as he left the cabin. He waited outside while Josh talked to Charlene for a few minutes.

When Josh joined him, he handed Hank a tub of sweet butter. The men walked together to where the trucks were parked. Hank waited until Josh got the old truck running smoothly, and then led the way to the meadow.

Ben and Josh hit it off right away. Josh told him he was a horseman and while training a colt, one the children of the man he was working for threw a rock at the horse, hitting him in the flank. The resulting explosion as the horse launched itself into the air threw Josh off into the fence, resulting in a concussion and compound fracture to his leg. Josh was unconscious when he arrived at the hospital. His employer did pay for the hospital expenses but let Josh go with a small severance payment. Josh and his family were lucky they owned their cabin and the ten acres of the box canyon. Since then, Josh worked as much as the limited employment opportunities allowed for a man with a lame leg. Immediately, Ben knew he had found a kindred spirit.

The next morning, Hank changed his mind and decided he would ride with Brent into Lone Horse. Josh and Charlene would take his truck with the kids to town. After breakfast at the town's café, Brent dropped Hank off at the truck dealer. He checked on the small fleet of 4 by 4 trucks including a black special custom 4 by 4. Most would be delivered except the special black F150 which would be picked up next week. He also made arrangements for Charlene to order the SUV. Hank drove one of the new F150 trucks back to the Lazy B.

Charlene's appointment to get her driver's license was at 3 p.m.; she took the children shopping and then Josh and the kids waited for her at the pizza parlor. Charlene ordered the new SUV which would be delivered from Missoula within the week. Charlene met her family at the pizza parlor and showed them her brand new driver's license. When they got back to the dealer he informed them the black F150 Hank ordered would be delivered along with the SUV. Charlene drove Hank's other new truck back to the ranch, and Josh drove a the new green F250.

It seemed like a crowded schedule, but it was the first time the Reynolds family had been out of the canyon in a couple of years. Cassie had never before been to Lone Horse and she sat quiet and wide eyed at first, then didn't stop talking except when a piece of pizza filled her mouth. It was the first time the children experienced pizza.

CHAPTER 14

The commuter airplane touched down onto the main runway of the Missoula airport. Hank pushed himself away from the half wall near the passenger exit he had been sitting on. He watched the turboprop plane taxi to the passenger apron and the propellers wind down to a stop. In the plane's windows he saw a wide-eyed Mary Ann: behind her framed by the next window Marjorie sat, her own eyes a match to Mary Ann's. Their eyes showed nervous excitement. Michael sat in the inside seat next to Mary Ann; he looked around her and his eyes too were wide with excitement. Susan sat next to Marjorie. Susan was leaning around Marjorie and the two girls' faces were plastered to the window. Hank did not immediately see Bess. Maybe something happened and she wasn't coming. His feelings began to tighten with disappointment.

The door opened and Hank was relieved when he spotted Bess next to the flight attendant. She stood near the clothes bag compartment. She and the children waited until the other passengers deplaned. When the children filed by her to leave the plane, Bess handed them their carry-on bags. Michael came first and stepped carefully down stairs and waited at the bottom for Mary Ann. Taking her hand, he followed the other passengers to the exit gate where Hank waited. Michael put out his hand and Hank shook it.

The older man leaned down and took Mary Ann's small hand in his large one. Hank gently shook her hand as she beamed up at him.

He turned his attention back to Michael. "Have a good trip Mike?"

"Yes sir, it was all right." The boy tried to act nonchalant but the excitement in his eyes betrayed him.

Hank turned his attention to the girls. He shook their hands and welcomed them to Montana, until it came to Bess. He surprised her when he pulled her into an embrace. "Damn, missed you." He released her but maintained light contact. He turned his attention toward Marjorie and Susan.

The girls had their heads together and were busily talking. Hank whispered aside to Michael. "They been talking like that for long?"

"Yes, since before we left Dutton." Michael looked around at what of Missoula he could see. "Missoula looks a lot like Dutton, maybe a little bigger judging from what I could see from the plane."

"Well Michael, this is the big town except for Spokane. Wait until you see Lone Horse. If you drive through town at the posted speed limit and sneeze, you might miss it." The luggage was unloaded from the plane and ready to be picked up. Hank pointed at the lone arriving baggage area. "Think you can identify everyone's bags?"

"Sure, no problem. Do you want me to get the bags?" Michael asked.

"Nope, just pull them aside. I'll get a cart to put them on."

Hank started to release contact with Bess, but she put her arm around his neck and pulled his head down to plant a kiss on his lips. "Humm good." She let him go and smiled at his reaction.

Hank shook his head and left to rent a baggage cart. He returned pushing a cart. "Bess, I'm going to help Michael then I'll get the truck from the parking lot. We can load at the curb."

Luggage all accounted for and in the back of the truck, Hank had the three girls in the back seat. Bess sat in the middle of the front seat and Michael rode shotgun. "If anyone is hungry, we can stop at the café on the way out of town or wait till we get to Lone Horse."

"I could use a burger. Hank," Michael said and got a smile from Bess.

"Okay, fast food or sit down?"

"I want a Happy Meal," Mary Ann said from the back seat, "and I want a chocolate milkshake too."

"We'll stop at the Crossroads Café, good food and good milkshakes," Hank said. He started the engine and drove the fifteen minutes to the café.

Leaving the café, Hank drove and in ten minutes was driving with five sleeping passengers. Bess laid her head on Hank's shoulder and was almost instantly asleep. Bess and Michael woke when Hank turned off the highway into the town of Lone Horse.

"How much further?" Michael asked.

"It's about sixty miles on this dirt road. There are only thirty or so families up this road so the state doesn't feel it's necessary to pave it. See those hills?" Hank pointed to the mountains in the distance. "The ranch is up there on a flat plateau."

Hank dropped Bess and the girls at the guest house and helped Michael get settled in the bunkhouse. The ranch hands were working with the cattle in the high country so Hank, Michael and Ben had the bunkhouse to themselves. The bunkhouse was set up for twenty men and the ten men currently employed by the Lazy B had their gear at the far end of the single barracks-like room. As foreman, Hank had the only private room. A double wall locker and a foot locker were provided with each bunk. There was a full bathroom with tub and shower at each end of the low building. A hitching rail stood in front as part of the wide porch which included an assortment of chairs and two round tables.

* * *

Bess and Charlene used Hank's truck and drove to Lone Horse with the children to shop at the general store. Michael and Marjorie had an appointment with the driver's license examiner, Marjorie at ten o'clock and Michael at eleven o'clock for their road tests. Michael and Marjorie were scheduled to take the written portion of the test at 9 a.m. The children were all up and ready to leave at the crack of dawn, excited about the coming day.

Marjorie and Michael practiced their driving the evening before on the ranch road and reread the driver's manual.

The carpenters asked Hank for a couple of days off while the cement footings cured to do some fishing in the stream. One of the carpenters didn't fish so he volunteered to build the power and pump house.

Bess planned to shop with Susan and Mary Ann for some ranch clothes while the older children were with the license examiner. Since the town wasn't large enough to have a license office, Hank had arranged for the examiner to come to Lone Horse for the day. There were three other new drivers from neighboring ranches scheduled to take the examinations. The truck dealer helped by loaning a vehicle for everyone to drive during the road test. Charlene had taken her test on the monthly scheduled examination day for Lone Horse the past Wednesday.

Hank gave Bess $1,000 for each of the children to buy ranch clothes and a good pair of boots. He did stipulate they would be Wranglers or Carthartt, shirts and a heavy work coat, a pair of rubber boots, a pair of roper riding boots and insulated coveralls. There should be enough left over to buy a hat. They didn't have to spend all the money but could save or spend the leftover cash. Each youngster, including Mary Ann, needed to set up a bank account at the bank branch in Lone Horse. He included Susan with the rest of the kids and set aside the same amount for Robby when he arrived with Ben and Wilma. Bess helped Mary Ann pick out the appropriate clothes, but left the other children to pick their own purchases.

Marjorie and Michael met Bess and the others at the Lone Horse Café where pizza and burgers were the center of attention. "Well, did you pass or do I have to do all the driving?" Bess looked expectantly at the twins.

"You are looking at the two newest legal drivers in Montana," Marjorie said, bouncing up and down excitedly. Michael smiled stoically, but Bess could see his excitement.

"Michael, you and Marjorie need to do your shopping and then before we leave Lone Horse we need to do a pick up for Hank. Do you want to order food before you go to the store?"

"No I'm too excited to eat," Marjorie said and then glanced at Michael. Bess motioned toward the food.

"I could use a slice." Michael picked up a slice of pizza and a fist full of napkins.

"Can Susan come with us?" Marjorie asked.

"Sure, if she wants."

Susan nodded enthusiastically.

"Susan put your packages in the truck and then you can go," Bess said. She'd watch Mary Ann and meet them at the truck dealer in an hour.

With the older children gone, Bess cleaned Mary Ann's face and picked up their packages to load into the truck.

"Where are we going Aunt Bess?"

"We are going to look at some big trucks and then we are going to have Michael drive one back to the ranch for Hank. Is that all right with you Mary Ann?"

"Yes it is. I think that's nice of Michael don't you?" Mary Ann asked seriously. She got a smile and chuckle from the woman she called Aunt Bess.

"Yes it is Mary Ann. Michael is a good brother isn't he?"

"Oh course, he's *my* brother you know." Bess buckled Mary Ann into the back seat and drove to the truck dealer. A black F150 4 by 4 with non-stock rough terrain tires was parked in front of the dealer. When Bess drove up the manager came out to meet her. He gave her the keys to the truck, an owner's manual and had her sign for the delivered truck. Bess carefully checked the truck over for any scratches, dents or other marks and found it immaculate, including the new car smell. The dealer included a set of floor mats and seat covers matching the truck's interior plus a full tank of fuel.

Bess finished her inspection as the older kids appeared after shopping. Susan helped Michael and Marjorie carry their purchases. Without the second truck the packages would not have been able to ride in the cab. With Susan and Mary Ann's goods the back seat was nearly full.

"Are all these packages going to fit in the truck?" Michael asked as he looked through the back window.

"I think we can manage. Michael, let me see your driver's license," Bess asked.

"All I got was a temporary license, but the guy said it was good until I get my permanent license from the Department of Licensing in the mail." He handed the small piece of paper to Bess. She studied it noting Michael's name, the address, issue date and the expiration date. "Yep, this will do. I need

you to drive that truck over there to the ranch. You follow me, understand?"
She handed Michael the keys.

"Yes ma'am." Michael proudly walked to the shiny new truck and opened
the door. Bess could smell the newness from where she stood.

"Michael, Susan can ride with you, Marjorie will ride with me and Mary
Ann and the packages. You two make sure you are wearing your seatbelts and
the gas tank is full. Michael, check the gas now; when you're done we'll leave.
I still have to fix dinner. We don't want Charlene to do all our work for us
now do we?"

"No ma'am." Michael, Marjorie and Susan answered in unison.

* * *

Hank sat in his favorite chair on the bunkhouse porch when Bess parked in
front of the guest house. Michael followed in the new black truck and parked
behind her, shut off the motor and got out and looked at the truck. Hank
walked over stood next to Michael. "What do you think of that there truck?"

"Wow Hank it's really something. Someday I'm going to get me a rig like
that."

"Say, did you happen to get the title and papers when you picked it up?"

"I didn't pick it up, Bess did. She was just finishing the inspection when
we got there after shopping. Oh yeah, both Margie and I got our licenses."

"Yeah, I sort of figured as you were driving. Marjorie got her license too?"

"Yes sir, she got a better score on the written than I did by one question,
but I got a higher driving score than she did," Michael said proudly.

"Great. How about getting the truck papers, they're probably in the
jockey box." Hank turned to Susan who had been standing beside Michael.
"How was the trip from town? Think Michael's a good driver?"

"Yes sir Mister Hank. I think he did real good. I hope I'm able to get my
license next month. Daddy said he would let me practice driving if we ever
got the chance." Susan smiled up at the man who had become an idol to her.

"Listen Susan, can I call you Sue? I think it'll be a lot easier you know."
She nodded. "Well it's this way: because of ranch work, you may be required
to drive here on the ranch. You are almost sixteen so that isn't a problem. You
can drive when a licensed adult driver is in the vehicle with you on the state
roads. Doing ranch work, you don't need a permit as long as you don't leave
the ranch property. Do you understand what I just said?"

"Yes sir, I can drive on the ranch while doing work but not otherwise
until I get my driver's license," Sue said seriously. "I turned sixteen last week,
so if Daddy will sign, I can get a driver's license now."

"Okay, we'll work on that; now I've got some business with Michael. Think he'll let me call him Mike?" Hank asked the girl. She giggled, smiled and nodded.

Michael handed the papers to Hank. "Did you look at these?" Hank asked.

"No sir, they weren't any of my business. They're your papers Hank, not mine."

"Well, I don't know if that's exactly true." Hank handed the papers back to Michael who looked at the title: Owner: Michael Anderson; Lien Holder, Rolling H Ranch.

"What's this mean?" Michael stared at the title.

"It means this is your truck, but the ranch holds the lien on the truck until you've earned it outright. It also means, the ranch pays the insurance and it is part of the ranch's assets."

"Wow, this is my truck?"

"Yep, yours and the ranch's until you pay it off. Shouldn't take too long if I know Ben and Josh. They have a lot of work needs doing around the ranch. Ben will be getting you a horse at Billings. You and Robby go with him to the next horse auction. I want you to learn as much as you can from those two men. They are two of the best cattle and horsemen I know. That's part of your job. You'll earn one hundred bucks a day while on the trip. You can use all of it to pay for the truck or a part, your decision. My suggestion is put some toward the truck, some in the bank and a little for spending. Gas is on the ranch. You'll be driving Marjorie and Sue to school in the fall." Hank turned extra serious. "If you abuse the privilege concerning the truck, I'll suspend your driving. Not a threat, that's a promise. I'm trusting you with two very important people. I don't expect you to let me down. Now, go sit in your new rig and get some of the new smell out of it." Hank slapped Michael on the back. "Oh yeah, can I call you Mike?"

"You can call me anything you want. Thanks Hank, thanks for everything." Mike hugged the older man surprising them both. Mike went to his new truck, climbed onto the driver's seat and started rubbing the dashboard, seatbacks, talking to the truck all the while.

Hank went up the steps of the guest house and into the kitchen. He poured himself a cup of coffee and sat at the table while he watched Charlene and Bess fix dinner. "Say, is Marjorie in her room?"

"I think so, you want her?" Bess wiped her hands on a paper towel.

Hank said, "If you don't mind. Did you get those pamphlets from the truck dealer?"

"They're in my room--do you want them too?" Bess paused on her way out of the kitchen to get Marjorie.

"I would please. If you've got a few minutes I would like you to sit with Marjorie and me. Charlene, we can go outside if we're in your way," Hank said.

"Not in my way, Hank," Charlene said over her shoulder. "Josh should be here in about a half hour. He's got the kids with him at the new ranch site and they are going to be hungry. I can never seem to fill those three up, especially Cassie. That girl eats like she's starving all the time."

"Charlene, why don't you, Josh and the kids join us for dinner? There's plenty, we can have a buffet," Bess offered as she came into the kitchen with Marjorie following her. She looked to Hank for approval.

The cowboy rolled his eyes as if that was a no brainier. He motioned for Bess and Marjorie to take a seat at the table. He took the pamphlets from Bess, holding them on his lap out of the girl's sight. "I made a deal with Mike. I can call him Mike now, and can I call you Margie?" The girl looked at Hank with her soft brown eyes.

"Please Hank, I'd really like that. Is that why you wanted to see me?"

"No Margie, at least not all of why I wanted to talk to you. I just made a deal with Mike. The black truck is his and the ranch's. He can pay it off with what he earns, no specific payments, just what he wants to pay. The ranch will pay for the insurance and the gas. He will be driving you and Sue to school in the fall." Hank glanced at the calendar on the wall next to the doorway. "That will be a bit over four months from now; if school still starts sometime after Labor Day. Well, here's the deal." He put the pamphlets on the table. They were for F150 4 by 4 trucks just like Mike's except there were different color schemes. "You will need transportation too, so I'm offering you the same deal Mike has. You will get paid just like he does, same wages and pretty much the same work. All you have to do now is pick out the color scheme you want for your truck." Hank smiled. "I would prefer if you didn't pick pink or some other awful color, but hey it's your truck, and no you can't exchange it for a sports car."

"You really mean it?" Margie said wide eyed. "You really are going to take care of us: me, Mike and Mary Ann?"

"Yep, that's my intention. I am not going to adopt you, you are Andersons not Springers. I want to be your foster dad and do all the things your dad would have done for you if he were here. I want to walk down the aisle to give you away at your wedding. I want only good things for you, Mike and Mary Ann."

"Now about Sue. She is the daughter of one of my friends. She is part of this family and I want you to treat her like she is, Robby too." He addressed himself to Charlene and she turned around to look at him. "Josh and Charlene are old friends, their children are my God children if they ever get christened. You don't have to call Charlene by a kinship name, like aunt or Josh uncle, but they are in all other respects your family just like Ben and Wilma are your parents also. Please explain this to Mike and Mary Ann. Bess, would you talk to Sue for me?"

Bess nodded. "Does Brent know your feelings?"

"Yes, Brent and I talked some yesterday and some before. He's all for the extended family thing. He's talked to Bev and she thinks it's great too."

Bess could only nod. Charlene was busy with a brush on the potatoes, and a small tremble passed over her shoulders. She dropped the potato she was brushing in the sink, and rushed out of the kitchen. Bess was right behind her. Margie stood, threw her arms around Hank, released him and grabbed the pamphlets and ran out of the room. Hank was left sitting by himself with a cold cup of coffee confused by the women's actions.

Pouring a fresh cup of coffee, he ambled out onto the porch and watched Mike crawl out from under the truck, a smile permanently plastered on his face. Off to one side, Charlene and Bess huddled together. Bess looked up and smiled; with her hand she shooed the man off the porch. Hank shrugged, descended the steps and walked across the yard to the bunkhouse. He sat down in his favorite chair, set his coffee on the wobbly table and put his feet on the railing.

CHAPTER 15

The construction of the ranch houses was ahead of schedule. All three houses be would complete around the same time. Jim loaned Hank his bulldozer tractor to disk up and plant a twenty acre hillside for alfalfa and orchard grass to provide feed for the horses. Another fifty acres were set aside for hay feed for the cattle in the winter. It was Ben and Josh's recommendation to drill another well to irrigate the alfalfa and hay fields. As soon as the snow was off the land in the spring, Josh intended to seed additional fields. Crops grow fast in western Montana and some feed and hay may be harvested two or more times. Josh thought he could get three cuttings from mature fields of alfalfa stacked and stored in the newly erected modular hay barn by the end of the growing season. By irrigating the alfalfa it would mature rapidly and produce an abundant crop.

Ben planned to go to Billings the same week he returned with Wilma, Robby, the horses and their household things. Josh would use Loco until Ben found him a couple of good ranch horses. Right now there was Jake, Loco and the mule. Jackson and Beany were Brent's horses. Brent made them part of the Rolling H Ranch. Frisky, the gelding Hank was buying from Ben, would be coming with Ben's family. Frisky would make a second horse for Josh. The two rope horses would still belong to Ben unless he decided to sell them.

The sun was still well below the eastern horizon when Hank woke Mike. The boy was up, showered and ready in fifteen minutes. The two walked to the guest house where Bess fixed them a ranch breakfast: a couple of eggs, ham, hash browns, juice and coffee. Hank didn't say a word when Mike poured himself a cup of coffee, but had to hide his smile when the boy made a face at the bitter ranch brew. Bess sat with them while they ate. She and Hank talked about the day ahead and shared their conversation with Mike.

Mike looked around the kitchen. "Where are Susan and Margie?" he asked with a mischievous grin.

"You know right where they are you scamp," Bess grinned. "Still in bed. Those two girls have talked constantly since they got here. It started in Dutton and they've talked continuously since they left. Last night they didn't stop until after midnight." Bess shook her head. "I don't think I can handle them right now, let them sleep."

"Susan talked all the way back here too," Mike added.

Hank laughed as he wiped the juice from his eggs with a final piece of toast while Mike wolfed down his second helping of ham and eggs plus a sizable portion of hash brown potatoes. Hank surprised Bess by kissing her and giving her a pat on the fanny as he scooted pass her on the way out.

"Hey, dirty old man, watch it." Bess laughed, her blonde ponytail glowing, caught by the light of the rising sun through the kitchen window.

"Don't you just love it?" Hank hurried out the door as Bess snapped a dish towel at his butt.

Hank and Mike helped Brent unload the turbine generator. "You and Mike set the generator up. Charlene will bring lunch later, around noon. Mike, you can ride back to the Lazy B with her or stay here with Brent and come back this evening for dinner. Brent, you are coming to dinner?"

"Yes sir, wouldn't miss a chance to eat someone else's cooking."

"I'll stay here with Brent, if he doesn't mind," Mike said and received a nod from Hank.

*   *   *

"Morning Hank, feels good to be working. What's on tap for the day?" Josh's toothy smile gleamed enough to be seen a mile away on a starlit night.

"Not much. Figured you'd ride to Missoula with Charlene and pick up the last F250 from the dealer there. Jim got a message last night the Missoula dealer has a truck somebody ordered but never picked up. Got a real good deal on it. You pick it up and it's yours. I would like Sue to drive the green F250 and get used to the bigger rigs. I've got a feeling she is going to be doing a lot of hauling of cattle and horses. That girl has a talent for ranch work." Hank paused and waited for a reaction from Josh; he got none. "That will probably take most of the day. Sue and Margie can watch the younger kids until Charlene gets back."

Hank paused. "Stop by the cell phone place and pick up a cell package that will work up here. Get one for each of the ranch trucks and the SUV. Be sure the chargers come with each one plus get a home unit for the house. We can put them all on the same frequency. Better get three base stations. I want the walkie-talkie feature on the phones."

"Okay, that's nine if you count Mike's truck and the SUV with intercom features and twelve charger units—nine for the trucks and three for the houses. Anything else?"

Hank sat quiet for a couple of minutes. "Think you can get away for a few days, maybe three?"

"Sure, what do you need?"

"I'd like you to go with Ben to Billings for the livestock sale. The boys, Mike and Robby will go too, feel free to take Jesse. The livestock auction is the day before the horse sale. You can take Jim's stock trailer so if you find any cattle worth buying or horses you'll be able to bring them back. Watch for a good bull. We've got lots of heifers and I don't want to keep breeding back to Jim's bull. The change to the gene pool would be good for his herd too. Actually consider two bulls, one for the north and the south herds I plan on."

"That it?" Josh asked, impressed.

"There is one more thing, the two boys; I want them along so you can start teaching them the cattle business. The boys will be working for you and Ben. Any problem with that?"

"No sir." Josh laughed. "You know, I'm beginning to like this family thing."

It was nearly 7:30 a.m. when Hank and Josh drove through the gate and up to the guest house. Josh went to the bunkhouse to a space he'd set up as an office for the cattle business. Ben followed Josh's example and fixed an office for the horse business until the stable and his permanent office were completed. Bess met Hank at the door with a cup of coffee. Entering the kitchen, he found Maya and Jim sitting at the kitchen table. "Those girls up yet?" Hank asked. "They've got work to do."

"Tell me you aren't going to make them muck out the stable you've been meaning to get to for the last couple of months." Jim looked at Hank with a mischievous smile.

"Yep, that's the job. Get them good and dirty right away. Good for them." Hank wiggled his eyebrows which started Bess and Maya to giggle like young girls.

"You're not going to make Mary Ann help them are you?" Bess asked, her smile vanishing.

"Nope, she going to supervise and then she is going to take a riding lessons with me and Jake. When the girls are through cleaning the stable we'll give them a riding lesson using Jake and Loco. Say Jim, I heard Sue is supposed to be a pretty good rider. What say I borrow that new ranch horse you bought a few months ago and see what he can do?"

"The girl or the horse? Oh yeah, sure. You going to use the arena?"

"Thought I would. I'll rake it up first. You got anything else you need raked while I've got the tractor and rake hooked up?" Hank asked, knowing there was always something else to rake on a working ranch.

"Yeah, if you've got time you could rake up the two branding pens and the round pen."

Sue and Margie walked sleepy eyed into the kitchen followed by a wide-eyed Mary Ann. The sound of Charlene in the F350 pulling up to the guesthouse woke them.

Hank turned his attention to the girls. "Morning ladies, glad you could make it while the sun's still shining. Better get a good breakfast, there's a lot of work to be done."

"Hi Mr. Springer, Mr. and Mrs. Sutterland. Bess, do you want me to fix some breakfast?" Sue asked. Margie bent over and looked out the window at the still rising sun.

"No, I'll make breakfast this morning, maybe you can tomorrow." Bess smiled.

"What do you want us to do today?" Margie asked Hank. In response Hank wiggled his eyebrows which set Bess, Maya and Jim to laughing again.

"Oh, not too much, better put on some old clothes though. You won't need any deodorant, it will be provided and don't forget your rubber boots." Hank smiled at the girls. "I thought we'd start you out in the stable. It could be a bit cleaner and after that we'll see how good you are with the horses." Hank poured himself a fresh cup of coffee and sat at the kitchen table while the girls sat at the other end and tried not to laugh.

"Do I have to work too?" Mary Ann asked seriously, big blue eyes wide open.

"Not today sweetie, you are the boss. Your job is to see that Sue and Margie do a good job."

"Oh I will. I'll make sure it's clean. What are we cleaning Hank?"

"When you've finished your breakfast, I'll show you. Okay?"

"Sure okay." Mary Ann turned to the other girls. "I'm the boss today, hurry up we have work to do."

Margie rolled her eyes at Hank. "You are creating a monster you know."

"Yep, ain't it fun?" Hank shooed Mary Ann out of the kitchen to get changed as soon as she finished her breakfast. "We'll be riding Jake when you're done being boss." Mary Ann ran out of the kitchen to return two minutes later. "I'm ready, can we get Jake now?" The little girl was barely able to contain her excitement.

After breakfast, Hank led the girls to the stable, got tools to clean out the stalls and showed them where to find the wheelbarrow. Mary Ann climbed up on a bale of hay and immediately fell asleep. The girls attacked the stalls and Hank went to hook up the tractor rake. When he finished raking the arena and the other pens he went to the pasture for Jake. He saddled the horse with the smallest saddle in the tack room.

* * *

Hank entered the stable followed by Jake without a lead rope. The man and horse found the girls had cleaned the stalls quickly and were busy loading the wheelbarrow with the last load of the muck to take out to the pile behind the barn. Mary Ann, awake and alert, watched the work. She looked around Hank to stare wide eyed at Jake who in turn was peeking around Hank's shoulder at the little girl sitting on his food. Mary Ann stared at the full sized horse.

Hank lifted her down from the hay bale and introduced her to Jake. The horse nuzzled her with his soft nose and nickered at Mary Ann, making her giggle in excitement. After lifting her and setting her on the saddle, Hank adjusted the stirrups up as high as they would go. They were still a bit long but Mary Ann managed to get her toes firmly on the stirrups so Hank decided to go ahead with the lesson. Later he'd shorten the stirrups another inch. He'd buy a couple of small saddles the next time he was in Missoula.

He led Jake with Mary Ann happily aboard to the round pen. Once inside, Hank let the horse take care of the little girl. Jake walked slowly around the pen making sure Mary Ann stayed centered in the saddle. Jake stopped whenever she slipped a little until she regained her seat. Mary Ann used the reins to gently steer Jake in slow circles first one way then the other. When Hank saw the horse was getting tired of being tense taking care of the little girl, he stopped them and lifted Mary Ann from the saddle.

"I think that's enough for the first day. Don't you Mary Ann?"

"Whew, riding is hard work. Did I do all right, did I do good Hank?" she asked excitedly.

"You did just fine—you are going to be a great rider someday, Mary Ann." Hank complimented her. "Now you have to thank Jake for giving you a ride." He lifted her up so she could pat the horse's neck and rub his cheeks. He was surprised when she leaned enough to kiss the horse on his nose; even more surprised when Jake let her without moving.

Sue and Margie came up to the fence and Hank lifted Mary Ann over the top rail to Margie. Once Mary Ann was settled on a bench, he addressed Margie. "You ready?"

"Yes sir."

"Good. Take the saddle off Jake, put it away and get the saddle you think will fit you and Jake from the rack. Did you wash the wheelbarrow?"

"Yes sir."

"Good, then you won't have to carry the big saddle. Use the wheelbarrow to bring it here, no sense wearing yourself out when you don't have too."

He watched Margie as she took the small saddle off Jake, removed the blanket and checked him for sore spots before putting the blanket back on the horse. She carried the small saddle back to the tack room and loaded one of Hank's smaller roping saddles in the wheelbarrow. The saddle still weighed 45 pounds, a lot of weight for the girl.

Margie put the saddle in the wheelbarrow and brought it to the round pen. Hank watched as she used her knee to help boost the saddle onto the horse's back. She didn't let it fall into place but guided it down on Jake's back. Margie checked the cinch, the latago and the back cinch before belting them around the horse's belly making sure the blanket hadn't bunched up. Hank was surprised when she used a cowboy knot to secure the latago and tighten the cinch. Margie measured the stirrup length; satisfied, she made sure the back cinch was snug but not too tight. Next she checked the breast collar looking for rub spots. Jake didn't need a tie down. Hank could almost see the horse was impressed too as he stood still while the girl moved around him.

Before letting Margie mount, Hank directed her to the large arena with the roping chutes at one end and the stripping chute at the other. On the way, he asked, "Where did you learn all about saddling? I thought you only rode English before."

"I did ride western a couple of times, but Sue told me all about saddles and putting them on while we were traveling here from Dutton. She is really good with horses, you know?"

"Yeah, I am impressed with the both of you. Now, check your cinch again and mount up. Do a walk around the arena first, then you can trot and then lope a lap each. When you're done come back here so we can talk."

Mary Ann and Sue joined Hank and watched through the rails as Margie rode Jake.

Margie did exactly as Hank instructed. When she was done she drew Jake up in front of Hank and started to dismount. "No stay up there, Jake needs a good run. The arena is three hundred feet by one eighty. Let Jake go, just remember he is very touchy around his mouth, don't saw the reins or yank on him."

"Yes sir, how many laps?"

"Oh I don't know, no more than ten, seven or eight should be enough to sweat him up some. Make it eight."

Margie grinned, clucked at Jake and they took off. She gave the horse slack reins and he set the pace, full out. The horse tested her by taking off on the wrong lead. She lifted his head, tapped his side with her foot and the horse did a flying lead change. Hank grinned as her pony tail flew out behind her and the horse's tail flowed out behind him. The girl brought the horse back to where Hank stood. They slowed to a walk gently so she didn't have to use the bit.

Her eyes wide, a huge grin on her face, Margie slid off the saddle to the ground, loosened the cinch and immediately went to the horse's face to rub him; talking gently Margie thanked Jake for the great ride.

Hank turned away. "Darn it, there goes another great rope horse. Jake will want to be ridden by girls from now on." He failed to hide the grin that almost matched the one on Margie's face. "Okay, Margie, put him away. You know the drill. Don't let him roll until you turn him loose in the paddock."

Hank turned to Sue. "I'm sorry, Jake has had his workout so you won't be able to ride him."

"That's okay Mr. Springer. I didn't need to ride."

"Oh I didn't say you won't be riding, you just won't be riding Jake. See that gelding in the branding pen? You go get him, saddle him up. You can use the same saddle Margie used. There is a fresh blanket in the tack room, get that and the right ear headstall with the short shank snaffle bit. I've used it on the gelding before."

He watched Sue run to the tack room and come out carrying the blanket and the headstall with reins attached, a tie down in her hand. "This tie down was with the headstall, should I use it?" Sue asked.

"Good thought, use the tie down. The gelding does toss his head if he thinks the reins are too tight. Remember you are the boss but you are on a three-year-old horse. He's still a baby and acts like it occasionally."

It took Sue less than three minutes to saddle and adjust the tack to fit the horse. She walked around him keeping one hand on him at all times. She went to his rear, patted him and rubbed his flank. She stood in front of him and let him smell her and his own smell on her. When she again went to the horse's rear he didn't even turn an ear; he stood quietly waiting for her to come back and rub his nose again.

Sue tightened the cinch, grabbed a handful of mane and climbed into the saddle. The horse started to walk out but she stopped him, backed him a step and sat for two minutes doing nothing. Laying the right rein against his neck, she gently pressured with her right knee; the horse moved forward and to the left. She walked the horse around the arena half slow and half at a fast walk. A cluck, loose reins and a soft touch of her heels and the horse moved up into a fast trot. Hank could tell when she kissed at the horse and he broke into a fast lope wanting to gallop. Sue eased him back into a slow gentle lope. She went to the left and then changed leads to the right. Hank decided the girl knew horses and he had another good horse trainer for the ranch.

After putting the horse through his paces, Sue finally slowed him to a walk to cool down before stopping. When she slipped from the saddle she went through the same routine Margie used on Jake. Tying the reins to the saddle horn, Sue walked across the center of the arena and back. The gelding walked beside her, his head at her shoulder. When she stopped, the horse stopped and waiting for her to tell him what to do next. Sue brought the gelding up to Hank; Sue untied the reins from the horn and handed them to Hank.

"Your horse sir." Sue smiled at Hank.

"Please put him away, not in the paddock with Jake but by himself." Hank pointed at a vacant paddock.

Sue tied one rein to the horn and used the other to lead the horse toward the tack room. Sue stopped beside the door and dropped the reins to the ground. The horse stood patiently while she removed the heavy saddle, took the tie down, headstall and bit from the horse. Sue put on a halter with a lead rope and dropped the lead rope to the ground. Hank didn't even know the horse ground tied; he was very impressed with the skill and the talent of the young girl.

After the horse finished his roll, he came to the fence for Sue to pet him. Hank was satisfied the horse was taken care of. He called Margie and Sue to join him.

"Girls, I need to talk to you both together so there is no misunderstanding. I am going to offer Sue a job as a horse trainer and riding instructor. Margie, you can see Sue knows a lot about riding and training horses. One of her jobs is to teach you to be as good as she is. Her dad will help if there are any rough spots. Margie, I'm offering you a job of seeing to the tack room. That is your domain; you will have a couple of the cowhands to help. One of their jobs will be to see you learn as much as possible about tack. Sue you can learn from these boys too. Both of you will work cattle with Josh; you'll get a man's pay for a man's day of work. You need to learn roping, branding and all the other jobs on a working ranch. Margie, your truck should be here next week. Sue, you will have to use one of the available ranch trucks if you need one; actually use the green F250. Consider it your truck unless one of the hands need it." Hank stood quietly thinking, and the girls waited patiently. "Sue, if you want a truck of your own, I will give you the same deal as Mike and Margie: front you the money to buy it, but you will have to pay me back out of the money you earn here on the ranch. Charlene is the temporary ranch payroll manager, and you can work a payment schedule with her. Fair?"

"Yes sir." Sue looked down at her boots, then looked up and smiled at the man standing before her.

"Sue, you can ride with me or use my truck too if you need to," Margie said.

"Mr. Springer, I talked to Dad and he wants me to wait another month before I take the driver's test. Dad wants me to get some experience driving here on the ranch. If the offer is still open after I get a driver's license, I'll take you up on the offer to front the money for a truck."

"Yep, after school starts sign up for the Defensive Driving Course when you register for school next month. You can use the green F250 around the ranch, but remember the rules." Hank changed the topic. "By the way, when Robby gets here I don't care if you tell him about our deals. Is he as good with horses as you are Sue?"

"Oh he's much better than I am. He taught me a lot. Dad's a great trainer, but he's not so good at teaching and Robby is great." A look of sadness came over Sue's pretty face. "I suppose you'll want him to train horses instead of me. He is better at it."

"Nope, I think offhand there will be plenty of work for everyone. I think I might have Robby be Brent's assistant. There'll be plenty of work for everyone." Both girls smiled at him; he knew he had two winners. "You know how to train cutters?"

"No sir, I know how to start them, but Robby knows cutters and so does Daddy," Sue said. "I can learn though."

CHAPTER 16

Two weeks after leaving the Lazy B, Ben Withrow arrived back at the ranch pulling his stock trailer. Wilma followed in a rental moving van. Ben pulled to a stop by the round pen, got the horses out and with Robby's help turned Frisky and the two rope horses out into an empty paddock. They watched the horses roll and run for a few of minutes. When the horses came to the fence, Ben inspected them for any travel injuries.

Wilma climbed down from the moving van and stood next to it; hands on hips, she rotated and stretched her back. She looked around at the buildings and empty stock pens. *The place seems deserted.*

"MOM!" Susan ran down the steps of the guest house into her mother's arms.

"Where is everyone?" Ben asked when Sue finished hugging her parents.

"They're up at the new ranch site. I've been cleaning house and waiting for you. Hank said you would be here today and he's always right you know. Oh yeah Dad, you are supposed to go up there after you put your bags in the bunkhouse. Mom's staying in the guest house with Bess and us girls. Robby is staying with you, Mike, and Hank in the bunkhouse until the houses are finished." Sue paused for air. "Mom, Hank says that truck over there is for you to use." Sue pointed at a new slate gray F150 pickup.

Wilma stared at the new truck. "Well." She gathered herself. "I suppose I'd better get my bags settled. Ben you show Robby what to do. Susan can show me where I'm staying."

Driving around a stand of trees, Wilma's eyes widened in surprise at the sight of the open area and the activity that surrounded the framed houses ready for siding. She drove out onto the beautiful meadow seeing her new home for the first time. Hank and Josh just finished roofing the Withrows' house. The main house was completed on the outside. The inside of both houses were framed with plumbing and electrical work completed, but still in need of drywall and insulation. The drywall would be done by contractors in the next few days. Painters were scheduled for Monday for the interior walls. The houses were half log and needed sealant and weather proofing for the natural wood.

Brent saw Ben, dropped his tools and left Mike holding a board in place. "Ben, did you see Bev? Do you think she'll need help? She won't say when I ask her on the phone."

Ben started to laugh, joined by Hank who came out of the pump and power shed; he'd been teasing Brent about being whipped into shape by an absent woman. "You should talk to Wilma, she's the one who's been talking to Bev. I didn't see her; I was pretty busy closing the house and clearing debts and stuff. Wilma was packed when I got there. It took a few days to get our business taken care of. Then we just loaded the horses, hitched up the trailer, threw the sleeping bags into the rig and took off for here."

Wilma took mercy on the poor man. "Brent, Bev has got the fever. She told the school board she was leaving at the end of next week, regardless if the new teacher was ready or not."

"Thank you ma'am. Talking to her on the phone is hard. I want to jump on a plane and go get her but I know it's not the right thing to do. It isn't, is it?" Brent looked hopefully at Wilma.

"No, you both are doing the right thing. Just be patient—that girl is so in love with you it's painful to watch."

"Yes ma'am," Brent said, his mouth turned down. He rebounded quickly. "Let me show you what we've done since Ben left us all this work." He led Wilma on a tour of the main ranch house and the foreman's house. "You'll be living in the guest house at the Lazy B until your own house is done. See those slabs over there." Brent pointed to a framed house on gray cement footings with plumbing sticking up through heavy plywood flooring; the bathrooms and kitchen could be easily identified. He led Wilma into what would be the back door and different rooms were marked by chalk labels, footings and some interior framing. There was a master bedroom with a huge bathroom. Wilma was stunned by the large rooms. A laundry room next to the kitchen would have a washtub and location for a commercial washer-dryer. The kitchen area Wilma could see would be bright with plenty of large windows overlooking the meadow and the stream winding through the land.

"What is that building over there. It looks like an outhouse." Wilma pointed at the ten foot by ten foot shed-like structure.

"That's the pump house for the water and the electrical equipment. We have a turbine generator in the stream where the water flows fastest so we have our own power plant," Brent explained.

Wilma looked around. "Where's Robby?"

"He went off with Mike. There's something Mike wanted to show him and Hank told them to take off."

"But how's he going to get back to the other ranch?"

"Mike has his own truck. Don't worry, I'm sure I know where they are," Hank said as he joined them. "There is an old gold mine up the hill there."

He pointed at a hill in the distance. They could just make out dust from the Forest Service road drifting above the trees.

"Why don't we all take the rest of the day off," Hank suggested.

Josh came out of the pump house. "I'll second that." He came over and introduced himself to Wilma. "Charlene should be back any time. She took the kids into Lone Horse for a checkup before school registration. Charlene is working full time for Hank, so she doesn't have time to home school the kids. Mary Ann and Bess are with them."

Brent pulled a large ice chest onto the tailgate of his truck. He opened the chest and handed the men each a beer, Sue a soda. Wilma accepted a beer. Hank excused himself and walked to the unfinished house. The rest gathered around the truck and the table from their first trip to the meadow. "Dad says we'll bring the rest of the horses up here in the next couple of days," Brent said. "Sue has been training two of Jim Sutterland's horses. The cement for the tack room has cured. Tomorrow Josh and I will build a temporary tack shed and it will be the base for the stable. The corral still needs some work. I thought Mike and Robby can work on that and get the paddocks ready for the horses. It's starting to look like a ranch." Brent raised his beer to toast the team effort.

Everyone turned when a horn sounded to announce Charlene and Bess's arrival. Wilma shyly went over to Hank. He smiled at her. "I apologize for not having everything ready for when you got here. I know the house isn't quite done. We will do the interior walls tomorrow and it will go fast after that. The mason will be here tomorrow to build the first of the house's two fireplaces. When the interior for your house is started, I'd like you to be here to answer any of the workers' questions. A set of plans are in that chest over there." Hank pointed at a large wooden box next to the main ranch house. "The kitchen appliances and cabinets will be here in the next few days, I called to have them rush the order. The finish carpenters will be here Monday, and the plumber. You should be able to move in within the next couple of weeks."

"Oh Hank, it's wonderful." She threw her arms around Hank. Ben grinned.

Hank guided Wilma around to meet everyone. "I think you've met everyone except Charlene." Wilma shook hands with Josh's wife. Ben introduced Robby when he climbed out of Mike's truck. "Ben, why don't you take Wilma over to the fire pit. I understand Bess and Charlene are cooking dinner and they can always use an extra set of hands. We thought we'd have dinner up here." Hank explained, "Jim and Maya are coming up later. Jim always seems to know when dinner's ready. Ben, I need to talk to you and Josh, the boys too, two hours."

Two hours later, Ben walked into the half-finished main house. He pulled up a stool to the large work table. Brent and Josh, not able to sit still when there was work to be done, finished the roof and were having a cup of coffee. Hank handed Ben a cup and pointed at the cream and sugar packets and the large commercial urn of coffee on a bench against the wall. Robby and Mike sat together on a tool chest by the framed picture window a few feet away.

"Ben, I know you just got back, but I'd like you and Josh to head over to Billings day after tomorrow. Jim got a call from a friend and there are a number of bulls on the block. The horse auction is the day after." Hank nodded at Josh. "If there are two really good bulls we can use them; your judgment. Ben, we need good ranch horses. If there is a good smaller horse suitable for Mary Ann buy it too. The boys each have a two thousand dollar loan from me to buy the horse they want. If they go over, I'll cover it if you think it's a good trade. Ben, see they don't make a mistake and buy dogs. I've heard Robby is as good as his sister around horses, so have him help Mike."

Ben laughed. "Between me and Josh, I think we can keep their money going in the right direction."

"I'd like to borrow your trailer, Ben."

"Sure Hank, anytime," Ben said.

"Okay, thanks. Josh use the green truck, if Sue can get along without it for a few days. The truck is already set up for Brent's trailer. Ben you can pull your own trailer with the big rig and Brent's trailer will give you a place to sleep in Billings, unless you prefer staying in a motel. It might be a bit crowded since you'll be taking Robby and Mike with you."

Josh and Ben looked over their shoulders at the two boys, excitement showed on their young faces.

"If you come back empty that's okay too. But be sure to bring those two back or Wilma and Bess will skin all of us." The men laughed and the boys looked disgusted.

"When do you want us to leave?" Ben asked.

"Hey, you two decide. The auction house and yard open tomorrow for viewing, the auction starts Friday. The yard opens at 0600 to check stock. The horses will start arriving in Billings tomorrow. Don't let those two bandits," Hank nodded at Robby and Mike, "eat too much junk food." Hank took out his wallet and handed Mike six—twenty dollar bills. "You still have a $300 credit for work you've already done. That's some of your pay for the last six days." He handed Robby another six twenties. "Robby, you get the same deal as Mike, he'll explain it. Half of those twenties are an advance. Any problems or questions? One other suggestion, have Robby ride with Josh and Mike with Ben. That way whoever is driving will get some peace and quiet not having to listen to those two ask, 'are we there yet?'" The men laughed at Hank's joke, and this time the boys joined in. "Tell them what you're looking for, they can be a second and third set of eyes."

"Good idea Hank. I think Josh and I can find something for them to do worth the cost of the fuel for hauling them to Billings and back."

"Okay, questions?" Hank looked around again.

"No sir, thanks for the money and the loan Mr. Springer." Robby held the money like it was gold.

"Robby, see Charlene, she has a check for you for the ranch clothes you'll need. You can visit the stores in Billings. Mike will tell you what you have to buy. Sue got the same deal. It's not a gift—for the ranch, it's an investment."

The following afternoon, Brent received his orders to report to Quantico in three days and it was back to a five week schedule.

* * *

Hank with Wilma and Charlene, watched the electrician throw the switch that powered the house's internal electrical system. The refrigerator began to quietly hum and the light over the stove came on.

"Welcome to your new home, Wilma," Hank said. The painters brought the wrong paint for the walls in the living room and two of the bedrooms. Those rooms still had the primer coat but basically the house was completed. "I wish you many happy years in this house." Wilma threw her arms around Ben. Ben's face said it all.

"Bess wanted to be here but she and Bev have a meeting with the State School Board in Helena. Bev is going back to Dutton for a few days to close her accounts and get the rest of her belongings, so she can be here when Brent comes home."

Wilma stepped back. "I'm sorry Bess isn't here but I understand. We can all get together later when Josh, Ben and the boys get back from the latest trip to Davenport and the cattle ranch Josh wanted to stop at." Wilma smiled up at Hank, kissed him on the cheek, and then hugged Charlene who had become a best friend. Bess, Hank, Josh, the girls and boys were all part of her family now.

"Welcome to the neighborhood." Charlene Reynolds greeted her new friend.

"Enough of this huggy, kissy stuff," Hank said in a gruff husky voice. "I suppose Sue would like to pick out her room now, don't you think?"

"Oh Sue did that before the inside walls were even up." Wilma laughed. "Sue and Margie are riding up from the Lazy B. They should be here pretty soon. They left the Lazy B this morning after breakfast." She glanced at her watch and then slowly looked up at the electric clock over the large window above the sink.

"Tomorrow if you talk nice and the ladies are back from Helena, you, Bess, Bev, and Charlene and the girls take the SUV and go to town for a girl's day and night out. The rest of the kids can take care of themselves for the day. I have a couple of things to do and I'll take Bea, Mary Ann and Cassie with me so you don't have to worry about them. Jesse can hang with the boys until you get back."

"Okay, if you insist." Wilma looked at Charlene. "If you'll excuse us we have plans to make." Wilma led Charlene to her bedroom where Hank could barely hear them talking excitedly. Two weeks before he had hired Charlene to be the permanent ranch household manager, chief cook and child wrangler. Everyone on the ranch had a job. Charlene's and Josh's children came to work with her each day they wouldn't be in school or taking extra credit classes. Bea and Jesse were often an extra pair of hands

* * *

Bev returned to the Lazy B and joined in the ranch work. Cassie spent time with Mary Ann and they became inseparable. Cassie found things for them to do; small jobs made the children feel helpful. Cassie talked Hank into putting in a chicken coop beyond the barn for fresh eggs.

Wilma expressed an interest in accounting and he suspected she would become his accountant. She enrolled in an accounting course at the University of Montana extension school at the Lone Horse High School. Wilma had completed three years of college before she married Ben. Once a week, she drove to town to attend class. Hank considered it a business expense. Bev helped Wilma with the math and Wilma did the rest. Charlene decided at the next semester she would take some classes too.

Brent wasn't due back until the end of the following week. Bev planned to meet him in Spokane and spend a couple of days shopping before coming home. Bess still had three weeks of her extended vacation and special work for Judge Hoskin before she returned to Dutton.

Hank sat with his second cup of coffee and talked with Bess in the kitchen of the guesthouse. Mary Ann, sleepy eyed and still in her pajamas, came into the kitchen carrying her backpack. "Good morning Mary Ann, are you ready for breakfast?" Bess greeted the child.

"No thank you Aunt Bess. I'm not hungry, I'm bored," The young girl said surprising the two adults. "I want to go someplace like Margie and Michael get to. They get to go to town and I always have to stay here."

"You need to eat something for breakfast, then we can talk about going somewhere." Bess insisted Mary Ann eat breakfast. Bess poured cereal into a bowl, something colorful and surgary and added fresh milk. Bess and Hank watched as Mary Ann reluctantly ate her cereal. "What would you do in town?" Bess asked smiling. Sometimes Mary Ann acted older than her six years.

"We could go shopping like we did when we first got here," the girl ventured, hope shining in her blue eyes.

Bess looked at Hank. "What do you think? Can we make a trip to town?"

"I don't see why not. The men and the teenagers have the day off. The teens are exploring that old gold mine on the mountain. I suppose we could find our way to town. Of course you're welcome to come along." Hank grinned at the light spreading over Mary Ann's face. "Why don't we make a day of it. We can shop at the general store and have lunch at the café. That sounds exciting, what do you think Mary Ann?" Hank glanced at Bess as the girl nodded excitedly.

"Okay, you get dressed while we finish our coffee and we'll go to town." Hank and Bess watched Mary Ann as she raced toward her room. A minute later they heard the shower come on. Since arriving at the Lazy B, Mary Ann had discovered showers and relegated baths to special occasions.

Hank rinsed his cup at the sink. Mary Ann came into the kitchen after being gone only a few minutes. She was dressed in her favorite clothes: pink Wrangler jeans and a blue sweatshirt with a rearing horse painted on the front. She sat in front of Bess, while the woman subconsciously began to comb and brush her hair into two ponytails. The girl handed Bess pink yarn to tie her hair in place. Bess pulled her own hair back into a blonde ponytail and used some of Mary Ann's yarn to hold her hair in place.

An hour and a half later, Hank parked across the street from the general store. "You ladies enjoy your shopping. I have some errands to run and I'll meet you in the store in 30 minutes." He watched as woman and child carefully crossed the street and entered the store. When they were inside, he drove two blocks to the hardware store.

Errands done, Hank entered the general store. He spotted Bess beside a dressing room door. "What's up?"

"Mary Ann found a new pink outfit with a blue shirt and she is trying them on." Bess rolled her eyes. "I wish she would wear something besides pink and blue."

"It's a phase, Sabrina went through the same thing when she was about that age."

"I thought I might try to get her to change a little bit." Bess held up a pretty pink blouse, a pink belt and a pair of children's sized blue Wrangler jeans. "When she comes out tell her how nice she looks and we'll show her this outfit. Tell her it would go well with her boots."

Mary Ann pushed open the dressing room door and stepped out. Seeing Hank she said. "Don't you like my new clothes? They are pretty, huh Aunt Bess?"

"I think they're beautiful, don't you Hank?" Bess hid a wink for Hank. "Did you see this outfit Mary Ann? It's almost the same only a little different. What do you think Hank?"

"Wow, now that's a nice set of clothes. Hey, won't they look good with your boots?"

"Humm." Mary Ann looked over the blouse and jeans. "Maybe you're right. Let me try them on." She took the clothes from Bess and returned to the dressing room. Five minutes later, Mary Ann came out dressed in the blue jeans and pink shirt. "What do you think, these are nice too aren't they Aunt Bess?"

"I think they are darling and just right for you. Do you want to buy them too?"

"No, I only get one set of clothes today. I think I'll take the blue pants and pink blouse. The blouse is the same color as my boots and the pants are more grown up." She handed her blue blouse and pink pants to Hank to hold. "I think I'll wear these home. Are we still going to get a pizza?"

"Yep, that's why I'm here." Hank followed the girl to the cash register and handed the clerk his credit card. "Now, let's go to the café for a pizza."

On the way into the café, Mary Ann saw a poster in the window of a bucking horse and cowboy. "What's that cowboy doing?" Mary Ann pointed at the poster.

"He's riding a bucking bronco in a rodeo," Hank explained. "Have you ever been to a rodeo Mary Ann?"

"Nope but I think Michael and Margie went to one. I was too little then. I'm bigger now—can we go to the rodeo?" She looked up at Hank with her big blue eyes expecting him to agree.

"Sure, why not? Let's all plan on going to the rodeo. I might even do some roping with Ralph. You remember Mr. Ralph from the ranch next door?"

"Oh yes, I like him. Is he a real cowboy?"

"Yes ma'am he is and if you can convince the bigger kids to go to the rodeo and the fair, then we'll go. That okay with you?"

"Sure is. I'll ask them as soon as we get home. It would be fun at the rodeo wouldn't it Aunt Bess?" Mary Ann squinted up at Hank. "What's a fair?"

Hank nodded. "It's like a big party with lots to do outside."

Mary Ann didn't waste time when she got home. She found Sue and Margie in the tack room and enlisted them to promise they would go to the rodeo.

*   *   *

Hank was at the kitchen table watching Charlene and Bess fix dinner, when the teen girls trooped into the kitchen. "Is Mary Ann right, can we go to the rodeo and fair in Lone Horse?" Margie ventured.

"Sure, I don't see why you kids can't go. I thought I might enter the Team Roping event. Maybe I can win enough to buy you all cotton candy or a caramel apple."

Margie left to tell Michael about the rodeo and Sue went to look for Robby before the boys left with Ben.

Sue found Robby working with one of the new horses in the round pen. As she watched, Ben came to stand beside her. "Are you and Robby going to enter the team roping at the Lone Horse Rodeo?"

"I don't know, that's why I'm here. I want to ask Robby if he's willing to rope with me. If he is, we need to do some practicing before the rodeo or it's just a waste of entry money." Ben smiled at his daughter. "I don't want to burst your bubble, but Robby might want to rope with George Honey or one of the other hands."

Together, father and daughter watched Robby work the green broke horse.

*   *   *

If Robby continued to practice and entered local jackpots to gain experience he could become a top roper. Hank talked to Ben concerning thoughts about Robby's talent and projected successes. After some discussion, Ben agreed Robby should pay his own entry fees as added incentive to win and rope with George Honey as his heeler.

Hank talked to the event manager and got Mike a job working the stripping chute for the roping events. Michael was so excited he didn't want to be late so he and Sue left early for the rodeo grounds to meet his boss. The first day of the rodeo, Sue rode with Mike in his truck to the rodeo/fair grounds.

The security guard at the contestants, gate directed Mike and Sue to where the animal wranglers gathered waiting instructions from the rodeo boss. Mike joined them while Sue wandered around the stock pens and grounds. She went to the holding pens where the stock for the events were kept. She looked over the roping stock and decided: in her opinion the Rolling H stock was better.

Hank met Ben at the contestants' entrance to the rodeo grounds, leading him to the assigned parking. Then Hank went to the office to pay their entry fees. Mike stood waiting next to the rodeo office. Relief showed on his face when he spotted Hank. "Have you seen Sue? I got her a job chasing the roping and bucking horse stock back to the pens. They have a horse she can use, a little green but a nice horse."

"The horse too green for Sue?"

"No sir, Sue can easily handle the horse. I saw him and he's pretty calm, seems to like people. The job pays fifty dollars for the day, but I bet Sue would do it for free." Mike was so excited he couldn't stand still as he waited for Hank's decision.

"Okay, I saw Sue over by the stock pens on our way in. You explain to Ben about the job and you go by his decision, right?"

"Yes sir." Michael took off at a run in search of Ben and Sue. Hank watched him run toward the stock pens and shook his head. He remembered his first job at a rodeo. In fact it was this rodeo and doing the same job as Michael, the stripping chute.

Most of the rodeo fans were in the grandstands; Hank looked over the back of the stand and saw Sue on horseback exercising a young horse in the warm-up arena along with ropers warming up their horses. Hank climbed up and sat on the top rail of a pen and watched Sue until the start of the rodeo. First came the introduction of the Rodeo Queen and the royalty from other towns with rodeos. After the introductions came a cowboy carrying the National Flag and the playing of the National Anthem. At the beginning of the anthem, the cowboy and flag were at a walk going around the arena. As the song progressed the man, horse and flag picked up speed until at the end of the song the horse was at a full gallop. The horse, rider and flag came to the center of the arena in a sliding stop and the flag was presented to the crowd and received an appreciative cheer from the fans.

With the flag ceremony and introductions completed, it was time for Hank to meet Ben and prepare for the roping event. The pace of the rodeo was quick: all preliminary and qualifying events must be completed on the first day. The second day of the rodeo was only for the short go's and any rerides if required.

After he finished warming up Jake, Hank ambled to where he could see into the arena. The bull riding was over and the first go saddle bronc riding was underway. Hank saw Sue on what appeared to be a young gelding in the corner of the arena. The horse stood quietly, the mark of an exceptional horse, particularly a green-broke horse. Looking down the length of the arena he spotted Michael standing on top of the stripping chute waiting for the roping events.

The saddle bronc riding event was to be followed by bulldogging; then the barrel racing and bareback bronc riding. Sue was in the arena for all the events except the bull riding and barrels. Hank watched her ride out from her corner, cut off one of the broncs and usher the excited horse to the horse exit. Hank watched until the pickup rider pulled the bucking strap from the horse and the horse was safely in the pen.

Sue, at a lope, rode toward the strap lying on the ground, leaned down and picked it up on the way by. She received applause from the crowd, unaware she had done anything extraordinary. Sue rode by the gate and dropped the strap onto the top rail and went back to her position in the corner. Sue did it all while the announcer was introducing the next rider and horse not causing a hiccup between riders.

Hank saw Mike on the stripping chute; he applauded along with the crowd. After each contestant finished, Sue picked up the strap and deposited it on the top rail near the gate.

In the team roping event, Hank and Ben came in second place behind Robby and George. Hank called them the RG team; not the very best but really good. Both teams were in the final go scheduled for the next afternoon.

After the rodeo events, Hank took all the children to the fair. Mary Ann and Cassie rode every ride and Bess thought they sampled every item made with sugar. The teens went their own way. Hank caught occasional glimpses of them on rides and as they stuffed junk food into their happy faces. Coming around the merry-go-round on the way to give Mary Ann a ride, Bess pointed out the girls on one set of horses while the boys were on the second pair chasing the girls around and around. Margie caught the gold ring for a free ride. When they were dismounted and noticed Bess and Mary Ann watching them, Margie gave the gold ring to Mary Ann.

When the young girl was in the line and it came time to present the gold ring for a free ride, Mary Ann wouldn't let go of the ring. She said it was a gift from Margie and it was hers forever. Bess handed the attendant a ride ticket while Mary Ann put the ring in her pocket. "Sorry about that," Bess apologized to the attendant.

"Don't worry, happens all the time." The attendant dropped the paper ticket into the box's slot. "We keep lots of spare gold rings in the chance one becomes a keeper."

For the next day, the finalists and the stripping chute operator and steer chaser needed to be there an hour before the first event. When Sue and Mike arrived and reported to the rodeo boss, Sue was asked to carry the National Flag during the opening ceremony. The normal flag rider experienced a small problem with a brown bottle the night before and was not suitable to present the "Nation's Colors" to the crowd.

Sue proudly saddled the horse she was using after spending time to clean and polish the tack. Sue was concerned the horse might have a problem with the flag flapping around him but when she mounted, the horse trusted her and ignored the flag. Wearing a blue denim shirt and blue Wranglers, Sue rode flawlessly around the arena and finished to the crowd's cheer. Many in the crowd recognized her from the previous day as the trick rider who picked up the bucking straps after rough stock riding. The rodeo boss hired her for next year and asked Mike to come back too. Sue introduced Margie to the boss and he hired her on Sue's recommendation. A highlight was when a group of preteens recognized Sue and asked her to autograph their programs.

The afternoon went fast for the family. When it was all over, the RG team was victorious while Hank and Ben again took second. Sue came looking for Hank. "That horse I used is for sale, cheap. I think we should buy it."

"Hey, don't talk to me, talk to your dad. He's the horse manager, not me."

That evening, a new horse rode with Jake and the other Rolling H horses. Sue rode in the cab with her father and helped unload the horses. Jake was turned out after a quick brushing. The other horses went into another paddock to spend the night. Sue put the new horse in a vacant box stall until she could spend some time with the youngster assessing his value and potential.

CHAPTER 17

Bess and Hank sat talking at the table on the porch of the unfinished bunkhouse. They were interrupted by the sound of light diesel trucks pulling up the road to the ranch. Hank looked at his watch: 11:30, still morning. It was early for Ben and Josh to be back with the boys from the Davenport, Washington, stock sale.

As the truck and trailer came closer they could hear livestock banging the walls of the long steel trailer. Hank and Ben discussed buying some mustangs from the Bureau of Land Management. Ben wanted to look over the BLM mustang stock in Spokane. The mustangs made good ranch horses. Mustangs were not very large horses but long on smarts and stamina. With the proper training they made great horses for new or inexperienced riders.

Behind Ben was Josh pulling Brent's horse trailer. Hank saw Ben's grinning face as he backed the trailer up to the large arena's gate with its high five rail Powder River pipe fence. Hank ran over and opened the gate and met Robby who jumped down from the passenger seat. Ben backed the trailer so the gate would shut off one side of the open gate and the trailer door would shut off escape on the other side.

Robby helped Hank and Josh open the trailer door. Twenty white-face cows burst out of the trailer and into the arena to herd up at the far end away from the people. Banging coming from the front section caught Hank's attention. "You want me to open the front?" Hank asked.

As Sue and Margie rode up to the arena, Josh pointed to the animals in the arena. "Ladies, if you would be so kind, would you run those critters through the stripping gate into the holding pen?"

"Sure Josh," the girls responded. Robby let the girls and horses through into the arena. Sue led and gave Margie directions and within a few minutes they had all the white-face cows in the holding pen.

Josh called them out of the arena. "Don't want you two to get hurt. Robby let the critters out." Robby climbed up on the side of the trailer and released the catch holding the steel divider shut while Josh untied a rope from the ceiling of the trailer and pulled the steel divider open. Three huge bulls snorting and jabbing at each other crashed out and into the arena.

"I got a two-fer," Josh explained. "The rancher I bought them off only had a small spread and the bulls were always getting out. He was about to sell them to the butcher when I offered him five hundred for the two of them.

He took the money. The third bull I bought at the auction cost a whole lot more but I think in the long run he's a good buy." Josh and Hank leaned on the fence rail to watch the bulls. "I'd like to keep him here for special breeding and turn the two ornery bulls loose, one with the north herd and the other with the south herd. The cows were almost a gift. Man couldn't afford to feed them and was offered ten cents a pound, I offered eleven."

"Don't we have enough white faces?" Hank asked.

"Well sort of, but these are a special breed. I recognized them from an auction I went to a couple of years ago. You notice their legs are a bit shorter and the barrel and flanks bigger. Most of them are pregnant by a bull with the same configuration. Lots of good meat there. I'd like to keep the open cows here until they are bred to that last bull there."

"Okay, you're the expert and they're your herds. What about the horses?"

Ben, who was standing and listening, asked Robby to move the truck and trailer so they could unload horses. The boy shut the trailer doors, jumped into the truck and drove it to the wash rack downwind from the houses.

Ben entered the trailer and came out with a buckskin gelding. He unhooked the lead rope and turned the gelding loose in the arena. The horse made a run around the arena's edges, slowed and walked to the center of the arena, lay down and rolled, ignoring the three bulls standing in the corner of the arena as far away from people as they could get. Meanwhile, Ben went into the trailer and came out with another gelding, a sorrel, large for a quarter horse. The sorrel followed the same routine the buckskin did.

Then Ben brought out a tall, blue roan mare. He turned her loose. She more sedately rolled first then made a loop around the arena. One more horse, a buckskin mare, fought Ben at first but he quieted her and after having her stand with him for a couple of minutes, turned her loose. She sprinted toward the end of the arena, slid to a stop and rolled. After rolling she got to her feet and walked slowly toward the bulls. She stopped fifteen feet away. Hank watched her lower her head, took one step toward the bulls and the three bulls started to move along the fence. Satisfied, she trotted back to where Ben stood. The horse nosed him after he invited her into his space. Ben turned to face Hank, a huge smile on his face.

"I suppose you are going to tell me these are the best of the show."

"Yep," Ben said, "we have three more mares coming and a smaller horse for Mary Ann, not exactly a pony but smaller than these other brutes. The geldings are Mike and Robby's; they got good deals on both of them. Both horses are four years old and have some training, a bit better than green broke. I think Robby and Mike will learn a lot training them. One of the mares still coming would make a great horse for either Margie or Sue, leggy and fast. I would like to keep Loco in the rider training cycle for Margie and Mike along with Frisky."

"Sounds good to me." He clapped the men on the shoulders. "You both did good, and I thank you for it."

Just before Hank could rejoin Bess, Ben caught up with him. "Hank, I've got one more thing to tell you about the horses. I bought a chestnut mare for Margie, no papers and paid a bit more than I wanted. Margie has been talking to me about learning to do barrels. The mare is leggy and faster than the other horses. She's a lot of horse for Margie but I think she can handle her. The horse is nine, a good age and has done barrels in competition. She was abused some and her manners suck but we can fix that. I want to be completely up front with you about the horse. If you don't want Margie riding her, she would make a good brood mare. I think she would throw good babies."

"That you're recommendation, put Margie on her?"

"Yes sir, I think they'll be a good match. If she doesn't work out I'll buy her from you." Ben stood straighter.

"Okay, she's Margie's and don't you ever slip back on your convictions. I hired you to run the horse operation and you do it the best you can. That's all I ask, fair enough?"

"Yes Hank, fair enough." Ben put his hand out and the boss man took it.

Hank saw Bess walking toward the guest house. "Come on, in I think we need a beer." Hank led the way toward the kitchen.

"I'll be right there; I got the bill of sale for the rest of the stock in the truck."

"Let Robby bring it in. When he sees it's still in the truck he'll bring it to me or give it to Wilma. Now for that beer." The two men went inside to be joined a few minutes later by Josh. No words, Hank handed him a beer. Josh had turned Frisky over to the girls. He said the horse was too light for the hard ranch work but would be great for arena or maybe barrels competition.

* * *

Ben returned from Lone Horse after meeting the horse transportation hauler from Davenport. Hank could hear horses stamping and shifting around. He walked to the rear of the trailer and helped Ben unload the new horses. Ben explained about each horse as they were led from the trailer.

"Don't worry, looks good. We're off to a great start."

After the transporter left, Ben found the boys waiting for him at the horse corral. "Where are we?"

Robby answered for both of them. "We fed the horses, half flake each and watered them."

Sue came to the fence on her new horse to thank her father. "Oh Daddy, I love the new horse." She had been riding him for the first time in the spare paddock. "He's great."

"Thought you might like him. What did you name him?"

"I named him Einstein because he's so smart."

"Einstein huh? Now don't you take him to school with you," Ben teased, and walked to the rear of the trailer to unload a stocky little white gelding about 14-2 hands. He tied him to one of the trailer's rings. Ben climbed back into the trailer to unload the new stallion.

Sue backed Einstein away from the trailer to give Ben plenty of room to work with the new horse. Soothing the nervous stallion, Ben talked quietly, rubbing the horse's neck. He walked the horse to his new stall behind the barn and turned him loose to investigate his new home. The horse rolled and trotted around the stall until Ben dropped a flake of hay into the feeder attached to the stall rails.

"Where's Robby?" Ben asked Sue.

"He left with Josh about an hour ago. Josh wanted to make sure the corral by Big Rock is ready for the branding tomorrow. Josh said they'd be back in a couple of hours."

"Okay, put your horse away. I'm going to get a cup of coffee. I'll be in the kitchen."

"Yes sir." Mike, who had come to watch the new horses, grabbed the manure rake from the rack on the inside of the trailer's door.

Sue tied Einstein next to the white horse. "Michael, I'll help with the trailer. I'll get the manure cart." Sue ran toward the tool shed.

Ben watched the teens for a minute, impressed with how they all were adapting and helped each other.

Sue and Mike entered the kitchen laughing together at some private joke. Ben came in and went to the coffee machine, poured himself a cup and stirred in some cream. He sat at the kitchen table to wait for Hank and Bess. Mike and Sue each got a Coke from the ice chest on the porch and snagged a couple of cookies from Charlene's cookie jar. They collapsed onto the floor next to the door.

Bess entered the kitchen first, poured two cups of coffee and joined Ben at the table. Hank entered and rinsed his hands at the kitchen sink before he joined Bess and Ben at the table.

"How was the trip?" Hank asked.

"Fine. The stallion is in the stall behind the stable. Mary Ann's horse is tied to the trailer. I would like you to check him over before giving him to Mary Ann."

"Why, something wrong with him?"

"No, I just think you should check him over and then you and Bess can give him to her. Works better that way I'm thinking."

"Okay, let's look him over." Hank stood and carrying his coffee headed for the door. "You coming?"

"Yep." Ben got to his feet and went out the door followed by Bess, Michael and Sue. The group walked toward the horse trailer where the white horse waited. The horse stood calm.

"My, he certainly looks big, not too tall but big," Bess remarked.

"He is or was a roping horse. Judging by his size, my guess he was a heeler," Hank said as he checked the white horse's back, legs and feet. "Think he's too tall for Mary Ann?" He looked to Ben.

Frowning, Ben replied, "I don't think so. I rode him and he was so mellow I'd put a raw beginner on him." Ben ran a hand over the horse's flank. "This little horse is bomb proof."

Hank turned to Bess. "What do you think?"

Bess patted the white horse's neck and ran her hands over the smooth white coat. She picked up each foot and gently put them back down. The horse stood quietly, indifferent to all the human attention.

Hank continued to rub the horse along his back and up and down his legs. The horse stood patiently; Hank untied the horse dropping the lead rope on the ground. The horse remained quiet. Hank picked up the lead and walked the horse around the trailer and returned to where Bess and Ben waited. "This horse has great ground manners." Hank jumped up onto the horse's back. Using only the lead rope as reins he loped the horse around in a wide circle narrowing it until the horse was loping inside a twenty foot circle. Hank stopped, dropped the lead rope and slid off the back end of the horse. Hank patted the horse, a wide grin on his face. "This horse is perfect for Mary Ann; you did real good Ben, thanks."

"You want me to get Mary Ann?" Bess asked.

"Sure, why don't you get her then we'll give her the horse."

Bess could barely hold her excitement. She went to the house and returned followed by two confused girls, Mary Ann and Cassie. As the girls approached, Mary Ann's eyes got bigger and bigger as she stared at the white horse.

"So Mary Ann, what do you think? You big enough to take care of a big horse of your own?" Hank asked the six year old. Her blonde pony tail swished back and forth as she looked at the horse, then Hank and then Bess, while Ben stood deadpan.

"Oh Daddy Hank, is he mine?" It was the first time Mary Ann had ever called him Daddy Hank. Mary Ann stared at him with her large blue eyes.

Hank heard a soft noise; he looked at Bess who quickly turned away. "He sure is, Bess and I thought you were big enough for a horse of your own. Ben will help you learn to ride him if you ask real nice," Hank said.

"You bet, Hank," Ben agreed. "I bet Mary Ann will be doing rodeo before we know it."

"What's your horse's name?" Bess asked the little girl.

"His name is Casper—you know, like the ghost," Mary Ann said with a shy smile.

"That is sure a good name." Hank agreed and got nods and verbal agreements from Ben and Bess. "Here, I'll help you put him away and feed him." Hank picked up the lead rope, folded it into flat loops and handed the rope to Mary Ann.

The girl put the folded rope in her right hand and offered her other hand to Hank. Together the cowboy, the horse and little girl walked toward the stable.

Bess and Ben returned to the house while the man and his foster daughter entered the stable with Casper, the gentle white horse.

CHAPTER 18

Bess, Wilma, Charlene and Margie stood or sat on the arena rails and watched Hank give Mary Ann her first riding lesson on Casper. Sue sat on Loco and demonstrated techniques as Hank explained them to Mary Ann. The six year old seemed to know what to do, pushing the horse left and right with her leg pressure naturally. The use of the reins she could work after having been shown once. Mary Ann possessed naturally gentle hands and held the reins loosely except when telling the horse what she wanted. When Mary Ann did make a mistake, the horse reminded her she had sent him a wrong signal. He stopped and waited for the right cue.

Hank ended the lesson and sent Mary Ann to the new stable with Casper. Margie and Sue went along to help teach her how to take care of her new friend. Casper followed the little girl, staying next to her right shoulder. The horse seemed to know Mary Ann was his to take care of.

Bess called her supervisor at the State Social Work office and requested to extend her vacation. Her assistant at the Dutton Orphanage could cover for her. She wanted to spend as much time with the children and Hank as she could.

Bev thought her mother might need a little extra help and called Judge Hoskin. He called the State Social Work office and soft-armed the supervisor. With the judge's help, Bess received an additional four weeks paid in Montana doing special work at the judge's direction. She would also get a month unpaid if she needed it. Bess planned to call the judge in the morning to thank him and for the special assignment. Bess was writing a proposal for the judge: a new program for fostering children using the example of Hank's plan of an extended family mixing fostered children with established large or extended families.

Hank decided the day for branding and culling of both the Rolling H and the Lazy B herds and put it on the schedule calendar. The men split into two sections and left the ranch to locate the northern and southern herds. Robby and Mike accompanied the older men for the overnight excursion. Sean Riley, Jim Sutterland's new foreman, searched out and moved most of the Lazy B herds to the branding corrals and pens.

Once the herds were located and moved to the branding pens, all hands would work until the branding and culling was completed. Bess volunteered to handle the branding irons. Marjorie and Sue would start helping Bess, trading with Robby and Mike with the roping and holding while Josh and Ben did the actual branding and banding of the three hundred plus Rolling H cattle stock. The work would be non-stop until all calves and were mavericks banded.

* * *

Hank gave permission for Margie and Sue to go with the men on the actual roundup and the cattle drive. He knew the girls could help on horseback and were actually better than some of the temporary hands he hired.

The teens worked roping and dragging; they practiced with the ropes and became good ranch ropers. Charlene took care of feeding the workers, while Wilma kept records. Charlene, with Hank's concurrence, turned most of the ranch's fiscal responsibilities over to Wilma, while Charlene continued to be the house boss. After the end of the first day of branding a group of tired, dirty wranglers lined up for supper. Charlene spent the day preparing the meal: steaks, corn on the cob, green salad and maple syrup baked beans, a cowboy favorite. Everyone looked forward to being able to sit down and relax. Coffee perked on the edge of the barbeque fire, sodas, milk and beer in ice chests near the table.

Margie and Sue started to walk off by themselves to leave the men alone for supper talk about the day and some of their experiences. Sean Riley saw them. "Hey, you two. Come over here with the rest of us, you don't smell any worst than we do." Sean grinned as he saw the light in the girls' eyes and smiles appeared on their dirty, tired faces. The cowboys made room for them at the crowded table. At first they were a bit shy, but minutes later the girls joined in the ribbing and storytelling like everyone else.

Hank and Bess watched the interplay between the girls and the other hands. The girls earned their place at the table on their own and were welcomed by their new peers. Mary Ann and Charlene's children sat at their own table. Robby and Mike arrived late after doing a special job for Hank and naturally moved to the big table and sat down to eat like they were starving.

When the combined hands of both ranches were through with the Rolling H cattle, they moved down to the Lazy B to do the same for Jim Sutterland's cattle; except Jim wanted his calves castrated the old way so he could have an old fashioned barbeque with authentic Rocky Mountain Oysters. The teenagers worked as hard, or harder than the other hands. Hank saw Sue motion to one of the men to move a particularly ornery steer and he did as she directed without hesitation.

CHAPTER 19

Bev paced in front of the arrival and departure monitors. She knew it wasn't going to make Brent's flight from Chicago arrive any sooner; according to the monitors, the plane already landed. Over the airport speaker system, the ticket agent announced Brent's flight waited for a gate space at the terminal.

Earlier the same afternoon, Bev arrived in Spokane and checked into the Davenport Hotel after driving non-stop from the ranch to Spokane.

Impatient, Bev stared up at the monitors, sighed and returned to pacing. She spotted a group of passengers on the stairs from the gate area. She noticed one man with a gym bag on his shoulder. The bag hid his face. While she watched he peeked around the bag: it was Brent. He wore a grin spread over his face as he lowered the bag. The two met at the closest point she could get to without the Transportation Safety Agency people ordering her to get back behind the line.

Brent came through the gate, swept her off her feet and kissed her, mindless of blocking a good portion of the passageway. "Where have you been? I've been waiting hours." Bev gasped before Brent shut her up with more kisses. He set her back on her feet and picked up his bag. He put his arm around Bev's waist, tucking her close as they walked hip to hip to the baggage claim.

"There was a weather delay in Chicago. When we finally did get here, a half hour late, there was another plane in our docking gate. We were on the ground here for over thirty minutes before we could deplane. Sometimes I miss the old days when you just went down the steps from the plane and walked to the terminal."

"Me too," Bev agreed.

"How have Dad and your mom been getting along? Dad's only letter didn't say much at all, talked mostly about the ranch and the kids."

"I see them every day. I finally got all my stuff last week. I had to stay in Dutton longer than I planned. Hank and Mom seem to be getting along but there's something bugging your dad. Mom notices but tries to ignore it." Bev stopped Brent and looked into his eyes. "You know they've been sleeping together?"

"No, but if Dad is sleeping with Bess, he is serious about their relationship."

"I think there is something really bothering him. Sometimes I catch him looking off in the distance with a sad expression, and he forgets to shave some mornings. When he's around the kids, he appears to be his old self, interested in what they're doing. He sold a couple of horses the other day to a roper from Oklahoma. We still have the horses and are boarding them until the guy comes to get them, probably next week."

Bev pulled on his arm in an attempt to hurry him along. "Sue helped Ben train one of the horses and Margie the other. Your dad gave them five percent up front for their work and another five percent went into a special fund for each of them. Ben got another ten percent. Hank had his money advisor set up accounts for both of the girls. Actually for each of the kids. He pays them half of their earnings, what they need for incidentals, and the rest goes into their investment accounts." Bev looked into her lover's eyes. "He is the most generous man I have ever known. He gives himself to everyone, but there is something bothering him. I'm afraid it has to do with your mom."

"Oh crap, I think I know the problem. You know he was a wreck when my mother was killed. They were so much in love we didn't think he'd survive. After we left California for the ranch with Jim and Maya, Dad turned to the bottle for a few days before he left to rejoin the MEU. After a few months, he returned with the MEU and put in his retirement papers. I'm sure Dad was always sober when he went to work but later when he was alone he drank. After a couple of weeks he quit drinking. Now, he doesn't drink except special occasions and a occasional beer or glass of wine with dinner."

Bev changed the subject. "I got a room at the Davenport Hotel downtown for two nights. Mom and Hank aren't expecting us until this Sunday night or even Monday. I drove one of the ranch trucks. Charlene needed the SUV for the little kids and all the running around Hank has her doing. You know Wilma is doing the ranch books and Charlene is running the house. Wilma is taking an accounting class at night school in Lone Horse and another through the Internet."

The couple held hands until they arrived at the baggage area and while they waited for Brent's Valpak. Bev tugged his sleeve. "Get your bag, I'll get the truck and meet you out front. Hurry 'cause I'm horny." She left Brent with his mouth open. A fellow passenger standing next to him grinned and shook his head as the two men watched her go out the sliding doors toward the parking garage.

Brent heard the squeal of tires and saw a new white Ford 4 by 4 with Montana plates exit the elevated parking garage. He watched as the truck crossed three lanes of traffic and stopped in front of him. Bev sat grinning behind the steering wheel.

Brent tossed his bags in the back and climbed into the cab. Bev drove away from the curb toward the airport exit before he could get his seatbelt fastened. She must have set some records because fifteen minutes later they were in the loading zone in front of the Davenport Hotel. A parking valet met them accompanied by a bellman who picked up Brent's bags and followed the couple into the hotel. She tossed the bellman a room key, "514 please," and handed him a ten-dollar tip.

"Come on, I'm starving and you are going to need your strength." Brent meekly followed Bev into the restaurant where a smiling waiter stepped up to greet her and led them to a table already set. He lit two candles and left to return with an ice bucket that contained a bottle of Chardonnay. The wine was opened and after Bev's approval, the waiter poured and left. "I ordered dinner, salmon in white wine sauce, baked potato and tossed salad. Oh yeah, and a large plate of oysters. After that, we'll see how the oysters work," she teased.

They talked quietly together until the waiter brought their soup and salad. When they finished dinner, Bev signed the check, and added a hefty tip for the waiter. Brent followed her not failing to notice Bev's nice curves and the turn of her bottom in her tight-fitting Wranglers. She picked up their room key at the desk, and everyone seemed to know her; she did make an impression in those Wranglers, sleeveless blouse with her blonde ponytail. They entered the elevator and were joined by a couple on a special evening out for their 50th wedding anniversary. Bev told them she and Brent were getting married and looked up into Brent's blue eyes. The young couple left the elevator after they exchanged good wishes with the older couple on their special day.

Brent put out the "Do Not Disturb" sign and locked the door to the room. He noticed the king sized bed turned down and the pillow mints had been set aside on each night stand. Bev stood next to the foot of the bed and pulled her shirt over her head. Without a wasted second the Wranglers were on the floor.

"My God Bev, you're not wearing any underwear." Brent stood with his mouth open. "If I'd have known that we'd never have had dinner."

"Yeah, I know." Bev began to rub her bare breasts against his sweater. "Here, let me help you get rid of this scratchy old thing." She tugged the sweater over his head. Better, but not enough. Next his pants: she stripped his underwear off with the pants. He stood in front of her wearing only his socks and T-shirt. "You look silly dressed like that—either put your clothes back on or get rid of the socks and T-shirt." Bev wore a smirk and a raised eyebrow.

"Okay." Brent reached for his pants, called her bluff.

"That's not going to work." She pushed him back onto the bed and rubbed her tongue over her teeth and lips, a wicked smile on her face.

After hours of round robin love making, they fell asleep holding each other. The T-shirt and socks had joined the other clothing on the floor. Brent woke long enough to pull the covers over them and returned to the dream of holding the world's most beautiful woman in his arms. His eyes cracked open and he found it wasn't a dream. He smiled, pulled her close, kissed her between her shoulder blades. She moaned in her sleep, sighed and slept. The sun broke the eastern horizon; no one in hotel room 514 cared.

Brent was the first to wake, his body still on East Coast time. He propped his head on his hand and gazed at the woman beside him. He drank in her beauty feeling exceptionally lucky to have found a woman like Bev. Young, vivacious, intelligent and beautiful, what more could a man ask? He slipped down and moved her hair aside to kiss the nape of her neck. Bev moaned again and slowly rolled to face him.

"I love you, let's get married," Brent whispered in her ear.

Bev's eyes popped open. She sat up and stared at Brent. "What did you say?" She was heedless of her bare breasts inches from his face.

"I said, let's get married, now on the way home. We don't have to have a big wedding. Unless you want one?" Brent asked before he kissed her lightly on the lips. His lips moved to her neck where they lingered until dropping to her breasts to nip and lick.

"That's unfair." Bev groaned, put her arms around Brent's head and pulled him into her arms. Slowly she eased herself back and pulled him down with her.

An hour later they shared the shower together, soaping, rinsing, and letting the warm water cascade over their bodies. Reluctantly, they left the shower, finished drying each other to dress before going down to the restaurant for a late breakfast.

"Are you serious about getting married on the way home?" Bev reached across the table; she put her hand into Brent's.

"Absolutely, meant every word. So we jump the date by a couple of weeks." He turned his hand over to hold her hand. "The wedding is scheduled three weeks from today. We'll get married twice." Brent moved his thumb over the diamond engagement ring on Bev's finger. He reached into his pocket and brought out a jewelry box to place in front of her.

"What's this?" Hesitantly she opened the box to discover the matched wedding bands of the same set as her engagement ring. Tears pooled in her eyes before cascading down her cheeks. Brent's eyes too were watery. "Okay, I guess you've got me. What, sir, are you going to do with me?"

"I am going to love you for the rest of my life, forever."

"That's it? Just going to love me?"

"No, I'm going to hold you and screw your lights out." He laughed. "There, now I've said it, can you live with that?" Brent was having difficulty holding a straight face.

"Well then, don't you think you better get started?" Bev stood, grabbed his hand and only waited long enough for Brent to sign the check before she led him across the hotel lobby to the waiting elevators.

The couple spent the afternoon shopping at the Riverfront Mall before a movie and late dinner. The following day they drove to Coeur d'Alene, Idaho, for a quick wedding at one of the marriage chapels. After the brief ceremony, they drove to Missoula for dinner before the drive to the Rolling H Ranch.

*　*　*

Brent was surprised by how much the ranch had changed in the five weeks he had been away. His face showed wonder as he drove through the gate of the now sprawling ranch complex. The main ranch house, completed with split log siding, gave the house a log lodge motif. The bunkhouse was complete except for the siding and some interior drywall. Three paddocks for horses with split rail fencing could be seen beyond the arena and round pens. Each paddock held at least ten horses grazing on the rich green grass. Further out he saw Jake and Loco grazing by themselves, no fences required to keep them near the ranch.

Brent spotted his horses Jackson and Beany as they grazed with some other geldings. A large bull was in a pen behind the barn and he wondered if his father had bought any others. A single bull to service the range cows would be a strain on the bull. He assumed Jim and his dad were working together to expand the gene pool.

After the planned wedding and honeymoon, Brent and Bev would stay in the guest house built as part of the ranch complex. Brent carried his bags and Bev's overnight bag and their purchases into the house. Bev told him about the week-long trail ride scheduled to start two days after the wedding and before their honeymoon in Hawaii. They needed to tell Hank and Bess about their elopement in Idaho. Guests from out of town and Marines from Brent's unit would begin arriving in two weeks.

They saw dust coming from the arena and the round pen. Bev pulled Brent in that direction. She explained, "Sue and Margie have been training some of the yearlings, teaching ground manners, tying, loading into trailers and having their feet handled. The girls each have three year olds they've been working with too. Ben continued to buy prospects and do some special training. The four teens have become the primary trainers. Ben was busy searching out and buying horses to increase the quality and quantity of the Rolling H Ranch. I think I told you they sold two horses for a few thousand each—Sue trained them from scratch. Ben used the profits to buy more prospects."

"Is Dad still guaranteeing his horses?"

"Oh yes, absolutely. He says he won't sell a horse unless he thinks the horse is ready and the rider is proficient enough with the horse. Hank personally rides each horse before he will sell it. He doesn't want spooky horses running around with his brand on their butt." Bev laughed. "You going to brand my butt Mr. Springer?" Laughing she stuck her fanny out for him. "The last horses sold are still here and Sue works with them at thirty dollars a day plus the board."

Hank and Bess sat on the top rail of the round pen and watched Sue exercise a bay colt. Brent and Bev climbed up and sat next to them. Hank grunted, but continued to watch Sue with the colt. Twenty minutes later, Sue led the young horse out of the pen toward the stable. The watchers climbed down; father and son put arms around each other. Bev was still awed by the strong relationship between Hank and Brent.

Hank started to bring Brent up to some changes about the ranch. "I hired two ropers we rode with to help out with the ranch work. You remember Leonard Honey, George's cousin, and Shorty Rau? They didn't have much work after last year and were looking for a permanent ranch job. I thought since we know them I'd hire them on. Both are out on the upper range, counting the late summer calves. They'll bring the calves down in October so we can brand and band the late arrivals and medicate them. Shorty said he would like to stay at the old line shack and work from there. Josh thinks it's a good idea, so if you don't have any objections, Shorty will be with the northern herd."

Hank led the couple to the old picnic table still in its spot from the first time they visited the meadow. The table had been strengthened and augmented by another table side by side connected to the original.

Brent saw Wilma and Charlene come out of the house with baskets and put them in a large green garden wagon. Pulling the wagon, Wilma came up to the table and shooed Hank and Brent away after she gave Brent a welcome home hug; she put a cloth on the table top, then Charlene arrived with a second wagon with an ice chest and coffee urn. After giving Brent a hug, Charlene put the coffee urn on the table with an assortment of cups. Wilma placed a basket of sandwiches and another with fresh-baked sour milk rolls and a jar of homemade butter. The rolls were still hot, covered by a white linen. Hank snagged a couple of rolls and quickly broke open the still-teaming bread. He spread butter to melt. Wilma added a jar of wild strawberry jam to the table. She scooted Hank down closer to Bess and joined the party. Charlene sat next to Bev.

"Hey, how come you didn't wait for us?" Sue and Margie sat down at the table across from Bev and Brent. "Yes Bess, we washed our hands, care to smell?" Sue presented her hands for Bess's inspection, while Margie presented her hands to Hank, who laughed.

"It's good having the family—here, hey where's Robby and Mike?" Brent looked around.

"Mike said they were going to check the south fence. They found one of the Foresters' steers on the south range," Wilma said. "Mary Ann and Cassie are napping, but they'll be up soon."

Mary Ann and Cassie arrived still rubbing sleep from their eyes. Mary Ann wore her favorite pair of pink Wrangler jeans and one of Margie's old blue plaid shirts tucked in with the sleeves rolled up so her small arms and hands could escape the cloth. Not exactly color coordinated, but the youngster didn't seem to mind. Mary Ann put her arms around Brent and hugged him for a minute, then sat next to him and crowded Bev to the side. "Brent, are you going to teach me to ride Jackson now? I'm bigger than when you left."

Bess rolled her eyes, Hank burst out laughing and Brent said, "Sure, as soon as Bess says, we'll take the old boy out for a spin."

"I'm a good rider, huh Daddy Hank? I ride Casper, but he's easy to ride." Mary Ann thought they were making fun of her. She stuck her lower lip out and seemed to notice Bev for the first time. Pout forgotten, she moved closer to Bev. "You going to ride with me and Brent, Bev?" She didn't wait for an answer; her mind shifted when Cassie sat across from them. Charlene buttered a roll for her and put strawberry jam on it, then buttered one roll for Mary Ann, handing it across the table to her.

The afternoon passed quickly, and everyone had something to share with Brent.

The sun began to sink toward the horizon; the summer evening was still warm. Charlene and Wilma went to the house and came back with steaks, pork chops and baked potatoes with French cut green beans. Charlene cleared the table while Wilma set the plates and utensils.

Brent saw Mike and Robby riding toward the stable. A half hour later the two boys joined the group who slid closer together. Brent laughed when they presented their hands to Bess for inspection. He did notice the boys took care of their horses before they took care of themselves: it was the cowboy way. Ben and Josh with Jesse and Bea joined them in time for dinner.

Hank's extended family sat at the table talking, sharing the enjoyment of being together. Mary Ann fell asleep with her head on Brent's lap. Bev watched the young man as he carefully picked up Mary Ann and carried her to the house. Wilma followed to put the girl to bed; it had been a long day for her. Josh collected his brood and loaded them into the truck for the brief trip to their cabin.

Margie, Sue and Charlene cleaned up, then Charlene went home. The children needed to get ready for bed but would wait for their mother so she could listen to their prayers. During the day, Charlene brought them to the ranch where seven-year-old Cassie played with Mary Ann. Bea and Jesse followed the older children and helped when and where they could.

Occasionally, Josh took Jesse with him when he checked the cattle or rode fence. The boy was a natural horseman and he learned about cattle from his father. Ben Withrow took a few minutes each day to teach Jesse one special thing about horses, cattle or nature.

Nobody said anything when they saw Bev wearing a wedding ring around her neck on a gold chain. The newlyweds hadn't thought of how they were going to tell Hank and Bess they'd eloped. They searched for an opportunity and found Bess and Hank at the table on the porch with cups of coffee.

Bev whispered, "Follow my lead." The pair stepped up onto the porch. "Hi Dad, thought we'd find you two together."

Brent smiled and leaned down to kiss Bess on the cheek. "Hey Mom, Dad, did you miss me while I was gone?"

Bess's eyes got big and Hank's head snapped around to stare at the two and he growled, "Dad, Mom? Not until you're married."

"Gee Dad, I thought you were smarter and quicker than that." Bev grinned.

"You didn't? You did!" Bess jumped out of her chair, threw her arms around Bev and then around Brent. "When, where?"

"Yesterday morning in Coeur d'Alene on the way home from Spokane. We decided to stop at one of the Love Chapels and do the deed," Bev said smugly. "Didn't want to give him a chance to change his mind and get away."

"Well, I'll be taken for a gelding," Hank said and made no sense at all. "What are we going to do about the wedding here?"

"Never you mind Mr. Springer," Bess said as she planted a big kiss on Brent's cheek. "You treat my little girl right now or you'll be answering to me, you hear?"

"Yes ma'am." Brent picked Bess up and twirled her around.

"Hey, put my woman down, son," Hank said. When Brent complied he slapped his son on the back. He reached out to Bev and folded her into his arms. "Welcome to the Springer family, Bev. I couldn't be prouder of two people then I am of you two. Here, sit down and tell us all about it." Hank got two more chairs from the other table on the porch.

The four sat and talked until the ranch became quiet. Only faint background noise from the movement of the grazing horses and the steady lap of the water in the stream could be heard. A lone wolf howled and from far away they heard an answer from his mate.

CHAPTER 20

Tuesday morning excitement surrounded the Rolling H. The children from Robby to Mary Ann were unable to sit still at the breakfast table. They could hear the cattle in the arena and the two pens holding new Black Angus calves purchased from a Central Washington ranch. The new calves needed to be branded and medicated, then combined with the northern herd's mavericks. At the stable, Brent saddled his horse Beany he would use to ride with Hank and Josh. When the men were finished, the teens moved in and saddled their mounts. Everyone joined in the work; the boys and girls rotated jobs so each would get a chance to gain experience for each job. Hank, Brent and Josh rode their horses in among the cattle, separating those to be shipped to market. Sean stood on the fence and pointed at marketable cattle the riders missed. The cattle would be loaded into the large double deck livestock carriers for the trip to Missoula stockyards.

To get the children out of the house, Charlene gave Cassie and Mary Ann the job of bringing water to the cowboys and cowgirls working the cattle. Margie and Sue worked in the arena with the ropes; Josh did the banding, Sean medicated and Bess helped with the branding irons. After the branding and medication of the new cattle, Ben with Robby and Mike drove the new purchased calves and the cattle not ready for market to the northern herd's winter grazing grounds and returned to take the balance of the cattle to the southern grazing grounds.

It took three days of dawn to dusk hard work to herd, brand, vaccinate and castrate or band the Rolling H and Lazy B herds.

*   *   *

The cowboys and cowgirls rode into the Lazy B ranch yard for a barbeque after all the cattle had been separated into lots and confined in pens to await load out and transport. Each rancher provided his truck and trailer if he had one. Convoys of beef cattle rolled down the highway from Lone Horse every day for nearly two weeks. Josh bought a large diesel semi-truck and livestock trailer for the Rolling H and with the Lazy B truck and trailer joined the convoys of trucks transporting cattle to Missoula.

Trucks from the Lone Horse Cattle Transport Company and trucks from some of the larger ranches delivered cattle to the Missoula Stockyard for shipment to markets. It was a hard week's work, and all the ranches in the area were doing roundup and branding at the same time. Everyone on a ranch worked. Hank planned to ship about 100 head of cattle, a modest beginning for the Rolling H Ranch cattle operation.

Hank and Josh were still building the Rolling H herd. The good news was they sold two of the horses Sue and Margie trained for a tidy profit after paying Ben and the girls their trainer's fee. Sue trained another talented horse as a cutting horse. Hank had been offered $25,000 for the gelding. Hank thought he'd keep the horse unless someone offered $50,000.

Hank returned to the Lazy B with the empty truck, Sue riding shotgun. There were two unfamiliar cars in front of the Sutterland ranch house. Jim stood on the porch and waved at Hank when he climbed down from the cab. Hank told Sue to park the truck in the lot behind the ranch house and meet him at the ranch house. Sean would have one of the temporary hired hands clean the truck and trailer.

Hank was met by Jim at the door. "There are a couple of folks here looking for you. I told them you'd be along sometime today. Both of the men are interested in your cutting horse and bidding against each other, or will be. You know the cutting horse your young missy trained. They already know your price is on the high side of $50,000. I kind of let it slip." Jim could hardly contain his excitement as he led Hank into the living room.

"Gentlemen, this is Hank Springer, the owner of the horse you're interested in."

The men shook hands, Hank excused himself, and went outside to wait for Sue. He explained what the visitors wanted and asked Sue to sit in on the meeting and keep notes. He wanted her input before he sold any horse she trained and it was good experience for her. Ben was at the Rolling H working with two of the new geldings. Hank decided to let Sue conduct some of this sale and see how she handled herself.

Hank returned to the living room followed by Sue. "Gentlemen this is Sue Withrow, she will be sitting in with us."

The men shook hands and smiled at the young lady when she sat next to Hank in a hardback chair. Sue accepted a notebook and pen from Jim and settled herself onto the chair.

The man from California started. "I understand Mr. Springer, you have a cutting horse, five years old and trained by the Withrow family. Is that true?"

"Yes sir, I do own such an animal."

"Is the animal fully trained and tested?"

"Sue, you've been at all of the training sessions. Would you say the horse is fully trained and competitive?"

"Yes sir, the gelding is very cow'y, quick and smart. He has not lost a steer in a fresh and spooky herd in the last fourteen sessions."

"Is there someone who can demonstrate the horse's abilities?" the California man asked, and both men leaned forward to wait for Hank's answers.

"Yes, I do believe there is someone who can demonstrate the horse. The horse is currently on my ranch a few miles from here. I'll ask Susan here to ride the demonstration." He turned to Sue. "Would you care to ride this afternoon?"

"Yes Mr. Springer, I'll ride Wind. Dad is better, but if you want I'll ride."

"Will that be agreeable with you gentlemen?" Hank asked.

"This I've got to see," Jim said and headed to the kitchen to tell Maya he was going to watch a cutting that afternoon at Hank's. He came back with Maya on his heels.

"Sue," Hank said, "would you call the Rolling H and ask Mike to bring the horses back to the ranch and put them in the small paddock. Tell him to have Margie's horse ready to be the holder for a cutting demonstration. Also have him put twenty head of the Corrientes range cattle into the arena holding pen. I'll ride with Jim and Maya. See if one of these gentlemen will give you a ride to the ranch," he said to Sue.

The man from California offered to give Sue a ride. Margie arrived with Robby as they were crossing the porch and asked Sue what was going on. Sue explained and asked Hank if Margie could come along with them since her horse would be used to hold the cattle. Sue and Margie rode with the California man. Mike finished hosing out the Lazy B livestock trailer and rode with Brent to return Hank's truck to the Rolling H ranch.

The girls climbed into the new-smelling car. "Whew, what's that smell?" the man said looking sideways at the girls.

"I'm afraid that's us: we've been on a roundup for the past five days only out of the saddle to sleep, eat and pee," Margie said with a straight face. "Oh a couple of other things started while we were out there."

"Things I don't need to know, entirely too much information." The man laughed. "Damn, I miss all this. I used to live about a hundred fifty miles over that way." He pointed in an eastern direction. "Our big city was Great Falls. I used to look forward to getting to the city. Now, I look forward to getting away from the city."

"You know you look a bit familiar," Margie said. "Should I know you?"

"You might have seen me in a movie or two. I got into movies while I was still in college at UCLA. Been lucky, now I can afford to buy good horses. I started cutting when I was still in high school and am just now getting back to horses and cutting. I heard Ben Withrow is the best trainer in these parts and I'm partial to Montana horses."

"Oops, turn here," Margie interjected. "The ranch is about two miles up this fire road."

Margie directed the movie guy onto the ranch and where to park. When she was getting out of the car, she asked. "Okay, what's your name?"

"You can call me Jeff, okay?"

"I guess that will just have to do then." Margie followed Sue who was already out of the car and looking for the horse she called Wind.

Sue walked toward the horse paddocks and whistled. A horse's head came up, ears forward looking for her. Sue put her hand into the air and whistled again. The horse trotted across the paddock to her. She rubbed the horse's nose and walked back to where the men waited on the other side of the split rail fence. The horse followed, staying at her shoulder. The horse stopped when Sue stopped, demonstrating the horse's ground manners. Margie went to another paddock and whistled up the horse she had been training.

Sue presented her horse. "This horse is called Wind. Would either of you two gentlemen care to inspect him? He stands fourteen hands two at the withers with some growing left in him. He is sound and balanced as you can see. He has had all the shots on schedule. A complete medical history is kept in the office and I'm sure Wilma will get a copy of his papers for you."

Sue watched Jeff lift each of the horse's feet and inspect the hooves for cracks or bruising. Jeff finished his inspection. "Where will you do the demonstration?"

"In the large arena. You may have noticed some cattle at the far end of the arena. You are free to inspect the cattle too. These are fresh Mexican Corrientes cattle used mostly for roping. We keep a herd of them for training and sell off older or stale cattle. Four of the hands working this ranch are rated ropers plus Mr. Springer and his son Brent. This herd is fresh; during training we change these cattle every two weeks from our own herd of two hundred Corrientes range cattle. The cattle were purchased from the rodeo market suppliers. Most are young and very quick."

"They look good to me," Jeff volunteered. "I'm satisfied there are no ringers in the herd."

"Well then, if you gentlemen will excuse me for a few minutes, I'll warm up Wind and we'll get to the demonstration." Sue opened the gate so the horse could follow her to the tack shack.

Ten minutes later, Wind was saddled and warmed up in the small arena. When Wind was ready, Sue rode him into the large arena for a couple of laps before putting him to work. The horse immediately noticed the cattle in the holding pen and wanted to go investigate. After a couple of minutes of riding, Sue signaled Hank to put the cattle into the arena. Sue rode Wind out of the arena, dismounted and checked the cinch and back cinch. The horse was wearing a light breast collar but no tie-down.

"Do you mind?" Jeff asked and looked in the horse's mouth, checking the type of bit. The headstall was a band bridle with a curb which was not tight against the horse's chin. "Thank you." As he inspected he noticed the saddle was a working ranch saddle not a competition cutting saddle. The ranch saddle would be a bit harder for the rider who had to use their hands on the shorter fatter horn. Jeff took his place with the others as Hank walked across the arena and went out when Margie rode into the arena to get the herd together at the far end.

Margie gathered the herd until Sue signaled her and Margie and her horse moved off into a corner away from the herd where she and her horse wouldn't influence the cattle.

Jeff called, "The brown with the white spot on the left hip, if you can."

Sue and the horse moved quietly into the herd, cut the selected steer out of the herd. She dropped the reins onto the horse's neck as soon as the horse knew which steer to keep away from the others.

"The black and white," Jeff called.

Sue picked up the reins and the horse was already looking for another steer. Sue cut three more steers all quickly and successfully with minimum disturbance in the herd. Sue sat perfectly still with her hands on the horn until she released the steer. The horse behaved perfectly. She returned to the men watching while Margie pushed the herd through the stripping chute into the holding pen.

Jeff met her as she passed through the gate and dismounted, but he was distracted by Margie working the cattle at the other end of the arena.

"Mr. Springer, is there a chance I can ride Wind and maybe cut a steer or two?"

Hank looked at Sue who shrugged. "You've ridden a good cutter before? Then okay." Sue whistled at Margie and signaled her to put the cattle back into the arena.

Jeff adjusted the stirrups. "I notice you don't use spurs—will I need a pair?"

"Nope, just ride the horse, watch your weight shifting, try to stay centered. Wind is very quick and if you're not ready he may put you in the dirt by cutting out from under you."

They watched as Jeff cut three steers from the herd and almost fell only once. He turned the herd over to Margie and stayed in the arena while she put the cattle through the chute into the holding pen.

Jeff returned with Wind. "Say Mr. Springer, is the horse that girl, Margie, rode for sale too?"

"All of my horses are for sale except for Jake and Loco and of course Mary

Ann's horse and my son's horses. Some of the horses are not mine, but those that are can be purchased if the price is right." Hank grinned at the younger man. He addressed the older man. "How about you Mr. Butler, do you care to ride?"

The other man, Butler shook his head, "No thank you. I represent a buyer in Texas. I myself do not ride cutting horses. I stick to easy trail horses. My client is also interested in roping horses both tie-down and team ropers."

"We do have some roping horses currently in training, but they won't be ready until spring. If your client has a horse in need of training, we have the trainers and facility available." In his head Hank thought how much a covered arena would cost him and how soon he would be able to recoup any investment.

"Yes, I believe he does have some horses needing training. I will discuss it with him when I see him tomorrow." Butler smiled. "Now, let us negotiate prices. I understand you want $50,000 for this horse, Wind? Is that correct?"

"Yes, $50K is the price, which is not negotiable."

"Fine, I offer $50,000 for the horse Wind," Jeff asked.

Sue watched Jeff while Butler had been talking.

"Excuse me, I will pay $65,000 for Wind." Jeff said. Sue's eyes widened.

"I'll match that and add $5,000," Butler said smugly.

"Sorry," Jeff said, "$75,000."

Butler looked at the younger man, shook his head. "I don't have the authorization to go higher than $70,000. I guess you've bought yourself a horse Mr. Price."

"Good." Jeff addressed Hank. "Do you think I can leave him here for a week or two until I have a stall built for him at my ranch?"

"Sure, no problem. The first month is on the Rolling H. If you leave him here longer, we charge board. If we didn't, our money manager would be all over me for giving the ranch away."

Jeff put his hand out for Sue to shake, closing the deal in both his mind and Sue's. "Sue, don't worry about him, he'll have five acres to run around in, all grass." Jeff smiled at her. "You trained this horse, not your father."

"Yes sir." Sue rubbed Wind's neck, as a tear escaped and rolled down her cheek. She wiped it away with the back of her hand. Margie rode up on the gelding.

"I'll offer you $25,000 for the gelding, same deal. Sue, did you train the gelding too?"

"Only a little. Margie really trained him. He's so gentle we call him Buttercup. He's a good strong horse, not a cutter you understand, but he can do anything else you want." Margie sat on Buttercup shocked to literally have her horse sold right out from under her. She still had her mare to run barrels, but she started and trained this horse.

"Okay, Mr. Springer, is there a place I can write you a check?"

Hank led them to the main house where Wilma, having seen all the men gathered at the arena, fixed sandwiches and coffee. Wilma made sure there was beer and white wine in the electric cooler and red wine on the table during business meetings.

Hank started into the living room, but Jeff asked, "Do you think we could sit in the kitchen? I miss that, being in California."

"Your call Jeff, the table is certainly large enough. If you don't mind, I'd like the girls to join us. Wilma, would you get the papers on the cutter Wind and the horse Margie calls Buttercup. It seems Mr. Price here just bought them." When she returned Hank said, "You sit down too, you're part of this operation you know."

Sabrina, home from working as a medical doctor at the Missoula General Hospital, entered the kitchen and was introduced to the buyers. The men rose and shook hands with her. When Sabrina left the kitchen Jeff remained standing and watched her leave and stood still wearing a stunned expression on his face. With an effort he turned his attention back to business.

Before she sat down, Wilma put the platter of sandwiches on the table, while Hank offered the group their choice of beverage. Jeff took out a simple folding checkbook and wrote a check for $100,000. Wilma handed Wind and Buttercup's papers to Hank who pointed for her to give them to Price. Price handed the check to Wilma. Her eyes went wide when she saw the amount of the check and the signature. When the girls joined them after taking care of the horses and tack, Hank offered a toast to the new owner of Wind and Buttercup. He smiled while thinking, *This place may make some money after all.*

The party broke up after Price and Butler left to drive back to Missoula to catch a late flight to Spokane. Hank invited Jeff to come back any time, but be prepared to work at $100 a day. He also invited Mr. Butler and his client to visit and look over the stock. The Texas man's particular interest was in horses raised and trained at a higher elevation; it gave them better wind for competition.

After the customers left, Hank asked Wilma to investigate the cost of installing an inside heated arena and how long it would take to get it in place and usable. Hank also told her to cut a check for $2,500 for Margie and another check for $7,500 for Sue, their wages for training the two horses. Later he'd have Wilma deposit a matching amount in the special investment account for each of the girls as a bonus.

CHAPTER 21

At the end of the day when Hank finally went into his master bedroom, he found Bess curled up on the bedspread asleep. He didn't remember her never being part of the ranch and it seemed to him she belonged there. A feeling of guilt washed over him, but it passed. Hank knew he needed to put the guilt away or it would ruin any chance at happiness he might share with Bess. He looked out the wide sliding glass window across the balcony and saw her ranch truck parked beside his. He remembered watching her work on the branding grounds as if she had always done the ranch work. He recalled when she climbed onto Jilly during their first ride together and the happiness that ride and evenings together brought. That woman is the best thing that's happened to me since Lori, he thought. I can't let memories and long ago promises spoil this thing we have.

* * *

The shower woke Bess. She undressed and slipped into the shower with Hank. She reached up and pulled his head down to her. After the warm wet kiss, he held her to him. He wasn't about to move and spoil the moment except a certain part of him was awake and it wasn't long before Bess noticed too.

* * *

Hank decided he should start taking the children to church in Lone Horse on Sundays. He thought it was funny the thoughts that passed through the mind after a night of love. It was just too warm and snug in the king sized bed to get up. Bess had one leg over Hank's waist, her breasts pressed against him. His thoughts slipped back to similar times with Lori and the guilt struck him again, not as hard as at first, but hard enough.

Bess stirred, reached for him, but he turned away and pretended sleep. She curled up against him and drifted off. Guilt ran rampant through Hank's memories. He felt he loved the woman beside him but also felt he was being unfaithful to the woman who bore his children. He slowly turned back so not to wake Bess. The sheets and covers slipped off her sleeping form. Hank gazed at her body, full breasts, and nipples in soft arousal, her stomach flat from workouts in Dutton and hard work and riding horses since arriving in Montana. He knew the feel of her breasts, the taste of her, her passion, and her gifts to him. Another stab of guilt caused him to get up and go into the bathroom. Naked he gazed at himself in the mirror, the gray hair on his head and chest. The muscles loosened in his once-flat stomach, a turkey neck beginning to show below his chin and beard now mostly white. Little color remained of his once dark beard with the red highlights. Lori loved to rub her hand through his beard when they were on vacation and he didn't shave. She would tickle his chest and lay her cheek on it to listen to his heart.

He looked into the mirror and sucked in a breath in surprise: Bess stood behind him. She moved forward and hugged him to her, pressing her breasts against his back. He didn't know what to do. He reached for the toothbrush, "Bad breath," was his excuse. Bess continued to hold him until he finished and she shooed him from the bathroom so she could attend to business.

Hank crawled back into bed, his mind awash in the guilt of being unfaithful to Lori. He was torn, what should he do? He and Bess would be leaving for a week-long trail ride after the wedding. Maybe with the ride the guilt would vanish. Bev and Brent's wedding was only a couple of days away. Sabrina and Randy would be coming to the ranch for the ceremony and to welcome Bev to the Springer family.

Bess's extended vacation and leave from her job would expire. She was scheduled to return to Dutton at the end of the week following the trail ride. Bess needed to return to Dutton; besides it was time for Hank to shit or get off the pot. Bess was too much a woman to leave dangling, twisting in the breeze.

Hank heard the shower come on and nearly went into the bathroom to join Bess, but he stayed in bed. His back against the pillows he waited for her, and the guilt bug bit him again. Bess came out of the bathroom a warm, beautiful smile on her face. She stood at the foot of the bed posing for him. When he didn't move she reached down and ripped the covers off and gazed at his erection, a smile spreading over her face. Kneeling down on the bed she scooted forward until she was spread legged over him. She slid herself down on him until he was completely buried in her. Bess leaned forward and put one nipple against his mouth and he began to kiss, moving back and forth between her breasts until each nipple was bright red, sensitive. He moved in her and she groaned. Hank didn't care about anything but the woman in his arms, the guilt pushed aside. He worked himself until he climaxed bringing her to orgasm. Their juices mingled as he held her tight against him and whispered his love for her; she purred in satisfaction and whispered her love for him.

* * *

Randy drove his old green International truck, purchased at a Forest Service surplus auction, through the gate and surprised his dad. Hank expected him later in the evening. Hank called Brent and they stood together and waited for son and brother.

Randy jumped down from the cab and looked around for his sister. "Where's Sabrina? I thought she'd beat me here."

"Bess and Bev are driving to Missoula to pick her up at the airport. You must have passed them on the way in. They only left an hour ago."

"The only vehicle on the road was a new white pickup driving like they owned the road," Randy said, slowly shaking his head.

"Yep, that was them. I'm surprised the Forest Service let you out on your own." Brent punched Randy on the shoulder resulting in a brotherly wrestling match. Charlene and Wilma came out of the house followed by Bea, Cassie and Mary Ann. Hank introduced everyone to his youngest and introduced Randy to his newest. "Margie is exercising a horse on a trail ride with Robby Withrow, Wilma's son."

"Who is the girl working the horse in the small arena?"

"That's my horse trainer along with her father. When she's done, I'll introduce her—she's Wilma's daughter so don't get any ideas."

"How can I not, she's awfully pretty. It seems I'm going to have to spend more time here. Wow, you have any more daughters Mrs. Withrow?"

"Watch it Randy, she's sixteen," Brent said and grabbed his brother's arm. "We need to talk. I guess we can talk later, but you behave. I'd hate to have to beat the crap out of you already."

"You misjudge me oh' brother mine. I am a changed man since high school. Besides I'm only twenty. Yeah, I know, she's under dad's protection too. You don't mind if we are friends, that's okay isn't it?" Randy asked with wide innocent eyes.

"Yeah, I guess so. Okay, come on, I'll introduce you." Brent led Randy toward the smaller of the two arenas. "Don't interrupt her until she finishes with the horse or she'll hate you without knowing you." The older brother laughed and slapped the younger on the back. "Hey, have you got any clothes other than that green Forest Service stuff?"

CHAPTER 22

Friday evening, Hank accompanied his sons and the male members of his extended family to the Lone Horse Cafe for Brent's bachelor party. The women were having a bridal shower for Bev at the same time and shooed the men out.

Randy decided he would throw a bachelor party for Brent on his last day as a single cowboy. Randy teased Brent about having to ride double from now on. As a wedding gift, Brent surprised Bev with a three-year-old mustang gelding barely fifteen hands. The beautiful cream colored palomino had a wonderful outlook toward life, sometimes you could just tell. Bev named the gelding Butterscotch. Hank said the name was too long so she called it BS for short.

After the usual roasting, teasing and toasting Hank ordered enough food for everyone. The owner put out a sign, private party and sent to the grocery store for steaks and chops for everyone. Randy brought a multi-color horse halter and made Brent wear it around his neck for the evening. Between Hank and Brent they knew everyone in the place. A newlywed couple on their way to Missoula, stopped by for a beer and sandwich, found the Private Party sign upside down and entered. They were welcomed to the party and received invitations to the wedding from a sincere and only slightly under the weather groom. With good cheer, the couple accepted Brent's invitation and received directions to the ranch.

Hank enjoyed himself as he watched his sons and friends, old and new, have a good time. Was it only months ago he rode fence for his foster parents? Jim was in a serious conversation with Ben and Josh. Hank let Robby and Mike join the men after the bar owner closed the front doors. The boys were the designated drivers and charged to bring the party goers back to the ranch safely. Sheriff Hal Worthington came in for the festivities; he took off his gun belt and badge, locked them in his patrol car and joined the party. Hank and Brent had already invited Hal, but a second invitation didn't hurt.

The party got loud but still orderly, only the groom became a bit too wobbly and Randy cut him off early in the evening on orders from Bess before the men left the ranch. When the pizza parlor owner heard about the party, he closed early and joined his friends. He brought a stack of pizzas to celebrate Brent's impending marriage. Ben saw the boys eye a bucket of beer and ice. He gave them a look that suggested they look at other things.

When the party finally ended and the men returned to the ranch, they found a special place for Brent ready in the bunkhouse. Randy, the boys, the hired hands and the Marine friends of Brent's, shared the Lazy B and Rolling H bunkhouses and made Brent go to bed.

Hank walked quietly into the house and slipped into his bedroom where he found Bess awake wearing a see-through black negligee. The wispy piece of net didn't hide any of Bess' considerable charms. He gently closed the door and appraised the woman who now stood in front of him. The man drank in the sight of Bess, her long beautiful legs, the swell of her hips and the rise and fall of her breasts as she breathed.

Hank stumbled forward, not from drink but from the sight of the woman he knew he loved. He dropped to his knees and pushed the flimsy material aside.

Bess gasped as Hank pushed his face against her. Her knees failed her and she would have fallen if Hank hadn't held her to him. Bess heard him mumble something, as he looked up into her eye.

"I love you Hank, I never dreamed I could love again. You are a beautiful man inside and out, with a heart greater than the whole outdoors." She gasped again when Hank kissed her.

Hank stood in front of her, his hands at his sides. Bess slipped the western tie over his head and began to unbutton his shirt, slowly. She made each move sinuous. She kissed his chest as she removed his shirt. She slowly folded the shirt and laid it on the clothes tree. Bess knelt down, undid the heavy belt and unzipped his Wrangler jeans. He reached down and pushed the dark filmy cloth from Bess's shoulders baring her breasts. Bess tugged his jeans down to the floor. He stood before her in his boxer shorts. Leaning forward he smelled her hair, inhaled the fresh smell of her perfume and shampoo, breathed in her essence.

Hank put his arms around her to hold her tightly against him. Involuntarily he groaned deep in his chest. She answered with a moan, her arms around his neck. She pulled his mouth to her lips.

The two held each other, bare skin against bare skin, lips to lips. Their love making was slow and sinuous. Hank never wanted the night to end or her to ever leave. His fingertips as light as a wispy breeze explored her body followed by his lips with feather light kisses. Bess gave herself body and soul to the man.

The lovers fell asleep in each other's arms. Twice more during the night they woke and made love, slowly, tenderly. First he spooned against her; then she spooned against him. The feeling of peace and contentment consumed them.

Knocking on the bedroom door woke Bess. She looked at the man sleeping beside her. "One minute," she softly called to the person knocking.

Bess opened the door to find Wilma with a tray of food. Wilma handed the tray to Bess and pulled the door shut, but not before saying. "You need to feed that man, we don't want him fainting during the ceremony. Take your time, it's still five hours away. Bev asked if you were up yet. I told her to come back in two hours." Bess looked down at her bare body. There were red blotches on her breasts and stomach where Hank's beard had scratched last night, or was it this morning? She looked at the tray of food and realized she was hungry. She put a piece of bacon in her mouth and chewed and returned to the bed. She dangled a piece of bacon in front of Hank's nose; he groaned but his eyes opened a crack. He sniffed and his eyes opened as he snapped up the bacon. He took the tray from her, set it on the floor, pulled her to him and made love to her again.

Later Bess sniffed, "God, I need to douche, I smell like bacon."

"Yep, you smell good enough to eat. Come here woman," he commanded.

"Not by the hair of my chinny, chin, chin you big bad wolf." She loved to see Hank his old self. He seemed free of whatever had been bothering him.

"It's not the hair on your chinny, chin, chin but your beard I love." Hank kissed her blonde curls. "Damn if you don't smell like breakfast."

*　*　*

The caterers arrived from Missoula along with a stream of cars and trucks. Robby and Mike directed the guests to the parking area, no one was turned away.

Bess argued she should pay for the wedding so Hank presented her a $200 bill for twenty gallons of maple honey barbeque beans brought by the caterers along with twenty gallons of potato salad and two bottles of wine. Charlene and Wilma baked and decorated the wedding cake plus one ten-inch square cake for each table. Hank felt he got off cheap. Bess was a nervous wreck and drove Charlene and Wilma crazy trying to help but more often getting in the way. Bev, smart lady she was, disappeared with Margie and Sue on their horses until it was time to get ready for the ceremony.

Brent dressed in the bunkhouse, putting on his dress-blue Marine uniform. The Sam Brown belt and his sword were ready to be placed on the dark blue blouse. His ribbons and medals, though not many, did represent honorable service to his country. The blue trousers with the red blood stripe down the sides were a perfect contrast to the dark navy blue blouse with the brand new silver bars of a captain. Brent's boots had also been replaced by the highly polished shoes of his dress uniform.

Bess helped Bev with her makeup while Wilma, Charlene, Margie and Sue fussed around the room and made nuisances of themselves. Sabrina, Margie, Sue and Mary Ann were the exception to the western theme: they wore floral dresses with white pumps on their feet instead of Wranglers and roper boots. Margie and Sue were sweet sixteen, and displayed the beauty of young womanhood. Hank dropped by, saw the girls, and asked Bess if he should get his gun to keep the boys away. The girls blushed prettily, giggled and rushed out of the room. Bev almost fainted when Bess pulled the bust of the wedding gown down and put strawberry rouge on her nipples. Pulling the gown back into place, Bess grinned at her daughter. "I might get a grandchild out of this relationship yet."

The uniform of the day, according to Hank, except for the bridal party and the Marines from Brent's reserve unit, was western clothing. Wranglers and western shirts were the acceptable and recommended dress. More officers in Brent's reserve unit arrived from Missoula in a rental car and stayed in the crowded bunkhouse with the Marines of the ceremony. They too brought their dress blue uniforms and swords to form the sword arch after the I do's. Instead of the usual six to eight officers of the sword arch, there would be sixteen officers.

Bess was going to give the bride away but Bev nixed the idea. Bev felt Hank should have the privilege. Sabrina was the maid-of-honor, Mary Ann the flower girl and Randy the best man. Sue and Margie were bridesmaids and Robby and Mike the groomsmen. Everyone but the bride and groom, and the bride's attendants, and the Marines were dressed in Western attire. Brent and Bev asked Hank and Bess to stand behind them as witnesses and along with Randy and Sabrina sign the marriage license. A Navy chaplin and good friend of both Hank and Brent conducted the ceremony.

The wedding went off without a hitch; Bev received the traditional sword swat by the last Marine in the sword arch as a welcome to the culture of the Marine Corps. A western band played dance music and some rock and roll for the younger crowd. Hank danced with Bev, welcoming her to the family, while Brent danced with Bess. Then the cake cutting and the traditional garter ceremony, and of course the bridal bouquet, which Sue caught and caused Hank a fit of coughing. Ben stoically watched Hank, shook his head and walked away. The garter had hit Randy directly on the nose. Wilma and Charlene ignored the whole thing, but Hank believed in omens.

Retiring to Bev's room to change clothes, the bride gave Brent his wedding gift, a gold plated nose ring for a bull. Brent gave Bev a gold heart engraved with, "My Heart is Now Your Heart." Bev pushed him down on the bed and he tasted strawberry rouge and wore a streak of rouge on his cheek.

Only Bev and Bess, Charlene and Wilma knew what the red on Brent's cheek represented. Dressed in jeans and plaid shirts, the new Mr. and Mrs. Springer joined the party.

Hank noticed the Marines brought Levi's or Wranglers and western shirts and changed clothes from their uniforms to western attire. The Marines were the hit of the party as the single girls of Lone Tree and daughters of guests swarmed around the young men.

Bess smiled. She found Hank's blue western style blazer jacket with his ribbons fixed to the left breast above the pocket. She had the jacket dry-cleaned and pressed for the wedding. Bess was amazed at the array of ribbons as she placed them on the jacket. She knew they represented awards earned and places served during his years in the Corps. Ralph wore his own blazer with his rack of ribbons. The two older men were pestered by the young Marines who hung on every word the old warhorses uttered.

Late Saturday afternoon the tired but happy family of the wedding party gathered at the Rolling H ranch house grounds. The men and boys took care of the livestock that needed feeding, while the girls helped Charlene and Wilma with the sleeping Mary Ann and Cassie. Charlene drove her children home and returned to help Wilma with the cleanup. Sue and Margie led those who wanted to ride on a short trail excursion. Some friends of the Sutterlands who were staying at the Lazy B rode horseback or on the hay wagon driven by George Honey on the short new trail to the Lazy B. Last week Hank had established another shorter trail with the bulldozer between the Lazy B and the Rolling H. The girls took care of their horses then helped the others to brush, feed and turn out the horses. A late supper snack was served and everyone turned in early. Sunlight still filtered through the trees where the sounds of snoring rode the light breeze.

Charlene used the leftovers for Sunday's supper buffet. The ranch was ready to resume work and the upcoming ride before Bess had to return to Dutton and Brent and Bev left for Hawaii on their honeymoon. The trail ride was scheduled for Monday morning and everyone turned in early Sunday evening to be fresh and ready for the start of the ride.

The Marines stayed until Sunday afternoon when most left for the long drive home, some all the way to the Washington coast. Jim and Maya played host to the Marines putting them on horses for a trail ride Sunday morning, led by Robby and Mike. When the Marines said goodbye, Hank and Brent noticed more than one Marine limped from sore muscles.

CHAPTER 23

On Monday, the day of the trail ride, Sabrina went into town to get her leave extended. Randy rode along to keep her company and catch up with her life before she left for Camp Pendleton. Before leaving Camp Pendleton, Sabrina received a warning order she would be deployed with the 1st Marine Division as part of the 1st Marine Expeditionary Force overseas to Camp Leatherneck in Afghanistan next month. When they returned to the ranch and set out to catch up with the group. Josh waited and joined them for the ride to the camp.

* * *

Bess admitted to herself the ceremony and celebration was probably the best wedding she'd ever attended. But now it was time for her to get on with her life until the man she loved made up his mind.

The extended family of the Rolling H Ranch assembled at the small arena. The horses and pack animals were tied to hitching rails. The freight wagon and chuck wagon waited next to the ranch house for ease of loading. Jim brought his and Maya's horses and tack up to the Rolling H.

Robby and Mike planned on taking turns driving the two-mule team. Their horses were tied to the back of the freight wagon with their saddles and tack in the wagon. Casper was tied to the back of the chuck wagon. Hank surprised Mary Ann when he told her she could ride Casper along the easier parts of the trial. She had started riding Casper bareback using only a halter to control him. Hank insisted Mary Ann bring along her saddle and a hackamore.

The first day, Mary Ann rode with Cassie in the chuck wagon. Jesse, who now wanted to be called Jess, sat on the ranch horse he'd bought from Hank, a nice horse Ben found on one of his frequent trips to stock sales. All the children were excellent riders including Cassie. Mary Ann promised Cassie she could ride Casper if Hank said it was okay or they could ride double.

Bess looked out the kitchen window and watched Hank walk across the yard toward the wagons. She didn't know what Hank was thinking. He seemed to have slipped into a dark mood and was distant this morning. The last few days had been a joy. Bess realized she had fallen hopelessly in love. The wedding night, Hank professed his love for her without any reservation, but today the old feeling seemed to have overtaken him again. Hank was still kind and thoughtful with her and the children. But his preoccupation pulled them apart again and he avoided her. Bess hoped the trail ride would bring everything between them out into the open. She knew he loved her. After last night she thought everything was settled, but now she was not so sure.

The wagons loaded, horses saddled and watered, Hank looked around at all the horses and people. Looks like those old movies with wagon trains or a gypsy caravan. He shook his head and walked over to help Bess mount Jilly. Brent held Bev's hand as they sat in their saddles. Mary Ann and Cassie sat on the tailgate talking and feeding Casper mini-cut carrots.

* * *

Sue led the way through the gate onto the trail up the mountain. Hank called the BLM and received a permit for the horses and wagons to use the campgrounds along the trail. Margie left with Jess an hour earlier and would meet them at the first rest stop.

Still early afternoon, the group arrived at the first campsite, and Sue called a halt and pointed to the spaces for the chuck and freight wagons. Charlene moved the chuck wagon to the designated spot, climbed down, stretched and began to unhitch the horses after placing blocks in front of and behind the wagon wheels. Cassie and Mary Ann were napping on an old bedspread and a sleeping bag in the space behind the wagon seat.

Sue watched as Mike brought the freight wagon to its designated place. Once the brake was set, Mike climbed down and began to unhitch the animals after blocking the wagon wheels. Robby helped Charlene and then joined Mike. The two boys worked well together. Mike ground drove the team to where the tack would be stored overnight. Robby put halters on the mules and led them to a grassy area and hobbled them so they could graze.

The animals were taken care of and hobbled, except Casper, Jake and Loco. Those horses wouldn't stray out of Hank's whistle range. Casper surprised Hank when he wandered over and joined the younger horses. Jake looked up at the white horse then returned to graze; he knew Casper was family.

After dinner and cleanup, Bess walked away by herself. She expected Hank to follow, but he remained by the freight wagon and watched her go. After last night she was confused by the man's actions—or non-actions. During their love making he had professed his love for her but now he was stand-offish, quiet and alone, consumed again by his demons.

Hank watched Bess leave the campsite and felt twice as guilty. Last night he knew what he wanted, now he didn't know if he could let Lori go. His promises and perceived unfaithfulness to Lori ate at him. He didn't want to be alone without Bess. Saturday night was the first time he had shared himself completely since Lori's death and it felt right and good. Hank's intellectual self knew he was unreasonable. Lori was the most unselfish person he had ever known until he met Bess. The one night stands through the lonely years meant nothing, and were only faded memories.

The time he spent with Bess lightened his soul, then the guilt came. His children loved Bess. She was like a mother to his foster children. Bess was the ideal mother-in-law for Brent. Sabrina, from the first moment she met Bess, had been confiding in her. The younger woman sought the opinions she would normally have asked her mother.

Hank watched Bess disappear into the trees and his heart failed him. He put his coffee cup on the tailgate of the chuck wagon and went to check on the horses. Hank's mind was in turmoil. He put Jake's foot down and stood quietly next to the horse. Hank was surprised when he discovered he had finished inspecting all the horse's feet. He looked around confused for a moment and then wandered back to camp. Hank looked for Bess; he knew he had been cold and indifferent. Bess didn't deserve the way he treated her. The thought of somebody else being with Bess brought other feelings and anger rushed to the surface.

Hank sat with his head down, his hat on the seat beside him, when Brent moved the hat and sat down. "Where's Bess?"

"She went for a walk I guess. I saw her go out that way." Hank pointed with his chin.

"Don't you think you should be with her? She might get in some trouble out there. I found a recently shed rattler skin right over there." Brent pointed. "You know the old saying, if there's one there's two and if there's two there's a lot more."

"Yeah, you're right. I'd better go find her." Hank rose, set his hat on his head and walked in the direction Bess disappeared.

Bess stood on a small bluff about two hundred yards from camp as she gazed over the open cattle country, her mind full of thoughts of Hank. She turned to leave and a whirring buzz stopped her. Bess stood still and waited— the buzz stopped. A faint rustling came from right in front of her. She stood quiet, not daring to move. She waited five minutes before she felt safe enough to start back toward the camp.

Hank stood beside a tree and watched Bess after he spotted her hair glowing in the moonlight.

Bess met Hank on the way back. "Hi, fancy meeting you out here," she said lightly.

"Yeah, I just wanted to check on you. Brent found a fresh rattler skin and this is good snake country."

"Yes, I know. I almost stepped on one a couple of minutes ago. I stopped and it moved and left me alone. Kind of like you do Hank." In the faint light, Hank's face was a shadow. "What's going on with you? You've been cold since this morning. For a few days you were great and wonderful, the man I've come to love. Now this morning and today you don't want me around you. You can tell me, I'm a big girl."

"Well, yeah I know and big in all the right places too." Hank tried to lighten things.

"That was crude Hank and insulting the way you said it. If you don't want to talk, then don't. I'm going to bed." She pushed by him.

Crap, what's wrong with me, he thought. I'm going to lose her if I don't get my act together.

Brent came out of the dark to stand beside his father. "Dad, what's wrong with Bess? She just came through the camp crying and went into her tent. Bev is with her but neither one will talk to me. Dad, talk to me; what's going on?"

"It's your mother Brent. I feel guilty being with Bess; I feel like I'm being unfaithful to your mom."

"Aw shit, I thought it was something like that. Listen Dad, Mom died a long time ago. I know you loved her, but you've got to let her go. Every time you meet a woman and I think you're going to start a relationship you break it off before it can get under your skin. Bess is different; she's more like Mom than anyone I know."

"I know, I know." Hank interrupted. "That's some of the problem." The older man put his back against a tree and slid down the rough bark to sit on the ground. "It's unfair. Bess is a wonderful person. I want to be everything she wants me to be and give her one hundred percent. I don't know if I have one hundred percent to give."

"Dad, give Bess a chance. Sabrina and Randy really like her." Brent sighed. "You know Dad, Sabrina is more like you than me or Randy. She's smart, you should listen to her. She thinks you and Bess are a match." Brent sighed. "Still your call."

The younger Springer sat down beside his father. "Dad, I hate to keep saying this, but the whole family approves of Bess. Know we're in your corner whatever decision you make."

Hank changed the subject. "I'm glad Sabrina and Randy will be able to make the ride. We can wait for them at the next stop. You still have your cell phone with you?"

"Yeah, but it's with my pack in the tent with Bess and Bev right now. It kind of looks like I'm going to be alone tonight. I'll sleep in the freight wagon, all I need is my bag." Brent put his hand on the older man's shoulder. "Don't worry about it Pop, it will all work out."

Hank stood up and stretched and they started back toward camp. He followed a step behind his son. "Brent, what made you so smart so fast? Wouldn't be that school teacher you married, would it?" He heard his son laugh.

* * *

The sun broke the eastern horizon with the smell of bacon frying. Hank stumbled out of his tent to find Charlene and Bess cooking; Maya set a large thermos pot of coffee on the table and a second pot over the campfire. A half dozen coffee mugs sat on the table. Hank picked one and poured himself a cup. "Good morning everyone, it's going to be a beautiful day."

Bess turned and smiled at Hank. "It is a beautiful day. Would you like eggs and bacon? The bacon is almost done and the eggs will only take a minute."

"That would nice, thanks Bess."

"You're welcome. Take a seat, Charlene will have a plate for you in a minute." Bess excused herself and left, rushing to her tent. A moment later Bev emerged and gave Hank a glaring look. "Good morning Mr. Springer. I hope you slept well. You haven't seen my hubby this morning have you?"

"He was sleeping in the freight wagon." Hank nodded at the wagon just in time to see Brent's head and eyes peek over the wagon's edge.

"Oh thank you," Bev said formally and walked toward the wagon with her arms and hands waving. She stopped and listened then turned and sent another glare at Hank. Bev stayed at the wagon until Brent pulled his boots on and hopped down.

Bev returned to the tent and Brent came over to where Hank sat. "Crap Dad, this is serious. Bess is crying again. You need to do something, right now." Brent took a deep breath. "Bev says Bess wants to go home."

Bess lay on her sleeping bag when Bev crawled into the tent. "I told Brent you wanted to go home. Is it that serious with you and Hank?" Bev sat on her own bag. "Last night you didn't tell me anything. You have to talk to me, Mom please. Brent is my husband and my life and Hank is his father."

"God Bev, I love that old cowboy. He is the nicest man I have ever met and I know he loves me but I think his wife is going to ruin any chance we might have."

"I thought his wife died. Brent told me she was killed." Bev's mouth was open in confusion.

"She died in an accident, nearly fifteen years ago I think. Hank retired from the Marines and brought his family up here to raise the children. He went to work for the Sutterlands. You know Hank's their foster son?" Bess reached for her daughter, to hold her hand. "Hank put all his Marine retirement into investments and made a lot of money, so: this ranch." Bess looked into her daughter's eyes. "Honey, Hank bought this land and built this ranch for Mike, Margie and Mary Ann because I kind of asked him to."

"Mom, you didn't ask him to buy land and build a ranch for those kids?" Bev asked seriously confused.

"Yes, I saw him with Robby Withrow at the Dutton Jackpot. I knew then he was the answer to the three children at the orphanage. I couldn't let them be separated and Brent let it slip he had a lot of investments himself. I thought if he had that much Hank would be pretty well heeled too, and it turned out he was." Bess looked down at her hands as tears rolled unnoticed down her cheeks. Bev reached out and pushed a lock of Bess hair away from her face. Bess smiled at her daughter and sighed. "When Hank was granted the court's permission to foster the children, I didn't think the judge would make me the court's advisor or observer. When we came up here together, I saw this land and knew the children would have a great life here."

Bess dropped back onto the sleeping bag and rubbed her eyes with the palms of her hands. "I never thought I'd fall in love with him. When we went back to Dutton to meet the judge and sign the foster papers we slept together. God Bev, you have no idea what that old man can do to a woman."

"Oh I think I do—I'm married to his son you know." Bev grinned and the smile reached her eyes and gave them an extra shine.

"Anyway, we made love and I fell in love: not just the physical stuff, it was great, but the man is great too. I know we can have a good life together but he won't let go of his wife. I can't compete with a saint and a bedroom devil. Like the song says, an angel during the day and a devil at night in the bedroom, that I can do, but I'm not a saint."

Bess rolled over amid fresh tears. Silent sobs racked her body in convulsions; a sob escaped. Bev left the tent looking for Brent.

Hank still sat at the table and looked miserable. When Bev came out of the tent and went looking for Brent, Hank got up and reluctantly walked slowly toward the tent Bev and Bess shared. He could hear faint crying coming from the interior and almost left, but his integrity made him bend down and crawl into the tent and lay next to Bess. He took her in his arms and she rolled over to face him, her eyes red and face wet, which nearly brought him to tears.

"Bess Honey, please forgive me. I'm really am trying to get over some of the demons left from when Lori died. I'm sorry you're the one paying the toll. I know in my heart I love you, but I come with baggage. I don't want you to leave, but if you must I respect your decision. Please wait until the children are on the way to Hawaii. Those two love each other almost as much as I love you." Hank pulled her into his arms. "Help me Bess, I'm lost and I need you to find me."

Bess put her arms around Hank. "I love you with all my heart. When Bev and Brent leave for their honeymoon I'm going back to Dutton. Don't try to talk me out of leaving because you probably can. When you have exorcised your heart and let Lori go, there will be room for us. Until then Hank, love of my life, we need to be apart."

"Bess, don't rip my heart out." Hank held her tighter.

She opened her shirt, took his hand and placed it on her breast. "Feel the beating of my heart. It is for you Hank, only you and I swear it will wait for you." Her nipple hardened under the palm of his hand as fresh tears leaked from her eyes.

They stayed together in the tent until they heard the sounds of the camp being broken down and the wagons loaded. Hank kissed her damp face, her eyes, nose and finally her lips. "Wait for me Bess—one day when you look up I'll be there, all of me."

Robby took over as Trail Boss for the second leg of the ride with Brent behind him. Bev just naturally moved into the position beside Brent. Hank rode drag side by side with Bess when the trail allowed. The wagons with Sue and Margie in charge stayed on the road while those on horseback followed Robby onto a trail to take them to a waterfall and pool higher on the mountain. Jim led one of the pack horses with the day's lunch and clothing for those who wanted to swim at the pool. Mary Ann and Cassie rode double on Casper, Maya accompanied them on her own horse. Hank decided the trail was safe enough and trusted the surefooted horse to carry the two girls.

Three hours after leaving the campsite, the riders rode out of the trees and there in front of them was a mountain oasis, the pool and waterfall surrounded by birch and aspen. For the past half hour they had heard the roar of the water falling into the pool; but seeing the waterfall and pool was breathtaking: a deep pool with a shale rock slide, rocks worn smooth by years of running water. Water plants provided the slickness of the slide that ended with a twelve-foot plunge into the crystal clear water of the pool. Robby, Brent and Hank established a picket line for the horses while Bev, Bess and Maya searched for a place they could change clothes with some privacy.

While the ladies changed, Sabrina and Randy rode up to the pool followed by Margie, Sue, and Mike. Wilma and Charlene stayed with Ben, Josh and the wagons at the next campsite. Sabrina had been there many times before with her brothers and father during vacations from school. Sabrina threw her horse's reins to Randy, jumped to the ground and launched herself into her father's arms. They hadn't seen each other since the wedding and he didn't get a chance to spend much time with her.

Sabrina jealously guarded her time with her father, but willingly shared him with Bess. When Sabrina arrived at the ranch the day before the wedding Hank was so busy she didn't want to disturb him, but she watched his interaction with Bess. Hank held her but she could feel her father held something back. She hoped it wasn't Bess. The woman had undoubtedly captured her father's heart.

The rest of the trail ride was uneventful. Margie and Mike each worked as Trail Boss for a day. Hank and Bess interacted normally around their friends. The gulf Hank had created with his demons lingered, like a shadow cast over him. Bess confirmed she would leave the day following the newlyweds' departure for Hawaii. Sabrina and Randy both talked to her and asked her to give their father the time to exorcise the ghost of their mother.

Sabrina and Randy would hang around the ranch for another two days before they returned to their jobs, Sabrina to the Navy hospital at Camp Pendleton and Randy to the Forest Service where he cruised the Kaniksu National Forest in Washington and Idaho. Charlene left to spend a day at home with her children and Josh. Wilma took over the chores of taking care of the ranch house. Ben and the boys repaired some small items on the wagons. They moved the wagons to the barn and lifted them into their storage place among the rafters out of the way.

CHAPTER 24

Bess packed as soon as they put the horses and wagons away and Bev and Brent departed for the airport. Bess spent the evening after she packed sitting in the center of the large bed thinking of Hank. When she wasn't thinking about Hank her mind was occupied with plans for packing what remained of Bev's things for shipment to Montana. Now all she had to do was tell Hank goodbye. Wilma decided to accompany Charlene when she drove Bess to Missoula to catch the 2:00 p.m. flight. The three women sat at the kitchen table and talked quietly. If Hank didn't show within the hour Bess would leave without saying goodbye.

Time slipped away and Bess was about to climb into the SUV when Hank came out of the bunkhouse. He looked exhausted from lack of sleep. "Bess, you leaving without saying goodbye?"

"I seem to remember another time when those words were used. I think it was you leaving then," Bess retorted.

"Yeah, well I am sorry about that. Bess, I don't like us parting like this." Hank quickly took her in his arms. She was stiff at first, but as he held her, her body betrayed her and she melted into his arms. "God, Bess I do love you more than you can possibly know. But I have issues to resolve—please wait for me, please," Hank pleaded, his eyes reflecting his pain.

"Of course I'll wait for you Hank, but don't take too long." Bess put her arms around his neck to kiss him long and hard. Without another word she broke out of his arms and climbed into the SUV.

Hank couldn't bear to watch Bess leave. He turned his head to hide the tears pooled in his eyes. He looked up in time to see the SUV pass through the gate as it carried Bess away from him. It's my own damn fault he thought, God help me find the answers. Hank went into the house, into the bedroom to find a note in Bess's neat handwriting.

He held the unopened envelop; he dreaded what the note might say. Finally Hank sat on the bed and carefully opened the envelop to read.

Hank, I love you more than mere words can say, but until you are ready I cannot be with you. The past few days were very hard. Being near you and not hearing the words of love I know you can say was torture for me. When you have confronted and found answers to your issues I'll be waiting.

Love Bess.

Hank carefully refolded the note and put it back in its envelope. He sat on the bed; her perfume lingered on the air.

* * *

Hank waited until the day after Sabrina and Randy left before going to Dutton. He returned a call from Judge Hoskin and made an appointment to see him. Hank drove to Missoula, caught a flight to Spokane and on to Dutton. He scheduled his return flight for the same night back to Spokane, an overnight at the hotel at the Spokane airport and out on the first flight in the morning to Missoula.

Judge Hoskin wanted a report from Hank personally without any influence from Bess. Hank left the Rolling H without telling anyone, including Bess, he would be in Dutton. The meeting with the judge was a private lunch where the two men discussed the children and what their wishes were. The judge received letters from Michael, Marjorie and Bess, and now he wanted time alone with Hank.

"Judge, you called this meeting. What's on your mind?" Hank asked when they were seated in a back booth at the local café.

Judge Hoskin leaned back on the black imitation leather seat and studied the man across the table for a full minute before answering. "I received letters from Mrs. Clemons and the children. I also received one from Beverly Clemons which I have to discount because she is or will soon be your daughter-in-law. The children have fully adapted to life in Montana but Mrs. Clemons has some questions." The judge leaned forward, put his elbows on the table and looked Hank directly in the eye. "Her concern is you may run out of money before you get everything finished and the ranch can pay for itself. I guess the question is: would you use the children's insurance money to pay for the ranch?"

"Well Judge, I understand you don't know me very well and your concern for the children is fair. First, I would never take any money that did not belong to me and that insurance money belongs to the kids. Second, I think the kids are enjoying the ranch. They are active members of the extended ranch family. Even Mary Ann has a job. She has one horse she takes care of and for that she gets an allowance of ten dollars a week. Mike and Margie both work on the ranch and are paid for the work they do. When they want to buy something, they buy it. I don't buy their 'I want that' stuff. One half of their wages goes into an investment account; they share in decisions about how the money is invested. Of course, my investment advisor and accountant make recommendations. Right now I think they are ahead earning about five percent per month."

"What about running out of money?" Hoskin pushed.

"I have one million dollars in reserve and another two hundred fifty thousand for operating expenses. I still have more than eighteen million in investments, not liquid assets, but available should I need extra cash or credit. All equipment for the ranch is paid for as are all the buildings. Currently we have twenty-five horses in training. We just sold two for a profit of over ninety thousand for which the horse trainers are each paid twenty percent of the net profit for the horse they trained. Margie has earned $4,200 for the horses she trained and Sue Withrow has earned $15,000 for the horses she trained. Fifty percent of each check went into their special account to be invested. The other fifty percent goes into the bank in a checking account they can use. Michael and Robby Withrow each have two horses they are currently training and should show a profit. I don't know what they will ask for the horses. Ben Withrow, my horse manager, helps them. The ranch gets paid first for the cost of the horse and fifty dollars a month board for the training period. When the horses are sold they get the same deal the girls do."

"Did you say Ben Withrow? I wondered where he and his family moved to. Ben came into town and squared all his debts and then just disappeared up the road."

"Ben and Wilma both work for me. Ben is my horse operations manager and Wilma is my ranch accountant and works at the house and with the children. She shares her time with Charlene Reynolds whose husband Josh is my cattle operation manager. Wilma has been going to an extended learning accounting class and I expect she will become the full time ranch accountant. We expect to show a reasonable profit this year; actually I would have been happy to break even. Next year is our big year. We have a couple of California horses and three Texas horses coming up for training with Ben.

"I guess I should mention Robby and Sue Withrow are attending high school in Lone Horse with Mike and Margie. Two of the kids already own their F150 4 by 4 trucks. Sue has ordered her own truck from the dealer and Robby has a couple of thousand toward the truck he wants. Looks like Robby will have the only Chevy on the ranch. I'm sure he'll take some ribbing about that. Right now, if he needs to drive he uses one of the ranch trucks."

"Sounds like you have a plan. I'm glad to hear it and it takes a load off my mind. The court took a big chance on you Hank and you've not let us down."

"Thanks Judge. Oh about the third thing: Each of the kids working must maintain at least a 'B' average to keep their job. If the grades drop below a 'B' they don't get to work until the grades come up. Education is a must for all of them. That goes for the Andersons, Withrows and Reynoldses--all the kids on the ranch."

"Hank, I do appreciate you coming down here and I have some papers for you to sign." Hoskins slid a large envelop across the table.

Hank opened the envelop to find final papers for the Anderson children to be fostered permanently by Henry (NMI) Springer in the State of Montana. The papers were already signed by the Judge for the Superior Court and the Director of Child Services for the State. "Does this mean we are no longer under the scrutiny of the Court?" Hank asked.

"Yep, you have three kids, they're all yours. If you want to adopt them I would sign the papers today."

"No, I think they need to remember their parents and carry on their own family name. Not that I wouldn't be proud to have them for my own but no, the Anderson children are on temporary loan until they can set out on their own or stay if they want."

"I thought you'd say something like that. I just won a lunch for two bet from the court clerk so I'm buying lunch. Order something good." Judge Hoskin lifted the menu and ran his finger down the steak side ending up with the lunch special. Hank ordered the same.

"Listen Judge, anytime you can get away you are welcome to come up to the Rolling H Ranch and spend all the time you want. We would be happy to have you."

"Thanks Hank, I just might take you up on that offer. Now for the food."

* * *

When Hank returned to the ranch he found it a lonely place even with the Withrows, Reynoldses and his foster children and his friends. The ranch was running itself with Josh and Ben making ranch decisions and Charlene and Wilma keeping the household run efficiently. Brent and Bev were in Hawaii on their honeymoon. The place without Bess felt incomplete. He was tempted to seek solace in a bottle of Jack Daniel's he kept for friends. He removed the bottle from the liquor cabinet and a glass. He set the bottle on the dining room table and stared at it and the glass beside the black labeled bottle. He sat thinking of Bess and Lori. He knew he loved them both. Lori's ghost rode his conscience and the feeling of guilt prevailed but the taste for the liquor didn't. Hank stood, picked up the bottle and put it back in the cabinet. There were many other things for him to be doing rather than feeling sorry for himself.

CHAPTER 25

Sue found Margie sitting on an upside down grain bucket and rubbing oil into her saddle. "What's up?" Sue tossed her coat over a saddle on a wall rack and grabbed another bucket, turned it upside down and sat down opposite of Margie. Sue used an old toothbrush to get dirt out of the leather designs and crevices then picked up an oil rag and began to rub the other side of the saddle.

Sue had started to wear her blonde hair in a French braid a month ago; Margie still wore her light brown hair in a ponytail. She didn't have the patience to sit and braid her hair. Margie had other things to do that were more important. There could be no mistaking these two young women as city folk. The ranch life was firmly ingrained in them and they liked the way it made them feel and the challenges Hank put before them.

"What's on your mind? You've got that look on your face: either Hank bought you a new horse or your dad did." Margie took a farrier hammer and tapped in a nail that had worked loose.

"I need to tell somebody and of course I thought of you being my best friend."

"Oh God, it's a boy." Margie dropped her rag into a plastic bucket. She shifted her position and gave her complete attention to Sue.

"No, it's not a boy, it's Randy."

"Randy! It's about time you noticed him as a person rather than a piece of furniture; he is a member of the family, you know. The two of you have been walking around each other like a pair of zombies since he came home."

"Margie, I think of him just like I do Robby. I never wanted to be with Randy or give him the wrong impression; so I talked to him and he feels the same about me. You know we did dance together at the wedding and all. He was with Dad and Ron Pratt the farrier and we went outside and talked. He was really relieved. We couldn't talk much—he was replacing some shoes and a couple of the horses needed trimmed. By the way, I asked him to trim those Texas horses and if he would look at Einstein. He wanted me to ask you if you wanted any other horse's shoes changed."

Margie grinned at her friend. "Yeah, Jeff Price's horse, Buttercup, needs to be trimmed. His last letter he sent to Hank asked if I could kind of watch and exercise him when I got the chance. He sent a check for two hundred dollars, seventy-five for the board and the rest for exercise and shoes."

Margie hesitated and spoke softer. "You have got to swear you won't tell." She waited until Sue nodded. "I met a boy at school. I haven't told anyone. He's a senior and we even have some classes together. I gave him my class schedule." Margie was normally shy; for her to give her schedule to someone was a commitment. Her face shifted from happiness and joy, to doubt and back as she confided in Sue.

"Is it serious, have you gone out with him?" Sue wanted to know everything.

The girls talked as their hands went about the automatic chore of oiling the saddle and tack. The conversation eventually came around to the relationship between Hank and Bess. Hank had been acting different, distracted. He forgot to come in for lunch and took off with Jake on rides when other things demanded his attention. "Do you think Hank and Bess will get married?" Sue asked the question on everyone's mind.

"I hope so," Margie said and leaned back against the saddle behind her. Sue picked up the oiled saddle and put it on its assigned wall rack. Margie retrieved her oil rag from the bucket, picked up a headstall and began oiling it. "Do you think because Brent and Bev are married and Bess is Brent's mother-in-law it makes a difference? Are they related so they can't get married like a brother or sister?"

"I think since they are not blood related it's okay if they get married. Maybe we should ask Charlene or my mom."

Margie rose from the stool and put the headstall she had absentmindedly oiled on a spare tack peg. She flipped up the stirrup and fender on a ranch saddle and checked it for cracks and if it needed to be oiled. If the leather cracked, it would be her fault. She was the one responsible for the ranch tack. Margie also kept track of the ranch hands' tack so she could tell the owner if the leather needed attention.

"Sue, it is really none of our business, but I feel responsible somehow. Bess got Hank to foster Mike, Mary Ann and me when our parents died. If it wasn't for Bess, the state would have divided us up and we might never have been able to get together again. A lot of people wanted us because of the insurance money. Bess kept those people away, especially from Mary Ann." Margie paused. "Did you know, nobody wanted Mike, only me and Mary Ann?"

"Why?"

"Well, I think they wanted the money first, but I also think there are people who want girls for their own personal reasons." Margie's shoulders slumped. "If it wasn't for Bess and Hank I don't know what would have happened to us."

"Yeah, Hank really saved us too. My dad was down to his last dollar when he won the roping against Hank and Brent. Knowing Hank, I bet he let Dad and Robby win. Hank and Brent are a lot better ropers." Sue lifted up a saddle to check the sheepskin under the saddle tree. She put it back on the rack and sat back down on her bucket. "Hank really saved us too. This job lets Dad hold his head up again. He makes good money, Mom has a job she loves and we're surrounded by the best people in the world." Sue started to cry softly, which was uncharacteristic for her. Sue was the strongest of all the teens, opinionated and loyal. "Hank has helped so many and so has Bess. They belong together."

"Yeah, what are we going to do about it?" Margie felt frustrated. "Ah come on, let's get the Texas critters and exercise them, if Randy and Ron are through with them. Next week we need to have the Texas horses ready for transport to Dallas."

The two girls took down their horses halters and walked out of the tack room toward the paddock where the two geldings waited for the day's lesson. Fifteen minutes of ground work and 45 minutes under saddle to work on neck reining and leg, heel and toe cues.

Charlene watched the two girls walk toward the horse paddock. Those two are more like sisters than most blood sisters. Charlene too was thinking about Hank and Bess when she stepped out onto the porch. It must be nice not to worry about what your heart is doing.

In the morning Hank planned an inspection ride with Josh to check the southern fence where cattle were disappearing, maybe getting out onto the BLM Federal Forest Open Range, a thousand square miles of rough country. Josh returned in late afternoon after the inspection of the fencing along the ranch's southern boundary. Josh and Hank inspected the fence line. They both thought the fence had been deliberately taken down. The wire was not cut, but the wire was off the posts and lay on the ground, both strands. The staples appeared bent, but neither man could see tool marks on either the wire, staples or posts. If this was a prelude to rustlers, they were both smart and cunning.

"Josh, remind me later to call the sheriff and report our suspicions and to check and see if other ranches have experienced the same fence problem."

"You know, Hank. We could bring the highland herd down to lower pasture," Josh suggested.

"Let's not do that until we get more information or if the fence comes down again suspiciously." Hank dismounted and took fence tools from his saddlebag.

Two hours later, the fence was restored, broken wire twisted together in splices and pieced out. The two men mounted and turned toward home. The horses knew the way home and the men let them have their way.

CHAPTER 26

Bess sat at her kitchen table, an untouched cup of coffee cooling in front of her. Images of Hank constantly popped into her thoughts. She found it difficult to keep her mind on her work. Bess would love to have stayed to watch the school being built, but she needed to leave and get away from Hank while she still could. *That cowboy owns my heart, damn it.* The thought kept repeating itself like an old song she couldn't get out of her mind.

Bess's mind replayed the conversation and events of the evening before she left. She sat in the kitchen having a last cup of coffee with Wilma and Charlene. Cassie and Bea came in to say goodbye. Mary Ann refused to say goodbye. She was adamant, Bess couldn't leave. Mary Ann denied Bess's imminent departure and ran to her room, slammed the door and refused to come out.

Charlene rinsed the coffee cups in the sink when Hank came into the kitchen. He went directly to Bess. "So you're really going to leave? Sure you can't stay?"

"No, I think this is for the best," she recalled saying.

"Bess, walk with me for a few minutes, please." Her memory played like a sad movie. Hank's eyes were so downcast it nearly broke her heart. But she needed to leave if they were ever going to be one hundred percent together. She wondered about having to leave so they could be together; it made no sense, but it was true.

Hank led her toward the horse paddocks where Sue and Margie watched the horses roll after cooling and brushing them. "The girls are doing a great job, don't you think?" Hank asked. "If those two keep washing and brushing they're going to rub all the color right off them."

"You're right, I think I see color coming off right now. Hank, you are very lucky to have them, the girls." Bess dreaded what was to come next.

"Bess, you know I love you. I've got to let go of the past before I can get myself to the future. Try to understand. I don't want you to go but I understand. Please, please wait for me, at least give me some time. If I don't make it in time, know I will always love you and thank you every day for helping me and helping these great kids."

"Hank, you are a good man and good father to everyone. Yes, I'll wait for you, but—" Bess left it hanging in the air between them. "If you ever need help with the children, please call me first," Bess hesitated. "I love you too."

She put her arms around his neck and kissed him with a little more passion than she intended. "I've got to go. I have to pack and I need some sleep." Bess put her arm through his and they walked back to the house where Charlene and Wilma waited to say goodnight.

Bess kissed him once more and went into the house. The memory was sweet but painful too.

Bess got up from the table and poured the now-cold coffee down the sink. She sighed and walked down the hallway to her lonely bedroom. Bess cried herself to sleep and dreamed of a life with her cowboy.

CHAPTER 27

Hank's phone woke him from a sound sleep. "Huh, what?"

"Hank it's Jim!" Maya said. "He's had a heart attack. I've called the doctor and ambulance; they're on the way. He wants to see you, can you come?"

"I'm on my way." After Hank's feet hit the floor, he grabbed his pants and a wool shirt. He was on the bed pulling on his socks when Brent knocked on his door. Brent and Bev were staying at the house with Hank since Bess left.

"Maya called me about Jim. Bev and I will be right behind you. Anything you want us to bring?" Brent's face showed the worry for the man he considered his grandfather.

Hank saw Bev behind Brent in a robe. His son was bare footed and wore a pair of Wranglers and a sweatshirt. Hank buttoned his shirt and asked Bev to call Charlene and then meet him at the Lazy B. Wilma could ride with Bev and Brent could go with Hank. Charlene and Josh were longtime friends of Jim having helped one another during times of stress over the years.

When Hank and Brent left the house two minutes later, Bev was on the phone. The two men took Brent's truck and sped toward the Lazy B.

Brent slid the truck to a stop in front of the main house steps. Hank was out of the cab before the truck completely stopped. He bounded up the three steps to the porch, rapped once on the door and entered the house. Hank found Jim and Maya on the living room floor. Maya held Jim's hand, his head in her lap.

Jim weakly turned his head to gaze up at his son. Brent came in through the front door, closed it and dropped to his knees beside his father. Hank recognized the pallor of death, he had seen it many times in the past and knew Jim was in the last hour of this life. He could tell Jim also knew this was his last hour on earth. Hank reached for Jim's free hand.

"Damn it Dad, Jim, don't you leave us. You've still got a lot of work to do around this place and Mom needs your worthless hide to keep her company." It was only in times of stress or intimate family time when Hank called Jim, Dad. He had worked for the Sutterlands as a ranch hand and foreman, and calling Jim, Dad would have been inappropriate.

"Sorry about that son. When the man calls you've got to answer. Maya and I have something we need to tell you right now, not later and don't argue with me."

"Okay Dad, lay it on me. I'm all yours." Hank sat cross legged on the floor. He held Jim's free hand, Maya held the other. Maya smiled at Hank and nodded. Hank watched Jim grow weaker, his life fading.

"Maya and I don't have any children of our own. The only relative is a nephew who ain't worth teats on a bull. Been in and out of jail all his life. Maya will take care of him. I want you to see after my two great loves." Jim weakly turned his head to gaze at his wife for a minute. "Hank, Maya is going to sell you all the land at a hundred dollars an acre and all the buildings for a hundred thousand. The livestock goes with the land."

Hank started to say something, but Jim cut him off. "Don't give me any grief. Hank you have started something here and we want to help you along the way. Me, I guess I'll just have to look down, or up depending." Jim tried to laugh but the effort nearly stopped his weakened heart. "Maya and I already have the papers done, signed and are at the lawyer's office in Missoula; there's a copy in the safe. The Lazy B Ranch and all she holds is yours twenty-four hours after my death." Jim began to cough. Hank could feel Jim's life slipping away. "Maya, the blanket," Jim whispered.

Maya kissed Jim on the lips and pulled the blanket up to cover his face. Hank and Maya held Jim's hands until they began to grow cold. Hank lifted the blanket only enough so he could close Jim's eyes. A tear dropped from Hank's chin onto the blanket leaving a wet spot to be joined by a another.

Hank and Maya still sat beside Jim's body when the ambulance arrived, red lights flashing. The EMTS came through the door to be intercepted by Brent who shook his head. The medics slowed and approached Hank and Maya quietly, respectfully with their emergency kits. They searched for any sign of life and made some notes. The medic who appeared to be in charge, used his radio to call the emergency room at the general hospital in Missoula and report the death. They were instructed to transport Jim's body to the hospital for the official death certificate.

As the EMTS placed Jim's body in the ambulance, the County Sheriff, Hal Worthington arrived. He checked Jim Sutterland's body, gave his condolences to Maya and escorted the ambulance with his light bar flashing red and blue on the first leg of Jim's final journey.

Bev, Josh, Charlene, Ben and Wilma arrived as the sheriff and the ambulance were driving through the gate. Charlene and Wilma went immediately into the house to be with Maya. In the morning, Wilma would drive her to the hospital and help Maya make arrangements for Jim's funeral. Hank said he would notify the American Legion and VFW who would render final honors at Jim's burial and provide the American flag to cover his coffin. Jim was an Army combat veteran.

The day after Jim's death was quiet around the Lazy B and the Rolling H Ranches. Charlene and the girls cared for the younger children while Wilma helped Maya with her sad tasks. Wilma stayed with Maya as long as she wanted the company. The next day Maya moved to the Rolling H and stayed in Hank's guest room until the day of the funeral. The evening hours were spent reliving stories of Jim's life and the building of the Lazy B Ranch in the early days after Jim's return from serving in the Pacific during World War II and Korea. Maya told how Hank came to the Lazy B and about some of his youthful escapades on the way to becoming the man he is.

The day of the funeral, the whole town of Lone Horse turned out to see Jim Sutterland to his final resting place. The funeral was held in the high school gym, the largest room in town. Sabrina in her Navy Officer's uniform and Randy in the pressed green uniform of the Forest Service flew into Missoula and drove a rental car to Lone Horse in time for the funeral and burial. Brent wore his Marine Officer's uniform and presented the flag to Maya. Marines from the Spokane Marine Reserve unit rendered honors and the Army sent a bugler. The Navy, not knowing an Army bugler was already assigned, provided a second bugler. The two musicians did one of the most stirring burial ceremonies. At the end of the preacher's rite, the riflemen fired the salute and taps began. Separated by a half mile from each other they played echo taps. The second bugler played as he heard the first bugler play and produced a sad echo. A KC135 tanker on its way to a refueling mission dropped in for a flyby just as the playing of taps was completed. The large plane passed over the mourners at a thousand feet and then climbed into the sky to disappear into the distance. There wasn't a dry eye among those who attended. Hank had not been aware Jim received the Distinguished Service Cross, the nation's second highest award for valor. The American military honored one of its heroes.

After the graveside service, a reception was held at the Lone Horse Bar and Grill. It was closed except to all Jim Sutterland's friends; it was almost the whole town. Everyone brought something to either eat or drink. Tubs of sodas were available for the children and anyone else who wanted one. Men and some of the women shared a whiskey or a beer while others talked over a glass of wine, cup of coffee or tea. All toasted Jim as a man of good deeds and a giant heart.

Maya put the little treasures she and Jim collected during their life together into storage. The following day she left for Hawaii where her sister lived on the Big Island not far from Hilo.

CHAPTER 28

Two weeks after the funeral Hank called a meeting in the Lazy B's large conference room. Included were all the members of Hank's extended family except the small children. The Lazy B's foreman Sean Riley was there as Hank read the provisions of the will. Sabrina and Randy were absent having returned to their jobs the day after Jim's funeral. The next generation—Mike, Sue, Robby and Margie—at in chairs along the office wall.

Hank sat at the head of the table and looked around at his family. "The two ranches have been melded into one large ranch. This meeting is to lay out our future plans and inform everyone where we are monetarily and the physical layout of the ranch and its assets. Instead of a 10,500 acre ranch with about 500 cows and thirty horses, we are now 100,500 acres, roughly 5,000 head of cattle and 65 horses belonging to the ranch. Maya and Jim set the standard by which we will operate, at least for the first few months. I have deposited a check for $1,000,000 in Maya's account and we have met the conditions of Jim's will. Maya will always be a part of this family and ranch and is welcome at our table whenever she chooses to bless us with her presence.

"We have two cattle wranglers who worked for Jim permanently who have agreed to stay on. Sean Riley will have a change in his responsibilities. He is still the Lazy B foreman but he will work for Josh who is the cattle manager. Josh will make cattle decisions that were made by Jim and me. Ben will pick up all the horse responsibilities for both ranches as the horse manager and trainer. Sean, you'll be expected to help Ben with the horses too. I suppose you have three bosses: me, Josh and Ben. Think you can handle that?" Hank waited until Sean acknowledged his new position before he continued.

"Ben will have at least one additional wrangler who will work for him and Sean. Before you ask," Hank addressed the youngsters sitting along the wall, "your jobs remain the same. Sue and Margie will continue to train horses and take care of the horses left in our care. There are five temporary cowhands who would like to stay on, I'll leave that decision to Ben, Sean and Josh. At least two of the hands should work for and with the girls. Ladies, that means you are the boss with the responsibility and authority for hiring and firing. Suck it up girls, you've been bucking for more control over the training, now you've got it. See Wilma for an operating budget. Ben will see to what is needed, but remember the first thing is education and schooling. Got it? Your grades slip and Ben will fire you." Hank raised his eyebrows as he waited for a response from the girls.

"Yes sir," Margie and Sue said together.

"Okay, Robby and Mike will continue to help with the cattle operation and if time permits train horses. Josh is your go-to guy, after Josh go to Ben, if both are unavailable find Sean. Sean, you will have to hire two more wranglers in addition to the ones still here from the Lazy B. George and Leonard Honey and Shorty Rau will continue to work for Josh and I suspect Josh, Ben and Sean will want to shift the help around some.

"Ben, you and Josh let Sean know what you want in the way of summer hands." Hank paused. "Oh yeah, Robby and Mike, only Sean, Ben, Josh and me will direct you or tell you what to do. Leonard, George and Shorty are advisors only." Hank paused for questions, then, "Any other questions, ask Josh."

The two boys nodded and looked to Josh who was smiling and stood up and spoke. "We've got a lot of calves to sort and rebrand with the cattle from the Lazy B. Counting Lazy B and Rolling H wranglers we may need help from everyone until Sean reaches the number of hands he thinks we need, so be flexible. Our teen helpers have school but the weekends are Ben's and mine unless something else requires their attention. I expect we can get everything done in three weeks." Josh sat down.

Hank nodded. "We will need all the help we can get for the next few weeks. I'm not counting on the girls to help that much with cattle. Sue, what's the take on horses in training?"

Sue stood and Margie rose and stood beside her. "We have three horses under contract for training. One cutter, a ranch and a rope horse. Robby has been helping out with the roper and Dad with the cutter. We can ease up on the time we are spending with them. We have ten trained ranch horses Brent is interested in. With the Lazy B horses added we will have over thirty unassigned horses, either fully trained ranch horses or prospects as sport horses. The rest of the unassigned horses are green broke ranch horses." Margie confirmed Sue's accounting. Sue looked at Ben for concurrence and received a nod and a smile from her dad.

"With school in session, we have less time for training. Margie and I have all our classes in the morning and have been using the wait time for the others to study and do homework. I suggest we finish by noon and come directly home. We can get at least four hours of work before supper and additional study time." Sue looked around the room for understanding and approval. "When possible, Margie and I will take the same classes and can study together."

"Good, thanks girls, I don't know what we would do without you. The horse and cattle operations seem to be in good hands. Now I've got a new wrinkle to add to the mix. Some time ago Brent and I talked about putting together a dude ranch or guest ranch as they are now called. But we'll get to that in a minute." Hank addressed Bev. "How goes the school project?"

Bev stood and looked around the room. "Hank has donated two acres for a school on the main road. I received my teaching credentials from the State School Board and I also asked for and received a license as school administrator. The plan calls for at least one additional teacher. I'll teach grades one through three, and we need a teacher for grades four through six. Grades seven and eight will still have to go to Lone Horse unless we can hire a teacher who is versed in math and science. But we will also need to equip a lab for the life science classes and I don't feel we're at the point we can do that."

"Do you think you can find teachers for four through six, and grades seven and eight?" Hank interrupted.

"I think we can find them, but their salary will have to be above the standard for the state. Probably at least three thousand per teacher higher per year or have some other perk to get good ones."

"Okay, advertise for two teachers; board and room will be provided for the right teachers. You have the point on this." When Bev nodded Hank returned to the previous subject.

"Now Brent and I talked a bit while driving around to different ropings. I think his ideas are sound. Since we now have two ranches, I propose we convert the Lazy B into a guest ranch. We will need horses and a few cattle. That is why Brent is interested in the girls' ranch horses. Currently we have a 200—head herd of Corrientes steers at the Rolling H. Combined with the Lazy B, I think we will have around three hundred Corrientes for training and roping. I hate to put those steers on you Josh, but they're yours. Investigate breeding a larger herd of Corrientes—I think we might be able to sell or rent out rodeo stock. Brent, you have the point on the guest ranch. Talk it up with everyone in this room, not now, but later over a cup of coffee, and be sure to include Margie and Sue. Sean, would you like to work with Brent on this project when your other duties don't get in the way?"

Sean Riley, standing near the door, was surprised Hank addressed him. "Sure Hank, you're the boss. I did work as a wrangler a couple of lean years on the rodeo circuit. Worked for a guest ranch in northeastern Washington for a couple of years. The job was fun and the owners made a lot of extra money using the guests as wranglers at brandings and roundups. Yep, count me in."

"Okay, that's about it. Wilma, our finances?"

Wilma stood, a little nervous. "We have $1.55 million in reserves. We are currently bringing in and outlaying almost identical figures. But we need to increase revenue by twenty percent to be safe. I would like to get with Brent and work up the books for the guest ranch and the futures. We have received inquiries about boarding and training sport horses. That's rodeo ropers and bucking stock. We currently do not have rough stock, but it is a possibility. By using our Corriente cattle either for sale or lease we will increase our revenue by about seven percent. Not much of a cushion but will keep us in the black. Our current monthly payroll and expenses is $57,350. Revenue $62,490."

Hank smiled at Wilma. "Great, it's black at least. I think we will have more coming in with the guest ranch in operation. We'll go into our reserve to make the changes to the Lazy B. The indoor arenas are already contracted and paid for." "Okay, Margie, how is the transportation to school in Lone Horse?"

"Pretty good Hank, Mike and I drive the little kids in Charlene's SUV when she isn't able to. She uses my truck around the ranch. But yeah, transportation is going good, but we'll have to tweak it a bit so Sue and I can get back to the ranch for the afternoons. I believe all the early grades are released at 1:30 p.m. right now. It will be better when Bev's school begins."

"Wait," Hank interrupted. "Wilma didn't you apply for a grant for the school? What's with that?" They all listened as Wilma explained she asked for both a federal and a state educational grants for the new school. When Wilma finished Hank complimented her. "Wilma, would you check on our insurance needs for a guest ranch and the school?" He then turned to Brent.

"Brent, will you draft some plans for the guest ranch operation? Wants, needs. Bev, would you check out the university for teachers who would like to live on a working ranch and teach multiple grades? Take Brent with you— he went to the university in Missoula and I'm sure he knows the campus." Hank concluded. "I think we're done here for the short term. Okay, we need everyone's input and help to meld the two ranches together and get everything paying its own way. Now let's have some lunch."

The next morning, Hank with his two managers and Sean headed up into the hills to start bringing cattle down to the Rolling H. Leonard and Shorty were at the old line shack and had most of the cattle rounded up and ready to head down off the high country to the arena, which would be used as the holding pen where they would be sorted and rebranded with the JH brand registered with the State of Montana. Hank used this roundup and branding as a rehearsal for the Lazy B cattle spread over 100,500 acres of the ranch and roughly 150,000 acres of open range. Hank also picked up the option on 5,000 acres Jim had planned to purchase. Hank decided to sell more than

2,000 cattle over the next few weeks. He expected a payday of $750,000 for the cattle. If the price of beef was up, he could see a substantial increase for the ranch's first large payday.

The girls would not be involved with the roundup; they had enough to keep them busy training horses. Hank decided to have Robby help the girls. He would take over the training and selection of the guest ranch horses with Brent's concurrence. Josh planned to have Mike work the roundup with George Honey and later join the other teens training horses.

CHAPTER 29

An inch of snow fell on the JH Ranch a week before Thanksgiving and melted by mid-afternoon on the lower elevations. The higher hills remained covered in white. The horses were invigorated by the crisp weather and ran about their paddocks, hooves tossing clods of mud into the air. Jake and Loco raced about like young colts, then stopped to graze before they began the process of rolling, racing and eating all over again.

Bess planned to spend the Thanksgiving holiday at the ranch. She wanted to visit with Bev who was pregnant. The whole extended family behaved like expectant parents and wouldn't let Bev do anything that might cause stress. The girls, especially Mary Ann, watched Bev and were ready to help her at a moment's notice. Along with Bev's pregnancy, the family was excited and looked forward to Bess's coming visit.

A lot had happened in the months since Hank first bought the Rolling H Ranch from the Sutterlands. The children were settled into their roles on the ranch and the ranch had reached the breakeven point. Wilma watched the finances closely making sure the ranch stayed in the black. She wrote expense checks like she was spending her own money.

The school building was completed the last week of October and furnished by the combined efforts of all the ranches in the area and with the help of state and federal grants. A grant from a Seattle Foundation allowed Bev to fully equip the school with the science equipment for grades seven and eight. Hank bought a used school bus, and had it completely rebuilt. Charlene collected the students in the morning while Wilma took them home after school.

At home in the evening, children lay on the floor to read and study. Each child's room was equipped with desk, books and computer. The sounds of clicking computer keys joined the soft music piped through the house. Sue and Margie studied together with Robby and Mike, who took many of the same classes. Each child had a student study partner. Third grader Cassie taught first grader Mary Ann to read. All the children competed against each other for the best grades and the one hundred dollar first prize presented by Hank to the top student at the end of each school semester.

A couple of the permanent ranch hands began taking extension courses via computer and entered into the good-natured competition. It wasn't long before the word reached the other families around Hank's ranch and they too became part of the education game. The first mid-term winner was Mary Ann. She received gold stars completely across her report card in all categories. When Hank presented her the check she immediately gave it to Wilma to put into her bank savings account. Teri Nightbrum from the Double G ranch matched Mary Ann's stars and received a check too. Teri followed Mary Ann's example and put the check into her college fund account. Each check was accompanied by a small framed certificate. The best student at the end of the school year would receive, in addition to a $200 check, a silver belt buckle. Winning a second annual award would be silver spurs.

When the schools in Lone Horse heard of the JH Ranch's scholastic competition, the school board approved a similar program for each grade at both the high school and the elementary school. The board invited Hank to present his awards at the same end of term ceremony as the state schools. The Lone Horse Chamber of Commerce got into the act by sponsoring the event, a win-win for the students and a win-win for the town.

Classes at the James Sutterland Elementary School, would commence after the first of the year, the day after Christmas vacation. At least two Saturdays per month the children spent at school so at the end of the school year in May the number of required state school days were met. Bev hired two elementary teachers who volunteered to live on the ranch and teach multi-grades. The state would pay their base salaries and Hank would provide living quarters and a bonus.

Hank visited Missoula and legally combined the Lazy B and Rolling H ranches into a single large ranch under the JH Brand. Josh found an old one-horse sleigh in a neighbor's barn while visiting and delivering foods for a rancher who was in bed with pneumonia. Josh bought the sleigh for the ranch as a gift for the children. He thought it would be good for the guest ranch too. Ben trained a couple of horses to harness for the sleigh.

Hank had a plow installed on two of the F350 trucks and he and one of the available hands plowed the roads the morning after each snowfall. Mike and Robby took turns driving the SUV to the high school.

CHAPTER 30

Margie began to spend her free time with Billy Carter. At school, she ate lunch with him every day and they walked around the halls holding hands. She invited him to the high school's Sadie Hawkins's Day dance as her date. Sue asked Mike to take her to the dance, an annual event for the students at Lone Horse High School since Hank attended classes there. All of the JH Ranch teenagers were juniors except Robby who was a senior. The Carter boy was also a senior and had in the past been in trouble with the sheriff for misdemeanor mischief. Nothing serious, but the sheriff didn't like the boy nor his parents who had been a thorn in the sheriff's side for years. Billy drove an older Chevrolet 2500 pickup painted in a green, brown and black camouflage pattern. A two-rifle rack covered the back window. An old Marlin lever action deer rifle occupied the top rack.

Carter frequently visited the JH Ranch to see Margie. Hank took an immediate dislike to the young man. If an adult male wasn't around, Charlene or Wilma asked Carter to leave. Hank tried to talk to Margie about Carter, but she discounted his advice and said Billy was all right, people didn't understand him.

Margie invited Billy to Thanksgiving dinner with the family. Unknown to Hank, Bess would be coming to spend the holidays. Judge Hoskin insisted the state hire an assistant for Bess.

Everyone but Hank called to invite her for Thanksgiving dinner. Bess almost refused the invitation believing Hank didn't want her there. Then thinking of the rest of the ranch family, Bess decided to fly up and spend five days visiting Bev, Charlene, Wilma and the children.

Charlene met Bess's plane at the Missoula airport. They drove to Lone Horse to meet some of the neighbors at the Lone Horse Bar and Grill. Minors were welcome before seven p.m. Sue, Margie, Robby and Mike met them at the café after school. Mike had to leave to take two of the high school students from neighboring ranches home.

Charlene followed Mike out to his truck. "Don't tell Hank, Bess is here. He doesn't know she'll be here for the holiday."

"Don't worry about that. Hank and Josh are riding the north boundary fence and won't be home till tomorrow afternoon," Mike told Charlene.

"How come nobody told me Hank would be gone. How long has he been away?" Charlene asked surprised.

"They left yesterday morning and planned on being out two nights at the old line shack. They each took two horses and one of the pack mules. Leonard, Barney, George and Shorty are supposed to meet them there. Two of the hands will be coming back down with Hank and Josh. They plan to spend the holiday with some friends in Lone Horse. Hank invited them to have supper with us but Shorty and Leonard want to stay up country." Mike's sense of humor got the best of him. He put on a confused look and said with a sly smile, "I thought you knew everything."

"Don't be a smart aleck. Sometimes Hank just decides to do something and leaves without telling everyone. I knew Josh had a three day trip upcountry planned, but not Hank. When you get home, tell Wilma I picked up Bess. I think she already knows but now I'm not sure."

"Sure, I'll tell her. Anything else?"

"No, Wilma will know what to do. You drive safe—I don't want to have to ground you." Charlene smiled at Robby who had become like another son to her and Josh. "Wait, ask Wilma to drive Bea home if I'm not there in an hour after you get home. Better, if I'm not back, would you mind going up to the cabin after chores until I get home? It would save Wilma some time I'm sure she can use for better things."

"No problem. Now if you would please let go of my truck so I can get these guys home today and deliver your messages."

Charlene laughed and watched Robby as he drove down Main Street toward home. When the truck disappeared, she returned to the café and her now-cold coffee.

* * *

Hank entered the living room after passing through the kitchen and saw Bess on the sofa talking to Wilma, Margie and Sue. His mouth dropped open; she was the last person he expected to see. Speechless, he continued to stare. Bess was wearing a pair of faded Wranglers, soft house boots and a loose-fitting sweater. Her blonde hair was pulled back into a pony tail the way Hank liked.

"Where did you come from? When, what are you doing here?" Flustered, he couldn't stop staring. His head felt like it was filled with sawdust.

"Why Hank, I thought I'd just pop in from Dutton at these ladies' kind invitation for Thanksgiving dinner. You don't mind do you? I could go home if you want." Bess teased, but there was a sharpness in her words.

"No, no it's good to see you Bess. How have you been?"

"Fine, after you stopped calling I sort of thought you had found another lady." Bess looked around the room. "Where are you keeping her?"

Bess couldn't help being amused at the look of panic on Hank's face. "I'm just teasing. I'm so sorry about Jim. He was a good friend to you and the family, to all of us. Margie has been telling me he left you all the land and the ranch buildings. I can see where you've been too busy to call."

"Gosh Bess, I've been meaning to call, I've just been busy, you know?" He stuttered, his mouth and brain not in synch.

"That he has, Bess. The old man has been really busy. We've been collecting a fund to buy him a motorized wheelchair for Christmas. Oops, did I let the cat out of the bag?" Margie looked wide eyed at Wilma and Sue before they began to laugh, all except Hank.

Bess rose and went to the kitchen to get the coffee pot and a cup for Hank. Returning to the living room she set the cup in front of him, filling it half full, plenty of room for cream. He stood near the coffee table across from the sofa. "Don't you want to wash your face and hands before joining us? Take the coffee with you, we can entertain ourselves until you return." Bess smiled at the cowboy's distress as he looked first at Bess, then Wilma and the two teens. "You might consider a shower too." Bess sniffed the air.

Hank rushed to his room, showered and changed into clean clothes, and put on a pair of house boots Bess had given him for his birthday. Conversation stopped when he returned and sat in his favorite rocking chair brought up from the Lazy B bunkhouse.

"It is good to see you Bess. Where are you staying? Your room here is not being used, I mean it's still yours," he said frustrated.

"Wilma has graciously offered the guest room in her house and I've accepted. I wouldn't want to put you out." Bess smiled politely. "I thought I'd help with the Thanksgiving dinner." She glanced at Charlene who came in and sat on the sofa with Wilma and Sue. "Where is dinner, here or one of the other houses?"

Hank interrupted, "It's here naturally. Oh yeah Charlene, Josh drove home as soon as the horses were tended to."

The front door opened and Robby came in. "Hi everybody, what's up?"

"Go wash up and come in and visit," Hank ordered, and received a raised eyebrow from Robby who shrugged and went to the small bathroom next to the kitchen. They listened to the water running not venturing to say anything until Robby returned. Not because Robby needed to be there, but as an excuse for Hank to gather his confused thoughts.

"Well, I've got to get home. Josh probably wants some dinner. I hate to leave it to Bea to feed her father. I'll see you tomorrow Bess." Charlene turned to Hank. "Now you don't keep her up all night talking. She's had a long day after traveling all day yesterday and helping around here today."

Hank looked up at Charlene where she stood in the kitchen doorway before leaving. "Yes ma'am."

"We haven't let him develop too many bad habits since you've been gone. Don't give him any ideas." Charlene pulled her sheepskin coat around her as she left the house.

"I think we need to go too." Wilma said to Bess, "I'll expect you'll be along shortly." Sue had to practically lift Robby out of the chair he'd just sat down on as she tossed his plaid Pendleton coat to him. She smiled and retrieved her own coat. Margie said goodnight and went to her room. They left Hank and Bess alone in the living room.

"Why did you stop calling me?"

"After the last time we talked I thought you didn't want to talk to me anymore."

Bess looked shocked. "Whatever gave you that impression? I never said I didn't want to talk to you."

"Well, you acted like you were too busy to talk and sort of hung up on me." Hank gave her a sheepish smile.

"Hank, I have a *job* to do and I was at the office. We had a murder, and a rape in town and one of the victims was a fifteen-year-old girl. The mother was killed and we needed to make sure the girl was being taken care of at the hospital and protected by the police. I didn't have time to talk and was on my way to the hospital when you called." Bess sighed. "I *always* want to talk to you, but sometimes events beyond my control take precedence."

"I'm sorry, I guess I'm just a little sensitive where you're concerned. Can we put it behind us and begin over?" Hank's eyes pleaded, his forehead wrinkled and he took a deep breath. "God Bess, I've missed you."

"Have you been able to put Lori to rest?" Bess studied him across the coffee table. She picked up her coffee cup, surprised to find it empty. Rising, she asked, "Do you need a refill?"

"Ah yes, please." He handed her his cup and watched as she walked to the kitchen. Her blonde pony tail moved with the sway of her hips. Hank wasn't surprised to find himself aroused.

Returning, Bess noticed Hank's arousal. "I see some part of you missed me." She laughed as Hank blushed. "Or maybe it's for the other woman you're keeping in the closet."

"Damn it Bess, you're the only woman I've been interested in for years. I really don't know if Lori is gone. I still dream about her sometimes. I dream about you too," he hastily added.

"Oh really, what kind of dreams?" Bess enjoyed teasing Hank. She knew he was in love with her but he was also in love with Lori.

"Hank, listen, I want to spend some time with Bev and Brent. It didn't take them long to get pregnant. I don't think Bev will have any trouble with the birth, but you know how mothers are." Bess rose, walked to the coat rack beside the door and put on her sheepskin coat and knit hat. "I'm going to Wilma's and get a good night's sleep. I hope you have a good evening. Night, Hank." She opened the door and walked out without waiting for him to respond.

Standing on the porch, Bess looked out across the ranch yard, at the corrals and pens, the barn and the horses in the paddocks. She heard the door open behind her and an instant later she was in Hank's arms. "I love you damn it." He kissed her hard and then released her and returned to the house. A smile crept across Bess's face. She skipped down the steps and quickly crossed the yard to the Withrow house. Wilma saw her coming, opened the door and recognized the smile on Bess's face. After saying goodnight, Bess went to the guest room, took a shower and climbed into bed.

When Bess woke the next morning, she replayed some of her dream. She was surprised to find her nightgown damp. "God damn you Hank Springer. I can't even talk to you in a dream without getting wet, crap." Bess mumbled to herself on the way to take another shower and get ready to face the day, and Hank.

Charlene, Wilma and Bess cooked the turkey and all the fixings. The younger children played together. Robby and Mike helped them build a snowman from the two inches of wet overnight snowfall. Later, Sue helped Mary Ann groom Casper. Mary Ann had some carrots Charlene gave her and she fed them to her horse as his holiday treat. Margie and Sue worked the horses they were training, cooled them down and brushed them. The owner was due to pick them up after Christmas and they wanted the horses ready. The heated indoor arena was scheduled to be completed the first week of December.

*   *   *

Thanksgiving dinner was wonderful; Charlene was a great cook and directed the kitchen efforts with faultless skill. Except for Margie's guest, everyone had a great time. The men and boys with Margie and Sue organized a touch football game in the snow. Bess called it the First Annual Turkey Bowl.

The only down incident was when Billy Carter knocked Robby down with a block in the back and then stepped on his ankle. Robby had to leave the game and it ended shortly after. Even though Carter apologized, the look in his eyes made it a lie.

When Carter went to his truck to leave, Hank could hardly contain himself; the boy grabbed Margie by the back of her neck and kissed her roughly. He glanced at Hank and smirked. Carter revved his truck's motor, spun his tires and fishtailed though the gate, his tires throwing mud and gravel at the watchers.

Bess saw Hank watch Margie and Carter and pulled him aside when he stepped up onto the porch. "Hank, you've got to let Margie see for herself what that boy is. Personally I see a candidate for the prison system. We don't want to encourage her to follow him. She's smart and she loves this family. I think she'll find herself."

"God, I hope you're right. I don't like that kid and don't trust him any farther than I can toss his truck." Hank entered the house. Can I talk to Margie about Billy Carter without losing her? he wondered.

When Margie came into the house, Hank motioned her to join him in the office. "Margie, I don't suppose you saw what Billy did to Robby?"

"I saw, it was an accident. He wouldn't hurt a fly. He is really a nice boy and I like him a lot. He treats me nice at school and at the dances." Margie was immediately defensive. "I wish everyone would get off his case. First Wilma, then Charlene and now you. I suppose Bess is on his case too." Without giving Hank time to respond, Margie bolted from the room. Hank heard her crying on the way out of the house. He followed far enough to see her with her coat in hand run to her truck. She climbed in and started the engine. She let the truck warm up for a minute, put it in gear and drove out the gate turning in the direction Billy Carter had gone.

Hank saw Robby limp toward his truck, joined by Sue and Mike. They followed Margie's truck toward Lone Horse.

Hank and Bess sat by the large window and waited for the teenagers to return. Three hours later, Bess saw Robby's black truck against the snow field coming back to the ranch. As the truck turned into the yard, Hank saw Mike was driving and Sue was supporting Robby.

Without getting their coats, Hank and Bess rushed out the door and ran toward the truck. Mike got out and went around to help Sue with Robby. Robby's face was bandaged across his nose and his lips were swollen and split open. Robby held his ribs on his right side, unable to stand without Sue's support. The three began to walk toward where Hank and Bess stopped halfway across the yard.

"What happened?" Bess pushed Mike out of the way to take his place supporting Robby. Hank motioned for Mike to join him.

They entered the house, and Hank pointed to the office. Mike followed him into the room. "Well, explain."

"Yes sir. We caught up with Margie just as she got to the Lone Horse Café. Billy Carter was outside the cafe with a couple of his friends. Robby tried to get Margie to leave but she refused saying she was going to stay with Billy. Robby tried to talk to Margie by herself when Carter blindsided him, knocking him down before we could do anything. Billy kicked Robby in the face and side. When I tried to get to them, Billy's friend tried to hit me and I blocked him and spun him to the ground. I think I might have broken his arm, or at least strained it. By the time I got to Robby and Carter, Carter had kicked Robby a couple of times. When he turned on me, his back was to Sue and she kicked him in the balls from behind. I don't want to get that girl mad at me." Mike's smile quickly disappeared. "When Carter fell to the ground, Sue put her foot on his butt and pushed him into the mud along the side of the road."

Mike shifted from one foot to the other. "The sheriff got there pretty quick and since it was all over by then he couldn't do anything without statements, which nobody wanted to give. Robby appeared really hurt so Sue and I took him to the emergency clinic. The doc thought he had a couple of broken ribs. He reset Robby's nose and cleaned his lips and face. He said the ribs will have to heal on their own." Mike stopped, then added, "The sheriff gave Carter a parking ticket and inciting to riot. I got a parking ticket too. Carter started to complain Sue attacked him. The sheriff laughed, told him to sign the ticket and get home before he put him in jail."

"What about Margie?" Hank stood with his eyes closed, a stern expression on his weathered face.

"Sue tried to get her to come with us but she said she wanted to talk to Carter. We couldn't convince her. If Robby hadn't been hurt so much we would have stayed. I tried to get Sue to take him to the clinic but she didn't want to leave me with Carter and his friends. Damn Hank, are women always that stubborn?"

"No, not always, you did the right thing. Where is Margie now?"

"After the clinic, we went to find Margie and she was in Carter's truck. They were arguing. I could tell Carter was pleading with her. I did get her to open her door and I told her we needed to get Robby home, he was hurt pretty bad. That bastard Carter laughed. I think that's when Margie got out of the truck. I saw her get into her truck and start to follow us out of town. I thought she was right behind us until we were almost home." Mike dropped into a chair. "Sue and I are going back to find her. Let us do it, please Hank. She's my sister."

Hank knew this was a crisis point in his relationship with his foster children, his trust in them. "Okay, I want to go with you."

"No Hank, we have to do this."

"Okay, how about taking Bess with you?"

"Yeah, Bess would be a good thing. Let me ask Sue." Mike was out of the room before Hank could respond.

"Sue told me what happened." Bess pulled her Sorrel snow boots over her thick wool socks. She tucked in her jeans and put on her sheepskin coat. She kissed Hank. "I think this is the best way. You are showing confidence in them. I'll go and do what I can." Bess went out the door and got into Mike's truck with Sue. Hank watched the truck disappear down the road toward Lone Horse.

On the way into town, Bess spotted Margie's truck alongside the road, Carter's truck behind it. She told Mike to stop. Margie's truck was empty but Mike spotted footprints and the track of something dragged toward a group of trees beside a stream. Mike ran ahead as he followed the tracks. Sue and Bess followed in the slippery snow. Mike broke out of the trees into a clearing and found Margie on her back in the snow, her jeans pulled down bunched on one leg, her panties torn into rags thrown aside in the snow, her coat spread out under her and her shirt in tatters. Her bra was pushed up around her neck. Tears flooded from her eyes; the bra was so tight against her throat crying out was impossible. Her lip was split open and a large bruise was forming on the left side of her face.

Billy Carter straddled her chest; his knees held her arms down, his pants down around his ankles, his penis standing out in front of him. He had a grip on Margie's hair and pulled her face toward his erection. He had his thumb in the corner of her mouth forcing it open.

Mike took in the scene and reacted. He hit Carter from the side as hard as he could with his whole body. He didn't see Carter's friend or know he was there until the boy landed on Mike's back and started hitting Mike on the side of his head. The boy was hampered by his pants around his ankles. He had been waiting his turn at Margie.

Sue arrived followed by Bess. "You just don't learn." Sue kicked Carter's friend between his legs from the rear as hard as she could. When he rolled off Mike onto his back, Sue put her boot on his hands covering his genitals and ground them into the snowy ground as hard as she could. Bess pulled Sue back but not before Sue got in another good kick. Mike, not hurt by the assault on his back, continued to hit Carter until Bess pulled him back from the semi-conscious would-be rapist.

Bess took off her coat and covered Margie. "Did he penetrate you?"

Margie shook her head slowly. "He wanted me to suck him Bess, then he said he was going to fuck me and throw me in the river. He hit me and ripped off my clothes."

"Here let me see." Bess gently lifted her coat covering Margie and inspected her looking for blood. "Are you a virgin?" she asked trying not to shock Margie but needing answers.

"Yes Bess, I've never been with anybody, I've never had sex." Margie began to slip into shock as her body began uncontrolled shakes.

"Okay, are you hurt anywhere other than what I can see?" Bess asked.

"No, he hit my face a couple of times." Margie started to sag into the snow and Bess supported her. With one hand, Bess took out her cell phone and dialed 911. When the operator answered she told him of the attempted rape and asked the sheriff be dispatched to the scene; she didn't know the location and handed the phone to Sue who gave directions.

"Margie, I want you to stay here, I'll be right back. Sue you guard these two. If they start to get up, kick them in the balls and don't let them dress." Bess returned with a picnic blanket from Mike's truck and another blanket from Margie's truck.

When Bess saw the reflections of the red and blue lights of the sheriff's car she went up to the road to lead him back to the scene. Mike sat next to Margie who held Bess's coat closed with the blanket around her shoulders. Tears rolled down her face, sobs racked her body.

"Sheriff, you'll need the clothes Margie was wearing as evidence. Do you have a large evidence bag?" Bess asked.

"I'll get one, but first let me put these handcuffs on Carter, I've got another set in the car for his friend there." The sheriff got a large plastic bag and put Margie's clothes in it after putting handcuffs on Carter's friend. "I'm sorry Bess, but I've got to take some photographs of the scene." The sheriff read the two boys their rights from a card and asked them if they understood. Not looking up the friend said he understood his rights, but Carter wouldn't say anything. The sheriff used his shoulder mike to record everything and took statements from Mike, Sue and Bess. Before they were allowed to leave, the sheriff took pictures of the scene, the victim and the two boys he arrested. Only then did he let them pull up their pants. He tried to get a statement from Margie; she was in shock and not very coherent, but he got the gist of what happened before, during and after the attempted rape.

Bess had Margie wrapped in the blankets; she wore only her boots. Mike picked his sister up and gently carried her to his truck. "I'm taking her to the clinic, "he told Bess and Sue.

"I'll ride with Mike and Margie. Sue you follow in Margie's truck." The sheriff made sure they were okay and, with the two boys in the back of his cruiser, left for the county lockup. He said he'd meet them at the clinic. They left Carter's truck along the side of the road.

The doctor at the clinic carefully examined Margie, did a rape kit which showed the hymen unbroken. The doctor took pictures of her wounds and recorded her test results and treatment. He recommended she see her family doctor and okayed Margie to go home.

Hank met them at the steps when Mike parked the truck. When he saw the bruising and cut lip Hank turned white with rage. Bess had to stop him from going back after the two want-to-be rapists. Instead Hank tenderly carried Margie into the house and to her room. Mike had a couple of bruises on his head and cheeks from Carter's friend's attack. He waited in the living room for Hank to return. After explaining what happened with Bess's help, Mike went to bed while Bess went to Margie's room and helped her take a warm shower and go to bed. Bess sat in a chair in Margie's room until the girl fell asleep and her breathing calmed.

Bess found Hank at the kitchen table. "I'm going to stay with Margie tonight. You should talk to Sue and Wilma before they go to bed. If you want to go right now, I'll walk over with you."

"Thanks, I think that's a good idea." Hank rose from his chair, took Bess by the arm and walked with her to the Withrows' house.

They found Sue at the table with Ben and Wilma trying to explain what had happened to Margie. Sue struggled to tell her parents about finding Margie naked and about to be raped. Bess explained what happened from her observations. She got some things from her suitcase and left. She intended to hold Margie and be at her side tonight.

* * *

Hank spent as much time with the teenagers as he could. Bess returned home to Dutton the third day after the incident. Margie, almost her old self, slept through the night without waking. Bess would have stayed longer, but she was needed in Dutton. Judge Hoskin telephoned and talked to her for some time in Hank's office. Hank drove her to Missoula where she used her return ticket to Dutton. On the way back to the ranch, Hank stopped at the sheriff's office.

"Sheriff, you still have those boys locked up?" Hank opened the conversation, no sense beating around the bush.

"No, the judge set bail and both boys are out. The judge also set a trial date in six weeks. The boy's father and mother were at court and the bail was pretty cheap considering. I wouldn't put it past that Carter kid doing something stupid between now and the trial." Hal Worthington was a good man, elected by a landslide in the last election.

"Hal, do you think there is enough evidence to convict them?"

"With Margie's torn clothes and the statements of Ms. Clemons, Mike and Sue, I think any jury will find them guilty."

"I guess that's all I wanted to know. You were at the scene, do you have any doubts about the boys' guilt?" Hank asked.

"None. The clothes are the most damning evidence. The statements are okay, but it is really Margie's and Mike's word against Carter and the other kid. Ms. Clemons didn't see any of the actions. The boy's statements were they were led on by Margie and she removed her clothes. Carter said Margie wanted to perform oral sex and he pushed her away and that's how the marks got on her cheek and lip." The sheriff stood and walked to the window overlooking Lone Horse. "You know how fickle juries are, especially around here. Every family's son is expected to work to support the family. It all depends on how the prosecutor handles the case. He has all the evidence locked up at the courthouse along with the statements and the torn clothes. I'm sorry Hank, I wish I could say it's a done deal, but it isn't. If Ms. Clemons had actually seen the assault then it might be different. There is no medical evidence that can't be explained away and the incident never happened. The DA wasn't too happy about it. I don't see him pushing for any long jail time. The DA wants me to put the clothes in my evidence locker for safe keeping."

"Okay, thanks Hal. I know you've done everything you can. I'm just glad Margie wasn't hurt anymore than she was. I've got to get back, let me know if there's anything I can do." Hank left the sheriff's office and drove back to the ranch.

CHAPTER 31

Brent filed with the State of Montana as a Limited Liability Company in preparation for the establishment of a guest ranch. The Springer Guest Ranch would be an independent enterprise but would share resources with the JH Ranch. Livestock, with the exception of the guest horses, would belong to the JH Ranch but the guest ranch would have access to the lands belonging to the parent company. The Sutterlands, Lazy B ranch buildings would be the base and plans called for twenty guest bungalows and an added second floor to the greatly expanded main house, consisting of single and double rooms on the second floor, a common room and restaurant. The guest ranch would operate year round and the restaurant would be open Thursday through Sunday for guests and customers for an evening out. The restaurant was open to guests for breakfast and lunch every weekday. Brent wanted to pour a covered slab for outdoor dancing and barbeques.

Hank had been dividing his time between the two ranch locations. When completed the first week of December, each indoor arena would have a pair of two—bedroom apartments overlooking the arena. Sean Riley would have one of the arena apartments and the other could be an apartment for the convenience of friends outside of the guest ranch's business. The contractor would use the same blueprints for both arenas, saving Hank a considerable amount of money in time, materials and shipping costs.

The first graduate student and teacher from the university elected to move into the second apartment above the upper ranch arena. Marlene Fields was a newly graduated elementary school teacher. She was from a large family and grew up on a working ranch. She agreed to work at the guest ranch as a wrangler escorting guests during holidays and summer vacations. The seventh and eighth grade teacher, Juanita Garcia, would share the apartment with Marlene. Twenty guest cabins were modular and quickly raised and furnished. The contractor and crew stayed in the bunkhouse. The work progressed at a rapid pace, four weeks from start to finish.

The children were still in school in Lone Horse until the Sutterland Elementary School opened. Christmas vacation began and permanent snow was on the ground until spring. The snow wasn't deep yet, but Hank expected at least a foot by Christmas. The sleigh Josh donated to the ranch was ready for use. Brent and Ben trained two horses to pull the one-horse sleigh.

Brent contracted with a group of California teachers for the holidays. It would be the guest ranch's first paying guests. Twenty teachers planned to spend Christmas at the ranch. Mike and Robby were hired by Brent to drive the sleigh for evening rides. Josh modified one of the old flatbed sled trailers with removable wheels for hay rides without snow.

Some of the guests expressed interest in horseback riding. Using the Internet, Brent had them fill out questionnaires on their experience around horses. He bought 25 new roping and western pleasure saddles for the guest ranch. The teens, with the help of two of the hands, rode and oiled the saddles so they were ready for the guests.

Hank received a letter from Jeff Price, the actor, asking if there was room for him over the holidays since his horses Wind and Buttercup, which he renamed Muddy, were still at the ranch. He volunteered to work as a wrangler for the guests, helping Margie and Sue. Jeff would use Sean's second bedroom. It promised to be an interesting first holiday at the Springer Guest Ranch.

Marlene and Jeff would wrangle for the Christmas guests. Brent gave them two ranch horses each to be considered theirs for the time they were at the ranch and one of the ranch trucks to share. Sean Riley would have one of the ranch hands help with the guests. Sue, Margie, Robby and Mike were additional wranglers when they weren't busy training or exercising contract horses. Hank insisted each family member have two horses with the exception of Charlene and Wilma. They insisted they only had time for one horse. Cassie was given a retired rope horse Ben found and brought home. Bea was assigned one horse and Jess two horses.

Hank made ownership papers for Jilly and put them in Bess's room. Ben went to the Davenport auction and bought good prospects and left for Billings where he made a tentative offer on six good prospects for the guest ranch. Each horse was a mustang and better than green broke. Margie and Sue, with Robby's help, would finish and test the new horses. Mike and Robby learned to drive the sleigh and the hay wagon. Mike supervised three of the temporary ranch hands riding the lower range at Josh's direction.

Brent went to Missoula and hired a cook, Roy Everett, as the guest ranch's chef. Leonard Honey came down from the line shack and hired on the guest ranch as a cook too. It seemed he had been a chuck wagon cook for years and enjoyed the job. After cooking a meal for Hank and Charlene with Brent watching, he was hired. His jobs were the outdoor chuck wagon meal on Thursday evenings, barbeques, and lunches during trail rides. Leonard would also be the breakfast cook every day. Brent hired two of Sue's and Margie's classmates as waitresses for holidays and weekends. When the word reached

Lone Horse and some of the other ranches, requests for special dinner parties and Friday and Saturday dinners nearly overwhelmed the cooks. Brent hired another classmate of the girls as a hostess and a neighbor's developmentally delayed son as dishwasher and busboy. The guest ranch was a success and it hadn't officially opened yet.

Leonard was loving life. His official chef's hat was a white Stetson, his uniform starched and ironed Wrangler jeans and colorful western shirt worn with a half apron tied around his middle. Brent had a large window installed between the kitchen and the dining room where people could watch the kitchen activity. Leonard made fruit cobbler and biscuits in his iron pots outside if the weather permitted; even if it didn't the old cowboy made due.

Mrs. Dolan joined the business by making fruit pies and sour cream pies when Leonard called on her. It wasn't every restaurant where desserts were delivered by the local sheriff. Brent's guest business was gaining attention in Missoula and Spokane. The four teens kept busy testing and training the horses and turning them into suitable mounts for green riders. Wilma dutifully logged and kept papers for each horse's cost, training and suitability for use on the guest ranch. Margie spent hours helping with the records to ease Wilma's work doing both ranches' books. Margie found she had a talent for bookkeeping. Margie's business sense kicked in and she became Wilma's assistant.

Margie maintained all the records for each horse at both the upper and guest ranch. Wilma was still attending accounting classes two nights a week and hoped to complete a bachelor's degree after the spring session. Margie's help became invaluable. She registered for precollege classes on line with the University of Montana and would graduate from high school and complete her first year of college at the same time.

CHAPTER 32

Josh sat in the kitchen nursing a cup of coffee and eating a hot ham sandwich while he waited for Hank. Charlene left for home after she put Hank's dinner in the oven.

Hank stomped the snow off his Sorrel boots on the porch and entered the kitchen. "Hank, we need to talk," Josh said.

"Sure, why are you all so serious. We got hoof and mouth diseases in the herd, what?" Hank got his dinner out of the oven and offered to share with Josh.

"No thanks, Charlene made me a sandwich before she left. Hank, I think we've got rustlers. I've been checking wintering places near the southeast corner close to the main road. There were twenty-eight steers there a week ago and now there are eighteen. The eighteen are right where they are supposed to be and I can't see a reason ten steers wandered off. Also, the missing are the biggest steers of the bunch and ready for market."

Josh got up and poured himself another cup of coffee.

"Rustlers?"

"Yes sir, the fence looks like it was taken down and put back up. Some staples are missing. You know how I like to double staple the wire to the posts. Well, there are only single staples holding the wire now and I repaired that section of fence last month."

"Anybody else missing cattle?"

"I called all our neighbors and we're the only ranch hit. Clem Harrison is going out tomorrow to check on his herds. As far as he knows all his cattle are where they're supposed to be."

"Okay, we'll get Ben and Sean and head out tomorrow. Can we drive to where the fence has been tampered with?"

"Yeah, I know I can find it from the road." Josh stood and rinsed his coffee cup in the sink before setting it on the drain board.

"Josh, why don't you come in with Charlene tomorrow and we'll go look at this fence. You have a rifle?"

"Yes sir, an old Model 94, 25-35 I inherited from my dad when he passed."

"Bring it. I don't want anyone out by themselves until we find out about this and I want everyone armed. There are some saddle rifle scabbards in the tack room at the lower ranch. We'll stop by there and pick up some and bring them back here. There's enough for you, Ben and a couple of extra. I'll talk to

Ben in the morning. I don't want the kids out alone. That goes for the teens too. If they go out of the immediate area there's one of our men with them. If Robby and Mike are together they can go out but I want them armed too. Robby's eighteen and Mike almost seventeen. They're old enough to be responsible and not shoot except in self-defense."

"Okay, anything else?" Josh was anxious to get home.

"No, get some sleep and kiss that wife of your—she's the greatest cook I've ever had the privilege of enjoying her cooking. Leonard's not bad though. Remind me to give her a raise. Hell, Wilma too, those women work harder than all of us. Now go home. I don't want to see you or Charlene before eight." Hank called Sean and Ben on his cell and told them the plans for the morning.

Hank didn't sleep well and was in the kitchen making coffee when Charlene walked in at 6:00 a.m. "I thought I told Josh I didn't want to see either of you before eight?"

Charlene ignored him and went about fixing breakfast: Four eggs whipped into an omelet with chopped ham, onions, diced celery and tomatoes, cheddar cheese and a couple of splashes of hot sauce.

"Josh told me about the missing cattle. He sat up half the night cleaning that old Winchester his dad left him. After nearly tearing the house apart he finally found a box of shells and then came to bed. What's going on Hank? Do we really have rustlers?" Charlene sat down across from Hank. "After what happened to Margie I don't feel safe around here anymore. I know it's not your fault. You do everything possible to keep us all safe." Charlene's eyes watered; she grabbed a dish towel from the oven handle and dabbed at her eyes. Hank stood up and she went around the table and put her arms around Hank's neck for a moment, then went to wake Mike and Margie.

Hank was finished eating when Josh entered the kitchen carrying his rifle. He leaned the Winchester against the wall by the door and touched Charlene on the arm. She turned and gave him a brief peck on the cheek. Hank mumbled, "I promise to do the best I can to protect everyone here. That includes you, Josh and the children." Hank put his hand out to Josh. After his friend shook his hand, Hank left the man to have breakfast with his wife. He went into his office, opened the gun safe and removed his .45 Caliber Long Colt Model 94 Winchester and strapped on his Colt pistol of the same caliber. Hank took his heavy sheepskin coat from the peg by the door and left the house.

Hank and Ben were waiting beside the truck when Josh came out of the house. "We need to wait for Sean—have you seen him this morning?" Hank asked Josh.

"Yeah, I saw him around six o'clock, said he talked to you last night and knew the place and would meet us there. He left on horseback and will probably be there before we are. It's only about three miles as the crow flies and more than double the distance by road. Actually he should be there about now." Josh glanced at the dashboard clock.

The men drove down the road throwing the overnight light snowfall up in a roster tail with the truck's passage. There were three rifles on the rack behind the rear seat.

Charlene sat at the kitchen table sipping coffee when Margie walked into the kitchen. "Good morning Charlene, what's on for today?" Margie hadn't returned to school since the attempted rape. She would return today accompanied by Sue, Robby and Mike. One of them would always be at her side. Billy Carter was out of jail on bond and Margie was afraid to go out alone. Sue and Wilma stamped their feet to dislodge snow from their boots before entering the house.

"For a couple of women, you two make enough noise to wake the whole mountain." Charlene tried to tease them, but it didn't work. Their eyes told a different story.

Margie saw Wilma wore a worried expression and concern was also reflected in Sue's eyes. Tears began to leak from Margie's eyes again and the older woman took the girl into her arms and held her.

"I saw Sean leave the ranch on horseback before six this morning. When the men left a little while ago, they looked like they were dressed for war." Wilma asked, "What's going on? Ben wouldn't say anything. He took his rifle with him when he left."

Charlene explained about the rustling of the ranch cattle. She looked at the cell phone charger and saw Ben, Josh's and Hank's cell phones were missing, which made her feel better. Charlene reached over the counter and flipped the switch on the base station and made all the cell phones into walkie-talkie phones. She picked up the base station cell phone and keyed the switch. "Hank, can you hear me?"

Ben's voice came from the base station speaker. "Yes Char, we can hear you just fine. Hank's driving so is a little preoccupied. It's kind of slippery out here."

"Listen, we are going to monitor here in the kitchen. You let us know how you're doing every fifteen minutes, you hear me Ben?"

"Yes ma'am. Hank is shaking his head. He said something about fussy women, but I think he likes it. Oops, got to go. We're here."

Josh carried his rifle and followed by the others jumped across the shallow ditch and limped through a two-foot snow drift before getting to the fence.

Josh pointed to where he thought the fence was laid down and put back up. As the men gathered around a fence post, Sean rode out of the trees.

"Gentlemen, I think you need to come see this." Sean turned his horse and retraced his tracks through the woods to a small clearing. The men followed on foot for about a hundred yards. They joined Sean as he dismounted and stood over a mound covered by snow.

Sean squatted beside the mound and carefully brushed the light snow off. Under the snow was a pile of intestines of at least a half dozen steers. He began to pull the frozen hearts from the pile until he had nine hearts lined up in the snow. "I think we've found our missing steers."

Hank pulled his cell phone from his coat pocket. "Charlene, you there?"

"Yes Hank."

"Charlene, call the sheriff and ask him to meet us. We'll wait until he gets here. He'll see the truck beside the road and our tracks."

"Will do." Charlene picked up the land-line phone and dialed the sheriff's office, left a message and then dialed his cell. When Hal Worthington answered, she told him Hank needed him and how to find the men.

Charlene used the cell to tell Hank the sheriff was on the way.

"Sean, you bring a rifle?" Hank asked.

"Yes sir." Sean pointed to the Winchester 30.30 lever action rifle in his saddle scabbard.

"Do you think someone could get a truck into this clearing?" Hank asked him.

"Oh yeah, but they would have to go away from the road before turning back to get on it. I think it went this way." Sean walked through the trees, leaving his horse tied to a tree far enough away from the steer guts so the gelding wouldn't smell the blood and spook.

Sean pointed to a mark of white paint on a tree about nine feet off the ground. "Judging by that I'd say it was a step van or one of those portable butcher vans. Some of them are dually four wheel drive." Sean continued through the trees. He pointed to a scrape on a tree with brown and black paint about fender high on a 4 by 4 truck. There were other paint marks on trees until they came to the fence where they crossed the shallow ditch to the road.

"We know how they got in and butchered the steers. I wouldn't be surprised if we don't find the heads in a different pile somewhere around that clearing."

They stood by the truck discussing how to prevent more rustling when the sheriff pulled up with lights flashing. "Didn't take you long to get here. You must have been at the widow's house having tea and coffee cake." Hank teased his friend.

"Damn Hank, without your business, I think I could retire and settle down with that widow woman." Worthington laughed, joined by the others. The mood lightened and the men returned to the business of the rustled cattle.

"Come on Hal, I need to show you this." Hank led the sheriff into the trees and followed their original path.

The steer heads were found away from the clearing. The men gathered around the sheriff's cruiser. "You know this isn't the only case of rustling we've had in the past few months. It all started last spring around the time school let out for the summer. We thought it must be some school kids, but it's way too professional. Whoever did the butchering was very good. The steers were strung up to trees, the heads removed and the carcass allowed to drain. By the time the last steer was strung up and head removed, the first was ready to butcher. Probably used an arm and hoist run out from the box in back of a step van. We know the van's at least nine feet high, probably a ten footer. It's got a track about the same as a 450 dually. There had to be at least two vehicles, the van and a four wheel drive pickup to break trail."

"Wouldn't they need a chain saw to cut up the steers here?" Ben asked.

"Nope, if they had a special set of batteries, they probably used an electric saw, quiet and quick. I've seen setups like that before, mostly legal. The State Police did catch a man butchering a steer along the side of a highway. Didn't have a sale ticket, but the steer was a traffic hazard and they let him go."

"Did they get his license number or name?" Hank asked.

"Nope, didn't do either. It was a rookie trooper and he just wanted to get off the road and home to his nice warm squeeze." The sheriff grinned.

"Yeah, just like you and the widow, huh Hal?" Josh slapped the sheriff on the back. The two men had known each other since attending grade school together. The widow was one of the girls in their school class too. Her husband was killed in a snowmobile accident two winters before, her children grown and moved away. Hal kept her company and supplied her with fire wood for the winter and helped with her cattle and small dairy herd on his days off.

"Hey, I've got to get back to town, I have a couple of things to check on. I'll get back to you Hank. If I can't get a hold of you, I'll leave a message with Charlene." Hal turned to Ben. "Good to see you again Mr. Withrow, I've heard some good things about you and your family. That girl of yours is really something—beat the shit out of the dumb friend of Billy Carter's." Hal laughed. "Gave Billy a couple of good licks too."

The sheriff climbed into his cruiser, started the motor before putting the camera into the secure box beside his seat.

Ben called Charlene to let her know they were on their way back to the ranch. Sean left for his horseback ride home.

The day after the discovery of the remains of rustled steers, the sheriff called Hank. "I've made some progress. I think I've identified the rustlers but I can't do anything. Let me know if you're missing any more cattle." Hank acknowledged the sheriff's effort, thanked him and hung up.

The feeling of doom invaded Hank's thoughts. He was afraid he wouldn't be able to protect everyone as he had promised. Billy had almost raped one of the girls he felt responsibilty for and frustration was beginning to set in. He looked up at the cupboard above the refrigerator where a bottle of Jack waited. He decided, taking a drink would be weakness. He stood up and walked out of the kitchen to his room. Hank imagined he could still smell Bess's perfume lingering about the room.

Hank lay down on the bed, but immediately got up and left the room. Entering the kitchen, he poured himself a cup of coffee and sat down at the table across from Charlene.

"Tough day," Charlene asked.

"Yeah, I worry about not being able to protect the people I care about. This thing about the girls being shot at has me spooked."

"Everything will work out fine, Hank." Charlene attempted to raise Hank's spirits. She rose and looked down at Hank. "Everything will be, fine. You are not the only man around here, you know." Charlene put the bowl of vegetables into the refrigerator after covering it with a damp towel. "Get some rest."

CHAPTER 33

The sheriff called the ranch and talked to Hank. "What's up Hal?" Hank greeted the sheriff.

"Bad news Hank. You know the evidence, Margie's clothes and the recordings I made at the scene?"

"Yeah, what about them?"

"The sheriff's office was broken into last night and they cleaned out the evidence locker."

"They took everything?" Stunned, Hank dropped onto a kitchen chair.

"Yep, they took all the evidence, some cocaine, about a pound of pot and the tapes. Pretty much cleaned out the locker. Broke the locks with a sledge hammer."

"Shit, we needed all that stuff to get a conviction. You talk to the Carter kid yet?"

"First thing I did. He said he was home watching TV with his dad and a couple of friends. An alibi I can't break if they stick together. I brought up the CSI from Missoula to see if they can identify the perps. The CSI didn't find anything. Gloves and rubber booties were worn. The same type you'd buy at Costco or Wal-Mart. Not a thing to identify who broke in."

"You call the DA?"

"Yeah, he said that pretty much blows the case against Carter. He has no choice but to drop the case if the boy's attorney asks. I'm sorry Hank."

"Is there anything I can do?" Hank felt frustrated and hamstrung.

"No, if you did find something, it would be tainted and inadmissible to the court."

"Listen Hal, I appreciate you letting me know."

"I'm sorry Hank." The sheriff dropped off the line. Hank went looking for Margie. He saw Charlene and asked her to accompany him to talk to the teens.

Charlene followed him toward Margie's room. They found her at her desk studying, her laptop computer open to the onboard encyclopedia. "Mind if we come in? You know where Sue and the boys are?"

"Sure, they're in the tack room, what's up?" Margie closed the computer without logging off.

"Would you mind getting them? Char and I will wait here."

Margie returned with Robby and Sue. Mike would be there in a few minutes. Hank had them sit while they waited for Mike. Mike arrived and sat next to Sue on Margie's bed. Hank brushed his hand through his hair, and told them the news. "The sheriff called, there was a break-in at the sheriff's office and Margie's clothes were taken, in addition to the tape recordings and some drugs. The CSI's from the Missoula crime lab checked the scene and weren't able to find any traces left by the perpetrators."

"Hank, what's that mean?" Margie asked. Her voice broke.

"It means the DA doesn't have the evidence to convict Carter and his buddy of a crime. He might be able to get a conviction of simple assault, a misdemeanor offense, and maximum thirty days in jail. Since he's still seventeen, he'll probably be remanded to Juvenile Court. I'm so sorry Margie, there's nothing the sheriff can do nor the DA without the evidence of your clothing."

Charlene sat on the edge of Margie's chair next to the teen and put her arm around her. Hank drew a deep breath. "It will be all right honey. We can get a restraining order against him and he'll have to stay away from you, and can't talk to you either." Hank looked Margie in the eye.

"Listen, because of the cattle rustling, all the men here are carrying weapons when they leave the ranch proper. Even Robby and Mike have their deer rifles with them. But they can't take them to school, so one of the men will be taking you to school and picking you up each day until we catch the thieves." Hank put his hand on Margie's shoulder and gave a gentle squeeze. He left Charlene with the teens. On the way out, he saw Sue punch the closet door in frustration.

CHAPTER 34

The upper ranch needed at least two more ranch hands and Hank decided to hire them and not wait until the spring roundup. A retired police officer from Spokane heard the JH Ranch was looking to hire ranch hands, called and talked to Charlene. He said he was interested in working for the JH Ranch. His wife had passed away, he was retired and needed a reason to get up in the morning. Hank called him back and hired him sight unseen. Pete Nelson knocked on the ranch house door the next morning after driving from Spokane.

When Hank returned from driving the kids to school, he spotted an unfamiliar pickup parked in front of the house. He entered the kitchen and found a man at the kitchen table chatting with Charlene and Wilma.

"Here he is now. Hank meet Pete Nelson, he said you hired him last night on the phone," Wilma said. The two women left the kitchen to the men.

"I suppose you want references and a little background," Nelson asked.

"Yeah, that would be a good place to start." Hank shook Nelson's hand and motioned to the coffee pot.

Nelson nodded and Hank lifted cups from the cup tree for himself and indicated for Nelson to begin. "I retired from the Spokane Police Department about a year ago, a little less. I, that is my wife and I, planned to see the country in a motor home but she developed an aggressive form of cancer and passed away last month. That pretty much wiped out our savings, but I still own my house and the truck you see out there." Nelson motioned with his thumb over his shoulder toward the Dodge Ram 2500 parked in front of the house. "I was raised on a ranch in southern Idaho. Rode horses most of my life until I joined the Marines and then the force. I did a little rodeo calf and team roping as a hobby until a couple of years ago. I still have my rope horse stabled in Spokane. He's pretty much a trail horse now."

Hank interrupted. "You on the circuit?"

"No sir, it was just a hobby like I said. We would have little jackpots on weekends. Did do a couple of rodeos in Deer Park and Ritzville. Didn't do much, was a heeler and my header missed both times. But it was a kick coming out of the box in front of a few hundred rodeo fans."

"I agree, it is exciting and we can use a good rider. We do a lot of work on horseback here. We have over 100,000 acres and more Federal Range where we graze cattle. Right now we have over 5,000 head of cattle and in the spring we're looking at a few thousand calves. I've got four bulls working four different herds spread out over the ranch. My neighbor to the east is Mrs. Dolan, a widow woman who lets me graze some cattle on her 10,000 acres. Her friend is our county sheriff, Hal Worthington who helps her around the place. For grazing rights we mix her beef cattle with ours and take care of them like they were ours except at market time. She has about 500 head and we have some grazing her land. She also borders BLM land and lets her herd graze there too. I loan her help when she needs it."

Hank went to the refrigerator and brought a pint of cream to the table. He poured some into his coffee and offered Nelson the carton. Nelson put some cream into his coffee and the carton back into the refrigerator. They sat silent for a minute and sipped their coffee. "That's about it, except we have a little problem with rustlers right now. We are taking turns driving our children to school in Lone Horse, so it's twice a day drive of a 120 mile round trip. We do have a grammar school on the ranch where all the younger kids will attend starting the first of the year." Hank laughed. "The next year the student population will more than triple when the older kids transfer to the new school. I even bet some of the kids will want to ride their horses to school." Hank laughed again and Nelson joined him as he pictured a horse hitching post instead of bicycle racks.

"The elementary school in Lone Horse is on an extended Christmas holiday. The high school holiday starts next week. For this coming semester my daughter-in-law who is the principal and two new teachers hired right out of the university will do all the teaching at our local elementary school. Bev hired them to teach grades four through six and seven and eight and hopefully a high school and college prep class. Actually, the teacher for grades four, five and six works here as a part-time wrangler with my foster daughters and sons, when not in the classroom. We are pretty much one large extended family. Do you prefer to work cattle or horses?" Pete indicated cattle, but would work horses if needed. "Because of the rustler problem all our hands are required to be armed while out of the main area and always work in pairs." Hank concluded by asking, "Any problem with that or questions?"

"No sir. I still have a valid weapons permit from Washington which is good in Montana. I have a Winchester 30.30 saddle rifle and a deer rifle, but I don't have a scabbard for the 30-30. I have my own sidearm too."

"Don't worry, we have plenty of scabbards. Do you still have your own saddle and tack?"

"Yes sir, I've got my roping saddle and roping tack."

"That'll do just fine. I'll introduce you to our foreman, Sean Riley. He'll take care of the rest of the introductions. I would guess you'll be working for

Josh Reynolds, the cattle manager. Sean functions as our go-to guy, kind of an answer man. The bunkhouse is around back of the ranch house about fifty yards. There are plenty of spare places. If you work out and are inclined, I will give you the space to build your own cabin. The ranch will pay for the materials. We have our own electric turbine and well."

Hank opened the refrigerator looking for something to snack on. He found his favorite finger food, a plate of fresh cut veggies. He set the plate on the table and indicated Pete to help himself. "You'll occasionally work at the lower ranch with my son Brent. He is putting together a guest ranch. We have over thirty horses that belong to the guest ranch with another twenty prospects, mostly mustangs. You can bring your own horse here and we'll cover his board and feed if you use him to work." Hank sat quiet for a couple of minutes inviting questions, but Pete waited for him to finish. "You will need two more horses; we work them pretty hard and I like to rest them whenever possible. Get with Ben Withrow my horse manager and he'll get you ranch horses or you can get and train your own. Either way is good but you will need the extra horses by spring."

Through the kitchen window, Hank spotted Sean climbing out of his truck by the stable. Hank and Pete left the kitchen and crossed the yard to the stable. They found Sean in his office looking over the list of horses available for guest and ranch use. Margie and Sue mounted a white board on Sean's office wall showing horses in training and prospects for different types of work on the ranch. Boarded horses were now Sean's responsibility, but the girls did most of the training and exercising for them. Two cowboys worked for the girls and exercised horses and filled in for them on occasion. Hank introduced Pete to Sean and left him with the foreman.

Nelson dropped his gear in the bunkhouse, and told Sean he would be back with the rest of his clothes and his horse. He needed a few days to close his affairs in Spokane.

* * *

Hank called a family meeting and discussed the dangers facing the ranch and Margie. Ralph Bentley dropped in to offer his support after hearing about the theft of the evidence at the sheriff's office. Ralph and the men of the ranch shared a couple of drinks from a bottle of whiskey and a beer before calling it a night. Hank didn't usually allow drinking on the ranch because of the children; booze, guns and horses don't mix.

The following morning Hank and Ralph Bentley traveled to Lone Horse for supplies at the Feed and Tack store. Hank was about to start the engine and head for home when Ralph pointed at a newly painted older black pickup with a scrape on the side. It looked as if there was a little bark discoloration mixed into the scrape.

The two men decided to wait and see who the truck belonged to. After an hour, Billy Carter strutted out of the café, climbed into the truck and drove off. "Well, don't that beat all. Isn't that the Carter kid who attacked Margie?" Ralph asked. "Think we should let Hal know?"

Hank pulled his cell phone off the truck charger and dialed the sheriff's office. Hal Worthington answered on the first ring. Hank told him what he and Ralph observed on the side of Billy Carter's newly painted black truck. "Let me get a warrant. I need a deputy and it can't be you. My two full timers are in Missoula testifying in a hit and run case. What is Ralph doing for the next couple of hours or so?"

"You up for doing some sheriff deputy work this afternoon?" Hank asked his friend.

"Yep, lead me to it," Ralph said patting the pistol he carried under his work shirt.

"You know you'd never get that pistol out of there before a half paralyzed centurion shoots you." Hank laughed.

"Hey, I'm quicker than I look. Where we going?"

"I'm dropping you off at the sheriff's office. From there you'll do whatever the sheriff tells you to do. If you need a ride home, call me."

When Hank arrived home that evening, he had a tale to tell. Billy Carter's father was a butcher with a white refrigerator truck with a hoist and generator power. The step van had a scrape high up near the roof with bark discoloration. The sheriff, with Ralph's help, arrested both the father and the son for rustling. The DA decided since this was the second charge against Billy he would charge him as an adult. The father claimed he paid for the sides of beef the sheriff found in the cold room at his meat business. He had a bill of sale positively identified as false. The elder Carter made bail but the judge held Billy without bail stating he was a flight risk. Billy was remanded to the Superior Court in Missoula for trial for sexual assault and livestock theft. The father was charged with grand larceny cattle theft, and released on bail. Billy tried to blame two of his friends for the cattle theft. The two boys, having enough of Billy Carter, turned state's evidence and confessed to the planning of Margie's rape. Billy's friend at the rape scene confessed to conspiracy and was released on bail. Billy remained in jail under a $100,000 bond.

CHAPTER 35

Things returned to normal around the ranch, and Hank received a call from Judge Hoskin in Dutton. After identifying himself, the judge asked a favor. "Hank I've got a problem here and I think you might be able to help me out."

"Sure Judge, what's on your mind?"

"Well, I really hate to ask, but Bess said you were the one with all the answers and the wherewithall to handle the situation." The judge paused before continuing while Hank listened to the static noise on the telephone line. "A few weeks ago we had a rape and murder here in Dutton. A woman, a single mother living with her fifteen-year-old daughter was attacked. The woman was murdered after being raped and sodomized. The girl was raped repeatedly and sodomized too. The girl was left for dead with multiple stab wounds and her throat cut. The girl lost a lot of blood and wasn't expected to live, but she did and is pretty much out of danger. She's been in the hospital undergoing reconstructive surgery. You follow me so far?"

"Yes sir." Hank was sickened by anyone harming a child, boy or girl.

"Okay, the girl is in the hospital and can only communicate using a pencil and paper; she's temporarily unable to speak. The danger being, she can identify her attackers: four men, two younger in their twenties, and two older in their forties, her guess. It's our opinion they're all part of the same family. They left no physical evidence of the crime and used condoms during the rape and wore gloves. The girl was seriously wounded in addition to having her throat cut, but should completely recover from the wounds. An assault on her life was made at the hospital. A Dutton police officer was stabbed and severely beaten while guarding her room." The judge was quiet for a minute. Hank listened to the telephone line noise.

"Luck would have it, the girl was in surgery at the time of the attempt. I currently have three police officers guarding her, a fair share of the Dutton Police Department. We have thirty-four police officers counting the chief. The assaulted officer is in the hospital, not expected to return to duty anytime soon."

"What do you need from me, Judge?" Hank asked.

"Well sir, you've probably figured it out. Bess says you're one smart, well I can't say exactly what she said. You've impressed her, but she seems to have a problem with your decision making." The judge laughed, lightening the mood.

"Come on Judge, spit it out. You and I can talk straight to each other you know. Bess is one good woman, what's her place in all this?"

"Bess is the social worker who will have to place the girl after the hospital. If something were to happen to the girl while in Bess's care I think it would destroy her. She cares too much for the job she has." Hoskin fell silent again. "Hank, I would like to send the girl to your ranch for safe keeping. We can pay fifty dollars a day for 120 days. Hopefully we'll have the criminals behind bars by then and she can return to Dutton."

"Okay. Will you send her up, or do you want me to come down and get her? What's her name? I don't want to have to call her 'girl' while she's with us." Hank chuckled. "I suppose you heard Margie was attacked by a boy at her high school. He turned out to be a cattle rustler too and he's in jail. His father was involved and is out on bail. My bet is the father will skip. Not a good example for the kid growing up. The boy is mean and you know girls kind of like the bad boys. I don't understand it but hey, we try."

"I would like to send the girl to you as soon as the hospital releases her, in the next couple of days. Her name is Gail Stratton, fifteen will be sixteen next month. There is some health and hospital insurance, enough to pay the hospital bills. There is also a $25,000 insurance policy payment available when she is well enough to claim it. The house was rented furnished and the state paid for the woman's cremation."

"Any relatives?" Hank asked.

"We don't know. We questioned the girl and she says her mother was an orphan and ran away from a foster home when she was sixteen. I wouldn't hold out much hope a family will suddenly pop up, a legitimate family not looking for insurance money."

"I'll get back to you." Hank wanted the family involved in the decision about Gail Stratton. "I want to run it past the family before we add another teenager to the mix. Oh God, another teenage girl."

"Hank, thank you from the bottom of my heart. I don't think I could take it if we lost this girl. She's been very brave considering what she's been through. I'll wait to hear from you."

"Great, out here," Hank said and disconnected the call.

Hank sat quietly at the kitchen table where Charlene found him minutes later.

"Charlene, would you please get Wilma and as many of the kids together as you can find. Meet me in the living room in half an hour."

"Sure Hank, is there anything else?"

"If you see Ben, Josh or Sean have them come too. I'll call Brent and Bev."

Hank used his cell phone to call Brent. Bev answered on the first ring. "Bev can you and Brent come up to the ranch for a meeting in about a half hour. It's important and concerns all of us." Hank signed off. "Out here!"

Sue and Margie were the first to arrive followed by Cassie, Mary Ann, Ben, Josh and Sean. They were sitting around the living room talking when Robby and Mike walked in. Wilma was the last to take a seat, except for Brent and Bev who arrived a minute later and brought chairs from the kitchen. Hank cleared his throat and looked around the room.

"I received a telephone call from Judge Hoskin in Dutton a while ago. He has a favor to ask of us and it's a decision we all must make together. If one of you doesn't think it's a good idea we won't do it."

"What is it Hank? You know we all go along with your decisions," Sue said.

"Well, this is not your ordinary favor from a judge. Let me start from the beginning. A mother and daughter were attacked in their home by four men. The mother was raped." Hank stopped. "Wilma will you take Mary Ann and Cassie to her room. I don't want them to hear what I have to say."

"Sure Hank." Wilma took Mary Ann's hand and led her to her room followed by Cassie. Wilma turned on the DVD of Mary Ann and Casper riding around the arena with Margie and Sue on their horses following her. The DVD was Mary Ann's favorite and she never tired of watching it.

When Wilma returned, Hank picked up where he left off. "The mother was raped and sodomized then murdered. The girl was raped and sodomized, stabbed and her throat cut. She survived and can identify the men who killed her mother and assaulted her." Hank noticed the tears form in Margie's eyes. The tears spilled over and ran down her face unheeded to drip off her chin onto her sweatshirt. "Do you want to leave Margie?" Hank asked.

"No, I think I need to stay."

"Okay, the girl's name is Gail Stratton. She and her mother lived alone in a rented house. There are no relatives. Gail's mother was an orphan who ran away from her foster home when she was sixteen. Never married and a single mother. Gail survived the assault but it was a close thing. While she was in surgery, someone attacked the police officer guarding her room, almost killing him. They were looking for Gail because they knew she could identify them. The judge wants to get her away from Dutton and has asked us if we can take care of her until its safe for her to return. Gail is fifteen, will be sixteen next month. Now you know as much as I do. Bess suggested the judge call here. That's it."

Hank looked over his family. "Do we open our home to this girl? It's your decision." Hank rose from his seat and went to the kitchen to get a cup of coffee.

He heard them discussing the girl: what if the men who did the evil things to her came looking for her? Hank waited another ten minutes before he returned to the living room.

"Okay, what do we do?" Hank stood in the middle of the room looking at his family.

"Do we have a choice?" Margie said. "What if it was me? It nearly was me. I say call the judge and get her up here."

The whole family was for bringing Gail Stratton to the ranch as soon as the judge could arrange it.

Hank called Judge Hoskin and gave him the family's decision. Hank left the kitchen and went to his room. He didn't know if he could face the family right now. He was humbled by their decision to take a strange girl into their midst to protect her from harm. Lori would have loved this place and these children and friends. Hank's dead wife had been occupying much of his thoughts the past weeks. He constantly compared her with Bess and what Lori would think of the relationship he had with the woman from Dutton.

*   *   *

Judge Hoskin was chewing the first bite out of his lunch sandwich when his secretary poked her head into his office. "Judge, Bess Clemons is here to see you."

"Send her in, I've been expecting her. See if she would like some coffee or tea please."

Bess knocked lightly and entered the judge's chambers. "You called Judge? The message I got was you wanted to see me this afternoon." Bess sat in the chair the judge indicated in front of his desk.

Hoskin picked up a folder, opened it. "Bess, about the Stratton girl. The doctors are willing to release her tomorrow morning. I want to get her out of town as soon as possible. Whoever committed the crimes against her and killed her mother are still out there. They have shown a willingness to do anything to keep her from identifying them. To protect her I've decided to go with your suggestion and send her to Montana and Hank Springer's ranch for safe keeping, at least for the foreseeable future."

"I think that's a good idea. I assume you have talked to Hank about Gail?"

"Yes of course. I talked to Hank and he returned my call yesterday saying the whole family is behind having Miss Stratton stay with them. What I need you to do is ride with her in the jet to Missoula and deliver her into Hank's care. Can you do that for me?"

"Yes of course. You said in the hospital plane, not commercial?" Bess was surprised. Using the local jet plane was expensive and unusual.

"Yes, I've arranged for the plane to leave Dutton and meet a Montana State Police helicopter at the Missoula airport. It will fly you to Hank's ranch and then return you to Missoula and you can ride with the jet back here. Shouldn't be gone from Dutton more than eight hours." Bess nodded her agreement.

"I understand. I know Hank's ranch is a good place for her to stay and heal. You don't need her to pursue the investigation until she returns to Dutton?"

"No, the police will be sending pictures of suspects for Miss Stratton to look at via overnight mail—almost as good as having her here. I understand Hank knows how to conduct interviews with victims and one of his ranch hands is a retired police officer. I'll rely on their expertise to get what we need from the girl." Judge Hoskin handed Bess the girl's folder, with a copy of her health and personal records. "Give these to Hank. You might ask Bev to help out while you're there. The Missoula sheriff said the helicopter crew is limited to an hour on the ground at the ranch so you won't have much time for introductions and getting Miss Stratton settled. Can you do it?"

"I think so. It doesn't give me much time to talk to Hank. Wilma his accountant and Charlene, his friend who looks after the house and domestic things, I'm sure they all will help. Sue and Margie will help Gail get past the memories of the assault. They are a wonderful group of people. You should feel good about letting Hank foster Mike, Margie and Mary Ann. You would never know they aren't his own children." Bess sighed, a tear started, and she brushed it aside.

"Okay, that's it then. The rescue helicopter will pick you up at the hospital, fly you to the airport and you're on your way. I want to see you when you get back."

"Yes sir." Bess stood, took the judge's offered hand and left her tea untouched on the side table.

*   *   *

The State Police helicopter landed in the yard in front of the ranch house. Bess climbed down and with the help of the crew chief assisted Gail Stratton from the aircraft. Gail was wearing a heavy long coat over her hospital gown. Bess carried Gail's bag until Ben Withrow took it from her and escorted them both to the house and into the kitchen, where Gail was introduced to Wilma and Charlene. Charlene took charge and showed Gail to her bedroom. When

Charlene returned to the kitchen, her first question to Bess was, "What are you going to do about Hank? He's been moping around here ever since you left."

"Charlene, I love him but he has to get over his first wife. I can't compete with a ghost, especially a saint-like ghost." Bess dropped into a kitchen chair and Wilma set a cup of coffee in front of her. "I only have a few minutes. Is Hank here?"

"No, he was called to make some decision about the school house. The first four grades started there this week with Bev and Marlene teaching; the school isn't officially open but Bev has started teaching anyway as part of the Lone Horse school system. About Hank, that man is too busy for his own good. He needs to take a break and live."

"I know." Bess drank her coffee and stood. "The helicopter needs to get back to Missoula. I hope I'll be seeing you again soon."

"You were supposed to be here for Christmas. Bev was expecting you and so were we. You'd better be here before Easter. I think there are some folks coming to the guest ranch over spring break. That would be a good time to come and you'd be closer to Bev's due date."

Over the Christmas holiday, Bess hadn't gone to the ranch. Hank went for a ride and spent Christmas with George at the line shack snowed in. Charlene and the children were able to talk to him on the cell phone, but they missed him too. It was five days before the storm passed and Hank was able to ride Loco through the belly-deep snow back to the ranch.

Bess smiled sadly at her friend and opened the door. Wilma and Charlene followed her as far as the porch. When the helicopter pilot saw Bess walk toward the plane, he started the engine without engaging the rotor. Bess climbed aboard and was helped to strap in by the crew chief. When she was set, the pilot engaged the rotor and lifted the copter into the sky. Bess waved from the window and her two friends waved back. They watched until the helicopter hazard light disappeared against the star-filled sky and the sound faded.

Hank saw the helicopter lift over the trees and disappear into the distance. Judge Hoskin had called him and said the girl was on her way and then came the call from the school. He thought he could make it to the school and back to the ranch before the girl arrived. The judge had neglected to tell him she was being delivered by air from Missoula. Five minutes later, Hank parked his truck and went into the house to be met by Charlene in the kitchen.

"I take it the girl is here?"

"Yes Hank, Bess brought her but had to leave because the helicopter needed to get back to Missoula. She wanted me to say and do this." Charlene came around the table and kissed Hank on the cheek. Charlene turned away and leaned against the kitchen counter.

"Where's the girl?" Hank asked, the sinking feeling in his gut telling him it wasn't the girl but Bess he truly wanted to see.

Charlene turned around. "Wilma is with her right now. Gail was still in her hospital gown. They must have been very anxious to get her away from Dutton. Is she in that much danger Hank?"

"Yeah, I think so. Some people want this poor girl dead. Charlene, doesn't Josh have a shotgun?"

"No, but I think Wilma said Ben has one, why?"

"Have Ben bring it here, put it on top of the refrigerator or someplace high up. I want you to have the means to defend yourselves and the small children while you're here. I'll have one of the men stay around the house for the next few weeks or as long as Miss Stratton is with us. I'll ask Sean to have one of the men pick you up and take you home. I don't want you traveling alone."

Hank left the kitchen to look for Sean Riley or one of the other ranch hands. He found Sean in his office surrounded by paperwork and notes from Wilma and Charlene. Hank also recognized Margie's neat writing on some of the notes and ledgers.

"Sean, would you pass the word to the hands, I want them armed and carrying their weapons wherever they go, including to town."

"Sure Hank, you care to share the reason?" Sean glanced toward where his rifle leaned against the wall beside his desk.

"The girl, Gail, we were talking about is here. The men who assaulted her and killed her mother have not been arrested. Just in case, I want the men armed. When you go to the ranch house be sure to let Charlene or Wilma know you're coming in. Charlene will have Ben's shotgun in the kitchen." Hank left to find Ben and Josh. Hank would tell the girls and boys the new safety rules later. Both Mike and Robby were old enough to be armed. But before they start carrying loaded guns around he wanted to set some Rules of Engagement for them to follow. Sean was in the Army Special Forces during his four year tour in the service and would cover the hands-on part of the ROE.

Dinner in the dining room was a little strained until Wilma escorted Gail Stratton to the table. Gail was wearing a soft faded pair of jeans and a plaid shirt. The swelling and discoloration on her face had faded, but the bandage around her throat underscored the extent of her injuries. Mike and Robby together jumped up from the table and helped her to her chair. The boys returned to their places and blushed when they found everyone watching them. Even through the bruising and bandages, Gail Stratton was an exceptionally beautiful young woman.

"Oh Lord," Hank said before breaking into a grin, "now I've got to watch you two to make sure you don't pester our guest. Wilma, you watch your son, I'll watch mine."

Everyone at the table was silent for perhaps thirty seconds. When everyone started laughing and talking at the same time, the tension broken. Even Gail smiled and there appeared a sparkle in her green eyes.

For the next two days Mike and Robby competed for Gail's attention until Sue finally, having enough of the male attention about the house, told them to stay out unless they were eating or washing up. Mike was a step ahead living under the same roof, but Margie saw to it he didn't take advantage of the situation.

While Gail pored over the picture albums the Dutton police sent by special delivery, the boys sat and stared at her strawberry blonde hair. Hank made a comment there were just too many blondes in his life: Bess, Bev, Wilma, Sue, and now Gail. Gail hearing his comment blushed and ran from the living room to her bedroom embarrassed thinking Hank didn't like her. Wilma saw the distress on the girl's face followed and corrected her impression. She told Gail about Bess and Hank's relationship and how he was torn between the love he lost when his wife died and love gained when Bess came into his life.

Using pencil and paper Gail wrote, "Hank is a wonderful man, I'd marry him if I was older." Wilma laughed, patted the girl on her shoulder. "There's no shortage of women who would marry Hank. He just happens to be in love with Bess and afraid to commit himself."

"Bess, the lady who brought me here?" Gail wrote.

"Yes, we all love her, including Hank, and wish she would stay here more," Wilma answered.

"But she's needed in Dutton too. When I go back there I'll be at the Children's Home where Mrs. Clemons works. I would miss her not being there." Gail scribbled.

"Enough of this, you come out and join the rest of the family. When you're well enough, Hank wants to show you the ranch and no you don't have to ride a horse. He has a very nice pickup truck you can ride in." Wilma helped Gail up from the bed where she sat. "Say, have you ever ridden a horse?"

"I petted a horse at the Dutton Fair this year but it was a small horse." She wrote quickly on the pencil pad held on her thigh. Gail stood and faced the older woman smiling.

"While you're here we'll just have to get you a horse to ride. There are some fine horses. My daughter Sue trains many of the them, Ben and Margie train horses too. The boys have other jobs around here. I just hope they come to their senses soon or those two will be pestering you. They aren't used to pretty girls they aren't related to."

Stopping at her desk, Gail wrote, "I'm not pretty, at least not anymore." She indicated the bandage on her neck and the bandages under her shirt.

"You are a very pretty girl and don't you ever forget that," Wilma said forcefully. "You are not to feel sorry for yourself while you're here. Everyone is equal and you are too."

Wilma followed Gail back into the dining room. No one mentioned anything about when Gail ran from the room. It was over.

CHAPTER 36

Gail continued to improve. Hank took her on a tour of the ranch, at least as much of the ranch as he could drive the 4 by 4 truck safely through the snow. Charlene took her to see the Reynolds cabin in the canyon and the new additions made to the original cabin. The girls each had their own room and Jess his private room too. During good weather, Josh used the bulldozer to make a road all the way to the cabin without having to cross the creek. He built a garage and shop building to keep the ranch truck in. The shop contained a heater so he worked on projects in warm comfort.

Sue and Margie took Gail to the—Lone Horse Café for lunch with Robby and Mike. The girls were followed by the boys in Mike's truck, Winchester rifles on the back window rack ready to defend the girls.

Hank didn't think the men who assaulted Gail and her mother would find out where Gail had been taken, but he was mistaken. On the way home, a bullet hit the windshield of Margie's truck in front of Gail but ricocheted off. Margie hit the gas and raced back to the ranch followed by the confused boys.

Margie's truck raced into the ranch yard. The three girls jumped out of the truck and ran into the house. "Somebody just shot at us!" Sue yelled at Charlene who looked up from the sink where she was peeling potatoes.

"What do you mean somebody shot at you?" Charlene stared wide eyed at the three girls. Gail's head was bobbing up and down not being able to speak above a whisper.

"When we were driving back from town, a bullet hit the windshield, but it bounced off," Sue explained.

Mike and Robby came through the door. "What happened to your windshield, a rock hit it?" Mike asked.

Margie looked disgusted at her brother. "No, somebody shot at us—there was no one in front of us so it wasn't a rock."

Charlene grabbed the walkie-talkie from the base station and called all stations. Hank, Ben, Josh and Sean answered then waited for Charlene's message. "The girls were shot at on their way back from Lone Horse. Mike and Robby didn't see anything and nobody shot at them."

"I'm on the way back to the house. Ben, Josh, Sean, I want to see you ASAP, kitchen. Charlene, keep the kids in the house, that means all of them." Hank dropped the phone onto the truck seat as the truck hit 50 mph on the snow-covered road.

"Okay, you heard the man." Before Charlene could reinforce Hank's orders, Mike was out the door followed by Robby. Five minutes later they were back in the kitchen with their rifles. A minute later Josh arrived with his rifle. Hank was the last to arrive carrying his own Winchester rifle. The kitchen took on the look of an armed camp. Margie went to her room and came back with her own 30-30 deer rifle.

Hank came into the kitchen followed by Wilma. "Charlene, call Bev at the school. Tell her to call the parents and have them pick up the kids. I'll call Brent and he can pick up Bev and Mary Ann. As of right now, nobody goes out without an over-watch. As soon as Brent and Bev get here we'll set up a game plan to protect everyone." Hank pushed the speed dial and brought Brent up to date on the shooting. Finished with Brent, Hank called the sheriff.

"Hal, somebody took a shot at the girls on their way back from Lone Horse." He listened for a minute, "Yeah, sure." Listened again. "We're all in the kitchen, all the men are armed and some of the women, be careful, we'll wait until you get here."

Hank ended his call. "Hal will be here in about an hour. Okay, this is what we are going to do. Ben, you and Robby take over-watch from your house. Josh, you and Charlene need to get home after you pick up the kids at school. Take one of the hands with you or have him meet you at your place. Is it possible for him to stay the night with you and Josh?" Charlene nodded. "Do not come back here until this is over, or you and the kids can stay here, your call."

"I'll take one of the hands with me and pick up the kids and bring them back here. We can use the vacant part of the bunkhouse."

"Great. Josh, is that all right with you about Charlene and the kids?"

After Josh agreed, Hank continued, "Wilma you can stay here or go home. I want Ben and Robby as over-watch of the house. I'll work out something so the other buildings and your home will be guarded." Hank addressed Sean Riley. "Okay Sean, it's you and me. We're going after these guys. Margie, I hate to ask you to do this, but I need you to come with us and show us where the bullet hit your truck. First, Josh call the bunkhouse, I think Curly is there right now, it's his day off."

"Sure Hank, no problem." Josh and Charlene communicated with looks at each other. Josh called the bunkhouse, and when Curly answered, Josh explained what was going on.

They were interrupted by the stamping of a foot. Surprised they all looked at Gail who stood in the doorway glaring at everyone. She held out her writing pad. Charlene took it and read. "I cannot have anyone hurt

because of me. Let me go out there and then they will leave and go home."
Charlene couldn't read the rest of what was written on the pad: tears blinded
her.

Hank took the pad and read the message. Hank reached out and gathered
Gail into his arms and held her tight.

*   *   *

Hank and Sean were about to leave the house when they saw a truck with a
horse trailer come through the gates to park next to the bunkhouse. "That's
probably Pete Nelson. Sean why don't you get him and bring him here." Pete
had experienced some trouble with closing his house and settling his affairs
and had called Hank to make sure it was okay to delay coming to Montana
for a few extra days. Everything taken care of in Spokane, Pete drove to the
ranch pulling his horse trailer with his clothes and personal things in his
truck.

Sean returned to the kitchen with Pete. "You get everything taken care of
in Spokane?" Hank asked, putting his hand out to shake Pete's.

"Yes sir, rented out the house put the furniture and stuff in storage. Got
the horse and I'm ready to get started." Pete noticed all the men were carrying
rifles. "Something happen since I left?"

"Yeah it has. Somebody took a shot at our newest family member, Gail
Stratton, who is staying with us for awhile. I'll fill you in on the circumstances
later, but right now I could use your help and expertise as a Marine and a cop.
You were in First Force Recon during your four year Marine career?"

"Yes sir, a year of training as a scout-sniper and three years in a platoon.
More training and some stuff around, you know. Maybe you ought to fill
me in now." Pete looked around at all the guns. "Things must be happening
pretty quick. The rustlers?"

"No, we caught them and one's in jail the other it seems has jumped bail
and left for parts unknown. Our little problem now is somebody took a shot
at Miss Stratton here. We are about to leave to meet the sheriff. He called and
said he would meet us on the road. The bullet hit the windshield of Margie's
truck and ricocheted off right in front of Gail. Definitely a shot meant to kill
her. I'll fill you in completely later, but right now we need to meet the sheriff.
I would like you to come along—we could use your experience."

"Sure Mr. Springer, let me get my guns and I'll be right back." Nelson
went out the door and ran toward his truck. He left his horse in the trailer.
The horse would be good for another couple of hours before he needed to be
let out and watered.

On the way back to the house, Mike and Robby met him. "Mr. Nelson, we'll take care of your horse and put him in a stable stall with a flake of hay. He'll be okay until morning."

"Thanks boys." Pete continued to run to the house with his holstered pistol and his rifle in hand. He had stuffed two spare ten round capacity pistol magazines in his coat pocket. Pete entered the kitchen, leaned his rifle against the wall with a couple of other rifles and proceeded to put his holster and pistol on his belt. "I'm ready any time you are." He addressed Hank.

Hank noticed the pistol was one of the new 10 mm pistols on a Colt 1911 frame. The rifle was a Winchester .32 Caliber model 94, well taken care of. "Okay, Sean and Pete take Sean's truck. I was going to take Margie, but Mike knows where the shot hit the truck so we'll go in my truck. As soon as Mike gets back from the stable."

Hank was interrupted when Mike came through the door. "Robby is taking care of Mr. Nelson's horse. I almost forgot you might need me to find where the bullet hit Margie's windshield."

"Mike you're with me in my rig, Sean and Pete will follow in Sean's truck. We better go or the sheriff is going to think we forgot him." Hank led his small posse out of the kitchen to the trucks. A minute later the two trucks left the yard through the gate onto the snow-covered road in the direction of Lone Horse.

"Right here Hank. This is real close to where the bullet hit the truck." Mike had his window down and was studying the side of the road. "I remember we just passed the bent down tree beside the road, when the girls' truck swerved then sped up for home."

Hank stopped the truck and waited until Sean pulled up behind him. They stood on the road and looked over the terrain. Pete approached Hank. "I would guess whoever made the shot was using that tree as a range marker, an old sniper trick." Pete asked Mike, "Where did the bullet hit the windshield?"

"Right in front of Gail about head high for her."

"Definitely Gail was his target, judging by the impact of the bullet. So it bounced off: the shooter was some distance away. I'd say over three hundred yards, maybe farther. Did anyone check the hood of Margie's truck? I would venture the bullet was short and bounced off the steel hood before hitting the windshield. What time was it and was the sun still up?" Pete asked Mike.

"Yes sir, but the sun was low on the horizon. I had my sun visor down so I could see the road. The sun was from the left front," Mike explained.

"Okay, the shooter was probably in a position where the sun's reflected light wouldn't interfere with his shot, but would interfere with the truck's passenger's vision. My guess his position was over there across the field in the woods, it looks like about 300 meters or so. I would be willing to bet he was also in a depression so he was shooting upward, adding to the cause for the bullet to bounce. I'd guess it was a slow moving hunting round, maybe a 30-30, a slow big bullet, big shock but not much penetrating power. It loses a lot of power over two hundred yards. The shooter was relying on the bullet weight to punch through the windshield. I'm surprised he didn't fire a second round. The muzzle blast might have blown up a lot of dry snow into the air and by the time snow mist settled for a second shot the truck was too far away. That is, if the driver hit the gas right after the round bounced off. The shooter also might have thought the driver was in shock when his passenger was killed." Pete studied the road and pointed out the tire tracks where the driver hit the gas and the truck swerved around before getting traction. Pete picked up some snow six feet from the road. He tossed it into the air the snow made a sparkling mist and slowly settled. "I'll go with, the shooter was semi blind for about five to ten seconds."

Pete thought for a minute. "The shooter must have seen Gail by chance. Was Gail in town any other time?"

"Only to buy some clothes at the general store," Hank said.

"That's probably when they saw the girl and knew there was only one way back to where she was staying. Easy enough to find out with whom and where. Everything would appear innocent."

As the men were talking, the sheriff pulled up to the front bumper of Hank's truck. Hal started to turn on the emergency lights but changed his mind and left them off. He walked up to the group. "What have you got Hank?"

"We've just been listening to Pete here do analysis of the shooter and the ballistics. I would like to follow his lead until we know different, okay with you Hal?"

"Sure Hank, where do we start?" the Sheriff asked Nelson.

Pete pointed to the woods across an open field. "I'd like to check that area first."

"Let's do it," the Sheriff said.

Twenty minutes later, the men were standing over a depression a few feet inside the tree line. They could plainly see where somebody had lain for awhile. The impression of a lever action rifle could be clearly seen. Hank would have expected some sort of rest for the rifle barrel, but he didn't see one.

Pete pointed to two holes in the snow. "He used a cross and held the barrel resting in the notch of two crossed pieces of wood. I bet the sticks he used are within fifty feet of here. He probably tossed them away after the shot. If he had a scope, he might or might not have seen the bullet hit and thought he had made his kill. Besides there were two of them—here you can see where the second man rested on his elbows." Pete pointed at depressions in the snow.

"Okay, what do you suggest we do?" the sheriff asked.

"If it was my case, I'd keep it a secret the girl wasn't hit, just in case. Is there a clinic where a wounded person can be treated waiting transport to Missoula?"

"Yeah, the clinic in Lone Horse can treat gunshot wounds and then transport to Missoula either by air ambulance or by road in the morning."

The sheriff said, "If we let it be known the girl was wounded but still alive, I bet those bastards would try again."

Pete interrupted, "A better idea is to get the doctor at the clinic to drive out here and get an ambulance from Missoula to come to the ranch too. Sort of set a trap. Make him or them try again. Actually a better idea is track them down. Hank you were a Marine and I bet you still remember how to move around in the woods. Sean, I can see you move well. If the sheriff will deputize us I bet we can find the shooter. My bet is they are within five miles of this spot right now. It is pretty cold, the snow is light and not too deep. I bet they have a fire going. It won't be seen from the road or trail or seen from the air, but in a cave or overhang. They'll move out at first light, so we've got about eight hours to find them and then they're gone." Pete grinned. "You want to try?"

Hank matched Pete's grin. "Yeah, I do. We can use the horses and cover a lot of ground. I bet I know just where the pricks are hiding too. Let's get back to the house." Hank started toward the trucks. "Hal you coming?"

"I'll be along shortly. I want to take some pictures and mark this off as a crime scene." The sheriff pulled a small camera from his coat pocket and a measuring tape.

Ten minutes later the sheriff joined the rest of the men at the trucks. Hank spoke. "Pete thinks the shooters walked up the shallow creek, under the road and into the woods before setting off cross country. Their track did go to the stream so they could have gone either south or north. With the overcast and darkness, it would be easy to become disoriented in the forest. It's another reason to support Pete's theory, but it is possible they'll head south toward the closer road. We need to follow that lead too."

"Listen Hank, I know you know this country as well as any man. I agree there is the possibility they headed toward the state road over that hill." Hal jerked a thumb toward the south and the state road six miles away on the other side of a small ridge. "It would be slow going but a better escape route than north, except it's the first place we would check too. There's nothing north for twenty miles or more and that's only a fire road."

Hank dropped his head and stared at the snow in front of him. "Yeah, Hal you've got a point. I suppose we should break into two teams of three."

"Hank, you seem to know the north escape route and I know the south so how do you want to divide us up?" Hal asked.

"Okay, there's six or seven of us if we count Mike. You take Ben and Sean. Mike stays at the ranch. Hal can you get a deputy to meet you on the state road?"

"Sure, I'll radio Charlie and have him meet us at the road. When we're ready Ben, Sean and I will take off over the hill. Better Ben goes with me than Josh with his bad leg—he should be on horseback with you and Pete. And he's still at the ranch, right?" Hal looked to Hank for concurrence and got the nod. "You are going to use the horses anyway, right?"

"Yeah, I haven't thought everything through yet, but yeah. From the ranch with a little luck we will pick up their trail pretty quick." Hank addressed the teenager. "Mike, you and Robby along with Curly will have to look after the ranch while we're away. Remember you've got the women and girls to protect."

"Yes sir, Curly, Robby and I can handle it." Mike stood a little straighter in the company of the men who looked at him and judged him as a man.

Hal called his deputy and had him heading toward a spot on the state road. Hal expected to reach the meet point in about six hours. Hank, Pete, and Mike drove back to the ranch. Hank took a few minutes talking to Charlene, Wilma and the girls to explain the plan for the search.

When Hank entered the stable he wore his pistol and carried his rifle, the .45 Caliber Long Colt. Josh had the three horses brushed and saddled, a rifle scabbard attached to each saddle. Hank noticed Josh saddled Loco for him; Pete rode one of the ranch horses and Josh saddled his own ranch horse. Pete's horse was saddled with Pete's own saddle.

Curly stood on the bunkhouse porch with Mike and Robby, their rifles in hand. They saw the men off. Minutes later, Mike climbed up to the attic and opened the window a few inches. He set a blind six feet back inside the room so no one could look into the attic and see him. Robby came up and he did the same with the back window. They completed their blinds when Sue and Margie climbed up into the attic and set up blinds in each of the side attic windows. Sue carried her own .22 Caliber WRF (Winchester Rim Fire) rifle, a slide-action Winchester with a lot of punch, a gift from Hank. A 30-30 rifle was in Margie's hands, also a gift from Hank. Both rifles were from Hank's collection of Winchesters. Hank started collecting pre-1964 Winchesters when the arms manufacturer stopped making classic rifles. Hank taught each of the teenagers how to shoot with accuracy and stealth. With the boys and girls guarding the house from the attic, all the approaches to the house were covered.

Mary Ann was in Gail's room with Wilma while Charlene guarded the kitchen and stayed near the telephone. She set the base station cell phone to dial 911 if the telephone circuit went open for any reason.

Hank led Josh and Pete out of the ranch yard onto the trail up the mountain. They'd leave the trail about two miles out in an attempt to cut the track of the shooters. After about two hours on the trail, Josh spotted tracks coming out of the woods and crossing the trail to disappear on the far side.

Hank pulled Loco off the trail to follow the tracks left by the shooters. After an hour of tracking, Hank held up his hand. "I think I smell smoke, anyone else smell it?"

Josh leaned his head back and sniffed. He detected the faint smell of wood smoke. Hank moved forward debating whether walking would be better but decided to ride a few more minutes before dismounting.

Pete smiled at Hank; he smelled the smoke twenty minutes ago, but it was faint and still some distance away. He was about to say something to Hank when Hank stopped and called their attention to the smell. They moved cautiously forward for another forty minutes.

The three JH men were as surprised as the two men camped at a sheltered fire against a downed tree. One of the men wore a white suit. He would be invisible against the snow. The other man wore a plaid jacket under a down-filled winter coat open with the hood back. Hank saw all this in the second it took him to level his rifle. He thumbed back the hammer when he saw a flash and felt a bullet hit him high in the chest. His vision flashed with sights of the snow-covered trees and then his body hit the ground.

Vaguely in his clouded brain, he heard four more shots before everything went black.

Josh and Pete saw the bullet hit Hank and the blood spray by the first shot from the rifle in the would-be assassin's hands. The man got one more shot off at the two mounted men before he was hit by a bullet from Pete's rifle. A second later a bullet from Josh's rifle hit the second man who was pointing a rifle at them and pulling the trigger over and over. Thankfully, the man hadn't levered a bullet into the chamber of his rifle. Josh shot him realizing the man's panic had saved them.

Both of the men were down. Pete ran to them and removed the rifles from within reach. With a piece of rope he bound the men's hands behind their backs. Josh knelt in the snow at Hank's side. He tore Hank's Carhartt coat off and ripped his shirt to get at the wound. Hank's wound began to bleed. The bullet was a through and through. It passed completely through Hank tearing a large hunk of flesh from his back, missing his spine by inches. The location of the shot didn't look good. Pete had seen similar wounds kill lesser men. Hank still breathed, but his skin was already a pasty color, he was going into shock. The cold slowed Hank's bleeding. Pete pushed a wadded up handkerchief into the wound as far as he could without causing more damage. He motioned for Josh to give him his handkerchief which he put in the hole in Hank's back. Pete stopped the bleeding, but it was imperative they get Hank to a hospital as quickly as possible.

Pete searched Hank's coat and found his cell phone. He handed the phone to Josh who pushed "talked."Charlene's voice came back immediately; she must have been holding the cell phone.

"Charlene, Hank's been shot. He's down but alive, we need a medevac as soon as possible. We'll get him to the ranch as fast as we can. Have Mike or Robby get the snowmobile out and start up the mountain trail. He'll see where we went into the woods, we'll meet him there. Hurry."

Charlene didn't waste a second. She yelled up at the ceiling for Mike and Robby to get to the kitchen, now. It sounded like a bunch of horses going across the ceiling, then Mike and Robby rushed into in the kitchen with the girls at their heels.

"Mike, who's the best on the snowmobile?"

"Robby is why?"

"Hank's been shot and we need to get to him as fast as possible. Robby, get your winter clothes on. Mike get the snowmobile out and warmed up while Robby changes clothes. Sue, you get your warm clothes on too. You ride with Robby and bring Hank's horse back. Mike, hook up the sled too." She yelled after the teenagers as they raced to follow her instructions. Mike pulled the canvas off the snowmobile, primed the motor and started the warm up. Mike checked the gas and topped off the tank.

Charlene called 911 and got the operator in Missoula. After explaining who had been shot and they need the emergency helicopter ASAP, she hung up and called the clinic to get the doctor on the way to the ranch but found the doctor was already on his way. Wilma and Margie came into the kitchen with a bundle of blankets; she put her coat on and went out the door to where Robby, Mike and now Sue were gathered around the snowmobile as Mike checked the attachments for the sled. With Margie's help, Wilma put the blankets on the sled and used bungee cords to hold them on during the ride on the mountain trail. Margie got four of the truck's keys and moved the trucks to form a box landing zone for the helicopter when the lights were turned on.

Wilma kissed her son and daughter on the cheek and sent them on their way. Wilma, Margie and Mike returned to the house. Charlene was on the phone with Brent. He was taking care of Bev, who suffered with a severe cold and was in bed. They were afraid her coughing might harm the baby. Bev was into her third trimester. Brent told Charlene to have Mike get some road flares ready to mark the landing zone approach and wind direction when the helicopter arrived.

The women, Margie and Mike sat in the kitchen. "Oh my God, Bess!" Charlene said loudly. She grabbed the land line and speed dialed Bess's number in Dutton.

Twenty-five minutes after leaving the house, Robby spotted the horse tracks where they left the trail and entered the woods, without the sled. He could have made it through the trees, but he decided to wait. Five minutes later, Pete came out of the trees leading Loco with Josh in the saddle holding Hank in front of him. The snowmobile was already turned around so it was facing back toward the ranch. Robby motioned for Pete to bring Loco close to the idling snowmobile. In less than a minute, Hank was on the sled covered by blankets. Sue decided she should ride with Hank. Josh and Pete could bring Loco back to the ranch with them.

Pete and Josh needed to go back to where they left the shooters. When Pete checked on them earlier, the younger of the men had died and the older of the two, looked like he would be fine with a flesh wound across his right hip and a wound high on his shoulder.

Robby started toward the ranch with Sue holding Hank, who hadn't regained consciousness. The blood loss had stopped but Hank's breathing was shallow and he was definitely in shock. Sue used her body heat to warm Hank by wrapping herself in the same blankets with him. Robby went as fast as he could riding the edge of safety. The snowmobile was clearing the trees when a helicopter swept across the yard. Robby could see someone lighting road flares and the four truck headlights lit the landing zone in the yard. He drove the snowmobile close to the landing zone as the copter settled to the ground and the main rotor idled. A car with a red and blue light bar came through the gate followed by another car.

Each new arrival pulled up close to the helicopter. The second car was the doctor from the clinic in Lone Horse. He was led to the ranch by a sheriff's deputy as fast as the road conditions permitted.

The doctor and the EMT who came with the helicopter strapped Hank into the air ambulance and climbed into the aircraft with him. The helicopter lifted, spun around and headed in a direct line toward the hospital in Missoula. With the aircraft's departure, silence came to the yard. Robby sighed and drove to the shed to put the snowmobile away, then remembered Josh and Pete had two criminals they were bringing in. He waved Sue off the machine and when she was a step away, Robby, with the sled still attached, retraced his tracks toward where he'd left Josh and Pete.

* * *

Bess was sleeping soundly when the persistent ringing of the telephone woke her. Who is calling me in the middle of the night? "Yes, what? This had better not be a crank call."

"Bess!" Charlene's voice came out loud and clear over the old push button telephone. "I'm sorry to wake you but I thought you should know something has happened up here."

"Gail, she's been hurt, those bastards found her." Bess didn't even think anyone else could have been hurt at Hank's ranch. He was so careful about everyone's safety.

"No Gail's all right. Someone did take a shot at her and the men hunted them down. There were two of them." Charlene's voice broke.

"Oh my God, it's Hank!" Bess screamed into the telephone. She jumped out of bed pulling the telephone off the bedside table and disconnecting it. She heard a dial tone and panicked. She picked up the telephone from the floor, and pushed the switch hook down just as the phone began to ring again. "Charlene, is he okay, is Hank okay."

"Bess you need to calm yourself, Hank is alive. He's been shot and is on the way to the hospital in Missoula."

"Is he going to die?" Bess cut Charlene off.

"We don't know, he was hit in the upper chest. It's lucky Pete was with him. When Hank got here, he had handkerchiefs stuffed in the bullet holes so he didn't lose as much blood as he could have. Josh and Pete packed the wounds with snow to keep the blood thick too. The helicopter left here about ten minutes ago with the doctor aboard."

"Oh my God, Brent. Is Brent okay and Bev?"

"They are both okay. Bev has a bad cold and Brent's been staying with her at the lower ranch. After you and I are done I'll try to get to Sabrina and Randy. Bess, are you coming?"

"You're damn right I'm coming. I'll be on the first flight I can get. I'm leaving for the airport as soon as I pack a bag. Do I still have clothes there?"

"Yes, all your things are in Hank's room. He sleeps smelling you. Don't you tell him I told you that, promise?" Charlene was serious. Hank was very private about how he felt about Bess, especially during the past few weeks.

"God Charlene, don't let him die, I'm on my way." Bess stared down at the telephone like it was an evil thing. She tossed it onto her bed and began to pack underwear, another pair of jeans, a couple of shirts into her travel bag and toilet items from the bathroom. Ten minutes later, she was in her car on the way to the Dutton Airport.

* * *

Robby drove the snowmobile slowly down the trail with the criminals tied on the sled. Pete and Josh led Loco and followed on the two hour walk to the house. An occasional moan came from the wounded man. The other, a boy of maybe eighteen or nineteen rode with the silence of the dead having bled out.

The snowmobile entered the ranch yard and Robby parked close to the sheriff's car. The sheriff exchanged the ropes used by Pete to bind the outlaw's hands with handcuffs. An ambulance arrived to transport the wounded man and the corpse to the clinic in Lone Horse where they would be picked up by the State Police and transported to Missoula.

"Gail said there were four attackers. I would think the other two are on their way out of the area or will be when they hear about what happened to their compatriots." When the sheriff heard on the radio Hank was shot, Hal, Sean and Ben returned to the road as fast as they could and arrived minutes before the snowmobile returned with the dead and wounded men.

"Do you think they'll try to hurt Gail again?" Sue asked.

"I'd guess they might. If I had any more deputies I'd leave a couple here until we catch the other two, but I don't. Mr. Nelson, you were a cop in Spokane. How about me deputizing you as a deputy sheriff until all this is over?"

"Sure sheriff, if you think it'll help," Pete answered.

"Yes, you're in charge until we end this. Brent is a reserve deputy already." Hal stopped and looked at the assembled family gathered in the kitchen. "Is that all right with you?" he asked. Hal didn't want to do anything to harm the solidarity Hank established bringing three plus families together.

Charlene looked around her getting silent concurrence. "Yes sheriff, if you think it's best, we'll go along with your suggestions."

"Thank you all. Hank is an amazing man. How's the little girl, Gail Stratton isn't it? How is she?"

"She's fine sheriff, I've been with her since this started except for a few minutes," Margie said from the doorway. "She still can't speak very well, but she is very concerned about Hank."

"I can't answer for Hank, but I'm sure he would say it's his job to take care of each of you." Hal said, "Listen, I have to be going back to town. Hank should be at the hospital by now. If you want to go to Missoula, I'll give you a police escort."

Charlene pulled Wilma aside. "Wilma, why don't you, Mike and Margie go. Take Mary Ann with you. Hank always smiles when she is with him. Bess is on her way to Missoula, but still has to go through Spokane to get there. I wouldn't expect her until the nine o'clock flight tomorrow morning, if she can get out of Dutton. Robby, Sue and I can take care of Gail with Sean and Pete's help." She turned to Mike and Margie. "Get your things and be back here in ten minutes. Sue you get Mary Ann up and ready to go." Charlene hesitated. "I haven't reached Sabrina yet. Randy is up near Colville and has about a six to eight hour drive to Missoula."

Thirty minutes later Mike drove and followed Hal's cruiser with its lights flashing. Three hours later Mike pulled the extended cab truck into the Missoula hospital's parking lot. Wilma went into the building ahead to get a report on Hank before the children entered the hospital lobby.

Wilma returned to the truck and sat in the passenger seat. "Hank's still in surgery, and there's a waiting room on the second floor. We can wait there."

Hal joined them in the waiting room. "I'd like to wait with you if it's okay?"

"Sure Hal, please, you should call Mrs. Dolan and tell her where you are, she might worry." Wilma watched Hal walk to one of the pay phones in the corner.

* * *

Slowly Hank returned to consciousness. He saw a blurry tear streaked face a few inches from his own. "Am I in heaven? Are you an angel?"

"No Hank, it's just me." Bess pushed a strand of blonde hair off her wet cheek. Bess loved his words. "God you old cowboy, don't you ever do that to me again. I don't think my heart could take another night like the other night."

Hank frowned. "The other night—what day is it?"

"You've been out for two days and nights. They didn't think you'd make it, but I knew you were too ornery to die. I would never have forgiven you for leaving me."

"Who's that in the corner?" Hank's eyes hadn't completely cleared and everything was fuzzy.

"Mary Ann, come kiss Daddy Hank." Bess called the little girl dressed in her blue Wranglers, pink blouse and boots.

Mary Ann jumped from her chair, rushed to Hank's bandaged body with its draining tubes, IV and oxygen tubes. She grabbed Hank's free arm and hung on like he would disappear if she let go. Bess looked up at the man's face and saw the emotion as he held onto his foster daughter.

Bess took a deep breath. "Hank, the doctors say you are out of danger of dying and should be out of here by the end of the week. You've got a line of visitors waiting to see you. I've got to get back to Dutton; so I'll say good bye, get well soon, they need you." Bess leaned over and kissed him on his chapped lips. "I love you God damn it; there, I've said it again." Bess stepped back and walked out of the room without looking back.

"I love you too," Hank whispered. Only Mary Ann heard his soft words.

The next week was busy with a stream of visitors and well wishers coming in and out of Hank's hospital room. The doctors released him to go back to the ranch on the following Friday. Based on the identity of the two men Hank, Josh and Pete encountered in the woods, a five-state all points bulletin was issued for the other two men, both with criminal records known to be associates of the captured felon.

The fugitives were captured west of Spokane when a State Trooper spotted their truck on the road with a busted tail light and stopped them. The trooper noticed the men acting suspicious, called for backup and the two men were taken into custody on warrants issued in Montana for suspicion of attempted murder; that would keep them in jail until the DA from Dutton could get extradition papers and have them transferred to Dutton to face murder and rape charges.

It was suspected the surviving three men would be put away for a long time for the crimes committed in Dutton. The dead man was buried with only two cemetery employees in attendance and a generous pastor of a Christian Bible Church to say a few words over the man's grave.

Hank called a meeting of the family. "We have something to make a decision on." He sat in his easy chair with his left arm in a sling and bandages showing where the top buttons of his plaid wool shirt were unbuttoned. Brent and Bev sat beside him on the sofa, Bev wrapped in a quilt wedding gift. Gail Stratton was with Sean looking at some new horses Ben bought from local horse ranches as prospects.

Hank started the meeting. "Okay, this is about Gail. She is an orphan, fifteen years old, no, she's sixteen, with some critical psychic damage to her because of the murder and the rape of her mother and the physical assaults on her. What do you want to do about her? This is your decision, I'm not going to make it for you, nor is Brent or Bev. I'm going to leave you with the able advice and assistance of my son and very pregnant daughter-in-law." Hank rose and left the room, going through the kitchen to swipe a hot roll Charlene had removed from the oven minutes before.

Margie stood up. "I don't think there is a question."

"I don't either." Mike stood up beside his sister.

Sue and Robby rose to join them and soon everyone was on their feet. "Who's going to tell Hank and Gail?" Margie asked the room.

"You are, you started this wave of emotion," Wilma said as she and Charlene returned to the kitchen and their gossip. "She stays!" Wilma gave the parting shot.

"We all tell them." Margie said, "Mike, me, Robby and Sue. We tell them."

Margie led the teenagers out of the house toward the arena where Hank was watching Sean help Gail up onto Loco. The horse turned his head and looked up at the girl on his back. Hank smiled as the ranch horse stepped out slowly. When Gail began to slip, Loco stopped and slipped himself back under her so she stayed centered. Everyone watched the girl and horse move slowly around the arena. They could hear the giggles coming from the horse's back as Loco trotted smoothly around in front of them. The next time around, Loco moved into a smooth slow lope and Gail was openly laughing, the first time Hank heard her laugh since she arrived.

"Hank, we have something to tell you." Margie motioned to the rest of the group of teenagers standing around her. "If you approve, Gail stays!" Each teen nodded, and as a group they walked away, the girls to the stable, Robby toward an unfinished job mending a broken panel at the round pen and Mike to work on replacing a wheel on one of the ranch trucks.

Sean laughed. "I guess you've got your orders, huh?" Brent, with Bev still wrapped in the quilt, came up and stood next to Hank. Brent took his wife by the arm. "Honey, I think we'd better leave Dad alone while he tells Gail. After all, he is about to become a father again. I bet he adopts her, officially." Brent whispered as he helped Bev into the truck for their return to the lower ranch and home, where Brent would be busy okaying and making changes to blueprints and plans for the ranch. Bev had lesson plans to finish for Monday, a school day. She had a scheduled meeting with Marlene to cover the other grades' class outlines.

Sean helped Gail slide off of Loco's back. "Do you want me to help brush him?" she asked Sean in her weak wispy voice. She no longer needed the pencil and notebook to be understood.

"No sweetie, I think Hank has something to say to you." As Gail looked up at Hank a stricken look came over her face, the joy disappeared. Slowly she walked to where Hank waited at the arena gate.

"Gail, just a little while ago the family had a meeting about you and your future. A decision was made and was just delivered to me by those teenagers that you see trying to make believe they are too busy to notice you and me talking. Margie gave me it to me in two words: 'She stays!'" Hank watched as the light came back into the hazel green eyes.

"Really, you mean it? You aren't just trying to make me happy are you?"

"No—yes, we want to make you happy and everyone wants you to stay and become part of our family. As you may have noticed, the Withrows, the Reynoldses and the Springers are all one big family. We take care of our own, always. From now on you are one of us. But only if you want to be," Hank quickly added.

"Oh God, I've wanted to be part of this family since I got here and met everyone. Everyone is so nice and they truly love each other." A sadness crossed her face. "Mom would have loved it here."

"She's here too. She lives in you, in your heart. Make room for us because we are knocking on your heart too." Hank put out his one good arm and enfolded her to him and listened to her sobs as she held on to him. He felt the release of tension as it eased from her body. The thought of adoption flicked through his mind and then the image of a smiling Bess came.

"Why don't you go with Sean and brush and love on Loco. Thank him for giving you a ride. There is a bag of horse candy in the tack room, give him a couple of pieces as a reward. Then I want you to go see Ben. Tell him to pick out a horse for you to train and ride. You can ask your sisters Sue or Margie to help you, okay."

"I love you Hank, thank you." The girl threw her arms around Hank, gave him a hug, then turned and ran toward the stable where Sean was leading Loco to his stall. She stopped only to grab some horse candy, a few more than a couple of pieces, made from alfalfa and molasses.

CHAPTER 37

Hank's next thoughts were what to do about Bess. Hank remembered the dream when Lori visited him while he was in a coma. She told Hank to get on with his life. He had too much to give to sit stagnant and alone. The dream had been haunting him since he woke up and Bess left.

Hank went to his room. Mentally crossing his fingers, he pushed the button to dial Bess's familiar number on his cell phone. When she answered, he was surprised at the feeling surrounding his heart. "Bess, it's me. I've got something to discuss with you. Please hear me out before you say anything."

When Bess saw who was calling on the call identification, her heart nearly stopped. Hank didn't let her say anything after, "Hello."

"Bess, I'm planning on a trip to Dutton. I wanted to ask you if you have any objections to my adopting Gail Stratton. I wanted to talk to you before I called the judge and asked for his approval."

"Hank, I think that's a wonderful idea. Gail is an amazing girl and she really loves everyone there. I'll call Judge Hoskin and use what influence I have to help. Now, I have someone in my office, so I'll talk to you later, maybe dinner when you get here."

"Ah yeah, sure. I'll call you when I get there." Bess had disconnected.

Hank felt a bit downhearted. He dialed the courthouse in Dutton and was soon talking to Judge Hoskin. Hank explained what he wanted, indicating he had talked to Bess. Hank accepted the judge's offer of assistance.

Hank, after talking to the judge, went to the ranch house kitchen. Charlene was cooking dinner and Wilma, with Margie's help, was going over the ranch books at the kitchen table, adding the latest acquisition Ben made buying eight new horses to replace the eight he sold to a rancher in Kansas. With Wilma's help, Margie made a new set of books for Brent's guest ranch enterprise. She also needed to transfer inventory. Margie became Wilma's right hand and assistant building the books and inventory.

Now the guest ranch was a business, books were kept on all transactions. Margie, after homework and exercising two horses, worked on establishing accounts. Brent opened an account at the local bank with $50,000 from his private account, buying an interest in the ranch legally, not just as a member of the family. Wilma would hold the checkbook until the bank issued a letter of credit backed by the JH Ranch. Brent smiled as he handed the checkbook to Margie. She solemnly accepted it and entered it into the ledger. Margie found her niche in two parts, horses and accounting.

* * *

"I'm going to be gone for a few days," Hank told Wilma. "I'll take my cell phone, but don't call me unless something happens to one of the kids, or, oh you know what I mean." An hour later, Hank was on the road, with Brent driving him to Missoula and the airport.

"Dad, what about Bess. Are you going to see her while you're in Dutton?"

"Of course. I think it's about time you, Sabrina and Randy have a new mother." Hank hesitated.

After a few minutes of silence, Hank began. "Brent, this might sound crazy but while I was in a coma, your mother came to me in a dream. She told me in a lot more words, but, to shit or get off the pot. Your mom thinks I need to stop mourning her. It's been long enough, I need to get on with my life."

"Dad, that's the best advice I've ever heard and no, I don't think you're crazy. It sounds just like Mom. She loved you with all her heart, but she always wanted the best for all of us. Do I tell Sabrina and Randy about this?"

"No please, let me ask Bess first. I also have to do the legal stuff to adopt Gail. You do want her in the family?"

"Yeah Dad, the whole family voted unanimously, we should adopt her. She has no one else. Just in the last couple of weeks she has been like a little sister. I never had a little sister until Margie and now I have two. Sabrina was always the leader, the big sister who took care of us." Brent sighed. "It's too bad Sabrina and Randy had to leave before you got out of the hospital. I would have liked to have them around when we decided to add Gail to our family. Not just fostered family but to the Springers."

"I'm sorry too, I would have liked them to stay awhile. I miss them."

Brent looked at his father and could see the sorrow etched there on his usually smooth face. "Come on Dad, Randy will be here in a couple of weeks and if Sabrina can get another leave before she deploys again, maybe we can have an old fashioned holiday, complete with sleigh rides before all the snow melts. Did you see the shop Josh built at his place?" The younger man shook his head. "Wow, I didn't think so many old wood working tools still existed. Whatever you're paying him isn't enough—the man's a genius with his hands. And Bea, I think I'm going to hire her away from Charlene and have her raise our brats." Brent laughed, joined by his father.

"I talked to Judge Hoskin. He doesn't think Gail will have to testify at a trial. All three men have pleaded guilty to the rape and to second degree murder. They're spared the death penalty but I bet the judge will give the max on the other charges." Hank adjusted his seat belt over his bandages to ease stress on the chest wound. "I really don't know how long I need to be in Dutton. If Judge Hoskin can help and I'm sure he will, I have to see Bess and convince her to forgive me and to marry us, yeah, the whole great big family."

Silence lasted until they reached the outskirts of Missoula. "Dad, will you call me or Bev and let us know what Bess says, please."

"Yeah, okay. You two are becoming pests you know. I hope your kid takes after his grandfather: strong, silent, a real he-boy."

"Dad, it's a girl. We found out at the last doctor's appointment. We didn't want to tell anyone, but me and my big mouth, I had to tell my dad."

"Another girl. What is the ranch becoming with all the women folk. I'm going to have to build two more bathrooms just so they have a place to hang their stockings. Hey yeah, I remember those things."

"Is that what those hangy things in the bathroom are, stockings?" Brent said with a straight face. "Mind if I share your bathroom?"

"Not on your best day after eating the food Bev's been feeding you. That reminds me, roll down your window, I need to breathe." Brent hit the buttons and rolled all the windows of the truck down.

"Okay, okay, roll up the windows; I'd rather die of suffocation than freeze to death."

Brent drove to the airport parking lot and carried Hank's Valpak to the ticket counter where Hank purchased a ticket to Dutton. He would arrive there at 3 p.m. Hank hadn't called Bess again. He was afraid she would refuse him.

Hank said good bye to Brent and went to the waiting room. Hank sat in the waiting room, his mind occupied with thoughts of Bess. In his memory he saw her asleep on his bed and remembered holding her as they made love. God, if she doesn't forgive me and accept my proposal . . . The thought was nearly too much for him. His mind was so preoccupied he missed the call for his flight until a steward came to ask him if he was going to Spokane.

* * *

Hank arrived in Dutton twenty minutes early, rented a car and drove to the courthouse. When he walked into Judge Hoskin's outer office the clerk took one look at him and announced him to the judge.

Judge Hoskin came into the outer office to greet Hank. "I am glad to see you Mr. Springer, Hank. I think we have some business to take care of. Come in and sit down." The judge led Hank into his office and closed the door. "Just to keep straining ears away." Both men thought they knew what the other wanted to talk about and both men were right: Gail Stratton.

"So what brings you to Dutton, besides Bess Clemons?"

"Well sir, the family voted that we should adopt Miss Stratton and make her a Springer. You and I talked about fostering her but I don't want to foster her like the other children, I want to adopt her."

"Well Hank, that's a big step. I know you qualify and have all the references you need for an adoption. But how's the ranch doing, making any money or is it all outlay?"

"Judge, last quarter we actually had to pay taxes, so I guess we're doing pretty good. Wilma Withrow is my accountant, you know she went to school just to learn how to do the books. Wilma says next year we should be solid in the black. I still have a few million in liquid assets if we need them."

"Oh hell." The judge retrieved an envelope from his desk drawer and slid it across to Hank. "Here, read those and sign. Then the kid's out of my court and in yours, a better place doesn't exist. Hank you never fail to surprise me, except this time I had a feeling and had these papers done yesterday after your telephone call."

"You say these papers are all legal, no surprises?"

"They are all on the up and up but feel free to read them before signing."

Hank borrowed the judge's pen and with a flourish signed the papers legally adopting Gail Stratton. Now, he and Bess needed to solidify their own relationship.

Hank left the courthouse with Gail Stratton's adoption papers in his jacket pocket. He had made the right decision. He drove directly to the Dutton Children's Home, pulled into the parking lot and saw Bess's car in her space. His heart did a double pump before it settled down to a steady beat. Walking up the steps to the main entrance, Hank felt doubt, not about loving Bess, but whether she would want him anymore. They didn't have a chance to talk when he was in the hospital and she left after hearing he was out of danger and on the road to recovery.

The doorbell rang throughout the building. Bess opened the door, stared at Hank and stepped back. "Can I come in?" he stammered.

"Certainly Mr. Springer, you're always welcome here." Bess opened the door wider and waited for him to enter before she closed it.

"Maybe this is a bad idea." Hank stumbled over the words. He turned to go.

"God damn it Hank, get your ass in my office, now!"

When he walked by Bess she shoved him in the back, gently, and followed him into her office. As soon as the door was closed, Bess Clemons was in his arm, the other still in a sling. She planted a lingering kiss on his lips, her hair wrapping around his face. "You have something to tell me?"

"Aw yes ma'am, actually two things. I have signed the papers with Judge Hoskin to adopt Gail Stratton so she won't be coming back here. The whole family voted for her to stay." Hank paused, almost afraid to look into her eyes.

"Okay, I kind of figured that. And why is the courthouse the first place you go when you come to Dutton?"

"I needed to get the adoption papers done." Hank was silent for a moment. "Also I have to apologize to you about the way I've been treating you, keeping you hanging on like I did. You didn't deserve that."

"That's it, that's the second part?" Bess pushed him away with a hand on his chest. "Well you can take your apology and you know what you can do with it."

"Well, actually the apology isn't really the second thing." He didn't know where to begin. "I aw, had a dream."

Bess interrupted, "You had a dream and here you are in Dutton adopting another girl. She needs it, more than you can imagine. So what's with this dream?"

"I was still on drugs."

"So this was a druggy dream, great, you're doing swell Hank."

"Damn it Bess, shut up and let me tell you about the dream." Hank moved around her desk and pushed her into her chair and made it lean back so her feet were off the floor. "Now, about the dream. I dreamed Lori came to me and told me I needed to step up with you. She said I loved you as much as I loved her and quit pussy footing around and ask you to marry me."

"You are only asking me to marry you because of a dream, drugs and a ghost?" Bess started to get up but Hank pushed her back.

"No damn it, I realized I love you with all my heart. I've known it for a long time, but I've just been too stupid to do anything about it. But here I am now, I'm telling you I love you and want to spend the rest of my life loving you and making you happy. Now?"

"Oh." Bess sat quietly. "You say you want to marry me, you love me?"

"Yes, that's what I'm saying. If I've screwed up my life losing you, well I guess it's something I'll have to live with. But I don't want to. Marry me Bess Clemons, make me the happiest man in the world. Oh yeah, the kids need a mother and you're the best mother this side of heaven. Okay, that's it. I've pleaded my case."

"I would like to hear you plead a bit more, Mr. Springer. But I don't think I can wait." Bess shot out of the chair into Hank's arm again. This time she didn't stop kissing him until he gasped for air. "Hey, do I get a ring with this proposal? You know there has been another suitor hanging around looking at my fanny when I walk by."

"Don't push it Clemons, love only goes so far. I guess it goes pretty far where you're concerned."

"I am going to close up the office right now, I'm on overtime anyway. I'm going to take you home and screw your lights out. Think you can stay with me old man?"

"Old man, I'll show you old man." Hank tried to slip his hand up Bess's dress. He got as far as the top of her stocking before she slapped his hand away.

"You get me all wet Springer and you'll pay."

"Pay, pay with what?" Hank was watching the gleam in Bess's eyes.

"Oh I'll think of some way."

Bess rode with Hank to her house; after opening the door she pulled him directly to the bedroom leaving discarded clothes in a trail down the hallway. Wearing only her bra, panties and black thigh-high stockings, Bess turned on Hank. "Why are you wearing all those clothes?"

"Because you haven't ripped them off me. Wait let me undo my belt before you ruin my trousers."

"Get those boots off right now, the boxers too," Bess ordered, dropping to the floor in front of him. "Damn, I'm going to have a soft carpet installed. These hardwood floors are hard on old knees." Bess laughed taking him in her hand and kissing him. "Just think, this little thing here is all mine now."

Their love making lasted into the evening. They got up and Bess fixed a dinner for them from a leftover meatloaf. Hank made himself useful fixing the salad, which only required one hand using a readymade salad package from the grocery.

While doing dishes, Hank lifted Bess's gown and it wasn't a minute until they were making love on the just-cleaned dinner table.

"God Hank, you're going to wear it out."

"Those parts don't wear out Bess my love, they only get better. Let's have Judge Hoskin marry us tomorrow." Hank glanced at the clock over the stove. "Well, today would be better."

"You really mean it? You're not just saying that to get laid?" Bess teased.

"Well now that you mention it, yeah it worked too."

"Cad!"

"God, I haven't heard that term since I was a PFC in San Diego. Did I ever tell you about—?" Hank was shut up by three fingers being stuck in his mouth.

"Cad." Bess whispered in his ear, "Show me how much of a cad you really are, make love to me Springer." Hank did as bidden, then staggered to the bedroom and collapsed onto the bed and was asleep within minutes with Bess spooning with him. She kissed his back and whispered, "I love you Hank Springer. I knew you would come eventfully and carry me off in your white truck. Hank you are a cad sometimes, but you are my cad and I love you." Bess was asleep seconds later.

On the way to the courthouse, Bess and Hank stopped by the jewelry store and bought an engagement ring and marriage band for Bess. Because wedding rings and ranch work, especially mending fences, are not conducive to safety, Bess bought Hank a small wedding band enclosed in plastic he could wear around his neck like dog tags or carry in his pocket.

When they were escorted into the judge's office, Bess wore her engagement ring; when they left she wore a wedding band with the engagement ring. Two people who were in the office to file their living wills with the county clerk served as witnesses. Neither Bess, Hank nor the judge had ever seen them before, but they were more than happy to witness the Springer vows. Mr. and Mrs. Springer decided to leave Bess's furniture and her car in Dutton and have it moved to the ranch later.

* * *

With the adoption papers in his coat pocket and his new wife on his arm, Hank left the rental car at the airport and the couple traveled on the commuter jet from Dutton to Spokane. After a two-hour wait between flights they boarded another commuter turbo jet to Missoula. Brent and Bev were at the airport to meet them when they deplaned. Bess carried only her overnight bag and Hank his briefcase. Bess's baggage and Hank's Valpak were in the back of Brent's pickup before they were through the terminal.

Bess and Hank were surprised to see two additional pickup trucks with all the ranch kids smiling through the windshield at the grinning couple. "Brent, did you tell everybody? I wanted it to be a surprise."

"Hey Pop, I didn't tell anybody except Bev," Brent said innocently.

"Bev?" Bess looked her daughter in the eye.

"Hey, I only told Charlene and Wilma. They have to get the rooms ready and supper made you know." Bev smiled her angelic smile.

"Okay, who is here?" Hank asked trying and failing to count noses through the glare of the windshield. "Wait, is that Gail with Mary Ann?" At that moment, Mary Ann got the truck door open and was in Bess's arms in a flash. She kissed Hank on the cheek.

"Enough, we'll all meet at the Crossroads Café." Hank helped Bess climb into Brent's crew cab pickup. Brent led a parade of pickup trucks toward the Crossroads Café.

When the noisy crew entered the restaurant, a waitress immediately got the manager. "Would you like to use the banquet room in back?" The manager asked.

When they were all seated waiting for their orders, Hank stood. "Miss Stratton would you please come up here, I have something for you." Gail stood in front of Hank and Bess, her eyes not able to fix for long on either one of them. Hank saw a little fear in Gail's hazel/green eyes, and didn't delay. "Yesterday was your last day as a Stratton, today you are a Springer. I hope that pleases you." Hank handed her a copy of the adoption papers. "That is your copy making you an official Springer."

Gail stared up at Hank and gingerly took the offered papers, glancing at them. She threw her arms around Hank and then ran from the room followed by Bess, Sue and Margie. Mary Ann tried to follow but Mike stopped her and whispered in her ear.

Bess was the first to reappear. "Did I do something wrong?" Hank wore a stricken expression.

"No you did everything right. Gail will be out in a minute. Margie is explaining why she, Mike and Mary Ann are still Andersons and Hank is their foster father. So Mike can carry on the Anderson family name. Oh you know what I mean." Bess kissed him on the cheek. "Wait till they get back and you'll see everything is perfect."

Gail returned followed by Margie and Sue. Her expression was one of wonder as she took in the image of her new father. Before taking her seat, Gail stood before Hank at the head of the table. "I'll try to make you proud of me, Daddy." She put her arms around Hank's neck and fresh tears rushed down her still-wet cheeks. Hank was the first person she had ever called, Daddy.

Hank patted her back, but held her tight. "I know you will honey. You just be you, that's enough for me." Gail stepped back from hugging Hank and faced her new assembled family while everyone applauded.

The trip to the ranch from Missoula was filled with happy conversation as Bess caught up on all the gossip and Bev's pregnancy. While Hank was in the hospital, Bess and Bev were unable to get together before Bess returned to Dutton. Bev and her mom were both excited about the little girl growing inside Bev. Brent was complaining about being in a house full of women, but loving it.

When the small caravan arrived at the ranch house, Charlene, Wilma and their husbands were on hand to offer the newlyweds congratulations. The master bedroom had been redone in Bess's favorite colors and a place in the bunkhouse was made up for Hank.

They hadn't been home an hour when the guests for a surprise bridal shower for Bess began to arrive carrying gifts, most of them handmade. Hank was sent to the bunkhouse until after the ladies' party, the first one ever attended by Gail, Sue, Margie, Bea, Cassie and Mary Ann. The ladies fussed over Cassie and Mary Ann. They planned Bev's baby shower. Robby and Mike acted as waiters for the affair, wearing clean Wrangler jeans and white long sleeve shirts. The two boys took a lot of ribbing about their outfits, but they wore them proudly.

Hank, Ben, Josh, Sean, Leonard, Shorty and Pete had a party of their own, a belated bachelor party complete with two of the ranch hands dressed as hookers doing a pole dance for the reluctant groom. While the two cowboys were doing a pole dance, they collided falling to the floor in their red long-johns and short skirts. Whiskey shots were called for and Hank and Brent had their share. At the end, Hank collapsed onto his bunk and fell asleep. He woke when the sun coming through the bunkhouse window struck his eyes.

Hank stumbled out of bed, went outside and broke the ice on the horse trough. He dunked his head and stood on the porch in his underwear before getting back into the warm bunkhouse filled with snoring cowboys. After getting dressed, Hank went to the house and tried to sneak into his and Bess's room only to find the ladies had padlocked the door closed. Looking at the hasp with the screws drilled into the wood of the door, Hank slowly shook his head. I didn't like the color of that door anyway he thought. He wobbled into the kitchen to find Charlene and Wilma preparing breakfast. "Where are the girls?" Hank asked meaning the younger kids.

"They all stayed in Mary Ann's room last night, a sort of slumber party for the under twelve set. They should be getting up pretty soon. Sue and Margie stayed at Wilma's and the boys slept in the attic loft bedroom. We didn't think they should stay in the bunkhouse from all the noise and laughter coming from there when the shower broke up."

Hank was finished with his second cup of coffee when Brent came into the kitchen. "Where's Bev?"

"She's in with Bess. They were having a mother—daughter talk when we left at ten last night," Wilma answered. "Don't worry, she is in good hands. You know there are other hands she can be safe in besides yours Brent."

"Yeah, I know."

CHAPTER 38

Interrupted by the ringing of the telephone, Brent reached over and answered. He was silent for a minute and replaced the receiver back on the base. "That was Hal Worthington. It seems the prisoner in the hospital overpowered the Missoula city cop and escaped. He killed the night nurse. Hal thinks he's out for vengeance and may be headed this way. He's got the cop's gun and his patrol car. The car has a shotgun and Mini-14 rifle in the trunk. There was also a bulletproof vest that would fit the killer. Hal said he would call us when he had more information." Brent helped himself to another cup of coffee. Hank sat still for perhaps a full minute before jumping up and storming out of the kitchen toward the bunkhouse.

Five minutes later he was back in the kitchen. "The men are getting up. Ben and Sean are getting their rifles to set up a guard around the house. I don't want Gail out of the house and keep her away from the windows. Actually everyone stay away from the windows. When Sean and Pete get here, I want to see them in my office. Charlene, is the shotgun still here?"

"Yes Hank, it's in the cupboard over the pantry. I'll get it. Someone will always have it in their hands until you say otherwise."

"Good, I'll be in my office. Send the men in when they get here." Hank went into his private office and opened his gun safe. He took out his .45 Caliber Long Colt pistol, put on his holster and belt and loaded the pistol with six of the heavy .45 caliber bullets. Removing his Winchester M70 rifle, he put four Lake City match .30 caliber rounds in it and laid the rifle on his desk. He left the safe open.

Pete Nelson, the first to arrive, wore his 10 mm automatic pistol in a holster on his belt and had a 30.06 deer rifle on a sling over his shoulder. Mike and Robby arrived next, each carrying his rifle. "Where do you boys think you're going?"

"We're part of this family too you know. This is our home and we want to help defend it." They were interrupted by the breaking of glass followed by the report of a high-power rifle being fired.

"Oh shit, pull all the blinds, get the women out of the kitchen. Are Sue and Margie in the house?" Hank yelled at everyone and no one in particular. "Wilma, where are the girls?"

Wilma rushed out of the kitchen followed by Charlene with the shotgun. "I'm pretty sure they're still in bed."

Hank peeked out the side window at the bunkhouse. He could see three men there, each man holding a rifle. "Where did the shot come from?"

Pete found the bullet hole in the wall, lined that up with the hole in the window. "My guess is he's at the edge of the woods if he stayed there after he made the shot. I would think he's moved though, maybe coming closer keeping the Withrow house between us and him."

"We need to get the girls over here or at least two of us over there. Thoughts!"

"Yeah, why don't we call them on from the base station. Sue has her phone in her room," Wilma suggested. They heard running footsteps cross the porch and Ben, followed by Josh, dove through the front door. Wilma nearly shot them before pulling the shotgun off her target.

"Where's the binos Hank?" Sean asked.

"On the wall behind the desk. What do you have in mind?"

"I'm going upstairs and see if I can spot him from up there or at least maybe his tracks." Sean was up the back steps followed by Robby after he retrieved the binoculars.

"Mike put your phone on walkie-talkie and take it up to Sean so he doesn't have to shout or come down to tell us what he sees." The boy was up the steps before Hank finished instructing him.

"Hank, you there?" Sean's voice out of Hank's phone.

"Yeah, what do you see?"

"There's tracks going toward the back of the Withrow house. My guess he is in the house with the girls."

"Yes, indeed I am and such pretty girls too. Here darling, talk to your daddy."

"Hank." Margie's voice came from his telephone still on walkie-talkie. "He surprised us, he's—" Her voice was cut off and a scream took its place with the sound of cloth being torn.

"Hey there Mister High and Mighty, lookie what I've got. Just to tickle your fancy, watch out the front window." An ugly laugh came from the phone.

Hank and the men looked out through the edge of the window and saw Sue pushed out the front door with a rope around her neck and her hands tied in back. She was naked from the waist up and Hank could see blood on her right breast and scratches across her thighs showing through the torn fabric of her pajamas. A bloody scratch crossed her stomach and belly.

"I'm going to kill you, you son-of-a-bitch." Hank snarled. All he heard was laughter. As they watched, Margie was pushed out onto the porch with similar scratches on her breasts and belly. A rope tied around her neck hung down in front of her; she stood still beside Sue.

Mike came leaping down the steps from the attic heading for the front door. Ben caught him before he could go outside and pushed him into a chair and had Charlene sit on him. "Damn it Hank, let me go. He's got my sister." Mike was sobbing, trying to push Charlene off him.

"Mike, he's got my daughter, don't you think I want to go out there?" Ben said through clenched jaws.

"Hey in the house, what's the matter, no guts?" the man yelled from the safety of the house across the yard. As they watched, Sue and Margie were yanked off their feet to lay sprawled on the porch. They were unable to get to their feet easily with their hands tied behind their back. "You going to leave these two little girls for my pleasure Mister Rancher Man? Ask that little red haired girl what I can do." Hank saw an arm and hand come out the door just above the porch and grab Sue by the hair and begin to pull her back into the house. Sue flipped around on her feet and stomped on the arm with her bare feet. A howl of rage came through the cell phone and Sue was loose. She was unable to help Margie because her hands and arms were still tied behind her, the rope around her neck hanging loose.

"How far do you suppose it is to the door over there?" Hank asked Pete who stood beside him.

"I don't know but I'd guess about 80 yards maybe a couple more."

Hank went into his office and came out with his M-70 match rifle. "I've got it zeroed at 750 meters with the scope. What do you think?"

"Well, if I were going to make the shot, I think I'd aim for the second button down setting the scope at 300 yards. That's the shortest range on that scope isn't it? Now you were telling me he may be wearing a vest. So it's a head shot or nothing."

"Yeah, I think so. The bullets are Lake City match. 30 caliber. I need that window out of the way though. Why don't you try talking to him through the window. Open it about a foot if you can without getting shot."

Pete went to stand beside the window, and opened it a crack when a bullet came through the window impacting the back wall above Hank's head. Pete turned to look at Hank and motioned as if to say, "I wouldn't stand there if I were you." The good thing was the window was now completely broken as the bullet hole spider webbed to the first bullet hole and broke apart.

Hank crouched behind a chair with the rifle resting on the chair's left arm. He lowered the scope to the 300 yard setting and zero windage. Hank looked through the scope and could see Margie clearly with the rope around her neck. He looked to the left and saw Sue standing against the wall looking directly back at him. She was trying to work the ropes binding her wrists against the corner of the house.

For the first time, Hank noticed Bess on the floor not far from him. He smiled at her and she smiled back. "Make the shot Hank. He's just a rabid dog and needs to be put down." Margie was on her feet standing in the doorway with the door open about three inches. The Mini-14 rifle rested on her shoulder, a rough left hand holding her still by squeezing her breast. Hank could see the anguish on her face but she stood still as if she knew the next minute may be her last.

Hank decided to aim at where the man's collar bones come together at the point of the chin. He thought the bullet would fly level but the crosshairs were set for 300 meters. He took the slack up on the trigger; out of the corner of his eye he saw Sue's hands were free. She crawled on her belly along the porch tight against the house toward where Margie stood. Hank watched Sue reach out and put her hands on Margie's ankles. Sue looked back over her shoulder at the ranch house. Taking a deep breath, she yanked Margie's feet out from under her and for a second the man was alone in the partly open door. The rifle in Hank's hands cracked. In the rifle's scope, Hank saw the man's head snap back and a red mist sprayed out into the room behind him. The Mini-14 dropped to the porch beside Sue who swept it up and charged into the house, only to return a moment later to signal it was safe.

Bess laid her hand on Hank's arm as he continued to watch through the rifle scope as Sue and Margie were swamped by family all running across the yard to meet in the middle of the parking area. Hank removed the remaining three rounds from the rifle and returned it to the safe in his office. He'd clean the rifle later when things calmed down.

Taking Bess by the arm, Hank led her out of the ranch house and across the yard. Sue and Margie were now covered by blankets Wilma brought from the house. Mike, after he made sure Margie was all right, held Sue as the events caught up with her and she sobbed against his chest. Margie was held by Wilma whose arms were around the older woman holding on as if she would never let go. Robby held Gail in his arms as she stared at the man, who raped her, killed her mother and wanted to murder her. Tears ran down her face and Robby held her and wiped them tenderly away.

Charlene, always the practical one, put an old saddle blanket over the body lying in the doorway of Withrow house. The killing bullet hit the man directly between the eyes, blowing out the back of his head. Hank would hire a special crew to come and clean up the mess.

* * *

Later in the afternoon, after the sheriff and the coroner left taking the body with them, Hank and Bess sat together in his office. Hank was behind his desk cleaning the rifle, Bess on the leather sofa against the wall opposite. "Did you notice who was holding who after the shooting ended?" Bess asked.

"Yeah, some of that was a big surprise. The only one who didn't surprise me was Margie. Let's see, Robby and Gail, Mike and Sue. I didn't see it coming and should have."

"Well golly, Hank my love, you've been a bit busy deciding your own fate the past few months. Gail just got here and she's a Springer, Robby is a Withrow, Sue is a Withrow and Mike is an Anderson. I don't see any problem as long as they don't start sleeping together."

"Don't scare me; I don't know what's in the future, but I'm sure it'll work out just fine." Hank finished cleaning the rifle, got up and took Bess by the hand and went to their room to change clothes.

Hank and Bess joined the rest of the family for the trip to the guest ranch for a late afternoon lunch put together by Leonard and Roy. Hank wanted the family to get back to normal as soon as possible.

* * *

The spring holidays came and went; Bev was busy teaching grades one through three and showed a much enlarged baby belly. Brent walked around like an expectant father. Last week Hank found Bess in the bathroom with a shocked look on her face as she stared at a pregnancy test kit in her hand. He got the faintest glimpse of the test window and it showed a blue plus sign, whatever that meant.